By D. C. Macey

The Temple Legacy - Published August 2015
The Temple Scroll - Published August 2016
The Temple Covenant - Published April 2018
The Temple Deliverance - Publication late 2018

THE TEMPLE COVENANT

(The Temple - Book 3)

Butcher & Cameron

D C MACEY

Published by Butcher & Cameron

ISBN 978 0 9933458 8 3

Chapter 1
TUESDAY 22ND OCTOBER - AM

The sun was nearing its zenith as the leading Land Rover, rocking and bouncing about, continued its slow passage along the rutted dirt track. It could have been any one of the vehicles based at the British Army Training Unit, Kenya, BATUK, but it wasn't. It was the lead vehicle in a little convoy that had been doing some very secret testing deep in the bush - far away from prying eyes. Now, job done, they were making their way back to the base at Nanyuki. Back to long overdue baths and cold beers all round - lots of them.

The matt yellows and browns of its camouflage were designed to merge into the surrounding arid bushlands but the vehicle was not concealed, its passage was marked by the great plume of dust thrown up from under its wheels. The dust rose and billowed into the hot afternoon air, exactly marking the Land Rover's progress across the landscape - like a white chalk steadily scraping across a blackboard. The two following Land Rovers were lost in the dust, but their presence was marked for the distant observer as their wheels kicked up more dust to boost and fill the plume.

A mile or so distant from the convoy, a slightly plumping Asian man stood stock still on the roof of his sand coloured 4 x 4. Smartly dressed in a well-tailored khaki safari suit, he was seemingly oblivious to the hot afternoon sunlight. From his raised vantage point, just above the height of the scrub-filled landscape, he used binoculars to follow the convoy's progress.

Abruptly he swung his gaze, tracing the line of the track ahead of the convoy. His shifting view came to rest on the cab of a flatbed lorry that was jutting above the bush line. Parked on the track, it blocked the approaching convoy's path. The man issued an order into his headset and continued to watch impassively, as moments later, his words stimulated a flurry of activity with men jumping from the flatbed's cab and dropping from sight into the bush below.

• • •

Steering his vehicle round a bend in the track the driver of the lead Land Rover stopped abruptly. Puzzled, he turned to the captain beside him, who was already calling a halt order into the radio.

The captain mirrored the driver's expression. 'I'll see what's going on. Just standby for a minute.' He swung out of the Land Rover and paced towards the abandoned flatbed.

'What the hell's this all about?' said a voice from behind him.

Turning, the captain nodded an acknowledgement towards the sergeant who had emerged from the convoy's dust cloud and was hurrying to catch up with him.

Hours spent following in the captain's dust trail had the sergeant anxious to see the journey finished, and now irritated that their progress had been halted.

The two men reached the tail of the flatbed and the mystery deepened. It was no old rebuilt truck, which was the norm in this part of the country. Yes, this truck was dusty but it was new, brand new. The sergeant looked at the rear tyres that showed scarcely any wear. He kicked one as he glanced meaningfully at the captain.

'Weird,' said the sergeant.

'Yes, odd. This shouldn't be broken down; it's brand new. And certainly shouldn't be out here on our firing ranges.'

'What do you think?'

'I'm not sure, and I don't know why it's abandoned out here. It makes no sense.'

'Too right, the locals will have it stripped down to its chassis in no time. I'll check in the cab, sir.'

The captain looked around, peering into the still and desolate bush as his sergeant paced towards the front of the flatbed. There was no sign of a driver anywhere. Glancing behind him, he could clearly see his little convoy as the dust began to settle. In the front vehicle, the driver sat patiently waiting for his signal. Behind that, two more Land Rovers. The rearmost was a traditional soft-top model identical to his own. It contained the guard detail, all uncomfortable in the hot still air. One solider had jumped out of the back for a quick smoke and to see what was happening. The front doors had both been swung open trying to catch any breath of breeze. Engines all turned off during the halt to minimise any risk of overheating.

Between the two escort vehicles was a third Land Rover. This one was very different; instead of the standard canvas strap-on top cover, it had a tall fibreglass superstructure that enclosed the whole vehicle. He knew its air-conditioning unit would be filling the interior with cold air. He could see the driver, sitting in comfort, isolated from the heat of the day.

The air was still and everything silent. Birds and even the cicadas were quiet, conserving energy in the afternoon, saving their efforts for the cool of twilight. The captain heard the truck's cab door click open as his sergeant investigated. He heard the sounds of the sergeant pulling himself up into the cab.

Then he heard another sound, an unnatural whoosh. Without time to respond or call a warning, his eyes could only trace the path of a smoke trail marking the progress of a rocket-propelled grenade. He saw the beginnings of movement in the rear Land Rover where the smoking soldier had also spotted the threat and shouted a warning to his mates - too late.

The grenade plunged into the front of the cab and exploded in the passenger seat so recently vacated by the sergeant. The driver was killed instantly, his body blown into pieces. A bright orange blast flash rolled over the seatbacks into the rear of the vehicle and engulfed the guard detail. Screams filled the air as three men jumped out, clothes on fire, exposed flesh melting beneath the unforgiving touch of the blast.

The captain's hand scrabbled to pull open the studded pouch flap that secured his pistol as he ran back past his own vehicle and down the track towards his men at the rear of the convoy. In the lead Land Rover, the driver hurriedly reached back to where his SA80 assault rifle was held firm in its travel mounting. His hand didn't even touch it before three rounds punched through the side window and shattered his skull.

At the rear vehicle, the smoker had pulled off his shirt and was desperately using it to wrap and roll one of his comrades in an attempt to extinguish the flames; it seemed to be working. Another man was on the ground writhing in pain, his screams rose to merge with the cries of the third man who was staggering away from the fire. He stumbled, dropping to his knees, burning arms reaching out for help that would never come.

The shirtless soldier looked about for support. Ahead of him he saw his sergeant leap down from the cab of the flatbed and unsling his SA80, saw the sergeant stagger and shudder as a burst of automatic fire punched bullets into his chest, the man dead before his knees buckled. He saw the captain raise his pistol to shoot at an unknown target in the bush. The pistol muzzle flashed and a cry confirmed a hit. Then the captain was hit by a burst of automatic fire that threw him backwards into the blazing cab of the rearmost Land Rover.

Helpless, still protecting his moaning comrade, the shirtless man watched as shadows amongst the undergrowth moved and rose, consolidating into human forms and stepping quickly onto the track. He saw them pull open the middle Land Rover's driver's door, saw them drag out the driver at gunpoint, saw the struggle, heard the shot, knew the driver was dead.

He watched as one man stood over the sergeant's lifeless body and put a bullet into his head. He watched the man make his way methodically down the line, shooting each body as he passed. As the man approached him, the soldier's shock seemed to pass, giving way to a rage. Unarmed, his weapon lost inside the burning Land Rover; he leapt up and with a scream of anger ran at the shooter. He saw the shooter smile. Saw the muzzle of the gun turn in his direction, saw a flash, and then saw nothing more.

For just a moment, quiet returned to the track. Then orders rang out. Men hurried to push the lead Land Rover off the track. Two other men lowered the flatbed's tailgate ramp while others dragged a thin tow wire down from the winch fixed behind its cab. They attached it to the middle Land Rover, its fancy fibreglass superstructure carefully left unscathed in the firing. The Land Rover was winched onto the flatbed and secured as the captain's body was searched for keys.

Methodical hands thrust in turn into each of the dead man's pockets. His body was rolled over in the dust to check back pockets to no avail. Finally, his legs were lifted and twisted to reveal a thigh pocket. Inside was a large plastic fob with a set of keys and swipe cards fixed to the ring. With a cry of triumph, the searcher lifted his find. Chasing up the ramp, he checked that the keys opened the rear door to the Land Rover.

Pulling the door open, he thrust his machine pistol into the doorway and screamed an order inside. Waving the muzzle of his weapon, he directed the occupants out. Blinking, two civilian technicians edged out into the sunlight, followed by a younger female technician. All three were scared, the two older men trying to shield the young woman who was now sobbing uncontrollably as she pressed in behind the men.

The muzzle of the machine pistol was jabbed into the woman's back, forcing her to move towards the rear of the flatbed. Her movement propelled the two men along and in seconds they were all clustered at the head of the ramp, arms supporting one another, fear in their eyes.

A short distance from the foot of the ramp, a man with a headset was listening to an incoming message. He nodded and replied in a language that none of the prisoners recognised. After another short listening silence, the man spoke to close his conversation. Then he turned his attention to the prisoners.

Pointing his pistol towards them, he shouted instructions and a man rushed up the ramp to search them. He checked their pockets, then ripped the ID passes from around their necks and quickly delivered them to his pistol-toting leader.

Having checked the cards with their magnetic strips, bar codes and security holograms, the leader smiled. He paced up the ramp, produced a little notepad and pencil. 'Password,' he said, thrusting the pad and pencil into the hand of the nearest technician.

'No way,' said the senior of the technicians, 'never.'

The leader did not hesitate. He raised a hand and slammed his pistol butt into the girl's face. She collapsed to her knees, screaming as blood poured from a cut opened across her cheekbone. He aimed the pistol at the kneeling woman's back.

'Password.'

The senior technician hesitated for just a moment before writing his password.

The leader waved his pistol towards the other technician. 'You now.'

The second technician quickly jotted down his password.

'You now,' said the leader prodding the young woman with his pistol. 'Quick, now.'

She reached up nervously and cleared tears from her eyes, so she could see to write.

Her response was too slow for the leader and he jabbed her between the shoulder blades with the pistol muzzle. 'Quick now, quick!'

Taking his notebook back, the leader climbed inside the Land Rover to check the login passwords were correct.

Stooping, the senior technician put an arm round the younger woman and helped her up; his colleague lent a hand. Standing in a cluster, they hugged her.

'It'll be fine now, don't worry. They've got what they want,' said the senior technician.

'You think?' said the young woman between sobs.

'Sure, it'll be okay. They have no reason to hurt you now.'

'Please God,' she said, 'I don't want to die. Look at all the dead bodies, all the soldiers are …' A fresh welling of sobs and tears stopped her talking, and the older man gently put his hand behind her head, drawing her face close to his shoulder.

'It'll work out, you'll see,' he said quietly in her ear. He felt her head nod in the slightest of acknowledgements.

Standing in the bright sunlight, they could hear the tapping of a keyboard as the leader checked their passwords were correct. Eventually the tapping was replaced by his voice speaking into the headset, the tone was jubilant. Moments later, the leader emerged from the Land Rover, he looked at the technicians and saw how they tried to shield the young woman, he laughed. Waving his pistol in the little group's direction, he issued an order.

One of his men immediately stepped up, placed his machine pistol against the senior technician's side and fired. Three bullets punched through his ribs, the lungs and on into his heart. The technician convulsed then dropped without uttering a sound. The muzzle rose, and the second technician was dispatched with a single bullet to the head. The young woman stood alone, now stunned into shivering silence.

The leader took the few paces to stand beside her at the rear of the flatbed. He laughed, gripped her hair and twisted, moving her face so he could look into her eyes, and shouted at her. 'Weak. Coward.' He shot her in the thigh, with a cry she fell down. He shot her other leg.

Bending, he gripped her and rolled her off the side of the flatbed, where she landed with a gasp on the dry, dusty trackside.

'Wait for lions, they eat you. You die. Tonight.' The leader looked around at his team, laughed, and they joined in, shouting obscenities at her and cheering. Then the leader issued more orders and they slipped into work mode.

As soon as the men had fixed a tarpaulin cover over the Land Rover, the flatbed's engine roared into life and the truck pulled away from the ambush site, leaving the dead untended and the wounded girl to her fate.

Chapter 2
TUESDAY 22ND OCTOBER - PM

Helen sat alone on the high ground and looked down on to the campsite. Around her, the scattered trees and bushes were comfortably greened, drawing water from the river's subterranean seepage. The more distant growth was tinder dry. Like a whole swathe of Eastern Africa, the land sat waiting for the rains; straw yellows, browns and blacks, branches bare save for a few determined leaves. Dried grasses and baked earth - everything waited. Switching her gaze away from the campsite, she looked over to the muddy brown of the Omo River, its sluggish, dry-season flow belying the power it normally boasted.

A little downstream, she could make out Sam. He was crouching beside the line of a rocky outcrop set perhaps a hundred yards back from the riverbank. Beside him were two other archaeologists, Eric Halpern and his wife Rosie. The couple were dedicated field researchers who had been working for years in Ethiopia, around the Omo River. This was their campsite and they had been only too happy to have Sam and Helen join them for a couple of weeks, on the first leg of his recovery and recuperation sabbatical.

Tomorrow, she and Sam would be moving on to Kenya then Tanzania. By the end of the trip, he would have undertaken a review of various sites linked to evidence of early human evolution. He would have recovered from his wounds too, which was all Helen was really concerned about.

She smiled to herself. Yes, it was frustrating to be taking an enforced break from her plans to investigate her inheritance in Edinburgh, but she had always loved Africa, and Sam was clearly benefiting from the break. The sun was high and the slim column of smoke rising above the camp carried the smell of cooking food up to her. It was after midday, and she began to think about heading back to camp.

Helen lowered her gaze to the camp. From beneath her broad brimmed hat, she watched an old and battered 4 x 4 bounce into the campsite. Two or three of the local tribesmen, who provided the security for their camp, closed in on it. After a short discussion that included some raised voices and plenty of arm gestures, the camp guards allowed three occupants to exit the vehicle; a driver, one older man and one who looked like he'd been hired as their escort. Like the camp's own guards, he had an AK47 slung across his shoulder. The driver abandoned his place to squat in the shade of his 4 x 4 and took a long thirsty drink from his water bottle. Accompanied by two of the camp guards, the old man and his escort began the climb up the hill towards her.

Helen stood up as the group approached. 'Hi,' she said. 'How can I help?' About five or six paces off, the group stopped as one. The older man took a single pace forward. He leant on a sturdy walking stick, was dressed in a plain black robe and a small black hat that looked for all the world like a little milk pan. Suspended on a shining chain around his neck was a large and highly stylised cross.

'Good day,' he said, bowing his head slightly. Close up she could see his skin was heavily wrinkled. He was a priest and looked too old to be making journeys into the bush for no good reason.

'You're a long way from anywhere. It's a hot day to be out and about - are you lost?' said Helen.

'Not lost, searching.' He raised his head and made eye contact with Helen. 'For you, I believe.' His eyes smiled from a travel weary face. 'And you are right. It is a hot day for travelling, but at my time of life, every day is too hot.'

Helen was suddenly a little cautious. She glanced beyond the old priest to where Sam had been crouched; he was gone. Casting about, she was relieved to see he and his companions were heading back towards camp for lunch; they would arrive back in just a couple of minutes.

'I don't know why you would want me, but let's go down to the camp and you can explain to my companion at the same time.' She pointed towards the little group walking towards the campsite below.

The priest looked out across the campsite and nodded. 'Yes, I was told you had a … a friend.' With a sigh, he started the climb back down the slope.

'Wait, can you manage? Here, do you want to take my arm?'

The priest waved her offer away and they both worked their way down in silence, closely followed by the escorts.

As soon as they returned to camp, Sam and his companions had spotted the newly arrived 4 x 4, and the three were gathered, waiting outside the canteen tent, when Helen led the visitor off the slope towards them.

As Helen escorted the old priest towards the canteen, Eric Halpern gave a loud chuckle. He thrust out a hand and stepped towards the man. 'Fana Iyasu, welcome. What are you doing out here?'

The men shook hands warmly and Rosie stepped forward to greet him too. 'Fana, come and eat with us. In all these years, I've never known you to get more than ten miles outside Jinka. Why on earth are you here?'

They guided Fana under the canteen awning and introduced him properly to Helen and Sam. More hands were shaken then they sat around a trestle table.

Rosie glanced between Fana and Helen. 'Two ministers at table. I wonder who would like to say grace?'

Fana stretched an open palm towards Helen. 'Please, you must.'

Helen obliged. As soon as grace was finished, Fana snatched up his bottle of chilled water and devoured it in one go. He waved the empty bottle at the cook's assistant who quickly provided a fresh replacement. Then the camp cook appeared and moved methodically round the table, ladling servings of an aromatic stew into the bowls before them. His assistant followed behind, placing warm flatbreads beside the diners.

They started to eat. The stew was tasty; though Helen did not recognise the meat, she didn't bother asking. She'd learnt that the Halperns gave their cook a lot of freedom over the menu and they invariably labelled the dish of the day as bush beef and tucked in regardless. Now she just followed suit.

Rosie looked across the table at Sam and Helen. 'Our base in Jinka is not far from Fana's church, where he's the senior priest. In fact, let's get it right, he's the senior Ethiopian Orthodox Tewahedo Church priest there.' She turned to look at Fana as she spoke, seeking his confirmation.

'Exactly so, Rosie. And let me tell your visitors that it has been a pleasure to have had you both as the church's neighbours all these years.'

Eric laughed a little deprecatingly. 'He wants something.' The others joined in the laughter. 'Seriously, Fana, what are you doing out here?'

Fana's smile remained on his face for a moment, and then the expression faded. Suddenly serious, he looked from

Eric to Helen and back. 'I've come to deliver an invitation to Miss Johnson, Helen.'

'But you don't know her,' said Eric. 'What's this all about, Fana?'

'You're right, I don't know her. Please allow me to explain.'

Eric nodded. Now cautious, Sam and Helen watched Fana; in their world, trust was a commodity that needed to be earned.

'I have come with a message from my Church, from Addis Ababa. From Bishop Ignatius, the patriarch's right hand. He would like to meet the Reverend Johnson in the cathedral of St George, at a time of her convenience, the week after next.'

'A church courtesy visit? You've driven all that way through the bush to deliver an invitation?' said Eric.

'But what a waste of time,' said Rosie. 'We'll all be travelling back to Jinka this afternoon. You could have just called round to our compound to deliver the message then.'

'Why would Bishop Ignatius want to see me?' said Helen.

'Yes, why? She's not even here on Church business, just accompanying Sam on his trip,' said Eric.

Fana shrugged. 'I am just the messenger. Bishop Ignatius is an important person; it's not for me to question him. I have just done as he instructed. Nothing more. But I would say he is not a man who expects to be ignored.'

'Sounds mysterious, or maybe they just want to be seen to be nice to an American Christian cleric. Everybody needs friends,' said Rosie. 'Seriously though, Ethiopia is a Christian country and the Orthodox Tewahedo Church is the State's official church, so Fana rushing out here can't just be on a whim. It must be important.'

Helen reached out a hand and squeezed Sam's forearm, then she looked at Fana apologetically. 'But we can't meet your bishop, Fana. We're flying up to Addis Ababa from

Jinka tomorrow morning and getting a flight out to Nairobi later in the day. I'm sorry, I won't be in the country to meet him when he suggests.' A real advantage of Helen's wealth was access to transport. She had chartered a little plane that would be waiting for them at Jinka's airfield in the morning to fly them up to Addis.

Sam nodded support. 'That's right, I'm afraid we'll be gone.'

Fana's face dropped. 'Are you sure? There are so many things to see in our country, so much history, surely a few days more ...' As his voice trailed off, his face reflected first disappointment then what might have been worry.

'Sorry, Fana, our onward flights from Addis are already booked and arrangements made in Kenya.'

He nodded and said nothing more. It was clear that Fana was a small cog in a big machine, and clear too, that he had never thought for a moment that he might fail in his mission. He had told all he knew and had no persuasive arguments to present. He shrugged, resigned. Then, in an attempt to lighten the mood, Eric ribbed his friend over his unnecessary journey into the bush, and it was clear from Fana's expression that he wished his bishop's instruction had arrived just a day later.

As the meal continued, the sounds of fresh activities reached them from outside. Tents being struck, transports loaded, and then somewhere out at the edge of camp, the diesel generator spluttered and stopped. It was immediately replaced by the sound of a 4 x 4 manoeuvring into position to hook up with it, ready for the tow back to Jinka.

'We'd better get moving,' said Eric, standing up from the table. He lifted the rear flap of the canteen tent and gave the cook and his assistant a thumbs up. 'Great food, thanks men.' The other diners started to stand, and they too called their thanks towards the catering staff, receiving cheery waved acknowledgements in return. Through the opened flap, they could see that the kitchen was already almost packed.

'You're taking everything?' said Helen.

''Yes,' said Rosie. 'We never leave anything unattended with the rains due. It's only what we call the Small Rains. The Big Rains come around March-April time. But last year they weren't so big, pretty much failed, and everywhere is really struggling for water now, though they've got it much worse further south into Kenya and Tanzania.

'Anyway, I know it looks like we're well above the river here, but when the rains come, even the Small Rains, water can do some weird stuff. The river can rise; water can flood down off the hills. Sometimes a little campsite like this can just fill with water from above and be washed away into the river. If it's not got roots, it's not safe to leave out. Really, I mean it, leave anything and it's likely to be gone when you get back.'

'Or stolen?' said Sam.

'Maybe, but unlikely here about. We are on good terms with all the local tribes. They frequently fall out amongst themselves, but we do hire local tribespeople.' She waved towards several men who were busy helping pack away the camp, the ubiquitous AK47s slung over their backs. 'They consider it a matter of pride that things aren't stolen on their patch. It's the rains that are our main problem.'

'Let's move,' said Eric. 'It's a long drive to Jinka, and I don't want to be caught out in the bush unprepared after dark. That's a recipe for disaster.'

A little while later, their convoy of assorted 4 x 4s pulled out, leaving behind an empty clearing, a space that the wild would almost instantly reclaim. There was a four-hour drive ahead of them and only slightly more daylight.

Chapter 3
TUESDAY 22ND OCTOBER - EVENING

His meeting over, Colonel Bob Prentice was at last off-duty. More than anything, he needed a shower and some sleep in a proper bed. The past month had been spent up at Nanyuki, the British Army's specialist live firing ranges in Kenya's remote northern bushlands. Until this morning, he had been roughing it in the bush with his team, carrying out field tests on the ACE system. The tests had come to a very satisfactory conclusion that morning. Immediately thereafter, he had been picked up by helicopter and flown to Nairobi, leaving his men to wrap things up and make the long drive back to Nanyuki base.

The rest of his day had been spent providing reports, answering questions and trying to dampen the wilder responses of a group of very senior NATO staff officers. Finally, when he was about ready to drop, they let him go as they all headed off for a celebratory dinner.

Walking along Kenyatta Avenue's pavement, he was enjoying the still warm but relative cool of the Nairobi evening. Even at this time, the broad street was thronged with vehicles hooting and jostling for position as pedestrians wove precarious routes through the traffic. The drivers' apparent disregard for any rules seemed to present a defiant challenge to the order offered by all the impressive new buildings that had sprung up in the years since Bob's first visit to the city. Here at least, the buildings gave every appearance of a modern capital.

In spite of appearances, he knew to be careful. The city was full of poor and desperate people. Young men and women, boys and girls, innocents born in the city's gutters and back lanes to grow up with only one future - to populate the street gangs. In growing up, they quickly learnt just two simple lessons. The only way to get food for today was to take it by whatever means came to hand, and nobody outside the gang could be trusted, ever.

Bob understood the situation. This might be a relaxed stroll but he remained alert. Life was cheap, and he knew there were plenty on the streets who would consider taking a Westerner's life a worthwhile risk for the contents of their wallet. Here in the centre of town, many of the old back lanes had been cleared away, making space for more and more new-build commercial buildings, but he wouldn't stray off the main drag at night unless he had to. That would be asking for trouble.

At the junction with Kimathi Street, he took a right, heading for the Hilton. Just five minutes' walk from here and he could finally relax. His bag had been dropped off earlier in the day. There, he had a room for the night, and tomorrow, he would fly back to the UK. He paused as a vibration in his trouser pocket flagged an incoming message. Shifting to the side of the pavement, he positioned his back against a hoarding, put up to shield pedestrians from the next big construction. He pulled his phone from his pocket. A text from BATUK.

ACE taken. Be alert.

Even as he read the text, his phone started to ring. It was Brigadier Starling, his direct commander, and one of the team who had spent so many hours grilling him.

'Prentice speaking, sir.'

'Good. Have you heard?'

'Just got a text from BATUK. What happened?'

'We don't know everything. The convoy was late getting back to base and had gone radio silent. Come evening, the commander sent out a search team. Thank God he did, or we'd still be none the wiser. 'They're all dead. Ambush. Complete slaughter. ACE has vanished.'

Bob Prentice grimaced. It was his team; they had worked together on the project for a long time. Losing his people was a personal disaster, a tragedy. Losing ACE might prove to be a military catastrophe.

'Who was it?'

'We have no idea. It could have been any one of a score of countries who'd like to get their hands on ACE. Right now, we're running blind.'

'What's the plan, sir?'

'Well, whoever it was, if they knew enough about the system to steal it, they'll know they need you too. So, at this instant, you're our number one concern. How far are you from the Hilton?'

'Corner of Kimathi Street and Kenyatta Avenue. Less than five minutes' walk to the Hilton. I can see it from here.'

'Go now, I'll meet you there. I'm on my way. I've asked for an escort to come over from Kifaru Camp, we'll keep you there tonight and get you back to the UK as planned in the morning.'

'Can't the Kenyan authorities help?'

'No chance. Political relations are bad enough with the Kenyans already. And our land lease agreement at Nanyuki is specifically for troop training. If they get wind we've been testing this new kit up there, they will kick off big style.'

'Okay, I'm heading for the Hilton now.'

Bob ended the call and gripped his phone tightly, glancing about. Traffic continued to roll past, horns sounding, and there were plenty of people about. All seemed to be going about their business. Most were ordinary folk, unthreatening. A few dangerous looking types, but that was normal for Nairobi. He set off walking along Kimathi Street. A fast pace but not so fast as to attract attention.

Almost before he'd started walking, he'd spotted them. Three Asian men, innocently crossing the road but on a course that would intercept his in about thirty paces. The uninitiated would have seen only three separate individuals moving independently in a similar direction. He saw the hunting formation, the staggered approach, preparing to encircle their prey - him. The middle man was making a phone call as he walked; there were more of them around.

Bob broke into a run. The nearest of the hunters caught him. An arm wrapped around Bob's neck, a hand clasped across his face. His legs drove him onward in a conditioned response developed through years spent on school and college rugby fields, Bob's momentum carried the man with him for a couple of paces. In those two paces, Bob had punched the man hard between the legs and turned his face to press his mouth against the man's cheek. He bit, hard, and with his legs still driving forward he turned his face to spit out a mouthful of flesh.

The man fell away screaming, his hands simultaneously clutching at face and groin. As the body fell away, Bob picked up speed, then dropping his shoulder slightly, he collided with the second assailant, sending the man and his phone clattering into the gutter. Bob's phone dropped too, and he cursed. No time to pick it up. Stretching his legs, he thought he might just outpace the third man, might make it.

Then his heart sank, ahead of him, running from the direction of the Hilton were five, no, six men, a bigger pack.

Even with his training, he was outnumbered beyond chance, and then suddenly he knew who they were. His heart sank as he recognised the sixth man, hurrying behind the pack, shorter than the rest, plumper, and smartly turned out in a safari suit. Bob's survival didn't matter now, getting the message out did.

Coming up on his right was the Stanley Hotel's entrance. If he played things right, there was still a chance. He stopped dead in his tracks and spun round. The third man suddenly realised contact was going to occur ahead of plan and desperately tried to adjust his approach, but it was too late. Bob took a half step to the side avoiding the third man's improvised flying kick, the boot passing where his chest had been a moment before. Sticking out a stiff arm, he caught the flying man square in the face.

With a cry, the man dropped to the ground, clutching his face.

Not waiting to assess the damage. Bob stepped smartly past the concierge, who was occupied guiding a wealthy guest to his limousine, and into the Stanley Hotel. Approaching the reception desk, he pointed at the phone and asked if he could use it. The receptionist looked uneasy and Bob was suddenly aware of uncomfortable glances from guests passing by.

He caught sight of his image in the large mirrored wall behind reception and understood why. Dishevelled, unshaven and unwashed, it would have been enough on any day to unnerve the reception team at the Stanley, one of the traditional grand hotels of East Africa. Throw in his shirt, soaked in somebody else's blood, a series of fingernail scratches raked across his face and fresh blood still trickling down his chin; calling security was the receptionist's only option. He saw the receptionist's hand frantically pressing a security buzzer; saw her eyes flitting back and forth from the madman in front of her to the discreet entranceway from where she prayed her salvation would emerge.

Bob turned and walked briskly away from reception, passing behind a large structural pillar and into the Stanley's Thorn Tree Café. The receptionist watched him go. A few moments later, security arrived, and she shouted directions to them, pointing after Bob. They rushed in, following his route. Shortly after they disappeared beyond a pillar into the café's entranceway, Bob emerged from the other side of the pillar and walked back into reception. The receptionist panicked, screamed, and suddenly guests and staff were running in every direction. Bob hurried past the reception towards the street exit. Pausing, he turned towards a high mounted security camera, and making a sign with his hand, he pointed back into the hotel and mouthed a few words. Then he turned and ran out into the street.

He reached the pavement and kept running, heading out across the road and directly into the traffic flow. As he ran, he was aware of the larger group to his right closing from the direction of the Hilton, much closer now. And he could sense those he had already clashed with coming in fast from his left.

Across the street was an opening, leading into a narrower side road. He took it, passed the less glamorous Oakwood Hotel where, years back, he had stayed on more than one occasion when off-duty in Nairobi. Ahead, the side street made a hard-right turn into Kimathi Lane. The chasing pack was closer now. He hoped he might find refuge in one of the gold and jewellery shops he knew lined both sides of the lane just round the turn, if he could make it that far. He kept going; he would find safety there.

Turning the corner, he ran towards the line of shops, his sudden approach triggering a flurry of activity.

'No, wait.' Out of breath, his voice scarcely carried.

Each shop had its own guard; some had two. All were tasked to stand by the shutters and control access. At the slightest sign of trouble - gold was an attractive target for street gangs - the guards' job was to step inside and roll down the steal filigreed shutters behind them. Then from their secure vantage points, the guards could fend off persistent attackers and provide covering support to the guards of other shops along the lane.

In just an instant, to the sound of slamming shutters, the street was emptied and the guards watched cautiously from behind their shutters as Bob ran past. Disappointed, he didn't bother stopping; trying to force entry would have elicited a violent response. Leaving the shops behind, he put on one last spurt of speed. If he could get back to the main street via the far end of the lane then maybe, just maybe, he could hail a taxi and escape.

Nearly there, Bob felt a hand on his shoulder, slowing him. He tried to shrug it off, but another grabbed him, and he was bundled to the ground. He struggled, but more and more men piled on, pinning him fast to the ground. Furious, Bob glared at the short plump man who had now caught up with the chase.

Producing a syringe from the jacket of his safari suit, the plump man pulled off the needle's protective cap.

'No. Don't you dare.' Bob struggled harder against his captors, to no avail.

In silence, the plump man bent over Bob and plunged the needle into his upper arm, squeezed down the plunger. Then he straightened up, discarding the used syringe and looking coldly at Bob.

'Welcome, Colonel Prentice. Your resistance is over. You are mine now.'

Bob couldn't respond, his voice would not articulate the words he wanted. His limbs stopped responding to instructions, then a wave of black swept through his mind and his struggle ended.

Chapter 4

WEDNESDAY 23RD OCTOBER - PM

Helen and Sam sat in one of the refreshment zones of the Addis Ababa Bole Airport. Each had a bottle of cold water set on the table in front of them and took an occasional mouthful. Their morning flight from Jinka on a little twin-engine Otter had passed uneventfully.

Once offloaded, they had checked their bags onto the Nairobi flight early and were now waiting in the airy concourse. High ceilings, clever use of glazed internal walls, and white colouring, provided a bright and welcoming atmosphere. They relaxed, just sitting quietly, watching the world go by while getting used to the hustle of humanity after their time in the bush, pausing for a little while before getting in line for the mandatory security checks.

Their peace was disrupted by a man who approached their table and rested a hand on the back of one of the empty chairs opposite. 'Sam Cameron?' he said.

Sam looked up at the man. He was smartly turned out in a white open-necked shirt and lightweight beige suit. One side of his jacket sagged slightly; weighed down with what

Sam guessed would be a phone and keys. 'Who's asking?' said Sam.

'Ah good, I thought I'd recognised you. Rupert Peterson, but please, call me Rupert.'

'And you want to speak with me because?' Sam was sitting up straight, paying attention, but he did not invite the new arrival to sit. The man's voice was English and accent free. Sam could not place him at all.

'Ha, good question. I thought you'd ask that one. Now look, old man, I really need a quiet word with you.' Rupert glanced towards Helen as he spoke, then rolled his eyes towards an empty table some yards away. 'Perhaps you'll allow me to buy you a beer?' He brandished a roughly furled umbrella in the direction of the table and then set off without waiting for Sam's reply.

Sam watched Rupert pause beside a chair at the empty table, saw him use a foot to push out the chair and beckon expectantly towards him. The umbrella in Rupert's other hand rose high like a signal mast and he waved it languidly in a signal towards the far end of the room. Then he raised his free hand too, making an open cupped hand sign that he tilted rhythmically at the wrist signalling drinks. His gesture morphed into two fingers held prominently aloft.

Helen and Sam traced Rupert's direction of gaze and saw a second man, a little younger than Rupert, wave back an acknowledgement, before heading for the bar.

'I'd better go and see what this is all about,' said Sam.

'Hmmm, must you? It's all a bit odd. What do you think it might be?'

'I have no idea. But they seem ready to wait us out.' Sam watched as Rupert sat, crossed his legs and then reached out with his umbrella to prod at the chairback opposite him, pushing it out invitingly. Then he leant back, folded his arms and arched his eyebrow in a slightly quizzical way towards

Sam. 'We've got an hour to kill still; I may as well go and see what he wants.'

'Okay, but be careful.'

Sam stood and walked slowly across to Rupert's table. He settled into the seat opposite him.

'Well?' said Sam, fixing Rupert with a blank stare. 'I asked you why you wanted to speak with me. You've got two minutes then I'm going back to my table.'

Rupert smiled at Sam. 'You're quite right to be cautious, I understand completely. In fact, I'm quite pleased to see that's the case. Unfamiliar places, difficult times, not to be cautious might prove hazardous.'

'Are you threatening me?'

'No, no, nothing could be further from the case. Look, here's my ID, see.' Rupert pulled his wallet from the sagging jacket pocket and picked out an ID card. He slid it across the table.

Sam recognised the diplomatic pass; he'd had one himself for a spell, some years before. 'Captain Rupert Peterson. Military attaché to the British Embassy in Addis Ababa.' He looked up at Rupert and handed back the ID card. 'Good for you. Now if you don't have anything to say I'll rejoin my companion, okay?'

'Here's the beer coming,' said Rupert, pointing across the room at his colleague who was weaving towards them, carrying a tray with two bottles of beer. 'You said two minutes, I've hardly had that.'

Sam was silent for a moment. 'Keep talking,' he said, focusing on Rupert and ignoring the assistant who placed the bottles of beer on the table and retreated.

'Right. I'll call you Sam. Unless you object? Good. Sam, I know you are over here on a sabbatical of sorts and you've been out of uniform for a few years, but I'm afraid HMG needs you. It has to be said, needs you rather desperately—'

'Save your breath. See her?' Sam pointed across towards Helen who was sitting watching them. 'I'm with her; we're on an archaeological study tour of the Great Rift Valley for my university. It's a tight schedule. Just finished Ethiopia, due in Kenya next and then we're scheduled to visit Tanzania. Sorry, I've no time and I'm not interested. Anyway, I can't think what I can do that any one of your people wouldn't manage in half the time.' He stood up.

'Please! Sam, sit. We are in big trouble. At least hear me out.' Rupert's voice was as smooth as ever, but Sam could see anxiety in the man's face - he really was worried.

'Just until I've finished this beer,' said Sam, sitting again. He lifted the beer bottle and began to drink.

Rupert's features relaxed just a little. 'Thank you. Now, what I'm about to tell you is in the strictest confidence. We've had something of an upset in Kenya, at the BATUK base in Nanyuki. I know you were there some years ago.'

Sam gave a little nod. Clearly, Rupert had full access to his old military personnel files. 'I know it. What's that got to do with me now?'

'Look, there's a lot to cover, and a lot that can't be said, but the key points are these. You know HMG and the Kenyan president have been at loggerheads for some time, over various threatened international corruption cases, crimes against humanity, the works really. You name it; he and his cronies seem to have done it. You'll have seen the stories bubbling along in the newspapers. Well, relations have taken a turn for the worse recently and the Kenyans have put significant restrictions on our staff moving in and out of Kenya.

'We've just suffered a significant loss in Kenya and can't do anything about it. We are not allowed to fly in the people we need who might be able to sort it out, and even my counterpart in Kenya, who between you and me, is a bit of a greenhorn, has just been restricted to Nairobi so he can't do much either. We're stuck.'

'I'm not a policeman. If you've had kit stolen, tell the Kenyans. They have a police force too; let them fix it for you.'

Rupert gave a short intake of breath. 'If only it were that simple. Look, Sam, we can't tell them what was taken since its presence in Kenya would have breached the terms of our land-use agreement. That would turn our current political dispute with the Kenyans into a nightmare and probably result in our being kicked off the land and out of the country permanently.'

'I'm sorry; I haven't got time for this. I've got places to be and certainly no time to go running around a foreign country searching for a piece of kit that I know nothing about …' Sam stopped talking, distracted by a movement at Helen's table. She had been approached by a smartly dressed man. They were talking; he couldn't make out what was being said but she was smiling, so at least that didn't seem too threatening. Two or three paces behind Helen's visitor waited three men, one middle aged, two young, all dressed as priests. He turned his attention back to Rupert. 'Can't help, I'm afraid. No, won't help, to be more precise. I'm not a recovery agent; you need to hire a bailiff.'

'This is not about the stolen kit. Well, yes, it is, it's top secret and half the countries in the world would like to get their hands on it. But there's more—'

Sam finished his bottle. 'Time's up, sorry, got to go.'

'They've taken one of our people. We need to find him.' Rupert's voice lost a little of its composure as he hissed out the words in a desperate attempt to keep Sam's attention.

'What do you mean taken? Kidnapped? Just pay the money; you'll get him back soon enough, job done.'

'It's not a ransom; he's been taken, because he's part of the kit. Somebody you know,' Rupert's voice had returned to its normal control.

'Who? And stop talking in riddles. What do you mean, part of the kit?'

'Colonel Bob Prentice. He's been snatched.'

Sam sat down. He was interested now. Colonel Bob Prentice had been his commander, then mentor and finally friend. 'Snatched?'

'Yes, snatched. I thought that name might catch your attention. Now it's not a riddle. The army's been developing a new piece of kit called ACE. I can't say what it does, but it's been taken from up at Nanyuki and the whole test team killed, all of them except Colonel Prentice who had been airlifted down to Nairobi for a meeting just before the attack.'

'If he wasn't there, how's he missing?'

'Abducted off the street in Nairobi later in the day. Whoever did this has a big team and is very organised to be able to pull off two strikes, well over a hundred miles apart, on the same day.'

'So, they needed Bob alive?'

'It would seem logical to assume so and hence we are not simply asking for your help to trace a piece of kit, rather to help find your friend, before whoever's got him manages to get him and the kit away to wherever.'

'Are you sure he's still in country?'

'We think so. Certainly been no unscheduled cargo flights out and our American friends have a little monitoring station at the port in Mombasa, so we know nothing's gone out by sea as yet. We just don't know where ACE or the colonel have gone.'

'Why have they taken Bob?'

'A lot of this is above my pay grade, I'm afraid. What I do know is ACE is miles ahead of the game and its operation is controlled by bio-security. The lead operator is preprogrammed for the equipment and his life signs are integrated into the system. None of the old iris scans or thumbprints. You can't dig out an eye or chop off a hand to work around the security anymore. This is based on an individual's life signs. Try to access or operate the kit in their absence, and the whole thing auto-fries into a mess of junk. Whoever has the ACE, has Bob Prentice alive.'

'Okay, I get it. Your people on the ground are unable to move about, you can't get anybody into the country quickly, and you want me to find Bob.'

'And ACE, of course. And let's face it; your file says you are the man for the job.'

'That was a long time ago; I'm a lecturer now.'

'Exactly so. A civilian with all the pre-issued visas you could wish for. Able to buzz to and fro around these East African countries looking at fossils and such. Perfectly legitimate. Nobody is going to turn a hair when you go past. Now, let's get more beers and I'll tell you what I can.'

For his friend's sake, Sam nodded agreement to Rupert, who promptly raised his umbrella to signal for more beers. Sam glanced over to Helen; she seemed to be managing fine with her stranger. He half raised an arm, waving towards her.

Helen spotted the movement and gave a little wave back, mouthing a word of encouragement before turning to address the man who still stood next to her table, she smiled. 'Please do sit down. This is a surprise but you're most welcome, your, your'—She hesitated for a moment, wondering desperately what form of address would be correct in his Church—'your Grace.'

Bishop Ignatius sat and waited for a moment, his assistant remained standing.

'Well, I'm glad Fana got my reply to you. It's just a pity that we're leaving Ethiopia today. Otherwise, I would have been very happy to visit you next week. But I'm a very small fish, I'm sure you could have found far more significant church ministers travelling through your country than me. Tell me, why me?'

Bishop Ignatius smiled gently at Helen. 'I think you underplay your status somewhat.'

'Not me. I'm just passing through on private business.'

'I wonder what that private business might be? We were very pleased when you came to Ethiopia, though more than a little worried when you vanished into the hinterland. I must say we wondered what you were doing. Then we learnt you were out in the bush at the Omo National Park. You can imagine we were very confused.'

Helen looked at the bishop, confused herself. 'What are you talking about? I don't understand. Why were you expecting me?'

The bishop gave a smile of understanding. 'Quite right, it's important to be careful.'

'Look, I really have no idea what you are talking about.'

'Come now, Miss Johnson. Here in Ethiopia we are far away from Europe but not so far that a news broadcast can't reach us. My colleagues and I have been watching events with some interest. The awful, awful things in Edinburgh and in Kefalonia too. And what exactly happened in Crete? That was a mystery, but our ecumenical contacts talk of some great success for Rome.'

Helen was suddenly on her guard. Her natural predisposition to give a stranger the benefit of the doubt had been tempered by recent events. She gave an involuntary shiver as the bishop's words drew back the thinnest of veils that she was gradually learning how to keep closed.

She thought of John Dearly, the parish minister of St Bernard's, Edinburgh, whose assistant she had been before his brutal death. Remembered the promise she had given John, even as he died; thought of the signet ring and the heavy gold chain he had begged her with his dying breath to take from around his neck.

It now hung around her neck. She recalled his desperate warnings to be careful with the unexpected inheritance and secret responsibilities that had accompanied the ring. And she shuddered again over all the subsequent deaths. Feeling uncomfortable, she looked across to Sam, but he was deep in conversation with Rupert, suddenly as if they were the best of buddies.

'What exactly are you getting at, your Grace?' said Helen.

'I just wonder, it seems your interests and ours might coincide.'

'How so?'

Bishop Ignatius looked around; making sure nobody was paying any attention to their conversation. 'I know you have to be careful, but we must speak now. It has been a long wait for your visit.'

'I don't understand.'

Bishop Ignatius gave a forced chuckle. 'Please, do not play a game with me. Your secret is our secret. We must come together now. It is why you came, I know this, it must be.'

Helen stood up. 'Your Grace, I don't know you; I don't know what you're talking about. Now I'm feeling uncomfortable, please can we let this drop, yes?'

Sam appeared at Helen's side. 'What's up?'

Sam's presence triggered action, and the three priests, who had been hovering a little distance off, quickly closed in to stand behind their bishop.

'This is Bishop Ignatius. He thinks he knows me. He's upset I haven't visited him.'

'I don't understand why you deny me. Please, like you, today I'm travelling away. To Arusha, in Tanzania, for the Christianity in Africa Conference. I will be back in a week. We must speak then.'

'Why?'

'Because we must. It is not my place to initiate this. It is written that the collector will call. You are the collector; you must take the first step.'

'Oh, come on, we've no time for riddles today. I've got bigger things to worry about, right now,' said Sam. 'Helen, we really have to catch our flight.'

'Just a minute, Sam.' Helen rested a restraining hand on his wrist while maintaining eye contact with the bishop. 'Explain, why am I to visit you and what am I collecting?'

Bishop Ignatius leant forward, lowering his voice so only Helen could hear. 'It must be you. Everything points to it. Tell me, one question, answer truthfully and we will know.'

Helen nodded slowly. 'Okay, ask away, but don't get your hopes up.'

The bishop pressed his eyes closed for a moment, muttered a little prayer then fixed Helen with an almost imploring gaze while stretching his hand across the table to take hers in what seemed a near desperate clasp. 'Have you got it? Have you got the ring?'

Helen held his gaze, not flinching, not giving away any sign of recognition. 'And what ring might that be?' She knew what ring he was referring to. It was hanging where it always did, on the end of a chain three inches above the tight knot that, until a minute ago, had been her stomach.

'You know. You must know.' His hand squeezed tighter. 'Please.'

Helen pulled her hand free. 'Look, I can see this means a lot to you but right now I can't help.' She pointed up at the flight information screens that were announcing her flight. 'That's our flight.'

The bishop was silent for a long moment. 'I must assume you are testing me.'

Helen knew she would have to speak with this man again. Suddenly, the ring weighed more heavily round her neck. What did he know? What did he want? She thought she had learnt all the ring's secrets. Had thought wrong. 'Perhaps, we should meet again.'

The bishop, composed again, smiled at her and stood. 'Thank you. Yes, there is reason to meet. But now you must take your flight to Nairobi and I go to Arusha to prepare for my conference. I will be in touch.'

They shook hands across the table. Bishop Ignatius turned and walked away, followed by his staff. Helen watched him go, wondering whether she had made a mistake.

'What's that all about?' said Sam.

'I'll tell you on the plane. Come on, let's go.' Helen fell silent as they hurried for the departure zone.

They had just reached the head of the queue for security checks when a woman immediately behind in the queue nudged Helen's arm. 'Hey, it's nice to hear a voice from back home, you're American, right?' said the woman; a broad and friendly smile crossed her face as Helen turned. 'Call me Tracy, honey.'

Helen smiled in return. 'Nice to meet you. Where are you headed?'

'I'm headed for Maputo, you know, Mozambique. What about yourself?'

'Nairobi,' said Helen.

'That's nice, on holiday or are you working?'

'Bit of both, I guess,' said Helen. Sam had stepped forward to be searched and, next in line, she turned, ready to step forward.

She started slightly as Tracy closed in behind her. The woman leant forward and whispered into her ear. 'Don't turn round. Beyond the security counter, there's a restroom about twenty paces off, on the right-hand side - be there in five minutes.' Tracy straightened up, still smiling to the world.

As Helen was beckoned forward by a security guard, Tracy called out. 'You take care, Helen. Hope I see you again soon, honey.'

Standing in front of the guard, Helen chanced a brief glance back towards Tracy. The woman had donned sunglasses and was busy looking in any direction but Helen's. Who was she? What did she want? How did she know her name?

Once through the security gates, Helen hurried over to Sam who was waiting a few paces beyond. They walked further into the departure lounge as Helen explained what had just happened. 'Do you think I should go meet her?'

'There's a lot going on that we don't know about. I still have to tell you what Rupert said. I don't think this Tracy means you any direct harm. If so, why bother announcing herself? In any event, I doubt it will be dangerous, certainly not here in public anyway. Look, you go in, I'll wait directly outside the entrance. At the least sign of trouble, shout, and I'll be there in a flash, ladies only or not.'

Helen looked at Sam intently. 'Okay,' she said. 'But I've got stuff to tell you too. Bishop Ignatius is a very interesting man.' She looked at the large digital clock set into the departures board, thrust her arm through his and started walking. 'Come on, I've a date to keep.'

Pushing open the door, Helen stepped cautiously inside. It was a long, quite narrow room. Immediately in front of her were a couple of wall-mounted towel dispensers and four hot air hand driers. Beyond that, a row of around a dozen sinks stretched to the end of the room. The whole wall was mirrored, creating a sense of space where, in practice, there was little. Opposite the mirrored wall was a row of cubicles. Most of the doors were open to varying degrees and Helen guessed they were empty.

A mother and her two young children were at the first sink, she was lifting the smaller of the children, so he could reach the taps. The only other occupant stood at the far end of the room. In one hand she held a lipstick, in the other a small travel brush with which she was rhythmically brushing her hair.

Tracy looked back along the line of sinks and smiled at Helen. 'Hey, Helen, I'm over here, come on over.' She beckoned enthusiastically, every bit the friendly tourist.

Helen walked past the mother who was too preoccupied with her children to register anything about the other women in the room.

'Well, here I am, Tracy. Now what's the big mystery?'

Tracy had stopped brushing her hair; she looked back into the mirror and pursed her lips. 'I'm thinking this pink is a little pale for travelling, what do you say? Would red be better? I have one in my bag.' She finished speaking and turned to face Helen just as the mother and children left; the door swung shut and they were alone.

'I don't care; I do want to know why I'm here.'

Tracy let the veneer drop and was suddenly very businesslike. 'Helen, you're an American citizen, so am I.'

'Yes, and ...' said Helen.

'Listen, honey, I'll cut straight to the chase. I work for the United States Government and there is some bad stuff happening in this part of the world right now. Stuff that's very important to us. But, as I'm sure your friend will tell you soon enough, like the British Government we're caught up in a political stand-off and our well-known faces are being denied access to the country right now.'

'Which country?'

Tracy paused before answering; it looked like she was wondering whether or not Helen was trying to wind her up. 'Kenya.'

'I see, and what has this got to do with me?'

'Your friend, Sam Cameron, has just spent the past little while getting a briefing from Addis Ababa's resident MI6 man. I'm betting Sam's now got a job to do in Kenya, something that's very precious to the British and, as their ally, we have a mutual interest, so it's just as precious to us.'

'I haven't got the slightest idea what you're talking about.'

'I know, and I haven't got time to brief you now. I trust Sam will give you the details, speak to him.'

'And tell him what? That I'm spying on him for you. You're CIA, aren't you?'

'Honey, you tell him what you like, but you're an American citizen and your country needs you to keep us in the loop. But from what I've heard, he's a solid kind of guy. He'll understand.'

'I'm not spying on Sam.'

'No, you're not. You're representing your country's interests, that's all. You have a duty to serve your country any way you can. We need you. And believe me, if there had been no political mess with the Kenyan president, we'd be in country, working on the ground with the Brits right now. We're on the same side, but everyone's in the dark here. All I want is for you to keep me posted. Right?' Tracy smiled her broad smile again and fished a card out of her bag. 'Call me any time, but only use the satellite phone, it's a little more secure.'

Helen glared at her. How did Tracy know that she and Sam had a satellite phone? Before she could challenge her further, an elderly lady pushed through the entrance door.

Tracy turned back to the mirror, pursing her lips again. 'You know, honey, I think I'll stick with the pink.'

Chapter 5

WEDNESDAY 23RD OCTOBER - EVENING

The sun was just dropping beneath the horizon as Helen and Sam exited Nairobi's Jomo Kenyatta Airport. He was pushing a trolley with their bags on, she was walking close beside him. It would have been an audacious thief who tried to snatch bags from under their noses, but they weren't taking any chances.

The heat hit them like a wave as they left the shade of the airport's covered foyer and stepped into the pickup zone. Almost instantly, they were hit by another wave, this time human. It seemed they were approached from every direction by taxi touts, all clamouring on behalf of their particular driver. Sam waved them away and pulled back slightly from the taxi queue, looking around for his ride. For a moment, he thought they'd been stood up, and then he spotted a hand waving from beyond the row of parked taxis.

'There's our lift,' he said. 'Come on, the sooner we're away from here the better.'

Susan Curtis was middle-aged, brisk and confident - the epitome of the middle class, post colonials who popped up in many parts of Kenyan life. She had grown up in the country and her parents and brother still lived on the family farm in the south, near the Tanzanian border. After university in England, she had returned to the country she loved. Not particularly career driven, Susan had been happy to take a job as assistant to an up and coming academic. Now, twenty-five years later, he was a senior professor and she was still his assistant. Assistant was a deceptive job title; in the professor's absence, she ran things. Clever and with a bark that was matched by a steely bite, nobody, neither staff nor student, wanted to cross her.

'You may as well both squeeze into the front with me. The aircon's great so you won't get too clammy. Got to keep my eyes on the road all the time hereabouts, so I can't be twisting round to speak to you. Incidentally, I understand you will want to get settled after your journey, but Professor Ngure is very keen to see you, Sam. He suggested we stop off at the university on the way to your hotel, only for an hour, he promised.'

Sam glanced at Helen, knowing she was not going to be interested in what the professor wanted to discuss. 'Perhaps we could drop Helen at the hotel first?'

'Of course we can,' said Susan while swerving to avoid a dog that had run onto the carriageway. She blasted her horn; the dog seemed unconcerned but several of the surrounding drivers hooted back in defiance of some assumed slight to their driving. 'Lunatics!' Susan braked again and flashed her headlights at the little van that had just cut in front of her. A futile gesture, the van was so overloaded the driver couldn't use his mirrors even if he'd wanted to. Amidst a stream of colourful language, she implied that he clearly needed glasses.

'The traffic is a bit high pressure here,' said Helen.

'This is nothing, wait for the morning rush, then you'll know all about it. By the way, madmen aside, you should be safe enough driving in the city. But if you're out on the highways, especially the coast road to Mombasa, don't stop if you're flagged down for an accident or such; there's always a chance it's a set-up and you'll be robbed, or worse.'

'Thanks for the tip,' said Sam, 'but I'll be okay. I've been a frequent visitor to Kenya in the past.'

'Really? What were you doing here? Work or pleasure?'

'Oh, work.'

'I don't recall you ever visiting the university before.'

'No, it was in a previous lifetime, before I took up archaeology.'

'Oh? What line were you in?'

'British Army,' said Sam, and then looked purposefully out through the side window, ending the conversation.

• • •

It was nearer three hours later when Sam finally joined Helen in the hotel room. She had soaked long in the bath, eaten a good meal and was now lounging on a sofa trying to make sense of the day's events. Sam's missing friend Bob Prentice, the slightly mysterious Rupert Peterson who Sam believed was MI6, Tracy who openly admitted to being CIA and, weirdest of all, Bishop Ignatius - what did he want from her? And he knew about her ring. By the time Sam arrived, she had not made much progress with the problem but had made a start on the bottle of rosé wine that room service had delivered.

Helen stood and crossed the room to meet him; a greetings kiss was followed by an anxious look. 'Sam, what's the plan?'

'I've agreed with Professor Ngure to postpone things for a day or so. That leaves us uncommitted tomorrow at least, so I can do a little digging into Bob's abduction. Then we're meant to head out of Nairobi, to see some work that's being done in the south of the country, and after that we will cross the border to link up with some of the Tanzanian academics he's working in partnership with. You know, what they're doing here is really interesting, only I can't focus on it just now.'

'I'm surprised you can be bothered with it at all right now.'

'I know. I've managed to avoid fixing a start date today but he's quite insistent I go back later tomorrow and make a plan. I'll do it because we daren't risk anyone in authority questioning the validity of my visas. Getting kicked out now would be a total disaster.'

He went to the fridge, pulled it open and lifted out a bottle of beer. Then he crossed the room to settle onto the sofa beside Helen. 'It seems we're in demand right now. Everyone wants a piece of us. But Helen, I want you to be careful. This can be a very dangerous place, and it's not your fight.'

She laughed at him and play punched his shoulder. 'Dangerous? Remember what we've been through in the past few months? You and I are always on the same side, Mr Cameron. If there's trouble, I'll be with you. Anyway, I spent three years in West Africa. Believe me, I know what dangerous Africa really means.'

Sam raised his bottle to her glass and they clinked together. 'Here's to trouble then,' he said.

'And don't forget I have to stay around; the CIA has demanded I do my patriotic duty and spy on you.'

They clinked glasses again. 'Okay, I can't argue with that Agent Johnson, you'd better do your duty.'

The phone rang. Sam answered it, identified himself, listened for a short while and then agreed to be collected at 09.30 next morning. He hung up.

'That was John Guthrie, Rupert Peterson's counterpart here. He's collecting us in the morning. We'll see what he's got to say, though, like Rupert said, he sounds a bit inexperienced. I want to make a start by visiting the scene of Bob's abduction.'

'I still don't understand what was stolen when your friend Bob was taken.'

'The events occurred several hours and nearly two hundred miles apart. So, they are linked but separate incidents. What it shows is great coordination, and nerve too. But that's the weird thing, Rupert Peterson wouldn't tell me what ACE is other than it has some sort of bio-security key built in that's linked to Bob Prentice. You know, I don't think he knows any more himself.'

'Is this John Guthrie likely to tell you anything more?'

'Perhaps, but I'm not convinced he will. It's a secret project and the whole system is in lockdown, which makes it hard to understand anything that's happened or predict future moves.'

'Why would they do that? Your friend needs rescuing.'

'Self-preservation. If this becomes public, there will be repercussions, and somebody will be left to carry the can. As sure as hell, it won't be the top brass. By locking it down they limit spread and can focus blame.'

'Surely, they'll want the ACE back, whatever it is?'

'Of course, but probably not at the expense of their own reputations. The Kenyan president's blocking of official movement provides our leaders with a perfect reason for their inadequate response. And sets up the fall guys nicely.'

'Who?'

'I'm guessing that novice who just phoned and—'

Helen sat up straight and looked at Sam. 'And what about you? Where do you fit in?'

'You know what I think? I'm doing two jobs. First, I'm what your American brethren would call a patsy. Rupert sets me up, he demonstrates he did what he could from outside the country, and as and when it all goes wrong, he's shown initiative and been proactive in getting me on the ground. And it's me that's blown it, not him.'

Helen scowled. 'That isn't right.'

'No. And I think the top brass are letting him do it, so they can legitimately delegate responsibility to the man making decisions in the field. When it all goes wrong, they can point to Rupert as having the lead role, and he can point to me.

'And if we do defy the odds and save Bob and the ACE, they'll all be quick to step forward and take credit for great problem resolution skills. Probably get promotions out of it.'

'But what about Bob? Is nobody actually trying to get him back?'

'Remember, all Rupert could tell me was, whatever ACE is, it includes some sort of direct bio-security link to Bob. Try to activate it without him and the system completely fries, self-destructs. I'm guessing there are one or two top brass hoping Bob didn't make it. That would fry the kit and wipe away all their security breach problems in a stroke.'

'That's shocking; surely they can't just write somebody off?'

'Shocking? Yes, why do you think I finished with the services? You don't get to be a big country by being nice. There's a lot of dirt washed under the bridge along the way.'

Helen drained her wine glass and Sam, anticipating her need, refilled it at once. Then he looked at his beer bottle. 'That's done,' he said, tossing it into the wastepaper basket. 'Water for me now.'

'Where does that leave you … us?' said Helen as Sam returned with iced water from the fridge. He let himself slump into the sofa.

'Sacrificial lambs as far as some are concerned, but I owe Bob Prentice a lot. He got me out of a tricky spot once or twice in the early part of my military career. In fact, I probably owe him my life, so regardless of what the generals are setting up, I'm going to save Bob.'

'No. You mean, we're going to save Bob.'

'Well, seems like nobody else is going to.'

Chapter 6

THURSDAY 24TH OCTOBER - AM

First thing in the morning, Helen had made a phone call back to St Bernard's, her church centre in Edinburgh, where Elaine oversaw all the day-to-day activity. Her request of the older woman was met without comment. Elaine's stoic, unflappable nature and her loyalty to Helen meant explanations were not necessary. She was asked to get Scottie Brown, their friendly IT security expert, to dig around discreetly to find anything he could about the ACE system, as quickly as possible.

Exactly on time, Sam and Helen arrived at the Hilton's reception and looked about for their contact. A smart young man stepped briskly across to join them.

'Hello, Sam Cameron?' he said, stretching out his hand in greeting when it became clear he had made the correct assumption. 'Pleased to meet you, really pleased. I'm John Guthrie, and you must be Miss Johnson, or is that "reverend"? How should I address you?'

'Just call me Helen, everyone does.'

'Okay, will do. But look, let's get away from here; I've got a car waiting outside. Why don't we get in and the driver will run us across to the end of Kimathi Street right away? That's where Bob Prentice was last heard from.' He leant in a little closer. 'Plus, it'll be better to talk in the car.'

Sam agreed, and they headed out of the hotel. 'There's the car, come on. By the way, I can't tell you what a relief it is that you're here. Truth is I'm a bit out of my depth on this one and the Kenyans have put restrictions on my movements. In fact, none of the High Commission's staff are allowed to leave Nairobi for the duration. It's a real mess.'

Sam glanced at Helen, catching her eye for the briefest of moments. 'Well, I'm pleased to help but don't build me up. I'm only here because no UK Government staff are allowed in right now. Believe me, under any other circumstances I would not have even been a candidate.'

John pulled open the car doors for Sam and Helen and gave a smile, 'Well you're the main man today and I really am pleased to see you.' He banged the doors shut, climbed into the front passenger seat and gave his driver an instruction. The car pulled away into the traffic.

'What exactly is a High Commission?' said Helen.

'Oh, just think of it like an embassy. High Commission is the name given to a diplomatic mission posted between Commonwealth countries,' said John.

An old car trailed along behind them. It was indistinguishable from the many other vehicles that served well beyond their intended lifespan on Nairobi's streets. The man behind the wheel was Asian. All morning he had followed John Guthrie in the High Commission's car, remaining inconspicuous while keeping tabs on the British military attaché's movements.

• • •

Sam stepped out of the car and Helen slid across the seat to get out after him. John instructed his driver to wait exactly where he was parked and then got out of the front passenger seat. Diplomatic plates had their uses.

'We'd have been quicker walking,' said Sam, looking back down the road to the Hilton. 'Five minutes max'.

'Yes,' said John, a little sheepishly. 'Since the abduction, High Commission staff have been given a strict instruction not to walk anywhere.'

'You're certain this is the last location we have for him?'

'Well, almost. He spoke to Brigadier Starling by telephone from here and said he would walk directly to the Hilton, where we've just come from.'

Sam stepped away from the others and stood at the kerb, first staring back along the street, then focusing on the foreground. 'So, he must have passed some of these buildings,' he said, more to himself than anyone in particular.

Helen gave John an understanding smile. 'Bob Prentice and Sam were close.'

John smiled back at her. The pair stepped over to rejoin Sam.

'What are you thinking?' said Helen.

'I'm thinking this is a busy street and Bob must have interacted with somebody. There might even be some CCTV cameras we could check. Have you considered that, John?'

'No, I'm sorry, it's all been about containment so far. I don't think the High Commission wanted to involve any third parties.'

'Okay, we'll look. That's the Stanley Hotel right there. It's the first place on his route back to the Hilton, so he must have passed it. Let's go in and see if their cameras caught any action.'

Across the street, the old car had drawn to a stop, almost invisible beyond the flow of traffic. Inside, the passenger held a camera; it clicked away. The photographer needed to report on the military attaché's movements, which had been unremarkable so far. Now though, he was standing in a delicate location accompanied by unknown people. It took only moments to forward the pictures, and then the driver pulled away into the traffic, retiring to a discreet distance to await instructions.

Standing outside the Stanley Hotel, John looked a little reluctant to proceed. 'I've been told not to cause a stir. Don't you think this might be a little excessive?'

'Probably,' said Sam. 'But I've got a friend to save, and if this all goes belly-up, don't think your superiors won't drop on you from a height for not pulling out all the stops. Damned if you do, damned if you don't. Come on.' He walked off towards reception. Helen and John followed him.

Sam stopped for a moment on the threshold. 'By the way, John, I don't suppose you have a photograph of Bob? His mobile phone number too?'

'They're in the file.'

Sam stuck his hand out. 'Great, may I have the picture, please?'

John flicked open his slim file and handed over an official photo of Bob.

'Thank you.' Sam looked at the picture of his friend, wondered if their investigation was starting a day too late, then slipped it into his pocket. 'Helen, would you take his mobile phone number and pass it on to Elaine, see if Scottie can get any information on its whereabouts? It's a long shot but you never know.'

Sam left the others to transfer the number and walked into the broad reception. Tall flowering plants, glistening black and white marble flooring, and high-quality, dark leather, upholstered seats screamed wealth. Beyond broad structural pillars were entrance and exit routes to a variety of the hotel's facilities. He passed the pillars and a little souvenir shop, making directly for the reception counter.

A man standing at one end of the counter had the carriage and demeanour that marked him out as the person in charge. Sam approached him, read the name badge - Joseph, Duty Reception Manager. Sam introduced himself and asked if he could speak with whoever was on duty during the evening of the 22nd. His request was met with polite obfuscation.

'Look, this is important to me. Nobody's in trouble, I just need to speak with whoever was on duty. You must have a rota. All I want is a name.' As he spoke, he realised what was happening. In this most traditional and expensive of hotels, guests and visitors were expected to tip for any service. Knowledge, it seemed, was no exception.

He pulled out his wallet and looked inside; pausing for just a moment, he calculated, then pulled out one of his emergency twenty-dollar bills and passed it to the reception manager. The man smiled politely, took the money and folded it away. 'Thank you, sir.' He made a play of searching through a sheaf of papers on a clipboard retrieved from beneath the counter.

After a little while, he looked up. 'That's lucky, sir. One of the receptionists from that evening is on duty this morning. Lucy's due back from her break any moment. Would you like to speak with her?'

Just then, a young lady in receptionist's uniform appeared from behind one of the pillars. She didn't give the duty manager's exchange with Sam a second glance until he beckoned her over and whispered frantically in her ear. Then she looked anxious. Glancing nervously at Sam, she gave her boss an unconvincing smile. Using her hands to smooth out imaginary creases in her immaculately pressed skirt, she turned to face Sam.

'Hello, Lucy. I'm called Sam and I'm looking for a friend who's gone missing, I wonder if you could help?'

'Of course, sir, but I don't know anything about any missing people.'

Sam smiled an acknowledgement. He had not expected any other response to his initial question. 'That's fine. I'm thinking about the evening of the 22nd, Tuesday, you were on duty here, I think.'

Lucy nodded. 'I was, sir.'

'Great. You see Lucy, the last known whereabouts of my friend was right here in Kimathi Street. I just wonder if you might have seen him by any chance.' He held the photograph of his friend out towards her.

Lucy took the photograph and looked at the smartly turned out army officer, clean-shaven and well groomed, the gold embroidered epaulettes on the shoulders of his dress uniform standing out brightly against the material. She shook her head. 'No sir, I didn't see this man. I can't help you.'

'I see. Is there anyone else from your reception staff here that was on duty that evening?'

'No, sir. We run a set shift system in teams; my team is on evenings this week. I'm just doing some overtime to cover for someone this morning. I hope you find your friend.'

Sam nodded and looked across the reception to beyond the pillars where he could see the Thorn Tree Café. In a different time, he and Bob had been occasional visitors to the café. He turned back to Lucy. 'Thanks for your time. I might see you again this evening when I come back to speak with your colleagues.'

'You're welcome, sir.'

Now he needed to negotiate access to the CCTV recordings. Sam looked about for Joseph, spotted him and worked his way back along the counter to where the man was busy studying a computer screen.

Another twenty-dollar bill got Sam access to the security room where Joseph introduced the security manager who was pleased to collect a twenty too.

As Sam waited for the manager to access the recordings there was an almost timid knock on the open door. All three men turned to see Lucy.

'Excuse me, sir,' she addressed her manager.

'Yes, Lucy, what is it? Can't you see we're busy?'

'Yes, sir, but I've just had a thought about the gentleman's question.'

'Well?'

Lucy turned towards Sam. 'Sir, I wonder if I might look at your picture again please. There was a disturbance at reception a little after eight on Tuesday night. Security had to deal with it. It was quite frightening.'

'Oh, that business, something and nothing, Lucy. We run a tight ship at the Stanley, sir. Nothing to be concerned about,' said Joseph, scowling at Lucy. 'Off you go now, you're needed out front.'

'Hold on a moment,' said Sam, handing over the photograph for Lucy to look again. 'Take another look and tell me about the disturbance. Can we find it on the recording?' The security manager nodded and set to work. Meanwhile, Sam could tell Joseph was unhappy. He guessed another twenty would be the best way to ensure Lucy didn't get into trouble.

'A middle-aged white man ran into reception, sir. He was covered in blood, scruffy, not like your friend. But there was something ...' Lucy paused for a moment, searching for the right word. Then her face suddenly brightened, and she pointed towards the TV monitor that was now displaying images from that evening. 'That's him, sir. That's the man in reception.'

Everyone looked at the screen and Sam saw his old friend hurrying across the black and white marbled floor. Scruffy, dishevelled, with a five o'clock shadow heavy on his chin - more worrying was the torn shirt, dark with blood, and the series of gouges across his face. Blood was running down his face to leave an intermittent drip trail behind him, visible on the white tiles, unseen on the black.

Sam noted Lucy's frightened response in the video, understood it. He saw Bob's attempt to use the phone, saw him turn away, frustrated, and then hurry off, exiting reception before security could arrive. Lucy stood alone in the frame, nervously glancing to and fro. After perhaps half a minute, Lucy started frantically pointing in the direction Bob had gone and security hurried through the frame, exiting in turn, after Bob.

For another half-minute or so, Lucy was alone in frame. She kept glancing anxiously in the direction that the men had gone while slowly composing herself. Suddenly, her demeanour changed again. She started screaming and guests rushed away out of the frame as Bob reappeared, running straight through the shot, heading for the hotel front doors. Shortly afterwards, the security detail chased through the frame, hot on Bob's trail.

Helen and John arrived at the security-room door and Sam beckoned them in.

'We've found him,' he said. 'He's not looking so good. Come and see this recording.'

They all stood in silence and watched the scene play through once more.

'Well at least we know he's alive,' said Helen.

'Or he was at half past eight. It looks as though he's taken a bit of a beating there,' said John.

Sam felt Helen move closer beside him, rest a hand on his shoulder. He turned to look at the security manager. 'Are there any other cameras? Where did he go to when he first rushed off? And why not head straight for the exit? There's something illogical in what he's doing and that's not Bob Prentice, believe me.'

'He ran into the Thorn Tree Café,' said Lucy. 'Then he came back out. I thought he was going to hurt me. I was very scared.'

'I'll bet you were,' said Helen. 'It all looks really scary.'

Lucy directed a nervous smile of thanks towards her.

'Why did he run into the café?' said Sam.

'I don't know, sir.' Watching the recording had rekindled Lucy's anxiety over the incident and she had started to cry - Joseph shooed her from the room.

'Here's the camera that covers our front doors,' said the security manager, tweaking the play settings so it would synchronize with the reception's camera. 'Coming up now,' he hit play and they all focused on the screen again.

In the background, cars were passing, and people hurried past unaware of their image being recorded. Mid-screen, the back of the concierge could be seen as he stood facing out onto the street, equally alert for arriving taxis and passing trouble. Then Bob hurried into the frame. He paused and deliberately turned to the camera. He mouthed some words and made a little sign with his hand. Then, as the concierge closed in on him, he ran off across the pavement and continued his run directly into the flow of traffic, and he was gone.

'Can we have copies of these recordings?' said Sam. He was alert now to the polite delaying process and circumvented it abruptly by pulling two fifty-dollar bills from his wallet. He waved them. 'I need two sets of copies, right now.' Sight of another generous cash gratuity, spurred the security manager into instant action.

'He made it out alive then,' said John.

'Yes, but where did he go to? And we still have no idea who was chasing him.'

Sam took receipt of two USB sticks proudly bearing the hotel's branding. Giveaways, he guessed, but was happy to hand each man their fifty-dollar tips in return. The payment was followed by a brief and polite exchange of formalities and then Sam found himself leading Helen and John across the reception area, heading for the exit.

He detoured to the far end of the counter where Lucy, having composed herself again, was standing. Sam thanked her and took her hand to shake it in gratitude. Then he left, and she had a twenty-dollar note held tight in her hand, hidden from Joseph's acquisitive gaze.

All three stood just outside the hotel exit and looked out across the traffic in the direction that Bob had run. Sam handed John one of the USB sticks. 'Here, you'll need this for your file. I'll keep the photograph for now, if you don't mind.'

'Thanks, that's going to be useful and do keep the picture, there's another copy in the folder. Where do you think Colonel Prentice went?'

'Well, he crossed the street, we know that, and he wasn't knocked down by a car so he must have made it to the other side. His destination was the Hilton - he could have got there by just walking along this side of the road. So, he'd changed his plan, he'd obviously been fighting before reaching the Stanley … was he still being pursued? I'm guessing, yes. As he crossed the road, his only option would have been through there.' Sam pointed to an opening between two buildings.

'What's over there?' said John, summoning his car and driver with a wave of his hand.

'Forget the car, we'll walk,' said Sam.

'But you know we've been told not to walk anywhere.'

'And how will we find anything out from the back of a High Commission car? You stay in the car if you want, I'm walking.' Sam started out into the traffic, Helen by his side. For a moment, John was undecided, and then with an exasperated grumble he signalled the car to follow and hurried after his companions.

He caught up as Sam and Helen made their way off Kimathi Street and through the opening. 'We really shouldn't be doing this, it's against current protocol.'

'We have to. And look - this isn't exactly the ghetto.' Sam pointed to the building on their right-hand side. 'See, an office block.' His arm swept to their left side. 'Shops, and that doorway over there, that's the entrance to the Oakwood Hotel, it's up above.' His hand swung up highlighting the first and second floors. 'It's not the Hilton or the Stanley, but it's clean and respectable.'

He stretched out and touched Helen's arm. 'It's got a friendly little bar. I'll have to take you for a drink there at some point.'

'Great, it's a date.'

'But where are we going now?' said John.

'We're following this route because it's the only way Bob could have gone. John, just trust me on this, okay?'

Helen's mobile phone rang, and she checked it. 'That's Elaine, I'd better take it.' They all stopped close to the entrance to the Oakwood Hotel and Helen picked up the call.

'Hi Elaine, how are things? Any news?' Helen fell silent, her face clouding over with puzzlement as she listened to Elaine's voice. 'Are you sure about that? It doesn't seem to fit with what we've found here.' Then another silence as Elaine expanded her account. Finally, Helen brought the call to an end with a dual promise, to avoid any trouble in the meantime, and of further talk later.

'That was a little odd,' she said.

'Who's Elaine?' said John.

'One of the team, back in Edinburgh. It seems Scottie was able to do a bit of trace work on Bob's phone. Scottie seems to have more connections than a brain cell. According to the records, Bob was stationary at the corner of the street for a few minutes before shifting position to stand just up from the Stanley Hotel where he stayed for the best part of an hour until a little after nine when his signal went dead.'

'That doesn't make any sense,' said John, 'and I didn't know you had a team behind you.'

'On the contrary, it makes absolute sense,' said Sam. 'Look, he's at the corner of Kenyatta Avenue and Kimathi Street when he hangs up on the brigadier after saying he will go straight to the Hilton. Then I think he takes a few steps into Kimathi Street, where he's attacked and makes a run for it. Dropping his phone in the process. Which is why he needed to go into the Stanley to raise the alarm. Probably it lay in the gutter for an hour until somebody found it and sold it on. When he was chased out of the Stanley, all he could do was run. I'm guessing his pursuers were outside waiting for him to emerge. And that's what we see in the external video. He's running for his life.'

'Why didn't he just give himself up to the security guards?' said Helen.

'Because security guards throw people out, and in places like the Stanley they do it in a nice calm and discreet way so as not to upset the guests - almost slow motion. It would have been like serving him up on a plate to whoever was waiting outside. His only chance was to hit the street at a run and keep going.'

'It's not looking so good then,' said John.

'Let's keep going, see what we find. Come on.' Sam set off with Helen beside him, John a hesitant step behind.

'Where to now? Shouldn't we report in?'

'Report to where? I'm not on the High Commission's payroll. Look, just tag along with us. See the turning ahead? That feeds us into Kimathi Lane, which runs parallel to and behind Kimathi Street. If he came this way somebody will have seen him.'

They turned the corner and immediately the reason for Sam's confidence became clear. On either side of the road was a whole series of little shops, each one brightly lit and each with a smartly dressed man outside. A group of white Europeans walking past was bait that could not be ignored.

As if by magic, from inside the shops, proprietors emerged to stand beside their guards, each one stepping forward in turn to assure the passing group that the best jewellery could be found only in their shop. And then, in turn, they assured Sam that they had seen no disturbance on the night of the 22nd.

Sam's Swahili was a little sketchy, having been developed while posted to East Africa years before and never used since. But it was enough to get the message that nobody of any description had been chased along Kimathi Lane that evening. Sam had almost given up hope of tracing a contact when one of the shopkeepers towards the end of the lane gave a little knowing nod and stepped in close, taking Sam's arm in what appeared to be an attempt to draw him into the shop.

'A white man ran past that evening after half eight. Ran fast, he was in trouble, a gang chasing him. I don't think he could have got much further.'

'Who was chasing him?' asked Sam.

The shopkeeper suddenly looked a little agitated. He checked to see the substance of his conversation had not registered with other shopkeepers, and then shrugged. 'I don't know for sure, but I do know they weren't local.'

Sam reverted to English to thank him and promise they would come soon to his shop and buy some jewellery.

As they started to walk on, Helen linked her arm through Sam's and squeezed for a moment. 'Perhaps we could find something nice to take home for Elaine and Grace?'

'Good idea. I'm up for that. But let's keep moving now. If they caught Bob it must have been just up ahead, after the shops and before the lane links back to the main traffic route.' They parted and carried on walking side by side;

physical closeness was not conducive to personal comfort in the rising heat of the day.

'Did you find out anything new there?' said John.

'Yes, it's certain Bob made it past the shops. After that, who knows? But what I can tell you is those men were afraid of something. Believe me, it takes a lot to put the wind up guards and shopkeepers like that. One thing the shopkeeper did say, the chasing gang was not local.'

They walked on a little further until Helen stopped them. 'Hold on, Sam, what's that?' She pointed into the gutter at the side of the lane. Here dust and debris had gathered over the dry months. Tucked away out of public sight, the accumulation had missed the cleaning gangs' occasional sweeps. The dirt would remain undisturbed in this quiet spot, continuing its gradual build up until one day soon the rains would come and wash everything away. Then, in an instant, the streets would be rinsed clear.

'What is it?' said Sam.

'Look at the dirt here, close to the wall. It's all scuffed about, like there might have been a struggle here.'

All three moved closer. 'I think you might be right,' said Sam.

'Do you think this is where they caught up with him?'

'Could be. Let's just have a careful look around, see what we can see.'

Here's something,' said Helen crouching down to get a better look. She flicked some browned leaves and scraps of paper aside to expose her find. On closer inspection, it turned out to be a hypodermic syringe discarded on the ground.

'Junkies?' said John.

'I don't think so,' said Sam. 'A junkie would want to keep his gear, and looking at this one, it's only ever been used once. So no, I don't think it's a junkie's. And see that. He nodded to a single shoe wedged into the recess where a fire exit door led out onto the lane. That's European style for certain.'

Helen knelt down to inspect it. 'You're right, Marks and Spencer. Did Bob shop at M&S?'

'No idea, possibly, probably. That's where I've started getting my shoes from, so why not him? It's not exactly uniform issue but then he's a colonel and he's been way out in the middle of the African bush. Perhaps he was choosing comfort.'

'Do you think this is where the chase ended?'

'I think it might be. There was a struggle here and the marks are all quite fresh. If it did, then maybe that syringe is a good sign. We'll get it checked. If it contains a knockout, it means the captors really wanted him alive.'

John turned and signalled to his driver to bring the car up. 'I can take the syringe and get it tested, find out if it's the right shoe size and so on. Now, if you don't mind, Sam, it's time to follow protocol and use the car.'

Chapter 7

THURSDAY 24TH OCTOBER - PM

Lunch at the British High Commission was a small and informal occasion, hosted by the deputy high commissioner, with Brigadier Starling and John the only other guests. Eating over, John's official car returned Helen and Sam to the Hilton. Outside the hotel, the occupants of the old car that had previously tracked John Guthrie's movements now focused on Sam. Analysis of their earlier photographs confirmed Sam as the sole target of interest.

Sam took three things from the lunch. First, nobody had a clue as to what country was behind the snatch of ACE and Bob. Second, the diplomatic corps were far more interested in patching up relations with the Kenyan authorities than saving Bob; though the deputy high commissioner had been at pains to stress his sole concern was, at all times, Colonel Prentice's safety and welfare. The third thing, he couldn't read the brigadier.

Sam couldn't tell what drove the man. Was it saving Bob or was it ensuring potential foes did not have access to ACE, which meant the unspoken though easiest solution was to see Bob finished off? Happily for Sam, both options demanded they actually find his friend first. He'd move heaven and earth to make sure the brigadier's easy option was not implemented.

The shoe and syringe had been immediately dispatched in a diplomatic bag to London and would be subject to scientific tests as soon as they reached the UK. They would have the results within a day.

• • •

Having showered and changed into fresh clothing, Helen took the lift down to join Sam in the poolside bar.

'I bagged this cool spot for us,' he said. 'Drink?'

'Nothing too strong if I'm to last the day in this heat. What's our plan now? You didn't say too much at the High Commission. Are you holding something back from John and the brigadier?'

'I'll get you an iced water, and I think we have to go back to the Stanley Hotel this afternoon. Now John's out of our hair, we'll walk.'

'Fine. Why are we going back?'

Sam didn't answer at once because the waiter arrived and took their order for four bottles of iced water. 'We'll drink two now and take the other two with us.'

Once the waiter had moved on, Sam pushed his phone across the table. 'So, now look at this.' Sam had transferred the film clips to his phone and he played them for Helen. 'Some things just don't make sense. First, if he was being hunted, why go for a wander through the hotel? Second, what's he mouthing to the camera? I can't make it out. And finally, what is that little hand signal he's making? See, just before he runs off. I think answering these three points will get us a long way towards solving this.'

'Well, I guess if you think the answer is in the Stanley, that's where we need to go.' Helen looked up and smiled at the waiter who had returned with their drinks. He put glasses on the table and broke open the first water bottle's seal before pouring it. 'Thank you,' she said, lifting the glass and letting its cold seep through to her palm while the waiter poured Sam's.

'Sam, what I'm struggling to understand is what is so important about establishing which country is behind the abduction.'

Sam took a mouthful of water. 'Well, different countries have various strengths and weaknesses in their capacity to function. Different resource capabilities when it comes to moving things illicitly. All round the world, there is a constant game of cat and mouse between friends and opponents. Who's doing what, who's moving what, and who's watching who? It's dynamic, always changing. Knowing which countries are involved will enable us to focus on their likely transport and access routes.

'So right now, with British diplomats confined to Nairobi and no new staff allowed entry, what few resources the UK has on the ground are stretched thin just watching exit routes. We have friends; you heard the Americans are watching Mombasa because they are there already. But they are caught up in the same fallout with the Kenyans. The problem is, in the short term, there is nobody actually able to hunt for the ACE or Bob. And that's where I, we, come in.

'The longer it takes to find them the more likely they will never be found.'

'Okay, so it's just down to us.'

'Just about. Come on. Let's walk over to the Stanley now. We can talk as we go.'

• • •

Helen and Sam left the Hilton and immediately afterwards a tall and smartly dressed young African man strolled out behind them. As they walked towards Kimathi Street, the engine of a small silver hire car revved a little and the young

African man got into the front passenger seat. The car stayed put for a little while, then pulled away as Helen and Sam started to merge into the pedestrian throng on Kimathi Street.

The occupants of a dusty old car noted the coincidental departure of Sam, Helen and the silver hire car. The dusty car followed the hire car at a discreet distance.

As Helen and Sam stopped outside the Stanley Hotel, the silver car paused a little further up the street. Still further back, its unseen companion eased to a halt. The occupants watched everything ahead of them with interest.

'This is where he stopped and turned to the camera,' said Helen.

Sam pulled out his phone and looked closely at the screen as it played back his copy of the security camera footage. Intermittently, he glanced up from the screen to view the hotel entrance before returning his focus to the phone screen.

Meanwhile, Helen engaged the concierge who was a little concerned about Sam's behaviour. Helen laughed at Sam, half waving a hand towards him and smiling at the concierge. 'We're going into the Thorn Tree Café in a minute. He's always checking exits before we go into buildings. Got a thing about fire.' The concierge was not convinced but did enjoy speaking with Helen, particularly when she slipped some money into his hand. 'Make sure you let us out first if there's a fire,' she said with another laugh.

The concierge smiled at her. Her companion was obviously not right, harmless but not right, but she seemed fine. He left them alone and went to greet a taxi as it drew up in front of the hotel.

Helen joined Sam as he looked again at the video loop playing on his phone. 'It looks to me as if he's definitely trying to say something. An insult maybe? He has just been chased out of the hotel,' she said.

'That's not Bob Prentice's style. Anyway, if he was being hunted, why waste time to speak to a camera? I know I'd just keep running.'

'Beats me. And what about that little sign he makes at the end. Is he imitating something? Pressing a light switch? What do you think?'

'I have no idea, but it must mean something. Come on, let's go in and have a walk round. We can have afternoon tea in the Thorn Tree Café.'

They entered the reception. There was no sign of Lucy but Joseph was still there. Although he was busy with a guest, they could tell he had spotted them, he would miss nothing in his domain. They kept walking.

'This way,' said Sam, leading Helen past one of the structural pillars.

'This is the route Bob followed, isn't it?'

'Certainly is, and conveniently it's where you want to be.'

'I do? Why's that?'

'It's the Thorn Tree Café, come on through, let's take a seat over there and look about a little.' They made their way to an empty table from where they could survey most of the café and its clientele.

Almost immediately, a waiter appeared, they ordered, then sat back to wait for their tea and inspiration to arrive. Helen liked the atmosphere. For such a high status hotel, the café was quite informal, lightly furnished with simple tables and chairs. Potted plants were positioned here and there, and she half thought she could hear a distant piano playing some easy listening tunes.

Across the café, she saw a tall African man enter, select his table and sit. He declined the menu offered by his waiter and just ordered off the cuff, she guessed just a drink. There was something distinctive about him, familiar. 'Sam, do you see that man who just came in?'

'Yes, I do. That shirt was in the Hilton's poolside bar earlier.'

'I thought I'd seen him before. Is he following us?'

'Probably. Followed us out of the Hilton and got into a little silver car.'

Helen looked as Sam indignantly. 'And when were you going to tell me all this?'

He smiled at her. 'I didn't want to worry you needlessly.'

'If you don't mind, Sam, I'll decide when I should be worried.' She kicked his leg under the table, only half in jest. 'In future you tell me what you know, right?'

'Okay, well here's an odd thing for you. Our friends and their little car have their own tail - much more professional, I've no idea who they are either, but at least they look the part. My guess is they're trying to get the whole picture by following them following us. And I'm guessing they hope if we spot anyone it'll be the amateurs.'

'But you spotted them both.'

'Yes.'

'So, what are we going to do now?'

Sam gave a little grin, pursed his lips then shrugged. 'Nothing we can do right now. Let's just wait and see what breaks with them - something will.'

They both fell silent and watched their waiter return with a tray loaded with teacups, teapot, milk and sugar. Another waiter was following him, this one carried a tray with the scone Helen had ordered and the most enormous cream meringue, which had taken Sam's fancy. He suddenly wished he'd paid more attention, it was meal sized.

The waiters left, and Helen asked again. 'What's the plan, Sam?'

Sam was eyeing up his meringue, not quite sure where to start. 'We're not going to do anything.'

'What, why?'

'Because the man over there knows we're here but he doesn't know we have clocked him.'

'So?'

'In this game, knowledge is almost everything. Let's just sit tight, enjoy ourselves and keep our advantage, for now anyway.'

'Well okay, it's your call but who is he?'

'No idea, but trust me the man's not a professional, so I'm pretty sure he's not a direct threat. Now sit back, enjoy the scone and let's focus on Bob.'

'You're right, Sam, and you know what too? Even if we have picked up a trail of spies, this is a lovely place. How did you know about it?'

'Used to pop in from time to time when I was posted out here. In fact, I used to pop in with Bob. He was my boss, but we got on well off-duty as well, which was good. You know, I owe him quite a lot. I had got myself into a bit of a fix and he was the cavalry coming over the hill, probably owe him my life. I promised then he could count on me in return.'

'And that's why you couldn't resist Rupert Peterson's request to come and help out. What happened back then?'

Sam paused to take a drink of tea and mount an attack on the giant meringue.

'Sam?'

'Right, well some of that stuff I can't talk about. It's all finished and in the past now but probably still classified. Let's leave the history where it lies.

'But what I can tell you is that back then you had to be careful where you ate hereabouts, and the Thorn Tree was always a good bet. High-quality and not at all fussy, a nice regular menu.'

'So, it's one of your old haunts then?'

'You could say that. Though I never actually slept here. If I ever came down to Nairobi on leave for a night or two, I'd stay across the road in the Oakwood; remember it? We saw it this morning, much cheaper but still nice. Then I'd come over here to eat.'

'Seems like you had it all organised in those days.'

'Yes, but I'm glossing over the hard bits. The café's got its own history though, quite romantic. When the Stanley was built, way over a hundred years ago, it was conceived as a stopping point for expats and it was close to the station for the new rail track the colonial administration was having built at that time from Mombasa to the Lakes.'

'Oh, I've heard of that, I'm sure I even saw a movie about it. *The Tsavo Lions* or something. Lots of the construction workers were taken by lions, weren't they? But what's romantic about being eaten by a lion?'

'Yes, the movie was called something like that; I think I saw it too. But although the hotel has a natural link to the railway, that's not the romantic part, not directly.'

'Well, come on Sam, what do you think is romantic?' Helen placed her elbows on the table, leant forward and cupped her chin in her hands.

'Being near the station and close to the government administration and the businesses that grew up here, the Stanley was very busy, particularly since it set very high standards. The movers and shakers of colonial society knew exactly what they would get when they came here, so it became the place to go for business and pleasure. A place to see and to be seen. It would be the first port of call for people getting off the train from Mombasa. It was a start point for people going up country - farms, mines, or tourists on safari, and a finishing point too.'

Sam paused for another mouthful of his cream meringue and Helen drank tea. She looked at him slightly disappointed. 'So, it's got a history, but it sounds like you could say the same about a heap of fancy railway hotels.'

Sam nodded, and then shook his head. 'Yes, you could, but the Stanley had something more. It really was such a hub;

they used to say if you sat long enough in the Thorn Tree Café, you'd meet everyone in Africa. Eventually, all the world passed through here.'

'Well alright, that's a little better, but I'm not at all impressed with your understanding of romantic.'

'I haven't finished yet, give me a chance.'

Helen resumed her chin in hand position and stared intently at him. 'Well, I'm waiting.'

'As I said, this was the place everyone passed through. There's a clue in the name; it's always been the Thorn Tree Café. Look over there; see the potted sapling and those noticeboards beside it?'

'Where those two women are standing?'

'That's it. Well it's been redeveloped in recent years but previously there was always a proper thorn tree growing right over there. I'm not sure, but it's possible in the early days, the café evolved as a sort of covered veranda facility incorporating an existing thorn tree. Anyway, that thorn tree's purpose was to act as a noticeboard. In those early days, there was no postal service here, no radios or telephones. When you were passing through Nairobi, you could write a message for your business partner, friend or lover even and pin it on the trunk of the thorn tree. Nobody would touch the message except the person to whom it was addressed. It would stay on the tree as long as necessary until it was collected.'

Helen was more impressed now. 'Oh, that's great Sam. Love letters, missed connections. Oh, and what about the people who never came back?'

'I don't know,' said Sam.

'You know, Sam, if the food's so nice here, why don't we come for a meal? How about tomorrow? It would be lovely.' She turned to look again. 'Do you think that's what those two women were doing? Sticking notes on the thorn tree?'

'Well I think that little sapling isn't up to carrying messages. The noticeboards beside it are probably intended for the messages now.'

'You know what Sam? I'd quite like to post a message.'

'Why not? Look, there's a box of pencils and note sheets over there. You could do one.'

'I will,' said Helen. 'I'll go do it now, while you finish that meringue … if you can.'

Sam stretched his hand across the table and squeezed hers. 'Great, and I'll get this finished if it's the last thing I do.' He watched Helen cross the room. Noted too that their tail was looking a little agitated, suddenly a little unsure of what to do. The man relaxed a little as Helen came to a halt beside the noticeboards.

Helen took a pencil, pulled a sheet off the little note pad and paused for a minute. Then scribbled something on the sheet, folded it and wrote Sam's name on the front. She pulled a pin from the board and turned to look and smile at Sam while pinning up the message. She saw him smiling back.

Helen turned back to look at her message on the noticeboard, Sam's name clearly printed on the front. Content, she turned and headed back for their table. As she approached, she saw that something had changed. Sam had pushed the unfinished meringue to one side and was thinking deeply. She had seen that look often enough before to know he was on to something.

'What's up?' she said, sitting down at the table.

'I think I've cracked it. Jesus Christ, I've been slow!'

Helen tutted at him, half in jest.

'Sorry, that just popped out. But it's been staring me in the face. I, should have seen it before.'

'Seen what?'

'What did you just do?'

'I stuck a message on the board.'

Sam mimicked Bob's sign from the video.

At once, Helen realised what it meant. 'He's pinning a message on the noticeboard!' she said.

'Exactly, and I, of all people, should have known. Occasionally, we'd leave one another messages on the tree, just for the hell of it. You know: when we'd be back, where to meet, in which bar, that sort of thing.'

'Who would he have left his message for though?' said Helen.

'Us, well whoever would be looking for him. It explains exactly why he did that circuit in here too. If I'm right, it will still be there now.'

'Let's go see.'

'Well hold on, I don't know what's in Bob's message, if there is one. I do know, whoever our tail is, I don't want him to know we've found anything of interest. The man almost tore himself in half when he thought you were leaving a few minutes ago. How about this: you leave the café, head out through reception and stop to chat to that concierge who took a shine to you earlier. I expect our tail will move too, probably to reception, so he can at least try to monitor both of us.'

Helen didn't waste any time. She stood again and leaned in to kiss Sam's cheek. 'Be careful, Sam.' Then, straightening, she strolled towards the exit. In passing, she caught the waiter's attention, made a scribble sign with her hand and then pointed back towards Sam. The waiter sprang into action hurrying to deliver the bill to Sam. She could see their tail signing to his waiter for a bill. Sam's plan seemed to be working.

Sam waited until she was out of sight, all the while monitoring their tail, who was once again showing signs of agitation and indecision. Eventually the man stood and walked into the reception. By watching through one of the pillar gaps, Sam could see into reception, and could just make out that the man had positioned himself, so he could both see

Helen speaking to the concierge at the entrance and pick up Sam when he eventually exited the Thorn Tree Café.

No longer under direct observation, Sam slowly strolled across the floor of the café, for all the world as though he were simply a tourist in no hurry and with no urgent place to be. He paid the bill then started his exit path, pausing to survey the noticeboards as he passed. He felt the café had lost something with the removal of the old tree, but this was not a moment for sentiment. His apparently relaxed movement belied the urgent flickering of his eyes, which were carefully scanning all the notices.

He saw his name, recognised the handwriting, stepped close to the board and unpinned the note. Smiling, he unfolded it and smiled again as he read Helen's message. He slipped the note into his pocket. Then he reached for a pencil and notepaper to write a reply to her. He pinned it to the board in the spot where he'd found his own note. His eyes continued their scan of the boards, there must be something here - it was the only solution.

As he was about to give up, his chest tightened, there it was. A note addressed to Bob Prentice. Of course! Who else could he address it to? Anyone following his signal would realise it was from Bob Prentice, not to him.

Sam unpinned the message, noted the dark smudge on the corner, a speck of dried blood. This was it. He ambled towards the exit, glancing at the note as he went along. The message was short, a quick scribble, nothing more:

Ro Soo-Ann

It was enough for Sam. His pace picked up along with his heartbeat. He knew who they were up against now and it was not good. Passing through reception, he ignored the tail who was still trying to be inconspicuous. At the entranceway, he nodded politely towards the concierge, and putting an arm round Helen's shoulder, he steered her into the street.

She moved along without resistance. 'Did you find anything?'

'Oh yes, and I need to get the word out quickly.'

They set off, hurrying back along Kimathi Street towards the Hilton. No talking, every bit of energy and breath invested in combatting the heat as they paced along. The little silver car was parked at the side of the street. Its driver spotted them and jerked to attention in a flurry of movement, straightening up, starting the engine and scanning beyond Sam and Helen for his accomplice. Having been caught napping by Sam's sudden turn of speed, their tail was now rushing up the street from the Stanley Hotel.

Further along, a dusty old car was desperately trying to manoeuvre out and away into the traffic flow as Sam and Helen moved up the street towards it. It pulled away and past them. Sam got a look at its occupants for the first time and didn't like what he saw.

Reaching the Hilton reception, they didn't break speed, just hurried on up to their room. Inside the room, they finally stopped and stood side by side in front of the air-conditioning unit, letting the cold air sweep over them. Sam got them bottles of chilled water from the fridge and they continued to stand cooling down and drinking water.

'Well? Are you going to tell me now? What was that mad dash all about?'

Sam delved in his pocket and pulled out the note. 'We were right. It's from Bob. He must have realised he couldn't outrun his pursuers, and I'm guessing since he had lost his own mobile phone, he decided this was his only way of leaving a message that might just get through.'

'It almost didn't. John would never have found it.'

'No, I'm not sure he's the right man for the job here. On the other hand, he's inexperienced and the Kenyan authorities have restricted his movements. Maybe he'd have eventually got round to checking Bob's route in detail.'

'Well, thank heaven you were on hand. So, what does the message say? What's the big reveal?'

Sam handed Helen the note. She looked at it, saw the little dark stain, guessed what it was and glanced at Sam with a questioning look.

He nodded back. 'Yes, that looks like blood. They may have needed him alive but were clearly happy to use a bit of violence to get him.'

Helen unfolded the note and read it. '*Ro Soo-Ann,*' she glanced at Sam. 'Who's she?'

'He, Ro Soo-Ann. He's what you might call a mastermind; formerly a key intelligence organiser for the North Koreans. At some point, he and his team appeared to go private. Highly skilled and heartless, the perfect combination for a mercenary.'

'Mercenary?'

'Well, apparently so. I've been out of the loop a long time, but I recall there was some scepticism at the time. North Korea never liked breakaways. They tend to snuff them out. So, if Ro Soo-Ann's team was operating privately, it might have been because it suited the North Koreans at that time to have a rogue team that could operate at arm's length from the state.'

'If this man is an independent, who's he working for now?'

'I don't know, but some country somewhere is always trying to get an advantage by theft, bribery or blackmail. Ro Soo-Ann is utterly ruthless and has no regard for law or life. I do know if he's involved, it's very important news. In my day, he only got involved in the biggest of things. I wouldn't imagine much has changed. He's as cruel and heartless as any of those we've had to face before.' Sam left the air-conditioning unit and headed for the wall safe. He accessed it and returned to Helen, carrying the satellite phone.

Helen looked at the phone a little quizzically. 'Who are you going to call? The High Commission?'

With a wrist shake, Sam highlighted the phone. 'This is more secure than our regular mobiles, so from now on, we'll use only this, but I don't want to put any message along the High Commission's open landline. Even if the Kenyans can't tune in, if Ro Soo-Ann is involved, it's almost certain his people will be able to. Last I knew, Ro's people had developed a strong IT capability, and I don't want to risk alerting him that we are on to him.'

'Okay, so what's the plan?'

'I've arranged to call in on Professor Ngure's office to fix my itinerary once the evening rush hour has eased back a bit. From there we'll go directly to the High Commission and brief John Guthrie face-to-face and Brigadier Starling too, if he's around. First, I'm going to call Rupert Peterson, he may have been a bit on the sneaky side, setting us up for a fall, but at least he knows what he's doing. Alerting him will ensure the right wheels start turning. We can't rely on John Guthrie knowing which buttons to push, or even if the high commissioner will allow him to act at all while the Kenyan authorities have imposed restrictions on the diplomatic staff here.'

Sam made his call while Helen got cleaned up and put on fresh clothes. As Sam took his turn in the bathroom, she leant against the doorframe.

'Won't be long,' he said as water sprayed in all directions.

Helen took a pace back and laughed. 'Careful, buster.'

'Sorry. It's safe to come back now, I'm under control.'

'You'd better be,' said Helen, returning to the doorway.

'What's up? You're looking a bit anxious.'

Helen held a business card in her hand. 'You know, Sam, I'm sorry but I've been thinking; I'd better call Tracy. If I don't, I'm letting down my country.'

Grabbing a towel, Sam stepped from beneath the shower and across to the doorway where he lightly brushed his lips against Helen's. 'I know, don't apologise and don't feel bad about it either. I'm the one who should apologise, I should have thought about it - prompted you. I'm quite certain that Rupert's superiors will involve the CIA anyway. In situations like this, you need all your friends. But go ahead. Only, make sure you use the satellite phone.' He stepped back into the bathroom.

Helen went to make her call. By the time she'd finished, he had emerged from the bathroom and was keeping cool near the air-conditioning unit.

Chapter 8

THURSDAY 24TH OCTOBER - EVENING

Sam had been watching Nairobi's evening rush of traffic from the window of their suite. At last, it showed some slight signs of easing back from chaotic mayhem to simply frantic. He gave a signal and they set off.

Earlier he had phoned Professor Ngure's office at the university. Susan Curtis had stressed again that the professor was anxious to see the arrangements for Sam's tour of their archaeological sites in place. Sam didn't have time for any field trips right now, but for the sake of appearances, and particularly to ensure that the authorities didn't start to wonder what his real purpose in the country had become, he needed to be seen to go through the motions.

The taxi journey to the university was brief, but long enough for Sam to confirm the Africans in their little silver car were back. Sam had the taxi stop at the main entrance and their followers paused a little further off. What Sam couldn't see, positioned some way beyond the Africans, was the dusty old car that had come to a gentle halt; its Asian occupants were very interested in Sam's visit to the university.

Sam left Helen in the taxi and went into the university alone. There he found that Professor Ngure had had to rush away to an important engagement. He had given Susan Curtis clear instructions to finalise a tour, and she was to be Sam's driver and guide to ensure he saw all the key aspects of the various locations that would inform Sam's visit.

Having quickly reached an agreement with Susan about an itinerary, which she clearly thought was too light, he insisted on a couple of days free at the outset, so he could deal with some personal interests. Realising he was not going to budge, she reluctantly agreed that the trip would start on Monday morning. Satisfied, Sam bade her farewell and hurried back to Helen.

The taxi journey to the High Commission was uneventful, though by the end of the journey Sam had established they had only one tail now. The Koreans and their dusty car had vanished.

• • •

Park Jae-In, Ro's second in command, stood in the empty university corridor; he listened to the sounds emanating from the half-open office door immediately in front of him. A man and woman were conducting a telephone conversation. For some reason, the woman had opted for speakerphone. Park was waiting patiently for the call to end. Glancing over his shoulder, he raised his open hand in a *we're still waiting* signal to his companions. He received curt nods in return from the two Korean men who stood in silence behind him.

'… Susan, are you sure he's been scheduled to see all our most prestigious sites? It will be good for the department if Edinburgh decided to link up with us for future research projects.' Professor Ngure's voice projected a metallic tone through the low-quality phone loudspeaker.

'Yes, I'm quite sure, though he was determined to keep his itinerary clear for the first few days. I think he's planning to slot in a little holiday break before we start touring round the sites.'

'Well, whatever he wants, try to accommodate him. Edinburgh is one of the richest universities in the world. A partnership with his department would be very useful.'

'I know, Joseph. Now stop worrying. I'm just going to finish typing up these details and then mail them to Sam. I'll copy you in too. Now go!' She hung up the phone and smiled to herself. Joseph worried too much and about the wrong things. The work the department was doing was first class - its quality spoke for itself.

Park heard her chair shift a little, heard papers being gathered across a desk and the sound of a keyboard. He looked back to the two men behind him. This time his hand beckoned them forward and they followed closely as he entered the office. Across the threshold, he paused and looked round the room. The middle-aged white woman behind the desk was so engrossed in her work that she had not noticed her visitors. He smiled, she would notice soon enough. Then he coughed politely.

'Can I help you?' said Susan, looking up, startled at the men's presence, but not alarmed - after all, this was the top floor of the university. 'Who are you looking for? I think most people have already gone home.'

'Yes, they have,' said Park. 'In fact, there's nobody else left on this floor. Just us.' He smiled, but there was no warmth in the gesture.

Park smiled again. He could see that Susan suddenly felt a little anxious and very alone. Her concern grew into alarm as the rearmost of the three men stepped outside the door, pulling it shut behind him.

'What do you want? Please leave now,' said Susan, starting to rise. Park's remaining henchman stepped across the office and pushed her back into her chair. Stepping behind her, he pressed his hands down on her shoulders, pinning her in place as Park picked up the telephone base station from her desk and ripped the linking cord from the wall.

'Get out, now,' said Susan, the volume of her voice rising in line with her anxiety. 'There are no valuables here. Just go.' She shook her shoulders, struggling in vain against the man who held her pinned to her chair.

Park gave a little laugh and sat himself on the edge of her desk. He leant over and turned the computer screen, so he could read what she had typed.

Itinerary - Dr Sam Camer—

'You have an arrangement with Cameron. What is it?'

'None of your business. Now get out while you can - security patrols these corridors all the time.'

'Well, we'll have to hurry then, won't we?'

'You have no right to be here, just leave …'

'Hold her head,' said Park and his man moved his left hand from her left shoulder to take a tight handful of Susan's hair. He jerked her hair back, pulling her head against the chair's headrest.

She gasped in discomfort. Her eyes rolled in anger and fear. 'Let me go now, or I'll scream the place down.'

Park swung his arm and hit her full in the face with the telephone base station. He pulled his arm back and smashed her a second time, this time just catching her hands which Susan had brought up to protect herself.

She screamed.

'Shut up!' Park took hold of her left wrist and pulled her hand away from her face. His man released her right shoulder and gripped her right hand with his to drag it away from her face too. All the while, he kept her head trapped against the chair's headrest by her hair. 'Shut up!'

Susan continued to scream.

Park took the telephone handset and drove it against her mouth. The first blow broke a tooth, the second blow loosed another. He struck again. This time he did not draw back the handset but maintained pressure, forcing it into her mouth, sliding it over her tongue and filling her mouth until the only sound she could form was a little throaty signal of distress.

Breathing with difficulty through her broken nose, little spatters of blood drops flurried out with each laboured breath. Her eyes were screwed tight shut. Park took a moment to admire his handy work.

'Will you be quiet now?' he said.

With her eyes still shut, Susan tried desperately to nod agreement against the tight hairlock her head was held in. He understood her message.

'Good.' He took hold of the handset, pulled it out of her mouth and placed it on the desk.

Susan gasped for breath. Desperately, she sucked in air through her mouth, the need for oxygen rendering her momentarily oblivious to the pain of air rushing across broken teeth and raw nerves. She had stopped struggling against the men's grip on her wrists, just needed air.

'I ask you again, what is your business with Sam Cameron?'

'I don't know what you mean. He's just here on a visit, that's all.'

'Liar! Why was he here? What is this itinerary you are planning?'

'Please let me go. Why are you doing this to me? I've done nothing to you.'

'I asked you what your business with Cameron is. Now tell me.' Park lifted the phone handset again and smiled to himself as he brought it close to his face to get a better look.

'He's here on a research trip. Inspecting fossil beds and the sources of our human fossils. That's all. Now please, let me go, I won't say anything, I promise.'

'Cameron has no interest in such things. My leader will not be pleased with your lies. I give you one more chance to speak the truth.'

'It's true, it's true. Please, I beg you, it's true. I know nothing more. Nothing at all.'

Park was used to hurting people. Used to reading the truth. He could tell it wasn't an act. She knew nothing. He frowned in irritation. 'I believe you,' he said.

Susan's eyes opened. 'Thank you, thank you. I won't tell anyone I promise—'

'I know. I believe you,' said Park. Watching as Susan's eyes sparked a little in relief.

Her eyes met his. She could see the coldness in his gaze and the spark of hope faded quickly from her eyes.

'No, no, no,' she protested, trying to turn her face away as Park again lifted the handset and brought it to her face. He smiled and stroked her cheek with it, wiping away big tears that were rolling down Susan's face. She tried to avoid the contact but couldn't move. 'Please no …'

Park drew the handset along her jawline, smearing her blood as it went. He bent closer to her face, listening to the little whimpered appeals.

'I know you won't tell anyone,' he whispered, as he pressed the handset between her lips and against her broken teeth. This occasion required much less effort on his part; as the handset pressed on her broken teeth her lower jaw opened automatically to avoid the painful contact and the handset slipped in. He pressed, and it kept sliding in; filling her throat.

Her eyes opened in a final panic, darted from side to side, looking desperately for a rescue that would never come. Legs kicked out under the desk and as the men held her wrists and head tight, urgent little squeals sounded from deep in her throat. Desperate pleas for life - unanswered.

When her struggling ended, Park straightened up, let Susan's wrist go, his guard did the same. She slumped forward, banging her head on the side of the desk as she fell to the floor. They left, turning off the office light and closing the door behind them.

• • •

John met Helen and Sam at the front doors to the High Commission and was quick to tell them London had reported that test results on the hypodermic were inconclusive. They were doing more tests. However, Bob's wife had recognised the shoe style and size; this had been backed up with a positive DNA sample from inside the shoe. Their instincts had been proven right - it was Bob's shoe.

The news had scarcely had time to sink in before they were guided through to an office where the high commissioner and his deputy met them. The high commissioner was not happy about the flouting of Kenyan Government instructions. However, following a break in their discussions, when he had used his secure phone line to London, he agreed that John could continue to support Sam and Helen, provided he still did not leave Nairobi or engage in any doubtful activities. Sam had accepted the terms though considered it was unlikely that their target was still in Nairobi.

'Why didn't they just take it straight out of the country at once?' said Helen.

The high commissioner nodded an acknowledgement of her question and stepped across the office to a big map of Africa that dominated one wall. 'They would if they could but it's simple logistics,' he said. 'Different countries have different capacities and different political friendships. Right now, Africa is a melting pot of influences, everyone wants to have friends here; Africa is so rich in minerals and natural resources.

'It's only a generation ago that Britain was the dominant influence in Eastern Africa. From the Horn right down to the Cape, Mozambique aside. Those days are gone now, of course. Though Mozambique bucked the trend - when it shook off Portuguese colonial rule, it opted to join the Commonwealth.'

'So, now we know it's Ro who snatched Bob Prentice and stole your ACE, how will he get out? Who are his friends and supporters?' said Helen.

'Hmmm, is Ro freelancing or not? We just don't know yet. But freelance or otherwise, Ro faces the same problem as his, maybe former, North Korean paymasters. Their greatest weakness is that not so many democracies like them. It's mainly authoritarian regimes that they have good relationships with. Unfortunately, those are the countries most likely to break the rules, which has always played to the Koreans' greatest strength. Right now, there are only a handful of countries that would facilitate export of whatever the ACE is and most of them are on the west coast. Angola, Equatorial Guinea and so forth. On this side of the continent, I'm guessing Ro's best bet would be Burundi.'

The high commissioner sat back at his desk and looked around the room. 'London thinks that too. If Ro gets to Burundi, we can probably kiss Bob Prentice and the kit goodbye. They will be beyond our influence.'

'I'm guessing the Koreans will have moved south, gone into Tanzania. It has a land border with Burundi,' said Sam.

'Yes, that's London's view too.'

'They'll be hard to find. They will probably have taken the main road south and then turned off into the bush before the national border, crossed out of Kenya and into Tanzania by bush tracks and then rejoined the main road further south, just in case we'd got our act together and the border guards had been alerted to their approach. That's what I would do. So, what does London want me to do?'

'Well, I argued that you'd better stay here for now, in case we've read the situation incorrectly. London and our allies are organising resources from elsewhere, I'm sure they will all click into place in the next day or two. Tanzania will manage without you.'

'No.' Sam stood up. His friend was being carried away and the diplomatic service seemed determined to allow it to happen. 'I can fly into northern Tanzania in an hour from here. It will take at least a day to get others on the ground, more. I have to go south now.'

'I'm sorry, London agrees with me. Your presence in Nairobi has been a godsend and it makes sense to keep you here, just in case.'

'Just in case? Just in case? They're almost certainly heading for Burundi through Tanzania. The job's going down the plughole and you give me, "Just in case"?'

Helen had never seen Sam so agitated. His friend clearly meant a lot to him, far more than she had appreciated.

'Thank you, Dr Cameron, your views are noted, but I've told you London's instructions and you are expected to follow them. You may think of yourself as a civilian now, but may I point out that you were awarded a regular commission in the British Army, which puts certain enduring obligations on your shoulders. Like it or not, you will do your duty.' The high commissioner stood, looked around the group.

Sam's jaw started to move; the high commissioner's hand rose to silence him. 'I believe that concludes our business for the evening. I'll wish you a good night, gentlemen, Reverend Johnson. John, would you be good enough to organise one of the cars to take our visitors back to their hotel, please? Thank you.' And he was gone.

Sam glared at the closed door, remembering all the reasons he had quit the forces in favour of academic life. Nothing had changed.

Chapter 9

FRIDAY 25TH OCTOBER - AM

Sam and Helen were woken early in the morning by a ringing phone. Sam answered it to hear a concerned hotel receptionist's voice.

'What time is it?' said Sam, trying to get his bearings.

'Half past four, sir. I'm sorry to bother you, but he's being most insistent.'

'Who is, what are you talking about?'

'A man from the British High Commission, sir. John Guthrie, he insists on being allowed to come up and visit you.'

Sam was silent for a moment, digesting the information.

'Hello, are you there, sir? Hello, should I send him up? I could have security ask him to leave if you prefer.'

Sam gave a sigh. 'No, send him up. Tell him five minutes, I'll see him then. Oh, and have room service send up some coffee please. Lots of it.' He hung up, and roused Helen. They hurriedly dressed and were ready just as a knock sounded on the door. Sam opened it and a very worried John Guthrie hurried in.

'Thank God, I've caught you. Major crisis, you have to move.'

Closing the door, Sam followed him into the room. 'What's the situation now?' he said. Sitting next to Helen he put his arm round her shoulder and waved John towards one of the other seats.

John ignored the invitation. 'Come on, it's all change, we really have to go. There's been a suspicious death and you're in the frame.'

Sam again pointed John to the chair. 'Sit down, John. Take a breath and tell me exactly what's happened.'

As he finished speaking there was a knock at the door. John almost jumped with shock. 'They're here, it's too late. I can't be found here with you, it's a disaster.'

Sam stood up and walked past him, heading for the door. 'John, sit. It's my coffee order.' He opened the door and a waiter entered carrying a tray with a large cafetière and three cups. 'Put it down over there,' said Sam, turning to point into the room. He noticed that John was now sitting, albeit on the edge of his seat. The waiter placed his tray and turned for the door. As he left, Sam pressed some money into his hand.

'Right, let's get some coffee and hear what you've got to say,' said Sam, striding back across the room. He poured coffees, handed them round and sat. 'So, tell us, what's happened?'

'On your way to the High Commission last night you called into the university to see Ms Curtis, Susan Curtis. How was she when you left her?'

'Fine, why?' said Sam. His tone was even but he already sensed what was coming.

'Well, she's not fine now. She's dead and according to the police, in a very nasty way. The university security staff insist you were her final visitor last night. The police traced you from there to the High Commission via the taxi you took.'

'How did you manage to get here ahead of the police?'

'They don't know where you are. At this time of night, it's always a junior on duty in the High Commission. Having been on night shift all week, she knew nothing of your visits. I happened to be in the office, trying to pull together some plans in the event our caper goes tits up. Luckily, I was able to feed her enough information to sound credible without tipping them off. I think they went away none the wiser, but they will be checking the hotels and this one must be near the top of the list. We really need to go.'

Sam finished his coffee. 'You're right.' He turned to Helen. 'We'd better move now.'

'Thank God, let's hurry,' said John, standing quickly.

Helen stood too, and then drained her coffee before heading to a wardrobe.

'There's not time to pack. We need to run.'

Helen ignored him and pulled out her case. Sam was doing the same.

'John, you can help. Phone down to reception. Ask them to get our bill ready, we're checking out now. Oh, and have them put out half a dozen bottles of chilled water, on the bill. We'll collect them as we leave,' said Sam as he lifted hangers of clothes off the rail and folded them directly into his case.

John snatched up the phone and called reception as Helen gathered their toiletries from the bathroom and stuffed them in the cases.

It took under five minutes to pack and leave the room.

They exited the lift together and Sam called a halt before they turned into the reception area. He offered his hand to John, who looked a little startled, then shook it.

'You've done well here, John, thanks. Now, I think we should leave separately; you should just go out quietly on your own. That way, nobody can accuse you of knowing where we've gone or assisting our flight.'

'But the receptionist saw me arrive, I spoke to her.'

'That's fine. If challenged, just say you came here on a hunch, and once you'd confirmed we were actually here, you went back to the High Commission to alert staff and contact the police. Oh, and be sure to do just that when you get back.'

'What if they don't believe me?'

'You'll be fine, you've got diplomatic immunity. Now get back to the High Commission.' Sam watched John's almost automatic head nod response.

'Good man, I'll call you when I can. Now go and look after yourself.'

John hesitated but was pulled from his momentary indecision by Helen's hug. 'Go on, John, quickly. We can't leave until after you.'

He drew away from Helen, smiled at her and left without another word. They watched him turn the corner into reception and waited, allowing him time to leave the building.

Two minutes later, Helen and Sam stepped into reception and paused to pay their bill and collect the bottled water, which they stuffed into their shoulder bags. With a thank you to the receptionist, they left the Hilton, made a hard right and headed for Moi Avenue. Though the sky was still dark, a combination of streetlights, office and shop security lights and the steady flow of passing vehicles ensured they were always in light.

'Where are we going, Sam?'

'To a bus station. Provided things haven't changed too much, we should be able to pick up an early shuttle bus.'

'To where?'

'Arusha, Tanzania.'

'Wow, we're going after Bob?'

'Too right. We can't stay in Kenya anyway now, or I will end up in jail. And that will involve months of unpleasantness while my innocence is proven.'

'Will this work?'

'Should be fine as long as we are discreet here. Buses run back and forth between Nairobi and Arusha umpteen times a day. They carry everyone and anyone. Safari trekkers and tourists, NGO staff, workers, market traders, families …'

'And don't forget fugitives from the law chasing a North Korean spymaster.'

'Some of them too. We'll be fine once we have tickets and get on board. Don't worry; you'll be having your tea safely in Arusha this afternoon.'

'How far to the bus station?'

'Less than ten minutes' walk. Now just stay close to me, keep your shoulder bag swung across your chest to the front and a good grip on your case. But if we do get embroiled in something, don't give up your life for your case. We can always buy new stuff.'

Helen nudged him with her elbow. 'Hey, mister, I'm no rookie. Remember, I spent three years in West Africa, and believe me, some places there make this place look like a kindergarten.'

Sam knew it. 'Sorry, just looking out for you, can't help it.'

She smiled to herself. 'Come on, let's get a move on.'

• • •

The shuttle bus pulled out of Nairobi, skirting the city's wildlife park, a few giraffes and zebras visible in the growing daylight. Then they were on the open road and heading south.

Helen and Sam spoke quietly, concentrating more on the lively conversations that were bouncing around the bus. What appeared to be a late-arriving, extended family had been split up into separate seats. Exercising her domestic control, the mother was calling out to children, keeping them informed and in line. A girl, aged about ten, had the task of ferrying drinks and food up and down the aisle to various family members, with the granny and the granddad, who were sitting near the front of the bus, getting priority service. There was no sign of a father. The constant babble was punctuated by occasional shouts from Granny when she needed anything.

The time passed quickly as Helen watched the countryside roll by. The urbanisation long gone, now they were travelling through rural Africa. Dry land stretched out into the distance, the horizon broken by occasional lines of far-off hills. Almost everywhere sported the same dry silvers, yellows, blacks and browns that had come to dominate the landscape in Ethiopia. Here, just as further north, the land waited for the rains.

This was not a completely empty landscape. Here and there were buildings dotted along the roadside, or farm steadings set back a little into the bush, perhaps just a roof visible. Occasional small communities flashed past, each sporting a quickly predictable mix of vendors' stalls, anonymous workshops, and some homes built with breezeblocks and corrugated iron roofs intermingled amongst others of traditional wattle and daub construction.

Eventually the bus slowed, pulled off the road and came to a halt for a comfort stop. Everyone got off. Some people went to the rather doubtful looking restrooms while others took the opportunity to stretch and to breathe the fresh air.

Sam gave Helen a little nudge to catch her attention. Beyond the restrooms were several cars parked in a rough line. A little silver car had managed to squeeze itself into the middle of the row. Helen looked to Sam who nodded towards the row of cars.

'So, we've still got company and it narrows the field. If they were Kenyan officials, I'm thinking we'd have been whipped off the shuttle back in Nairobi,' said Helen.

'I don't know, but as they're not trying to arrest us or kill us, let's let sleeping dogs lie. Come on - everyone's getting back on the bus.'

The shuttle pulled back out onto the road, followed by the little silver car. A few moments passed before an old dusty looking car followed them out and also took the road south.

A while later, they arrived at the border. Along with everyone else, Helen and Sam left the bus and stepped into the Kenyan border control office. Queues formed as each passport was checked and stamped. Helen glanced at her passport. It was in order, but she still felt a sudden twinge of anxiety. Sam had said there would be no problem at the border; nobody would have realised yet that they had left Nairobi. It would be some time before anyone would think to inform the border guards down here.

Progress was slow. Once they reached the official at his counter, Sam was obliged to pay a few shillings for something and nothing. Then they were through and hurrying back towards the shuttle bus.

All aboard again, the bus rolled forward a short distance and stopped once more. The administration process was repeated on the Tanzanian side of the border. Less stressed here, there was now no threat of a phone call ordering that they be hooked out of line and driven back to Nairobi in custody. Once again, their passports had been pre-stamped in London with the appropriate visas, so this was just a long-drawn-out formality.

They joined the queue that snaked back and forth within the building. The smell of travel weary bodies perspiring into the hot still air became progressively more oppressive as they slowly edged their way to the head of the queue, where a pair of officials sat behind a wood panelled counter reminiscent of a 1950's British office. At last, they were through immigration and free to carry on the search for Bob Prentice - almost.

A further half hour passed while customs officers satisfied themselves the bus was carrying nothing more than it should.

All the while, the area outside the building was abuzz with people waiting their turn to get into the immigration office. Others, having got out, were waiting for their cars, trucks and buses to receive clearance to proceed. Vendors offering refreshments moved amongst the crowd. One little group of enterprising women had a patch staked out and were cooking hot food, others were brewing bush tea. Their calls mixed with those of the other vendors, the noise of half a dozen idling truck engines, screeching children scurrying about, and two competing portable stereos playing different tunes.

A little gust of wind brought light relief for a few moments then it lifted and mixed together the smells of the cooking, diesel fumes and an endless variety of produce, fruits, spices and herbs. This was much closer to the Africa Helen remembered; the concrete of central Nairobi and its luxury hotels suddenly seemed a long way away.

Helen looked across to the far side of the road. The traffic heading out of Tanzania into Kenya stretched away into the distance, for as far as she could see. There were soldiers on their side of the road, but many more were stationed around the customs and immigration post on the northbound side, heading out of Tanzania. Other soldiers were posted at strategic points on the little bluff that overlooked the road and yet more strolled up and down the stationary traffic queue. The soldiers' relaxed and slow movements under the midday sun were belied by the weapons they all carried unslung and ready for action.

Many northbound drivers and passengers had abandoned their cars; instead, opting to stand in the hot dry air, fanning themselves and covering their heads with any available artefact, from umbrellas to cardboard boxes. As ever, vendors had appeared from unknown places and were working the traffic jam for all it was worth: water, fruit and even cups of what she guessed was tea from a portable urn.

'That looks like hell over there,' she said.

Sam had been watching the scene on the other side of the road too. 'Absolutely. I'm guessing it will take a day to get to the head of that line. I wonder what the problem is.'

He approached one of the customs officers who had just signed off their shuttle bus driver's entry permit. At last the bus was free to drive on.

In faltering Swahili, Sam tried to find out what the problem was.

The customs officer smiled at him. 'You speak some Swahili,' he said in functional English.

'Just a little, I haven't used it for years.'

The customs officer laughed out loud and wagged an exaggerated finger at Sam, again replying in English. 'Very good you try but I can tell, it is many years. How can I help, sir?'

Sam reverted to English. 'What's causing the delays over there, it looks like hell.'

'Hell, yes. Very hot, very bad. We're happy to be on this side of the road.' Then, for the first time, the smile vanished from the man's face. 'Very bad. Terrorist attack in Arusha on Thursday. They tried to attack the vice president while he was visiting.'

Sam and Helen looked concerned. 'That's bad,' said Sam. 'I hope the vice president is okay.'

'Yes, but four guards were killed, many soldiers hurt. Those madmen.' He waved a hand towards the north and Sam guessed he was meaning the terrorist groups based up in the Horn of Africa. 'Three terrorists escaped, and the president has locked down the borders while we search for them. They won't get away.'

'I hope not,' said Sam, as Helen adopted a sympathetic expression. 'Seems that madness is everywhere now.'

The customs officer nodded, and then turned his head to look at their bus; the driver was sounding his horn, revving up the engine a little. Stepping to one side, he waved them forward. 'Have a good journey.'

Helen smiled a thank you and, as she climbed onto the bus, she had a last look around. She could not see the little silver car. Possibly, the occupants did not have papers to hand to get them across the border. Anyway, they seemed to have vanished.

Chapter 10
FRIDAY 25TH OCTOBER - PM

There seemed no difference in the landscape on the Tanzanian side of the border. After a short silence, Helen nudged Sam. 'What do you really think the chances are of finding Bob?'

'Up until we spoke to that customs officer, I'd thought not good. But there is a slim chance now.'

'How so?'

'Timings. The ACE and Bob were snatched on Tuesday morning and evening, respectively. Based on the message Bob left at the Thorn Tree Café, we know it's Ro's Korean boys. The good news is the nearest country from where they could ship their prize out without any questions being asked is Burundi. Of course, the bad news is it's Ro Soo-Ann running the show.'

'Hmmm,' said Helen, pensively. 'How long does it take to drive that far?'

'There's the question. Ordinarily, you might allow a day, perhaps a little less, to reach Arusha from Nanyuki, which is a good way north of Nairobi. But I'm guessing Ro and his men drove at night, which can be pretty dodgy here, so they would have gone slowly and then laid up through the day, just to minimise their exposure. Plus, throw in the fact they would have used bush tracks to get across the border, bypassing the border posts will have added more delays. I'm reckoning they didn't come out of the bush on the Tanzanian side until maybe Thursday morning.'

'When you put it like that they are still way ahead of us.'

'You'd think that. It's near as you like a thousand kilometres from Arusha to Burundi, with some very wild ground to cover and some pretty dodgy roads. You have to allow one and a half days, perhaps even two to reach Burundi.'

'They'd maybe make it over the Burundi border sometime later today then.'

'Ordinarily, yes. But perhaps not right now. See that queue?' Sam pointed to the line of stationary northbound traffic that they were still driving past, all waiting to exit Tanzania. 'That's going to be repeated on all the other border crossings, including those into Burundi.'

'And Ro won't want to risk sitting in a line like that or being caught up in any checkpoint search of their vehicles.'

'Exactly. So, I'm guessing, hoping, they're still in Tanzania. Probably holed up somewhere, waiting for the heat from that terrorist attack to subside.'

'Couldn't they try for a bush crossing into Burundi, like you think they did to get from Kenya to Tanzania?'

'They could, but if I were in Ro's shoes I wouldn't risk it. The Tanzanian Government has closed the border tight, so they will have made sure all the smaller crossing points are guarded, too, for sure, and probably mobile patrols on border bush tracks.'

They lapsed into silence for a little while, each thinking about their close shave in Nairobi and what was to come next. Their reverie was interrupted by the phone ringing.

Helen looked at the incoming caller display, recognised the Edinburgh number and answered.

'Hi Elaine, it's Helen here. Good to hear your voice.' Helen was silent as Elaine responded. Pressing the phone to her ear, she struggled to hear over the noise in the bus. 'Speak up, Elaine,' she shouted into the phone. 'It's noisy at this end.'

Helen was silent again, listening carefully. Sam handed her a little note that he had scribbled down.

'Okay, Elaine. I'll tell Sam. He'll be interested to hear the news. And thanks to Scottie, I hope he won't get into trouble for finding that out. Look, Elaine, here's something else. You had set us up with an accommodation base in Arusha, for the Tanzanian leg of our trip. We're going to need it earlier, if at all possible. We've had to leave Kenya in a hurry. I can't explain while I'm on the bus, but we'll be arriving at Arusha in about an hour.' The telephone conversation ended, and Helen hung up.

'What's the news?' said Sam.

'She'll try and shift our booking now. Failing that she'll make a fresh arrangement elsewhere and get back to us.'

'Great. But what about Elaine's news? It sounded interesting.'

'It does. Scottie has really pulled out the stops, but I think somebody is going to be annoyed with him. He's found out a bit about ACE. It all seems weird to me. But remember, Elaine's not a science buff and I'm not a fan of weapons, so if it all sounds garbled … well, it probably is.'

'Okay, tell me.'

Helen lowered her voice and leaned close to whisper into Sam's ear. 'Turns out ACE is an acronym. It stands for Autonomous Combat Entity.'

'Sam nodded, 'So ACE *is* a weapon then.'

'Scottie had to break into some very secret defence websites to find out for us. I'm hoping they can't trace it back.'

'He's the security wiz. I'm sure he will have covered his tracks. What did he find?'

'Well, apparently, it's a system that can replace soldiers on the ground in certain environments.'

'Robots?'

'No, Elaine didn't say that. But it was a bad line and hard to hear with all this going on,' Helen waved her hand about.

'She did say it operates independently but has a human programmer or director who is linked into the system's master controls. She said Scottie had described the set-up as a human ignition key. And whatever ACE is, it won't function unless that living key is to hand. Trying to operate it without will trigger a self-destruct mechanism. He told her it's designed to completely fry itself instantly.' She paused, pulled back a little and looked at Sam. 'What do you think?'

'Well, that fits with what Rupert said. Though I've never heard of that type of security before. Yes, thumbprints, iris recognition, even voice, but what is it measuring? Maybe biorhythms, heartbeat patterns, I don't know, but very clever. And Scottie mentions this self-destruct mechanism just as Rupert did. I can see why they need Bob alive too. That's useful, a real sign he may still be alive.'

The heat of the afternoon had finally tired the passengers out. People had said all they could and now they mostly sat quietly sleeping, reading or just gazing out of the window, waiting for the journey's end and watching the continuing pattern of the dry and dusty bushlands. The scene was broken by occasional streaks of green where distant trees marked the route of near-dry riverbeds. Helen's eyes would trace the lines of far-off hills then would suddenly be drawn to the foreground as the flash of ramparts signed the bus's passage across yet another bridge.

In the quiet, the satellite phone rang again. Helen answered it quickly. She listened, thanked and hung up.

'That was Elaine again. She spoke to the accommodation. It's fine, they have space free right now, so at least we've sorted that out. They will send their driver to collect us from the shuttle stop. All we need to do is look out for an orange Land Rover.'

'Orange?'

'That's what she said - bright orange.'

• • •

Stepping off the shuttle bus Helen and Sam spotted the orange Land Rover at once. The shuttle had pulled to a halt in the parking area of an impressive hotel. There were less than twenty paces from shuttle bus to Land Rover.

Helen went directly to the Land Rover to introduce herself while Sam waited for their cases to be hauled from the shuttle's undercarriage.

Climbing out of his vehicle the driver gave her a welcoming smile. A huge man, the proverbial barn door. Scrunching a wrapper in his left hand, he hurriedly swallowed down the last of his chocolate while wiping his right hand against his trouser leg. 'Hello, miss. Welcome to Arusha. My name is Mauwled. You're coming to the Mount Meru View Guesthouse with me,' he said while shaking Helen's hand. He let it drop, and opening one of the rear passenger doors, he waved her in. Then he stepped over to help Sam with the bags.

Mauwled was a forceful driver, which proved useful in Arusha's heavy traffic. It took about a half an hour to turn his Land Rover, run a little south along the main road and then swing off to his left on a road leading out of the city. Here the road began to rise. It didn't take long before they had left behind the city and its metalled roads and were moving slowly up a rutted dirt track onto the lower slopes of Mount Meru.

The track was fringed with groves of trees. Beyond those, Helen could see homes built of corrugated iron and wood. Some set in little clearings cultivated for market gardening, most with larger cleared patches of land for farming. Filling the skyline ahead was Mount Meru, the great volcano that dominated the landscape and whose height created a microclimate that kept its slopes green even in the height of the dry season.

Breaking up the run of homesteads were high-walled compounds behind which could be seen more substantial buildings - large villas with outhouses and properly constructed staff homes. The Land Rover slewed off the dirt track into a yet narrower lane, completely shaded by the trees; it ran just twenty paces before ending at a solid metal gate. Mauwled sounded his horn several times. The blast was immediately met by a cacophony of barking, then a voice from beyond the gate shouted and the dogs fell quiet. The voice called out an enquiry. Leaning his head out of the driver's side window Mauwled bellowed a response.

Mauwled's voice recognised, the gate opened a little and a watchman's head appeared to check all was in order. Satisfied, he swung the gate wide. Dressed in what may have been old military fatigues, he waved Mauwled forward and stood by, ready to close the gate as soon as the vehicle was through.

Helen saw the guard's friendly nod towards Mauwled as he passed, and she saw their driver's hand raised in response. Immediately inside the gates was a pack of dogs, all tethered by long chains. They were watching the arrival with interest. She counted five, maybe six. Big dogs, sandy red in colour with a dorsal ridge running down their backs from neck to hip. Rhodesian ridgebacks - lion hunting dogs, animals not to be messed with.

'That's Joseph, the watchman,' said Mauwled as he revved the engine and moved the Land Rover forward.

Helen saw three happy little children playing in the dirt at their mother's feet as the Land Rover passed the guardhouse, which was set immediately inside the gates. The children all waved to Mauwled as he passed, and he tooted his horn in response, which the children clearly loved. Helen and Sam received friendly waves from the children too just as Mauwled stretched an arm out of the window and tossed chocolate bars towards the youngsters. They scrambled to collect them as the dogs launched into another round of barking and the Land Rover pulled away up the drive, which was in much better condition than the rutted public lane. Helen saw it had been topped with gravel. Mauwled brought their vehicle to a halt near the entrance.

'Here we are. Welcome to Mount Meru View Guesthouse.' He jumped out and pulled open Helen's door, pointing her towards the front door while he began wrangling the cases. The door opened, and a smiling teenage girl greeted Helen and Sam, waving them into the vestibule.

'Come in please,' said the housemaid, pointing Helen into the cool shadows of a corridor beyond the vestibule. 'Come in. Come in. Welcome to Mount Meru View. My name's Val, I'm the maid.'

Val bustled past them in the corridor. 'This way. I'll show you your room and tell Miss Jeanie you've arrived.' The corridor contained six dark wood doors, three evenly spaced to either side. Beyond them, at the corridor's end, were double doors, one side had been left open, giving a partial view into what seemed to be a large lounge.

At the third door on the right-hand side, Val stopped and opened it, inviting them in. 'This is your room, I hope you like it. There's a bathroom and shower inside too. I made the bed for you just now. Please, go in. I'll fetch you drinks … cold water?'

'Water would be smashing,' said Sam, allowing Helen to lead into the room as Val hurried away. He followed Helen in and looked around, his eyes making contact with Helen's as she glanced back from the bathroom doorway. She smiled an approving smile.

The distant voice of an older woman reached them from somewhere in the public space beyond the double doors. 'They're here? Why didn't you tell me?' They couldn't quite make out the maid's response but did hear the sound of approaching flip-flops slapping on the marbled floor. This was the voice of another of the colonial era matriarchs, clinging on in her personal corner of Africa. Helen shuddered; they had known Susan Curtis only twenty-four hours and she had died.

A well-rounded white woman appeared in the doorway, smiling and puffing. Her shoulder-length hair, once brown now mostly silver, was held back from her face with a hair band. 'There you both are! Welcome, welcome.'

She gave each a hearty handshake. 'Jean Albright, call me Jeanie, everyone does. Sorry I wasn't here to greet you, I was making sure the gardener had done the grass the way I like. He's very good, but I like to let him know I'm around. You really must sit out on the patio later. He keeps everything so well. Lovely views.'

Jeanie clapped her hands and gave a chuckle. 'Now I know what that shuttle bus is like. What are you drinking? G and Ts?' she turned to Sam. 'Or would you prefer a lager?'

'I think there's some water on its way,' said Sam.

'Well, whatever you want. You must treat this place as your own. You're quite lucky - I was full until this morning when the group I've been hosting, a film crew and some animal experts, lion people mostly, packed up and headed off. They had been here for a little while, waiting for the Small Rains. Something about recording the change in hunting behaviours as the rains begin. The long-range forecast is for rain, at last. It's very overdue. So off they went to get to wherever they're meant to be.'

'Yes, we noticed. Everywhere is so dry up in Ethiopia and Kenya too,' said Helen.

'Oh! You've been getting about, what have you been up to? But never mind just now, you can tell me over dinner, if you like. Please, get cleaned up and come on through and I'll show you round. You're the only guests tonight.'

Chapter 11

FRIDAY 25TH OCTOBER - EVENING

Helen and Sam sat in easy chairs on the patio. Helen had been delighted to discover that Jeanie had a stock of South African rosé, and an almost empty glass now rested on the occasional table in front of her. Sam held a lager bottle in his hand. The warm air carried just the faintest of sweet flowering scents - courtesy of the gardener who, taking advantage of the microclimate effects on the slopes of Mount Meru, still managed to produce a few blooms in the garden, in spite of the wider drought. A few bees still buzzed, stragglers busy on their final pollen gathering trips before nightfall. Otherwise, just the sound of cicadas clicking away in the undergrowth lulled them both into a moment of peace.

'Doesn't that look lovely,' said Helen, looking up to where Mount Meru's highest slopes glowed, caught in the last shafts of sunlight; while the lower slopes and the garden's colour had already faded into the shades and monochrome of the deepening twilight.

'Impressive,' said Sam. Jeanie's villa was set on the lower western slopes of Mount Meru, positioned above Arusha City. Though only a few minutes from the city, it was surrounded by smallholdings and almost on the edge of the protected mountain park. 'You'd pay millions for a property like this back home.'

They heard a chuckle behind them. 'Yes, it's lovely, isn't it? I've been here for more than forty years and I love it just as much as ever. It originally belonged to my husband's family. I don't know how much it's worth. One or two people have approached me in the years since my husband died, but I won't sell.

'It's nice now, but I think you'll like the morning too. My favourite time is when the sun rises over the mountain and fills the garden with sunlight. You can feel the dew lifting, the birds go wild with song and every sort of insect is buzzing about their business. Always have my coffee out here in the mornings. You must join me tomorrow. Now are you coming in to eat? Mama Grace is ready to serve and it's bad form to keep her waiting.'

They rose to follow Jeanie through the glass sliding doors into the guesthouse's public lounge space. Immediately inside the lounge was a cluster of comfortable chairs, set around a pair of coffee tables and arranged to provide their occupants with a view out through the glass, across the gardens and on up the slopes of Mount Meru.

Jeanie walked on deeper into the broad lounge. To their left, the closed double doors that opened onto the corridor off which the bedrooms lay. To the right, a doorway - shielded by a long fringe of hanging beadwork that blocked out any light from beyond but not the sounds and smells emanating from within. Jeanie didn't need to tell them it was the kitchen. Then, reaching the far side of the lounge area she waved Helen and Sam towards a long dining table - one end was set for three.

'Oh, by the way, we don't go out after dinner without telling Joseph, our watchman, first.'

'Wild animals?' said Helen.

'No, big dogs. Joseph normally lets some of his boys run loose in the grounds at night. All the locals round about here know; it makes sure we have no pilfering.'

They sat and were immediately attended by Val, the young maid who had welcomed them earlier in the day. As she hurried back and forth from the kitchen, they became aware of Mama Grace's presence, signified by banging pots and shrieked outbursts.

Suddenly realising just how hungry they were, Helen and Sam were happy to set about the generous portions of braised beef, rice and vegetables that Val served to them.

Meal over, Val cleared away the dishes, leaving them to sit around the table with mugs of strong African coffee and glasses of Drambuie. Jeanie proved to be a mine of local information. She expected the extra border controls to be in force for several more days as everyone was on edge. Sam was happy to hear that - it might yet give him time to catch up.

His big problem was he wanted to maintain the cover of being in Tanzania on university research business but had arrived two weeks ahead of his planned rendezvous with Professor Malangwa who was based at the university in Dar es Salaam. Jeanie suggested that, next morning, he should present himself at the office in Arusha University that Professor Malangwa and his team were using as a base for their fieldwork. She thought there was bound to be somebody there, if only a caretaker, who could at least report Sam's presence, and then he would be on the professor's radar. Sam recognised it was a good plan.

Eventually, Helen stood and muttered about a long day and needing to get sleep. Just as the others rose, the quiet of the evening was shattered by the barking of angry dogs somewhere out in the darkness of the grounds.

All three turned to look across the lounge to the great windows that afforded views out across the lawn and gardens to Mount Meru during the day. Right now, they were nothing more than shiny mirrors preventing any sight of the outside action.

'Val! Switch off the lights,' Jeanie's voice filled the room. 'Let's see what's going on.'

Val scurried out from the kitchen and flicked the light switches off. The whole area was plunged into darkness. They waited while their eyes adjusted.

'What do you think it is?' said Sam.

'No idea. Could be nothing, maybe an animal come down scavenging from the mountainside, perhaps an intruder. We'll know soon enough.'

As his eyes adjusted to the darkness, Sam had watched Jeanie working her way across the room to a bureau. Once there, she had folded down the front leaf and pulled open an internal drawer. She lifted out a handgun.

'Are you going to need that?' he said.

'I hope not, but sure as hell, nobody is coming into my home. You don't want to know what house robbers will do to women out here.'

'Is it loaded?'

'Always.' Jeanie raised the weapon for Sam to see. 'And I'm a dead shot with it, believe me.'

'Have you ever actually used it in anger?' said Sam.

Jeanie didn't answer.

Sam looked closely at the gun. It was an old British Army service issue revolver, an Enfield No 2, World War Two vintage. 'Where did that come from?'

'My husband's father served in the King's East African Rifles during the War.' She turned her attention back to the gardens where they could now make out the shapes of shrubs and bushes around the patio. 'It's always been kept in the bureau, ready. My father-in-law always said, "Better to have it and not need it than need it and not have it." And he was sure one day it would be needed.'

There was no movement, but the sounds were clear and coming closer. Running feet, little shrieks of fear and the sound of determined hunting dogs forcing themselves through the shrubbery to reach their quarry. Suddenly the figure of a man burst into view, running for the sanctuary of the house. A hand grabbed the patio door and attempted to slide it open. As part of her duties, Val had locked it while the guests ate dinner.

The hand jerked frantically on the handle and they could clearly hear his cries of fear. This was not an attacker; this was a man scared for his life. The reason for his flight manifested itself in a series of low shapes emerging from the dark. They manoeuvred and paced, methodically boxing in their prey. The dogs emitted long throaty growls that ended in gruff half barks as they steadily closed on their target. He now stood resigned to his fate, back pressed to the window, arms outstretched towards the ridgebacks.

'Are you going to let them attack?' said Helen.

'I can't stop them. Only Joseph can do that,' said Jeanie.

'Where is he?' said Sam.

'Well, house robbers normally come in a pack; there are probably others to be flushed out.'

'Strikes me, he's on his own and I'm not keen on seeing somebody ripped apart by dogs. The man's terrified.' Sam stepped over to the patio door, slid the bolt back and cracked open the door. He reached out, grabbed the shaking man by the shoulder, jerking him backwards through the doorway and slammed the door just as the dogs launched their attack.

The man cried out anew in fear, and this time, in pain. As he'd been pulled through the door, one of the dogs had just managed to seize his foot, which it held clamped tight in its jaws, keeping it caught beyond the door. The man toppled, pulling Sam down too. The ankle was preventing the door from sliding fully shut, leaving a gap through which the remaining dogs were competing to thrust their muzzles, forcing the door further open in a push for their prize - the man's soft fleshy calf, and the rest of him.

Helen stepped up quickly, placed both hands on the door handle and pressed the door tight against the man's ankle, causing him more pain but preventing the dogs from getting through the door. She could feel the dogs' breath, felt drips of drool as the tongue from the highest muzzle licked round to taste her fingers on the handle. She shuddered but held the door tight.

'What now, Sam?' she said, flinching as one of the snarling hounds threw itself at the glass beside her shoulder, its muzzle open, teeth kept from her face only by a quarter inch of plate glass. The dog fell back and the glass in the patio doorframe shook again as the dog bounced back for another attempt. 'We need to do something now; this glass won't hold for much longer.'

Sam released the prostrate man and stood up. Immediately, the man's ankle, lubricated by his own blood and pulled by the blood-crazed hound, started to slide out through the gap in the doorway. A second dog forced its muzzle down against the newly exposed expanse of calf muscle and bit. The man's screams redoubled as the weight of two dogs pulling together threatened to drag his entire leg outside. Helen pressed her whole weight against the handle; the extra pressure temporarily putting the brakes on the man's slide.

Helen glanced at Sam, needing action now, knowing the pressure she was applying on the handle was either going to break the man's leg or snap the handle off. She hoped it was the leg breaking; without a handle to hold the door the dogs would force it open in seconds.

Sam reached across and took the service revolver from Jeanie's hand. For all her earlier bravado, she was now transfixed by the scene and the weapon slipped out of her grasp without any resistance. Sam stepped over the crying man and knelt down, bringing the gun to within a few inches of the nearest dog's head. Its fevered eyes rotated up to look at Sam whose hand was now only a muzzle's length away from its teeth. The intensity of its snarl grew, but the dog had a good hold on the calf and nothing would induce it to let go.

Sam waited, unflinching as another dog lunged in above the others, throwing itself at the gap in a desperate attempt to take Sam. Its muzzle forced through the gap, snapping and snarling, trying to reach him. Then, as it fell back to ready itself for a further lunge, Sam took his chance. He thrust his arm forward, pushing the barrel of the revolver through the doorframe gap, putting his hand into the bite zone. Sensing the dog was already moving forward again for its second attempt to take him, Sam brought the revolver to within an inch of the calf-locked dog's jaws and fired.

The report of the revolver reverberated round the room, the calf-biting dog let out a howl and whine and the man on the ground continued to scream.

'Don't shoot the dogs! Joseph needs them,' shouted Jeanie, coming out of her trance.

Sam raised the revolver, pointing through the gap and fired three times more in quick succession. Startled by the close proximity gunshots, the dogs had released their bite and pulled back a couple of paces. Sam threw down the revolver and stooped to grab the wounded leg. 'Door,' he shouted to Helen.

She released the pressure on the door handle and Sam jerked the mauled leg inside. Helen slid the door fully shut and flicked the door latch on, just ahead of the returning pack. The two biggest dogs reached the glass first. It vibrated under the shock of their impact, and they growled, snarled, scratched claws against the doorframe in frustration and pressed muzzles against the glass as they were joined by the rest of the pack, all angry that their prey had escaped. Suddenly, they fell silent and instantly vanished into the night.

'Lights on,' said Sam, and Val responded immediately, filling the room with light and excluding the night as the windows once again acted as mirrors reflecting the brightness back into the room.

Helen was kneeling, looking at the man's leg as Sam picked up the revolver and handed it back to Jeanie.

She took the weapon, looked at it absently then focused her attention on Sam. 'You shot the dogs. They're our protection. What will Joseph do? What about his children, they love the dogs.'

Sam put an arm round Jeanie, guided her towards one of the sofas that were dotted around the lounge. She allowed herself to be led. 'It's okay, Jeanie. I didn't shoot the dogs. Just gave them a little scare. I aimed over the first one's ears. Knowing ridgebacks, there was no point in shooting it once it had clamped its jaws on the leg. Wounded, it would have almost certainly died biting, shooting it wouldn't have deterred any of the other dogs. The shock tactic of a huge bang beside their ears was our best bet, it moved them all back for just a moment.

'Now you sit there for a minute while I fix you a G and T. Looks like you could do with one.'

Jeanie nodded absently, content that Joseph's dogs had survived.

Sam squeezed her arm. 'Well done, Jeanie.' He pointed at the wounded man. 'Watch him while I'm gone. If he tries anything, shout for me, and if you have to, use the gun this time, okay?'

'I might have a drink myself,' said Helen, looking up from where she was applying pressure to the man's bleeding wounds with her tee shirt, which she had just peeled off. Swinging gently as she bent over him was the signet ring suspended on its heavy gold chain. 'See if you can find a medical kit while you're at it.'

Moments later, Val hurried up to Helen and placed a big first aid kit on the floor beside her. The man had regained some composure now that it had dawned on him he was not going to be savaged to death by the pack of dogs.

Helen looked up at the maid. 'Thanks. Now I need some fresh water and then perhaps you'd go to my room and get me a clean top please?' She turned her attention back to the wound and lapsed into a near automatic process. Her first career as a nurse and three years spent in a mission hospital in the Congo had conditioned her responses.

The medical kit was impressive, and she could see everything was there for her to do a full treatment on the spot. The water arrived allowing her to rinse away the blood and dog drool from the leg. The calf had several deep lacerations, it was going to need some serious needlework, but not by her. She used a bottle of antiseptic fluid to clean the wound and then dressed it securely. Her intention was to get him fit to travel to hospital where they could do the sewing. He was going to need some precautionary injections too. While she guessed the compound dogs were not rabies carriers, that too would need to be considered.

Then she turned her attention to the foot. It had been grabbed at the onset of the attack and been the subject of constant savaging. She wondered what was left of it. Taking a pair of scissors, she carefully cut the man's bootlace and began to ease the boot off his foot. He cried out in pain and slapped his hand against the flooring.

Helen looked at him. 'I'm sorry but we really need to see the damage,' she said.

He ignored her, rocking his head from side to side and moaning.

Val returned from Helen's room with a clean top just as Helen decided to get it over with. She pulled the boot off; the maid covered her face with a hand and gasped in fear. The man cried in pain. Helen looked at the exposed foot as Sam arrived with the drinks.

'How is he?' said Sam.

'Whimpering,' said Helen. Throwing the boot down, she reached out and jerked her top from the mesmerised maid's hand. While the casualty was distracted by the pain in his ankle, Helen pulled the top over her head, pushed her arms through the sleeves and collected a glass of rosé from Sam in one seamless movement. She took a mouthful from the glass, held it for a moment then swallowed and repeated before setting the glass down on the floor beside her.

'Look, the boot has taken the full force of the attack. It's full of holes but his foot is fine. A bit of bruising but nothing to write home about,' she looked up at Sam. 'True, his ankle is a bit messy but that's down to me forcing the patio door against it. I'll just put a strapping on the whole thing and that will do him till he gets to hospital.'

The strapping took only a couple of minutes to complete, and then Sam sat the man up, propping him against a sofa. He sat opposite the injured man. 'So, what have you got to say for yourself?' said Sam.

Helen retrieved her wine glass from the floor and sat next to Sam, taking her first opportunity to take a proper look at the man's face. 'Just a minute, Sam. I know this man,' she said.

'What do you mean? How do you know him?'

'Look past the messy hair, and the tears and the drool. Look at the face. He's the man from the Thorn Tree Café; he's been following us halfway across Africa.'

Sam studied the man's face. It took just a moment to realise Helen was right. 'You're spot on. Great call,' he said. 'So, now maybe we'll find out why we've picked up a travelling companion. One thing's for sure, he's not on Ro Su-Ann's payroll. He's not made of the right stuff.'

'I think we'd better call the police now, don't you?' said Jeanie. Like a ship's sail catching a sudden breeze, she was starting to billow back into her confident colonial matron mode.

'Yes, but perhaps we should wait a little while,' said Sam. 'This one's been following us, and I'd like to ask him one or two questions.'

The man looked anxiously from one to the other. He shook his head and was starting to speak when he suddenly dissolved into nervous tears and an incoherent stutter while staring at the window.

Helen looked over to the patio door. Pressed so close against the glass that its proximity overcame the mirroring effect of the glass was a ridgeback. As she looked, it was joined by another. 'Sam,' said Helen, as a third dog arrived and sat silently, staring through the glass. 'They're back.'

Everyone was staring in horror as more dogs arrived. The pack sat in silence staring back at them through the glass.

A little above the line of dogs, the room's reflection vanished from the glass as a face appeared. It was forced unwillingly against the glass and a couple of the dogs looked up towards the face and growled. It was a frightened face.

Then two other faces appeared, and a huge hand rapped on the glass door.

'It's Mauwled, and Joseph too,' said Jeanie. 'Thank God they're safe, the dogs too.' She threw a look at Sam. He wasn't quite sure what it conveyed but suspected there was something of a reprimand in it. 'Open the door then, let them in.'

Val hurried to open the glass door. Mauwled thrust his prisoner through the open doorway and down onto the floor. He stepped in and was closely followed by Joseph, who slid the glass door shut behind him. The dogs sat in silence, watching their master through the glass.

Helen and Sam recognised the second man, who was now sprawled on the floor. He was the driver of the little silver car who had become so flustered when they had hurried past it in Kimathi Street only the day before.

Jeanie stepped across the room to Mauwled and Joseph. 'Thank God you're safe. Is everyone else all right? The children, your wife?' She squeezed Mauwled's upper arm, at once happy and relieved. Then she turned to Joseph and gave him a full-blown hug. Sam stretched out and once again relieved Jeanie of the revolver, easing it from one of her hands that had arced round to embrace Joseph's neck. The crisis over, this was not a moment to risk accidental gunshot wounds.

'They're all fine, Jeanie, everyone's fine. I caught him outside the gates. His friend had climbed in.' Joseph threw the injured man a look of disdain. 'He's a lucky man, the dogs wanted him.'

'Yes, he is. Now the question is, what are we to do?' said Jeanie.

'I think we'd agreed I'd ask some questions, and we can be guided by the answers. Half an hour's delay won't matter to the police and these two are in no fit state to cause us any more bother.'

'Agreed,' said Jeanie. 'Joseph, go see if Mama Grace has any meat in the fridge, your boys deserve a treat tonight.' She glowered at the injured man. 'Though I doubt it could taste as good as that.'

Sam nodded an acknowledgement to Joseph, rested his hand on the man's shoulder, and grinned at him. 'Thank you, Joseph. Your capturing this man will be very helpful, and I'm impressed by your dogs. Glad we're on the same side.'

Joseph smiled back and allowed Sam's hand to slide down his arm where their hands met to link and shake in a full greeting. 'It's my job, sir.'

'Call me Sam.'

Joseph nodded, gave Jeanie a broad smile and accompanied Val to the kitchen and Mama Grace's fridge, from where a low buzz of chatter rose to reach back to the lounge.

'Right,' said Sam, 'let's get down to business.' He stood over the driver.

The captured driver was eyeing Sam nervously; he could see the distress of his companion, the damage done to his leg and knew the dogs were still around. Sam's revolver was threatening too.

'Please, don't hurt us. We are your friends,' said the driver.

'Oh? Perhaps you'd better explain why you're breaking in during the middle of the night then,' said Sam.

'Yes, yes. I will explain. We have been watching over you.'

Sam arched an eyebrow. 'Really? Guardian angels? Why would you do that?'

'Because the bishop instructed us. He was concerned that Reverend Johnson did not come to harm.'

For a moment Helen was shocked, exchanged glances with Sam, then she took a sip of wine, needing to cover the involuntary smile that had crossed her face. She had seen these two in action, they were not guardian material. She took another sip of wine as the smile returned.

'Explain,' said Sam in his calm tone. 'Why would the bishop think Helen needed watching over?'

'I don't know exactly. We're only juniors; we know nothing. We only came out of training seminary last year. The bishop said we were to watch and keep him informed of your progress. Where you were, what you did, who you spoke to.' The man's voice had a pleading tone. He was frightened and clearly had not been trained for the role he was fulfilling.

Helen looked as Sam. 'What do you think? If it were true, why would we be followed like this? Can it be anything to do with your problem?'

'I doubt it; these boys are a thousand miles from Ro Soo-Ann.'

'So, you're priests?' said Helen.

'Yes, we are on Bishop Ignatius' staff. All I know is we were to watch over you and report.'

'Right, two questions,' said Sam. 'One, why would the bishop want Helen watched? And two, if you were meant to be watching why did you and your friend end up breaking in and on the wrong end of Joseph's guard dogs?'

'You didn't go to a hotel when you arrived in Arusha. We followed you here to this private compound. The bishop didn't understand why. When you didn't come out again he told us to make sure you had not been tricked here and taken prisoner.'

'Okay, so again, why?' said Sam.

'We don't know. It is not our place to question him. He is second only to the patriarch of our Church. He is the patriarch's right hand.'

Helen knelt down beside the young priest and proffered a glass of water. He took it enthusiastically as she held a second glass out to the injured priest.

'So, you must be in touch with your bishop. You can ask him, can't you?' Sam waited while the man took a draught of water.

'Yes, we can speak with him, by telephone. But it is not our place to challenge our leader's intentions.'

'Even if it ends in your friend getting his leg half chewed off?'

'Even anything.'

'Here's a suggestion,' said Helen. 'Why doesn't he speak with me?'

115

The injured priest moaned a little and the other squeezed his hand before looking back to Helen. 'That is what my bishop wanted. He asked that you wait for him, but you refused.'

'No, I didn't refuse. I just said I couldn't hang around in Addis Ababa waiting for him; we had business to attend to in Nairobi. Remember he was going away too.' Helen fell silent for a moment. 'Hold on, he said he was going to a conference in Arusha. Is he still here? Now?'

'Yes, of course. We met with his assistant earlier this evening.'

Helen straightened up and looked across at Sam. 'Well, I reckon there's a bishop of the Ethiopian Orthodox Tewahedo Church who's got a lot of explaining to do. Fancy attending a church conference tomorrow?'

The young priests were only too willing to telephone their bishop. He in turn was delighted that Helen now wanted to speak with him and had his juniors convey the offer of an appointment at the conference building next morning. Then Joseph held the dogs back as Mauwled escorted the two priests back to their car.

At last, the lounge was quiet. Jeanie poured herself a large G and T and put it on the coffee table. Then, while letting out a great sigh, she slumped down beside Helen. 'Well that was unexpected,' she said. Helen let the understatement pass.

'I think I need one of these now,' said Jeanie. She leant forward over the coffee table and pulled a silvered box towards her. Opening it, she took out a lighter and selected a cheroot. She rolled the slender cigar between finger and thumb for a moment and looked longingly at it. 'Would you like one?' she said.

Helen pursed her lips for a moment. 'You know, I think I'll join you,' she said stretching out to take one.

Jeanie flicked the lighter and both women lit their slim cigars, then relaxed back into the sofa, drinks in hand.

Chapter 12
SATURDAY 26TH OCTOBER - AM

Mauwled swung the orange Land Rover into the side of the road and came to an abrupt halt directly outside the Arusha International Conference Centre. Facility attendants looked at him disapprovingly, pointing in the direction of the parking spaces provided. Mauwled waved to them with a cheery smile and then simply ignored their directions.

'Here we are,' he said, looking out at the impressive white building directly in front of them.

Helen surveyed it and then turned to Sam who was in the rear seat. 'I'll go in then,' she said.

'Are you sure you don't want me to come?'

'No, I'll be fine. You go with Mauwled to make your link up with the university; your work is way more pressing than mine is right now. Anyway, you saw the bishop at the airport in Addis; he's not exactly a threat ...'

'Here's your man,' said Mauwled, pointing towards the open doors of the conference centre.

Helen turned to look and spotted the driver priest of the previous evening hurrying towards the Land Rover. She turned back to Sam. 'His sidekicks are hardly a threat either.'

Sam gave a little laugh. He couldn't argue with that. 'Okay, but I won't be far away, and I'll only need a short time with Professor Malangwa. Either that or I'll just leave a message for him. Then we'll come straight back, say one hour maximum. I'll wait for you just through those doors in the reception area.'

'Great; I'll see you in a while. And Sam, don't fuss.'

His hand reached forward and gently squeezed her shoulder. 'I know, but believe me, of all the bad guys we've had to face in the past, Ro takes the biscuit.'

'Right, he must be pretty bad then! But whatever this is, it will have nothing to do with Ro Su-Ann. I'll speak with the bishop, see what he wants and finish it off for good this morning, so we can focus on finding Bob Prentice.' She smiled, turned, opened the door and slipped out, waving towards the approaching priest.

• • •

'This way, please,' said the driver priest, waving her inside and towards a row of alcove sections that led off from the far side of the reception area. She could see each alcove was equipped the same, fitted with a low table in the middle and three sofas ranged around it, their backs to the walls of the alcove. The fourth wall was glass with a door opening into the foyer. 'The Bishop has reserved a meeting space, so you can talk with him.'

She knew which alcove to head towards; standing outside the glass door was a sore-footed priest. Since she had last seen him, his lower leg looked like it had been treated properly in hospital and was now encased in a plastic moonboot to support the ankle she had crushed between door and frame. She hoped it was just soft tissue damage and he hadn't fractured any bones.

'Good morning, how's the leg?' she said, approaching the man. He bowed his head ever so slightly.

'Good morning, Miss Johnson. My leg will be fine, thank you. Only, I can't run for a week or two.' He gave a wry smile and pulled open the glass door. 'Please do come in and sit. You will see iced water is provided and coffee too. Let me pour you a drink.'

'No, I'll be fine thanks, but where's Bishop Ignatius?'

'My colleague has gone to announce your arrival. I'm sure the bishop will be along directly.'

Helen sat at one end of the middle sofa; it provided her with a full view through the glass wall of the comings and goings in the reception.

She had barely sat down when a bustle of activity on the far side of reception caught her eye. Hurrying towards her cubicle was the bishop, moving with the confident step of a man who expected a clear path in front of him. At his side walked the assistant who Helen recognised from Addis Ababa Airport.

Bishop Ignatius smiled broadly and extended his hand to Helen. 'Well, Miss Johnson, I am delighted that we meet again so soon. It is not how I had anticipated our meeting would be but welcome in any event.'

Helen was struck by his good English; here in the calm of the enclosed alcove it was far more noticeable than it had been at the airport. She stood and stretched out a hand to shake his.

The bishop hesitated for a moment before selecting the sofa to Helen's right, sitting in the seat immediately adjacent to her. His assistant pulled the door shut and sat on the sofa beside his bishop. Beyond the glass stood the two junior priests, providing a guard, which made Helen smile to herself.

'Welcome for you, your Grace, but I'm only here because you've had your boys follow me halfway across East Africa and they nearly got themselves killed in the process. How about you tell me why our meeting is so important. I can spare you a little over half an hour. I'm afraid after that I'll need to link up with my friend again and get on with the business we're actually here for. Now, please tell me how I can help you.'

Bishop Ignatius looked slightly pained. 'But surely you know who I am?'

'Yes, your Grace. You're the bishop who won't leave me alone and I don't know why yet. And I'm not very happy about it.'

The bishop's voice remained calm. 'I am the right hand of the patriarch, do you understand?'

'Yes, I guess. You are number two in the Ethiopian Orthodox Tewahedo Church. But what would such a high placed churchman want with me?'

The bishop turned and spoke quietly to his assistant in Amharic, the dominant language of Ethiopia. Helen did not understand but did pick out the word Edinburgh repeated several times along with the sound of her name. She registered the consternation in their voices and noted the occasional glance in her direction.

After allowing the side discussion to run for a couple of minutes she cut in. 'Really, your Grace, I'd like to understand what your interest in me is. Now would be a good time.'

The two men stopped talking, and after a moment of silence, the assistant nodded earnestly to his bishop. He might have been signalling agreement or perhaps encouragement. The bishop turned back to face Helen, took a moment to compose himself, then smiled. Suddenly there was just a hint of nervousness about his demeanour.

'You are Helen Johnson. Priest of St. Bernard's in Edinburgh?' he said. She detected a hint of anxiety in his face, but his tone expressed hope.

'Well, almost,' said Helen.

She saw the confusion spread across the faces of both bishop and assistant and hurried to explain.

'In my church we call priests, ministers.' She decided it would be too complicated explaining the Church of Scotland had just closed St Bernard's and she had bought the buildings using her Templar trust fund - she was not sure she had a full understanding of all the finer legalities of that process herself yet.

'A minister. Of course.' The bishop turned and shoved his assistant's arm with some vigour, a reprimand for an information failing. 'Minister. Minister,' he said to his assistant before lapsing into a short run of Amharic that left the assistant looking uncomfortable.

'So, you know who I am, happy now? How about telling me why you've had your boys hound me across three countries.'

The bishop looked back at her. This time worry was the dominant tone. 'You do not know? How can this be? I am the patriarch's right hand.'

'Yes, and?'

He pursed his lips and sat in silence for a minute, then turned back to his assistant. They exchanged a few quick-fire phrases, again in Amharic, before the bishop turned back to her.

'As I said when we last met, Addis Ababa is a long way from Edinburgh, but we are not backward here, just distant from you.'

'Okay,' said Helen, cautiously. Recent events in Edinburgh and her Templar inheritance should have no relevance in the middle of East Africa. Involuntarily, she thought back to the brutality and butchery they had struggled against. The bishop even knew about the ring. How was it possible that she was linked with Bishop Ignatius and his Church? A shiver ran down her spine and the air conditioning suddenly seemed much colder. What was this? She was beginning to wish she had kept Sam with her. 'What exactly do you want?'

Glancing at her watch, she realised there was still some time before he would return, certainly too long to stall. 'Sure, I'm from St Bernard's. Why would that interest you?'

The bishop looked at her, held her gaze. 'I am the patriarch's right hand.' He detected no response in her eyes. 'I am the patriarch's right hand. The hand that keeps the key …' the bishop paused, searching Helen's eyes for a reaction. He was visibly puzzled now.

Helen had no idea what he had expected from the exchange, but it was clearly not going as he had anticipated. Though she could tell there was something he considered important in his riddle; something she should know and didn't.

'Your Grace, if you have something to say, say it. Because as things stand, when my friend gets back, I'm gone.'

The bishop averted his gaze and his hand gripped the ornate cross that hung around his neck. He intoned a little prayer under his breath. Then, still gripping the cross like a security blanket, he looked back at Helen.

'I am the patriarch's right hand. The hand that keeps the key. I await the keeper of the lock - the bearer of the ring.' His words had the rhythm of an oft-repeated chant.

Helen's stomach tightened, and her mind started to race, trying to process the bishop's meaning, all the while struggling to keep her face expressionless. Yes, this linked directly to her role as the Templar ring bearer, which she had inherited from the previous minister of St Bernard's Church. Poor John Dearly, he had died a horrible death without being able to properly explain her responsibilities or his church's links. Until this morning, she'd thought she finally had a handle on it. Clearly not. And like so many other aspects of those inherited responsibilities, they appeared when least expected and invariably trailed trouble like a ship's wake. More than anything right now, she needed to speak with Sam.

The bishop and his assistant were both watching her intently; waiting for a response. She decided honesty was the only workable policy.

'I'm sorry. There's only one possible link between us and I know that's the Templars. You are right, I'm not going to deny it, I am from Edinburgh and I know the ring. But I don't know you or your key, and I certainly don't have a lock.'

'This cannot be!' said the assistant. 'She must be an imposter, must be!'

The bishop raised his hand and the assistant was quiet.

'I'm afraid I don't understand how you can be the ring bearer and not know what is required. It is not possible.'

'Well, it is. I'm afraid I took up the mantle in difficult circumstances and my predecessor died before he could provide a full account of my duties.'

There was a long uncomfortable silence, which was finally broken by the assistant leaning close to his bishop and whispering in his ear. The bishop responded in hushed tones. Their whispered exchange became heated for a few moments. Finally, both men seemed to reach an agreement and nodded assent to one another. The bishop turned again to face Helen.

'Well?' she said.

'I think we might consider this a stand-off of sorts. Neither party knows for certain who the other really is, their motives nor what the outcome should be. If, as you say, your predecessor died without telling you that which you needed to know, then you cannot respond appropriately to me. I have seen recent reports of the cruel and dreadful deaths of churchmen in Edinburgh. So, it may be the case that you do not know, and if so, then our arrangement would seem lost for all time. In such circumstances I can understand your not knowing, but it does not break the impasse.

'However, my assistant has made a very sensible suggestion. One that I am happy to endorse if it can take us to a solution.'

'Go on,' said Helen, 'I'm listening.'

'The one sign that will prove you are bona fide to me is the sign over which our covenant was made. Come, prove yourself and I will share what I can with you.'

'I'm sorry, your Grace; I'm not going anywhere. If you want resolution, let's reach it here or let it go.'

'No Helen, I meant come forward. If you are the ring bearer, show it. Let me see the proof.'

'You want to see the ring?'

'Exactly.'

Helen weighed up her options. She would have preferred to discuss the whole thing with Sam first. She did know that the papers and television news had had a field day over the previous killings; they were pretty well all public domain, but the ring was not. Only those at the very heart of the Templar secret had knowledge of the rings. If Bishop Ignatius knew about her ring, he must be privy to at least part of its secret. She decided it was worth the risk. The bishop already believed he knew who she was; proving it would provide her with access to information. Identifying herself had to be a chance worth taking.

'Forgive me, your Grace, but how do I know I can trust you?'

'Ah yes, cautious as ever, very sensible, I think. Now, I have something I want to show you before we go any further.'

'Fire away.'

Ignatius turned his assistant. 'The plaque?'

From his pocket the assistant drew a slim wooden case about the same size as a modest hip flask. He passed it to Ignatius, who placed it on the occasional table in front of him. Before opening it, he looked at Helen again. 'When we first met I had a feeling that you were not fully aware of your connection to my Church.'

'Spot on, I'm completely in the dark.'

'Well I can tell you something of what you need to know.'

'All right,' said Helen, a note of caution returning to her voice. 'So … how do we proceed?'

Ignatius carefully opened the hinged lid on the slim wooden case and slid the box towards Helen. She sat forward to get a closer look. 'You show me this,' he said.

Helen looked at the sheet of gold. An engraved plaque. She recognised the engraving and gave an involuntary shiver.

'May I?' she asked, gesturing with her hands.

'Please, be my guest, but do be careful. It is a very delicate object.'

Helen lifted the box to get a closer inspection. She sucked on her lower lip a little then moved her hands to bring the object closer to her eye. 'This is interesting,' she said. Then fixed Ignatius with a stare. 'Where did you get this from?'

'I got it from my predecessor, who got it from his and so on, back a very long way.' He pointed at the gold plaque. 'We must compare originals now.'

The gold plaque carried a perfect engraved representation of the face of Helen's ring.

Ignatius smiled at her. 'This is what I think you would call the crunch point. If you pass the test, the key is returned to you and I will tell you what I can. For I see you do not know what you need to know. If the test is not passed, then you may go on from here with my best wishes and an assurance that I will deny ever having had this conversation.'

He laughed again and leant back into the chair as his assistant nervously echoed his laugh.

'So, what's the test?'

'Simple, your ring must fit exactly into the engraving on the plaque. I trust it will fit but ...' he shrugged, 'Rules are rules - we must check. Yes?'

She let her finger trace across the surface of the plaque. 'They are the same,' she said quietly, almost to herself.

She could tell the engraving was a perfect representation of the face of her ring. The ring suddenly felt very heavy. This was real confirmation of association. A photo could always be mocked up, this couldn't. How did Ignatius have this? What did he know? What did he want? Did everything always have to come back to this? The rings, the Templars, the ...

She looked up to see that Ignatius and his assistant were taut, leaning slightly forward in hope and anticipation.

'Okay, I'm in. But don't play any silly games. I show, you tell.'

The bishop bowed his head very slightly. 'It is your decision and you are in control. As you have always been.'

Helen placed the little plaque on the table. She stood up and slipped a finger beneath the collar of her top. The bishop and his assistant watched as she pulled the gold chain out into the electric light. She saw their eyes sparkle with anticipation. As the ring emerged into view on the end of its chain, they leapt up as one, exclaiming with glee.

Helen had to take a step back and swat their hands away as excitement got the better of them.

'Whoa there,' said Helen. 'Hands down, I'm not public property.'

Ignatius sat, raising his hands and making a little nodding gesture. 'I'm sorry, I'm sorry. Nobody really thought this day would come. Certainly not in my lifetime. Please continue, I am composed.' He leant across and pushed his assistant's arm, admonishing him for his part in the transgression.

The atmosphere calmed, and Helen sat too.

'Helen, if my engraving matches your ring exactly, I must accept you as the ring bearer.' He opened his palms towards Helen. 'May we?'

Helen extended the chain to its limit. She allowed the assistant to turn the ring on its chain to complete his checks. He placed the ring against the face of the plaque and rotated it gently to and fro. Almost at once the two artefacts slotted together perfectly, a lock tight fit. A moment later, he let the ring go and confirmed it was the ring represented in the engraving.

Ignatius clapped his hands in excitement. 'This is my brightest day. Our Church can fulfil its promise and it is me that has the honour of completing the circle.'

Helen was about to let the ring slip under her collar when Ignatius stopped her. 'Please, Helen, may I touch it? The ring. Just once, it would be my honour. We have waited a long time for this to come.'

She lifted the chain a little towards him and he reached out to touch, taking the weight of it in his hand, and then rolling it with his fingers. His smile beamed.

'Right, I think we have reached an understanding. There are things you promised to share if the ring fitted your plaque. It does. This is probably the time to explain what has been going on, and about this key you mentioned?'

Ignatius released the ring and leant back in his chair, pressed his hands together and lapsed into silence as though praying. The silence continued for some time and Ignatius' assistant sent a smile of understanding towards Helen as her frustration began to show. She responded to his attempt at empathy with a tight smile.

Finally, Ignatius spoke. 'I know who you are. The news reports I have seen coming from Edinburgh first were simply brutal killings, then a religious theme developed and then the name of St Bernard's Church emerged. I knew it must flag the re-emergence of our benefactor and so the opportunity to redeem our promise.

'My assistant was less convinced. He is a sceptic in such matters.' Ignatius reached out a hand to his assistant and squeezed his upper arm. 'But to be careful is an important thing. One day he may well rise to fill my shoes, but not yet.' He released his grip on the assistant's arm and let out another laugh, which his assistant dutifully echoed.

'So, everybody knows who everybody is,' said Helen. 'Now we agreed you'd tell me what it means.'

The bishop smiled. 'I did, but first let me take your hand, let me kiss the hand of the ring bearer.'

Helen was taken aback by the request but after a moment's thought she proffered her hand. He lent forward, took it in his and pressed his lips against the back of her hand.

Done, he released her hand and straightened up. 'This is a day I and all my predecessors have waited for. Look, see here, this cross is one of the symbols of my office, passed down from one to the next for generations.'

Helen looked at the cross. It was clearly made of gold, heavy and so extraordinarily ornate that she had to look twice to confirm it was indeed a cross. She smiled at the bishop. 'It's lovely, very intricate.'

'Look again, look at the very centre.'

She looked again and this time she saw it, set deep within all the patterns and imagery was fashioned a representation of a ring, her ring. It was her turn to feel a thrill; she looked at the bishop and smiled.

The bishop nodded. 'Now I will tell you a story. I am Bishop Ignatius, I am the assistant to the patriarch, and one of my titles is the patriarch's right hand. I have many public duties, and a few very private, very secret ones. The oldest of my duties is to watch and be ready for your coming. It is the uppermost of my private duties and it has been so for generations.

'The history of my Church is not like the Church of the West. Ours was a big and successful Church, already strong when the Church of Rome was just an emperor's whim. But our story is tied to that of the Coptic Church and its birthplace in Egypt.

'As a country, Egypt was fabulously wealthy, in spite of successive generations of looting by Alexander and the Greeks, the Roman Caesars and finally Byzantium, which inherited control of Egypt when the Roman Empire divided. The Christianity of Byzantium and the Eastern Roman Empire was different from Rome and the West and different again from the Coptic Christians. As so often seems to happen, difference leads to persecution. The Copts suffered badly under Byzantine rule; brutality, bias against their form of Christianity, taxes and seizure of wealth. It was not a happy story.

'As Islam's leaders grew in strength, by various means, they seized control of Egypt from Byzantium. Once Byzantium gave up on Egypt, the Copts, who had suffered so many debilitations under Byzantine rule, were so weakened they were in no position to resist the caliphs.

'The Copts were still the great majority of Egypt's population but dominated by a small Muslim ruling elite. Over hundreds of years, the Copts were taxed and brutalised by a long succession of caliphs, with the next one always wanting more than the last. Islam allowed the Copts to continue because they needed their administrative and accounting skills to manage Egypt, in order to strip its wealth.'

'It sounds awful,' said Helen. 'How did they survive?'

'Over hundreds of years, they were bled almost dry. Too weak and disorganised and constantly harassed by the caliphs, the Copts were never in a position to help Christian Europe in the crusades. In fact, the taxes and penalties they paid would have helped pay for the Muslim war efforts.'

'Okay, Ignatius, but where are we fitting in?'

'It had become a practice to blame the Copts for whatever ill befell Egypt at any given time. The result would always be the same. The arrest and imprisonment of the Coptic Pope who would be held until demands for reparations were met.

'When the caliph decided that he needed a new fleet his next decision was obvious - the Copts must pay for it and the Coptic Pope was seized. The Copts had protested they had no money left to pay the caliph's demands; as a result, he took his extortion efforts to new heights.

'The families of many senior Coptic officials were seized; the wives and daughters were to be sold into slavery as the playthings of any who had the money to pay, and the boys sold as field or galley slaves. There really was no wealth left so the caliph allowed the Coptic officials a year and a day for full settlement, after which the families would be sold to pay for his fleet.'

'That is awful, but what's this about a pope?' said Helen.

'Yes, awful indeed. The patriarch of the Coptic Church is also known as the Pope. And now, this is where you, or rather your predecessor, came in.

'The Coptic Church decided to seek help and sent a secret envoy to the Pope of the Catholic Church in Avignon. They needed support, a Christian army to drive Islam from their lands. The Pope was weak and gave nothing. But just when the Coptic envoy thought all was lost, he met a man from another delegation, also visiting the Pope's court, a man of integrity and strength. He was a priest and a truly good man.

'The priest's home church was St Bernard's in Edinburgh and he was in Avignon as an envoy of his King, Robert the Bruce of Scotland.'

'He was my predecessor,' said Helen. 'I've heard about him.'

'You are the ring bearer so that would be expected.'

'What happened? What did they do together?'

'It seems your predecessor had something he needed to hide. He had in mind to hide it as far from the grasp of the Roman Church as possible. But the Coptic Church and its peoples were tired. Stripped of their wealth and dignity, it was no place to hide anything. But they did have one safe place, my land, Ethiopia.'

'And?'

'The Edinburgh priest saw how poor and broken the Copts had become, and he felt for the officials whose families were to be sold as slaves. He met again with the Coptic envoy and struck a bargain.

'Your man was returning to Edinburgh, to his church, St Bernard's, but he promised to send another priest back at once with sufficient gold to free the Pope, the families, and bolster the Coptic Church's fortunes. In return, he wanted a promise that a bishop would take into Ethiopia a package the priest would bring with him from Edinburgh. Even then, my Ethiopia was solidly Christian and forever safely beyond the rule of both Rome and Islam, and it was subject to the Coptic Pope's religious oversight. That package, the key, was to be held secretly in Ethiopia until the ring bearer would return to collect it.'

'You have a package for me?'

'Indeed, I do. The priest left Avignon for Edinburgh and was as good as his word. Some months later his ship returned to Alexandria, this time with a younger priest on board. He appeared as a merchant. His cargo was unloaded and, concealed within it, was a cache of gold, just as had been promised. The Pope and the families were freed and there was more gold besides to sustain the Coptic Church again.

'As soon as he was released, the Pope sent my predecessor personally to the sister church in Ethiopia with the package and sufficient gold to maintain an office for its preservation. Over time, that job evolved and was absorbed into the wider Ethiopian Church. And here I am,' he threw back his head and laughed.

'Right,' said Helen. 'So where does that leave us? You have a key for me?'

'Not exactly, I have a box.'

'I see. Is the key in the box?'

'I don't know, it is sealed and forbidden to be opened - except by the collector, the one with the ring.'

'So, what happens next?' said Helen.

'It's not here. It is hidden in our most secret place. But we can make an arrangement. Though if you do not know of this, presumably you do not have the lock that the key should open? The covenant demands that the key and the lock are brought together - it is the only way to turn the lock.'

'What do you suggest?'

'That is for you to resolve.' The bishop pulled out his wallet, flicked it open, and took out a picture that he passed to Helen. 'This is the key. It is held ready for you.'

Helen had no idea where the lock was, but she was interested to see the key. She looked at the picture and was puzzled. 'It really is a box.'

'Yes, and yet it is the key,' said the bishop.

'Well, I don't know what lock is opened by a box,' she said and then looked again. The photograph clearly captured the design on the box. Its swirling symmetrical pattern, exquisitely executed, seemed to owe much more to Islamic art than to anything from the Christian tradition. As she was handing the picture back, something stirred in the back of her mind. She held on to it for a moment, then pulled it back and looked again.

Then, she knew it, or thought she did. Couldn't be absolutely certain. But she knew where a box very like this was kept. In a Swiss bank vault. In her Swiss bank vault, which she had inherited from John Dearly. It had been a couple of months before when she had visited Switzerland and inspected the contents of the security box. At the time, it had been an interesting artefact, nothing more. A box she couldn't open so had just put to one side in the rush to deal with the pressures of that moment. Now she wished she'd paid more attention.

Just before she handed his picture back to the bishop, a thought occurred to her. When in the vault, she had photographed everything for Sam. She excused herself, checking her phone on the pretext that Sam may have sent her a message while she quickly flicked through her picture archive. Slowing then stopping. She studied one image very carefully, glanced discreetly at the bishop's photograph - a pair! Putting her phone away, she looked up and smiled at the bishop while returning his photograph.

• • •

Mauwled slammed on the Land Rover's brakes and it came to a halt, with the nearside wheels on the kerb. He jumped out and hurried directly into the conference centre reception, a trail of protesting attendants following behind. He ignored their frantic shouts while casting about for Helen. There was no sign of her anywhere. Just as he was about to give up and hurry home to consult Jeanie Albright, his eye chanced on Helen's distinctive auburn hair in one of the glass fronted alcoves.

He sprinted over, the pursuing attendants raising a clamour of protest in his wake, and as he reached the glass door into the alcove they were joined by the junior priests attempting to bar his way. Mauwled had no intention of stopping for anyone and the growing commotion attracted security who came running across just as the bishop's assistant opened the door to demand an explanation. He was bundled aside as Mauwled forced his way into the alcove.

The sheer weight of bodies eventually brought Mauwled to the ground and then a security guard's weapon pressed against his head brought the struggle to a close.

Helen had been watching the melee as it unfolded but only now could she get a good look at the perpetrator. 'That's my driver,' she said. 'Mauwled, what are you doing? What's going on?'

One security guard was shooing the pack of facility attendants out of the alcove while his colleague kept Mauwled flat on the ground. He realised this was not a simple intrusion, and a little puzzled, he looked about for guidance.

'Big problem, Helen. Big problem,' said Mauwled.

'What is it?' Helen waved the security guard back; the man did not move. She turned to the bishop. 'He's my driver. I need him freed at once.'

The bishop turned to his assistant and gave a little wave of his hand.

The assistant responded with a volley of instructions to the guard, who initially looked startled and then called over his shoulder to his partner. That triggered another round of shouting from the bishop's assistant. Almost immediately, the guard backed off and left the alcove with his partner. Deprived of the prestige of their prisoner, the two guards ensured the facilities' attendants suffered as they shepherded them out of the reception.

'How did you manage to move them on so easily?' said Helen.

'Easy,' said the assistant, 'my bishop is today's conference chairperson. Nobody is going to go against his word today.'

Mauwled was climbing to his feet, brushing himself down and grumbling to himself.

'Gentlemen, I'm sorry for this disturbance. I know Mauwled will have an explanation.' She looked at him expectantly.

'I need to speak with you privately, Helen.'

'Whatever the reason your driver may have, I'm sure we all need to hear it, since if it were not for my bishop your driver would already be on his way to Arusha Police Headquarters.'

Helen looked at the assistant and looked again at the bishop, who had resumed his seat and was waving his hand to indicate that Helen and his assistant should also sit.

She sat, as did the assistant while simultaneously pointing the two junior priests towards the glass door.

'Well, Mauwled? What's the story? And where's Sam got to?'

'He's been arrested.'

'What? What's happened?'

'When we got to the Arusha University offices, we were directed to the unit which has been allocated to your professor from Dar es Salaam. As Sam had expected, he's still in Dar, only a support worker was there, and Sam reported to him, asked when the professor was likely to arrive.'

'Right, that's what we planned. So, what went wrong?'

'The support worker asked us to wait while he made a call. We sat down, and he went into the back office. A few minutes later the police burst in and took Sam.'

'But why?' said Helen.

'I guess somebody must have been chatting between the universities. When Sam appeared this morning, the support worker called the local police. Now he is to be transferred to Nairobi to help investigations into a killing at the university up there.'

Helen felt a sickening knot tighten in her stomach. 'Oh, heaven. This has to be a mistake. Where is he now?'

'I don't know. The police station, I expect. They took him away in the police chief's car. He was there so it must be an important case.'

Helen turned to the bishop. 'Sorry, I'm going to have to leave you now. I have to get to the police station.' She turned to Mauwled. 'Will you take me please?'

'Of course, we can go now.'

'Wait, wait a minute. Let's think about this before you rush in,' said the bishop.

'I can't wait,' said Helen.

'Look, I don't know anything about your Sam, but I'm sure of three things. If he's with you, he's our friend. You can spend all day sitting in an African police station without finding out a thing and, most important, you need a lawyer. It would be my privilege to help you if you will allow it.'

Helen could tell the bishop was talking sense. 'So how do we start?'

The bishop turned to his assistant and rattled off a series of instructions in Amharic. The assistant stepped out of the room and repeated the instructions, ending with a shouted exclamation and an arm waved towards the bowels of the conference centre. The driver priest ran off in the direction of the assistant's gesture.

The assistant came back into the room and carefully closed the door before sitting. He nodded to the bishop.

'Before acting, we need some local knowledge,' said Bishop Ignatius. 'Fortunately, we have a church here in Arusha, to serve our diaspora and to reach out to help the poor of the city, of whom there are very many. I have sent for our local priest who is attending the conference too. His local knowledge will be of use.'

Helen paced about the alcove. 'How can this have happened? He's innocent, you know?'

Before the bishop could respond the young priest with the wounded leg tapped on the glass and pulled the door open, pointing across reception from where his colleague and another man were hurrying towards the cubicle.

'Sit now,' implored the bishop.

Helen sat as the local priest arrived, anxious not to keep his bishop waiting. Entering, he bowed his head slightly and the bishop invited him to sit. The priest took a seat on the empty sofa. Introductions were kept brief and were it not for the pressing circumstances Helen might have found pleasure in the priest's name, Angel Eli. The bishop got straight to the point, explaining the problem to his local priest. Then he asked Helen to provide the background, which she did as concisely as possible, including their flight from Nairobi.

Angel sat quietly for what, to Helen, seemed a long time. Finally, he broke his silence, addressing his bishop.

'This is a difficult situation. I will be happy to help. A member of our congregation is a solicitor, a good man, a friend too. With your permission, I will engage him to make contact with the police chief. In this part of the world, much of the legal system is a direct inheritance of the British colonial system. As a structure, it is quite predictable. But I know from previous dealings with this system that the problem we face is very real. There is an agreement that certain types of criminals and terrorists can be transferred between East African Community countries without a full extradition process, though officially a case must go to court and be considered by a judge before the prisoner is transferred.

'Unfortunately, there have been many complaints in the news during the recent past that the police simply ignore the court appearance requirement and transfer prisoners between countries as quickly as possible and to suit their convenience.'

'That can't happen. If Sam ends up in Nairobi, he's going to be in the frame for a murder he didn't commit. There must be a way to stop this?' said Helen.

Angel looked from Helen to the bishop, saw the bishop's encouraging nod and turned his gaze back to Helen. When he spoke, he measured his words very carefully. 'There are rules. There are people who work within the rules. And there are people who enforce the rules. The police chief is an enforcer of rules. Not every rule is enforced with the same rigour in every case. The solicitor I mentioned has actively fought against some of the actions of the police in Arusha. He has few friends in the police force and that makes him a poor go between. But he will know who amongst the legal fraternity might best represent us to the police chief.'

'Okay, that's good. How quickly can you make the enquiries?'

Angel looked a little embarrassed as he resumed. 'First, might I enquire, how extensive are your resources?'

'I beg your pardon?'

'Do you have money? The law is the law. However, we live in a society where almost everything has a price.'

'You mean we could buy Sam out?'

'I don't know for sure. I do know he has committed no crime in Tanzania, so this is not the police chief's personal problem. The right approach by a trusted face might encourage him to look the other way. It's certainly worth a try.'

'Okay, we have no resource problem. Whatever it takes, just get him out.'

Angel nodded acknowledgement, then turned his attention back to the bishop. 'With your permission, I will go at once to start an engagement.'

The bishop nodded.

'I'm coming too,' said Helen.

Angel shook his head. 'It would be best if you didn't come. A worried woman will be seen as a weak link and, worse still, if we don't deliver what they ask quickly you might become a target.'

Helen started to protest but saw Angel was determined to go alone. She bit her tongue for a moment and then nodded. 'Okay, if you're sure it's the best way to achieve a solution … but keep me in the loop, and when it comes to money, I really meant it: whatever is required, it's yours.'

Angel stood, inclined his head towards the bishop, then to Helen, and with a final nod in the direction of the assistant he left.

The bishop stood up. 'I think there is nothing more that can be done on this matter until we receive Angel's report. Perhaps this would be a good moment to break. I have a full meeting of the conference to address shortly. Let's put the business of the key to one side for the moment. And I suspect you might benefit from some time to rest and think.'

Helen didn't need to rest but she did need to start thinking about her response to this latest problem. They all shook hands and agreed to meet again, as soon as Angel had reported back with news.

Helen had Mauwled drive past the police station on the way back to the guesthouse. The journey in the Land Rover felt strangely lonely.

Chapter 13
SATURDAY 26TH OCTOBER - PM

Helen sat amidst the dappling sunlight watching it play across the patio beneath her feet as the sunbeams filtered through the overreaching boughs of an acacia tree. It had been carefully pruned and trained over decades to create the perfect natural parasol. Deep in thought, Helen was oblivious to the beauty around her. A sudden round of dog barking signalled visitors at the gate. Silence fell again, and she stood, hoping the visitor was for her.

A couple of minutes later Jeanie led Angel out to join Helen, closely followed by Val who enquired about refreshments. The priest welcomed cool water; Helen did too.

As soon as they were alone, she pressed Angel for news.

He gave her a stony gaze. 'I'm afraid that police chief represents all that is bad in Africa. He is big, and he is bloated, and he should look for no rewards in heaven. Though I doubt that's where he will be going.'

'Tell me what's happening, exactly.'

'Our solicitor knew there was only one person to approach. One of the senior solicitors in Arusha is on very good terms with the police chief. He agreed to work as an intermediary for us.'

'That's good.'

'Well, yes perhaps, but unfortunately, he and the police chief are more than good friends, they are cousins.'

'How's that a problem?'

'They are family, can rely on one another. It makes them confident and greedy too, I think.'

'Tell me. How much?'

'It's not just what they want. It's when they want it. Today is Saturday; they have put Sam in the police station cells. I think at present his arrest is unrecorded, so the police chief has some flexibility in how he deals with the situation. Come Monday morning, he must have the situation regularised.'

'Oh?'

'Right now, Sam is not officially recorded in the system. The Kenyans don't know; nobody does. The cousin of the police chief spoke to him and thought an arrangement might be possible. If the whole problem were to go away before the law offices open on Monday, there would be nothing to report and nobody to transfer.'

'What does that mean?'

'It means the police chief and his cousin have an eye for the main chance. If we can give them money before Monday, Sam will walk free.'

'How much?'

'One hundred thousand.'

'Shillings?'

'Dollars. US dollars.'

'That's serious money. Are you sure they will deliver?'

'Can you afford to pay it?'

Helen suddenly looked worried. 'Yes, I can afford it. But as you already said, it's Saturday. Where can we get that sort of money before the banks open on Monday? Even if the local banks were open, I doubt an Arusha branch would hold that many dollars.'

'I know, that's what's worrying me. Our solicitor tried to get an extended deadline, but they wouldn't have it. They said, money by Monday morning or he must be transferred to Kenya. Take it or leave it.'

'How do they expect me to find the money over the weekend, Angel? I don't know this country.'

'Perhaps they think, if you want to free Sam enough, you'll will find a way. After Monday morning, they have no leeway to bargain anyway, so they are all in now. Even if you came up with twenty thousand dollars, I'm quite sure they'd accept that.'

'Finding any thousand dollars is the problem. And I'm not risking turning up with only twenty thousand. I'll get the money, somehow.'

'You will?' said Angel, the doubt in his voice was clear.

'I will. Give me ten minutes and we'll see what can be done.'

She hurried into her room to collect the satellite phone and returned to sit at the patio table. There she made a call.

Five thousand miles away in Edinburgh a mobile phone rang and was answered almost immediately - the line clicked open.

'Hello? Elaine here, what's up? I wasn't expecting to hear from you today.'

'Hi Elaine. Look, I don't have time to explain. Where are you right now?'

'I'm at home.'

'Great. Please, go online and check when the next flight is from Arusha to anywhere in Europe.'

'Okay, I'm at my computer. I'll do it now. Are you guys cutting short your trip?'

'Not exactly, I'll explain later. It's a flight for me only.'

'Right, I'm in now. Here we are. The next flight out of Arusha's Mount Kilimanjaro Airport is the 17.35 for Amsterdam but it's not direct, you won't get to Amsterdam Schiphol until after six on Sunday morning.'

'Any others starting later but flying direct?'

'Hold on …' the line went quiet for a moment as Elaine scanned her screen. 'No, it's all much the same.'

'Okay, book me on it right away, while I'm holding the line open. One-way ticket, no return.' Glancing up, she could see that Angel was looking very disturbed, almost distressed. 'What's up?' she said.

'You're leaving, not coming back?'

'What? What do you mean?'

'One-way ticket?'

Helen frowned a little and shook her head at him. 'No, I'll be coming back a different route; it's the only way I can hope to get sorted over there and back in time.'

Angel nodded, still unsure.

'Helen, are you still there? That's it all booked. I'll text you the reference numbers for your tickets. But what's going on?' The normally calm lilt in Elaine's Scottish accent carried a hint of concern.

'It's a mess. I need to get a lot of money back here by first thing Monday. We'll speak later once things are underway. Please bear with me for now. I need you to do a couple more things for me. Contact Xavier in Sardinia, ask him if I can use his plane for a few days, and make sure he understands it's ultra-urgent. Tell him I need it to meet my flight at Schiphol on Sunday morning. I'm going straight on to Switzerland, to see Franz Brenner, and then I want it to fly me directly back to Arusha.

'Then phone Franz, tell him I need to get into the bank on Sunday. I'll happily cover any staffing costs. Make sure he understands this is an emergency; it can't wait until Monday.

'Thanks, Elaine. Got to go, I'll phone once I'm en route and everything's underway. Love you, and love to Grace too.' Helen hung up the line and sat still for a moment as her mind raced over the life changes she had experienced since first becoming John Dearly's assistant. Not just the killings and the evil, there were good things too - Elaine and her daughter Grace. Francis and Xavier, the wonderful old priests who had been John's long-standing confidantes. There was Franz Brenner too, the Swiss banker and custodian of the secret trust fund, access to which she had inherited, and what a trust fund. And Sam. She stood taking a deep breath of air and held it in for a moment.

Angel had stood up; he had followed the conversation with growing excitement. 'You are coming back! You really think you can get the money?'

'The money's not the problem it's the shortage of time.' She reached out her hand and squeezed Angel's forearm. 'Thank you, Angel, this is a mess, but you've offered me an opportunity to fix it. I'm very grateful.'

Angel gave a shrug, almost embarrassed. 'My bishop says. I do.' Then he smiled. 'I will be waiting, ready for your return. Phone me, we can make arrangements.' He took Helen's notepad and scribbled his mobile phone number on it.

Helen smiled in acknowledgement and turned, heading indoors as she called out to Val. She needed Mauwled ready to set off for the airport in five minutes.

Chapter 14
SUNDAY 27TH OCTOBER - AM

The police lockup had been empty when Sam was first put in it on Saturday morning. The basement room had seemed quite spacious then. Fluorescent light tubes were fixed all along the centreline of the ceiling providing an even, if unforgiving, light throughout the space. The room was thirty feet long and half as wide and set with narrow unglazed but barred window slots high to the ceiling along one long side. Outside, where the slots just showed at ground level, they faced into the police station's courtyard car park.

After the steel door had banged shut on him, Sam had surveyed the space. There was no furniture in the room, the cement walls and floors were raw and grubby. The only concession to comfort was an eighteen-inch-high cement step that ran down both long sides of the room, doubling for both seating and sleeping space.

The short cross wall, nearest him, hosted the steel door. Fixed in the further away cross wall and offset to one side was a tap. At the middle point of that cross wall was a small hole in the floor - the toilet. Otherwise, the room was bare, save for occasional decorations formed through rough etchings in the cement work where bored and angry prisoners had passed their time.

He chose his spot. In the far corner, close beside the tap and beneath one of the high window slots. It wasn't much of a base but in lockup terms, it was prime real estate. Sam had hunkered down and watched as the hours ticked by and the cell gradually filled up. He spent most of his time crouched on the cement step, backed into the corner so he could not be surprised from behind.

Many of those being locked up just staggered in and collapsed into sleep. Clearly, there were some with drink problems for whom the lockup was a second home. The air had become more foul and muggy with the passing hours. By the steady trickle of drunks, he guessed it was well into the early hours of the morning when things took a turn for the worse.

A commotion suddenly kicked off beyond the steel door. Several raised voices clashed in an argument that was punctuated by the sounds of kicking and banging. Finally, the door opened, and the police forced four men through the entrance before banging the door shut. The new arrivals hammered on the door. Their shouted insults through to the guards woke some of the sleeping drunks who were ranged along the step to either side of the cell.

Eventually, the men gave up on the door and turned their attention to the cell. They swaggered up and down, kicking at any unfortunates who had spilled off the step and into their way. One man was small, almost dapper in appearance; the other three were bigger, muscle. Sam watched the men carefully, keeping his head down, but it didn't take long for the gang to spot him. Particularly as he occupied the prime spot next to the water tap.

'Hey, you, mister, I'm speaking to you,' said Dapper.

Sam raised a hand in acknowledgement. 'All right. How you doing?'

Dapper approached him. 'You American?' said Dapper.

Sam kept his head down, avoiding being drawn into a staring contest. 'No. British.'

Dapper turned to his friends. He spoke in Swahili, which Sam just managed to follow. 'He's British. And he's in my seat. Let's get him moved.'

'Hey, British, I want that spot, it's mine. Move now,' said Dapper in English.

Sam looked at Dapper then glanced at his friends. A long time ago he'd been in a very similar situation, knew how it would unfold. He always hated conflict, tried to avoid it, but he knew if he gave ground they would come after him again for some other reason or none at all. 'I don't think so,' he said slowly, for the first time allowing himself to make eye contact, first with Dapper and then with the heavies - a giant, a scar face and what he guessed was the junior gopher of the group. Then his gaze settled back on Dapper. He pointed towards the far end of the cell. 'You're mistaken. There's space up there. This is my spot.'

There was a rippling through the gathered humanity as an instinctive awareness of brewing trouble saw even the apparently comatose amongst the inmates somehow able to edge away from the epicentre.

Dapper's friends stepped in front of him, penning Sam into his corner spot. Dapper spoke to him from behind the human wall. 'Come on English, move.'

'I'm Scottish.' Sam didn't want a fight, wasn't so sure about the odds, four to one, but he had some advantages. His attackers had all been drinking, they all thought he was drunk and a soft touch, and he had plenty of targets to hit.

'Ho, he's Scottish. Whisky man! Hey, your bones will break just as easy if you don't move.' Then Dapper gave a short order in Swahili, which Sam understood quite well. 'Break him!'

The attackers closed in. The first and biggest was much taller than Sam; he had the muscular frame of a man who does a lot of physical labour. He rolled in with a great piston of a punch that would have broken Sam's face permanently and knocked him out cold had it made proper contact. But Sam had guessed the big man would lead and had been waiting.

In conflict involving sober versus drunk, sober nearly always wins. As the giant fist flew towards him it reached the point of no return and Sam, with perfect timing, pulled his head to the right, and instead of meeting a welcoming face, the fist crunched into the cement wall that Sam's head had been resting against. With a cry, the big man reeled back, leaving his blood and knuckle skin ground into the cement. He trailed blood across the floor and carried away a broken hand that would keep him out of trouble for several weeks.

Sam went on the offensive. By just straightening his legs, he elevated from his crouch position and suddenly stood eighteen inches higher than his assailants. In just a moment, scar face's expression switched from raw, confident aggression to surprise and, finally, to pained confusion when his advancing face met Sam's knee, and his nose slumped back into his face. Sam pressed home his advantage at once, banging his fist into scar face's broken nose and pushing him sideways hard against the short wall. As scar face's shoulder reached the wall, Sam put all his weight behind a second thrust, banging the man's head against the wall. The crack reverberated round the cell and scar face dropped like a stone, unconscious.

Sam turned his attention to the gopher who was suddenly looking unsure; backing away even as Dapper tried to push him forward.

Sam pointed to the far end of the cell. 'Your place is up there. And take him with you,' he said while pointing down to scar face, who was coming round and starting to groan.

There were no further incidents.

Chapter 15
SUNDAY 27TH OCTOBER - PM

Helen walked down the little stairway, exiting Xavier's private plane that had collected her at Schiphol Airport and carried her directly to Zurich, Switzerland. She shivered. Autumn was biting hard in the Alps and she suddenly wished that she had a coat. All she had brought from Arusha was a shoulder bag with a few essentials; it was left behind her in the plane. Like everyone else, she had to pass through immigration control but had no desire to add any time to the transit process with customs delays.

A little while later, she exited the arrivals zone and looked about for a familiar face, hoping Franz had been able to send his personal driver, Simon, to collect her. She could not see him anywhere, perhaps it was his day off.

Just as she gave up and scanned the signs for a taxi rank, a familiar Scottish accent caught her attention. She turned to see Elaine waving from near the main exit doors. They hurried to one another, and Helen hugged and kissed Elaine warmly. Elaine's hands slid round Helen's back and patted twice in what represented a huge show of affection from the older woman.

Then they both leaned back a little to regard each other. For Helen, it was a joy to see her most trusted of friends. She knew there would not be much speaking on Elaine's part, but she was already feeling better, more confident just through the older woman's proximity.

She and Sam had left Edinburgh only three weeks before, but the wounds Elaine had received during the summer were at last starting to show real improvement.

'Elaine, what are you doing here? You're meant to be back in Edinburgh.'

'Did you think I was going to stay back there with you travelling halfway round the world to get here? Grace wanted to come too, but I made her stay in Edinburgh just in case there was anything else you needed doing.' Grace was Elaine's daughter; the three women had been through a lot together and, in spite of some very tricky times, had come out on top.

'Well, I'm glad you're here.' She kissed Elaine again, and they turned to walk to the exit.

'Franz is outside. He's driving us today. Simon is away on business for him until next week,' said Elaine.

Helen was a little disappointed; she'd been looking forward to seeing Simon. They too had been through a lot together, and she knew he could be relied on when things went wrong. She had secretly hoped that Franz might send Simon back to Tanzania with her.

Outside the cold hit her; she shivered and was pleased to see Franz standing beside his big Mercedes, waiting to pull open the rear door as soon as she reached the car. She laughed through the cold and hugged him. He hugged her back and then hurried her into the back seat, closing the door behind her. He escorted Elaine to the other door and showed her in.

'Franz, it's wonderful to see you and thanks for coming to meet me yourself. We're in a spot of bother.'

'So Elaine explained. And no need to thank me. Even if I'd wanted a lazy Sunday afternoon, you don't think my wife would have allowed it, do you? Now, you must tell me what you want, and I will see what can be done.'

'Elaine has told you I needed some money.'

'Yes, and rather a lot it would seem. I can organise that for you. My chief clerk is waiting in the bank. He will deal with it once we are in the building.'

'Wow, thanks Franz. You know, it seems you always come up trumps. Though I hope I haven't ruined your clerk's Sunday too.'

'Don't worry, he doesn't mind. Remember, yours is a very special account, and besides, I'm sure there will come a point in the year when he wants time off and will be quick to remind me of this favour.' He drove on, the familiar landscape flying past in their rush to the city centre, where they crossed the Limmat River by the Quaibrücke and entered the financial quarter.

Franz pulled up outside the bank; there was little traffic about and fewer pedestrians. He tooted the car horn and waved up at a security camera. They all got out and approached the closed doors, waited for a moment. The noise of locks being opened sounded through the wooden outer door.

A security guard edged opened the door. Helen noticed that a second guard was positioned a little further back, standing ready to hit the seal locks and sound alarm buttons at the slightest provocation. That it was their boss entering the building was no excuse to lower security protocols, and they didn't.

Once the guards were happy that Franz was entering the building of his own free will and the doors were all secured again, the atmosphere relaxed a little. Franz paused to exchange a few words with the guards about their families and interests.

It was very hard to get through the recruitment interview process at Franz's bank, but once in, staff were rewarded well and treated properly, and staff turnover was very low. People left because they were retiring or leaving Zurich. To leave for any other reason was considered quite remarkable.

After a few minutes' conversation, Franz took Helen and Elaine in the lift up to his penthouse office. There, they all sat and, shortly afterwards, coffee and cakes appeared. Helen shared her East African experiences and explained why she now needed the cash quickly.

Franz took the hint and called in his chief cashier who was delighted to be introduced to Helen. He took great pleasure in telling her that for several years, since his promotion to chief cashier, he had held personal responsibility for day-to-day oversight of her accounts and he hoped there would be many years still to come.

He disappeared and, shortly afterwards, returned to announce the money was counted and ready. He just needed to recount it with Helen and have her sign a receipt. She thanked him and asked if he might do the recount with Elaine. There was something else she needed to attend to.

Alone, Franz looked at Helen inquisitively. 'Is there something else I can help you with?'

'Well, I mentioned I had some contact with the bishop from Ethiopia. He showed me a picture of an artefact he has in Addis Ababa, something of interest. I think they have a link to John Dearly's past, another one of his secrets that I never got a chance to learn about before he died. If it's possible, I'd like to go down to my security deposit box and check something.'

'Of course. Please go straight down now. You know which button to press. I will telephone ahead and alert the security detail that you are on your way.' He guided Helen from the door of his office and stood with her until the lift came. As the doors closed, she smiled to herself in response to Franz's strict adherence to traditional European form. He bowed his head very slightly, and just as happened months before, she was sure she heard his heels clip together.

Following a rapid descent, the doors opened to reveal a familiar corridor, the glazed wall at the end and the security detail watching her from beyond the bombproof glass. She reached the doors and waited, knowing the guards could not open their security doors until the lift had returned to reception level.

After a few moments, once the lift had gone and the security requirement had been met, one of the guards opened the doors and welcomed her by name. Then he guided her into a private room. It had rich wood panelling, cut from the same tree as the table that sat in the centre of the room. Helen sat at the table and waited while watching the spot on the wall where she knew a discreet panel would open shortly to reveal her security box.

It took only a few moments for the panel to drop and there it was. She caught her breath, remembering the first time she had come here. Innocent and unknowing. Those days were long gone. Recalling how heavy the box was, she crossed to the door and pressed a buzzer. One of the guards entered and carried it to the table for her. The man did so in silence then immediately left the room and closed the door behind him.

Alone again with her security box, Helen let her hands glide over its surface. She allowed herself a minute to think of her predecessor, John Dearly, and of all those that had gone before him. Now it was just her. Pulling out her keys, she selected John Dearly's old key and unlocked the box. She lifted the lid and felt a shiver run down her spine. What was she about to find? Just as importantly, how would her box link with the box in Ethiopia?

She carefully unpacked items, each one triggering reminders of her agreement with Sam that he would come and properly appraise the contents. She needed to get Sam back here - she needed to get him out of jail first though.

Helen reached in for the ornate wooden box and lifted it out. It was just as she remembered, like a jewellery box, polished, the sides worked with an intricate marquetry pattern. Just as when she first saw it, she felt its design owed more to Islam than Christianity. No sign of any openings, but by its weight, she knew it was not solid. After satisfying herself there was no doubt that her box was the same as the bishop's she put it back. On an impulse, she took it out again. Putting it aside on the table, she packed everything else away and locked the security box. Then she pressed the buzzer to call the guard who quickly transferred the security box back to the open wall panel. As he left the room, the panel slid shut and Helen stood alone with the ornate artefact.

Arriving back in Franz's office, she saw that Elaine now held a neat little briefcase. Elaine promptly placed it on Franz's desk and opened the lid to show Helen a thousand one hundred-dollar bills, all neatly bundled. Helen smiled at her and then tried to squeeze her ornate box into the briefcase too.

Franz stopped her; he made a phone call and requested bubble wrap and a larger briefcase. His requests were delivered almost at once. Helen transferred the cash and then, carefully wrapping the box, she placed it beside the cash. Franz leant in to pack more bubble wrap over everything and then she closed the case, locked it and looked up at her friends. 'Well, time to go.'

'Won't you stop for an early evening meal?' said Franz. 'Just a little something. Sara is keen to see you again.'

'No, but thank you. There's no time, and anyway, Xavier's plane is always stocked with eats. Now I must fly.' She smiled at her own joke. Franz gave a polite laugh and Elaine remained her usual impassive self.

Franz bowed his head very slightly. 'Now Helen, if I may ...' He lifted his perfectly tailored overcoat down from a coat stand and draped it around her shoulders.

Chapter 16
MONDAY 28ᵀᴴ OCTOBER - AM

Helen carried her shoulder bag and briefcase as she stepped down from the plane at Mount Kilimanjaro Airport. The case was a little lighter now since she had taken out the box and had the cabin crew lock it in the plane's safe. The sun was already illuminating the eastern sky. Helen looked at it with some anxiety, hoping she had returned in time.

The airport was quiet, and her pilot had been able to taxi to the most favoured executive landing spot. Here, the airport was used to VIP arrivals, rich people dropping in for safaris and other private business. The ground staff had long been schooled in the art of not delaying VIPs, and a member of the incoming flight crew would invariably leave a little something in return for the airport staff's considerate treatment. Not leaving something would result in a very difficult and protracted exit process.

Consequently, Helen's route through customs and immigration was smooth and unhindered. She exited the executive arrivals doors and walked quickly into the main passenger hall. This area was single storied with white walls and what appeared to be marbled floors. Cleaners were dotting about, preparing for the new day and a smattering of passengers were arriving for the early morning flight down to Dar es Salaam.

Angel met her at the exit and pointed towards the car park that was immediately adjacent to the airport entrance. A Land Rover sat in the nearest space, engine revving. No colours showed up in the predawn monochrome, but she knew it was orange. Angel opened the front door and she got in. He climbed in behind, and immediately, Mauwled manoeuvred out of the parking bay, allowing a chocolate wrapper to flutter out of his open window as he pulled away. They headed in the direction of Arusha.

'Did you manage to get the money?' said Angel, leaning forward, hands gripping the front seat headrests.

Helen half turned her head and raised her hand holding the briefcase. 'It's all in here.'

'Praise God,' said Angel. 'Praise God a hundred times.' He leant further forward and prodded Mauwled's arm. 'Faster, we must not be late.'

'Will we make it?' said Helen.

'No problem.' Mauwled glanced quickly at her then back to the road. It was a good road, properly built, but it never paid to take your eyes off it. Anyone and anything used these roads, and most did not bother with lights, meaning there was always the threat of unlit carts or stock-laden bicycles appearing out of nowhere. 'We'll be there before eight.'

'Where are we making the transfer?' Helen turned to look at Angel in the rear seat.

'I have arranged to meet our solicitor in the town, at the clock tower. We will go to see the police chief's cousin outside his office building and then do the handover in there. Then we must drive to the police headquarters where he will go in and the police chief will release Sam. Simple.'

'It sounds it,' said Helen.

Angel leant forward again. 'For you, this is a dirty business, frightening, worrying for you and your friend. But I think the police chief and his cousin are naughty men. For them, this is just another day's work. If they get their money, all will be well'

'Let's hope so.'

The drive to Arusha continued in silence, Helen deep in thought, the others reluctant to disturb her. With each passing minute, the darkness lifted a little and the start of morning business got nearer. She wished they had made better time but knew everyone had done their best.

The Land Rover slowed a little, and she watched absently as they passed a pickup truck, half off the road, its front buried in the rear of a donkey drawn cart. The collision had dislodged part of the cart's enormous load. At the front, the donkey had regained its footing and stood quietly between the shafts, quite happy with the break from dragging its near impossible load. On the road beside it, the drivers haggled and, as always seemed to happen, a crowd had formed from the empty landscape to jostle and argue or just to enjoy the spectacle.

• • •

The traffic had proven slower than normal, and Mauwled had been obliged to drive faster and more aggressively than was safe. They needed to meet with Angel's solicitor by eight o'clock if the transaction was to be completed in time. At a couple of minutes after eight, the orange Land Rover finally pushed through the traffic on Old Moshi Road and the Arusha Clock Tower came into view. Here, at the centre of old Arusha, the buildings were low-rise: two, three and four floors.

Helen heaved a sigh of relief. 'There's the clock tower,' she said. Mauwled nodded in acknowledgement of what he already knew and kept the engine revving slightly more than he needed, trying to unnerve the driver in front.

'I don't see our friend said Angel. He's not at the clock.'

'Look again, he has to be here,' said Mauwled, focusing on keeping the Land Rover going around the broad sweep of the grass-verged roundabout, at the heart of which sat the Arusha Clock Tower. To keep on the inner lane of the roundabout, he forced the Land Rover into an impossibly small gap between a van and a commuter's car. The car driver gave ground and hooted in frustration. Mauwled ignored the protest and kept turning. 'Look! Can you see him?'

Angel was shaking his head disconsolately while peering out of the side window at the clock tower.

They would soon be making a third circuit. 'Where exactly did you say you'd meet him?' said Helen.

'At the clock tower, right here.' Angel pointed frantically through the window. 'He's not here.'

Helen looked about. 'Could he be anywhere else? Where else might he be?'

Angel gave up staring at the roundabout's clock tower and began desperately to look about. And almost at once, he saw his friend standing in the petrol station forecourt on the junction of Old Moshi Road.

'There, there,' he said, leaning into the front and pointing across Mauwled towards a small man in grey flannels and a neatly pressed, open-necked, white shirt. 'In the petrol station.'

For the second time, Mauwled generated a tide of bad feeling from his fellow drivers as he forced the Land Rover across lanes and directly into the garage forecourt.

Angel hurried out to speak with his friend whose displeasure at their lateness was equally matched by Angel's annoyance that the solicitor had not stood where he had said he would.

Helen witnessed the bickering exchange through the glass windscreen; saw the mime of mouthed recriminations and the arm gestures. It all came to an abrupt halt when Mauwled rested his finger on the horn and pressed. He kept it sounding until the two men stopped arguing and turned to see why the horn was sounding. Mauwled beckoned them to get in the Land Rover and they both hurried to get aboard.

Angel was quick to introduce his friend Mr Kasanda as Helen leant round and shook his hand. She wished there was more time for her to speak with him before the plan was implemented, but that wasn't to be.

'Change of plan, take the Boma Road exit. We're picking up our man at the Palace Hotel. I'm worried that we will be late,' said Mr Kasanda.

Mauwled bullied his way back through the traffic and right round the clock tower for the third time, now taking the exit before the petrol station. 'We'll be there in two minutes,' he said.

'We collect the police chief's cousin from the front of the hotel and drive to the police chief's home. We'll count the money there; he'll take it in and phone his cousin at police headquarters. Then he'll release Sam.

'Will we get all that done before nine?' said Helen.

Nobody answered; it was going to be tight.

As they drove along Boma Road, Helen scanned each side in her search for the Palace Hotel. She noted how many of the building heights were beginning to rise. The properties here seemed newer, higher, and brighter. And then they were at the Palace Hotel. Disregarding the parking restrictions, Mauwled stopped directly in front and immediately a man approached. He was smartly turned out, similar to Angel's friend but with a necktie neatly fixed around his neck.

Angel opened the nearside rear passenger door and got out, holding it for the police chief's cousin. The man climbed in beside Mr Kasanda while Angel got into the front, squeezing beside Helen.

'Where to?' said Mauwled. There were no introductions or small talk. The man gave directions and Mauwled followed them; otherwise, silence.

Pressing through the rush hour grind it took more than thirty minutes to reach their destination. Helen noted they were in roughly the same district as Jeanie Albright's guesthouse, driving up a similar long and winding dirt track fringed with trees. Here too, occasional walled compounds dotted along its length while elsewhere between the trees, were patches of cultivated land and clusters of shanty style houses for the local poor.

'Turn off at the next turning on your left; it opens into a small clearing. Drive across the clearing and stop directly outside the compound gates.'

Mauwled followed the instructions and in the quiet of the clearing, Helen felt vulnerable. This was the perfect spot for a double-cross.

'Mr Kasanda and I have some business to transact. I wonder if all of you in the front seats of the vehicle might like to get out and take a stroll around the clearing. We will let you know when we're done.' The man spoke with a perfectly structured English accent that really would have been quite at home in any court in the UK. He smiled politely, but for all his nice phrasing, it had been an instruction that did not brook resistance.

Helen looked at her watch. 'It's getting close to nine o'clock. There's not much time.'

'I am aware of the time, young lady. Now, if you wish we lawyers to conclude the transaction you must go and allow us to do our work.'

Helen passed the briefcase and key to Mr Kasanda and then got out. She wanted to slap the police chief's cousin for his arrogance and for his crookedness. She contained herself. Time was all that mattered now. When the law offices opened, the police chief would be obliged to have Sam's detention processed into the system.

Getting out with Mauwled and Angel, Helen threw a final worried glance towards Mr Kasanda before walking quickly away from the Land Rover. They headed for a spot that was still shaded from the new morning sun and stopped there. Helen and Angel turned and looked back at the Land Rover. Mauwled concerned himself with the possibility of things he couldn't see in the undergrowth beyond the clearing. It all seemed quiet.

'They're taking too long, we're not going to make the deadline,' said Angel.

'There are a thousand bills to count, that takes time,' said Helen, forcing herself to believe there was time. She couldn't let Sam be transferred to Kenya.

As the minutes continued to tick away, all they could make out were little movements in the rear of the Land Rover. She glanced at her watch. It was after five to. They were going to run out of time.

With just a minute to go, the two men climbed out of the Land Rover. There was no shaking of hands. The police chief's cousin held the briefcase. He waved to Helen with his other hand and called out. 'It's been quite the pleasure to do business. Thank you, and goodbye.' Then he banged on the compound gates. A round of barking went up, it was quickly silenced by shouts from the watchman who pulled open the gate and the police chief's cousin stepped through. The gate banged shut behind him.

Helen and her two companions broke into a run, crossing the clearing in seconds.

'Was the money okay? There's never going to be time for him to make a call now,' said Helen. 'It's nine o'clock.' The frustration in her voice was clearly audible.

'Then I'll be going in there to get your money back. I'll take him and the dogs. Don't worry, he won't get away with it,' said Mauwled. He rested both arms high up on the compound wall and pressed, exercising his frustration.'

Mr Kasanda was looking a little perplexed. 'Please, there is nothing to be concerned over. It is done.'

Helen stood in front of him, just managing to restrain herself from jabbing a finger in his chest. 'No, it's too late. He had to phone before nine. That didn't happen so Sam will be sent to Nairobi.'

Mr Kasanda waved his hands in front of him. 'No, no, I said it is done. As soon as I opened the briefcase, he flicked through your bundles of notes. He was happy you weren't cheating him and then made his call, even before we counted it. Your friend will be free already!'

• • •

Sam was sitting on a bench a little way down the road from police headquarters, just enjoying some fresh air. A weekend spent in a rank smelling cell with he didn't know how many others had made this little moment a treasure he'd value for a long time.

It had not been easy. A white European man alone in a cell full of African prisoners, mostly drunk, many of whom blamed European exploitation for their own poverty. He had become a focus for that discontent and understood it.

He closed his eyes and tilted his face towards the sun, enjoyed its warmth. Though he didn't understand why he had been released, he was just glad the ordeal was over. He'd think about what to do next in a little while.

A car horn sounded, and he opened his eyes to see an orange Land Rover approaching. He knew there could only be one of those in Arusha and he waved, stood up and stepped forward as it came to a sharp halt in front of him.

Helen jumped out and hurried over. She hugged him hard. After a moment she pulled back, looked at his dirty, unshaven face and then kissed him. 'Heavens, you smell awful. No more hugs until you've had a long shower.'

Then she linked her arm with his and guided him to the vehicle, she pushed him into the rear seats and turned to thank Mr Kasanda who had already explained he needed to go about his business once they were back in the centre of Arusha, as did Angel. She thanked them both, hugged them, kissed their cheeks and then climbed in beside Sam.

'Let's go Mauwled, the Mount Meru View Guest House as soon as you like,' she said.

Chapter 17
MONDAY 28TH OCTOBER - EVENING

Sam emerged from the bedroom. He'd showered, shaved and slept; awoken, showered again and donned clean clothes. Hungry now, he walked into the communal area. Everyone else had eaten but Mama Grace had hung back without a grumble, waiting to cook for him.

As Sam appeared, she swung into action and the sounds and smells of good cooking quickly spread again through the living area, accompanied by faint, though distinct, sounds of disquiet from Mama Grace, restored to her normal grumpy disposition once the cooking began.

With no intention of sharing his bad experience, Sam skimmed over most of what had happened. He did make sure Helen knew how grateful he was. Then he asked about the men who had been in the Land Rover. She explained it all to him carefully: Angel and his solicitor friend Mr Kasanda, the bishop and the box. As she finished, Val appeared to announce Sam's dinner was ready. Helen crossed the room with him and sat at table while he ate.

'So to be clear, there is no arrest warrant out for me in Tanzania and no formal extradition request from Kenya?'

'That's right. Your arrest wasn't logged here so the Kenyans don't even know you're in Tanzania. And we've made sure the chief of police here doesn't want you to be transferred now. So, you're as free as anyone else to do as you wish.'

Sam grinned at her. 'I'm pleased you thought I'm worth so much. But my being locked up has given Ro Su-Ann more time. I wonder if he's out of the country yet. What do you think?'

'While you slept I've had to field two calls, one from my CIA friend Tracy and one from Rupert Peterson. Neither was that impressed with your being locked up, and apparently, I should have checked with Tracy and got permission before leaving the theatre of operations.'

'How did you respond to that?'

'How do you think? I'm sure she's beginning to think I'm a bad citizen now.'

Sam laughed.

'After Tracy had finished moaning about my unauthorised trip to Switzerland, she did tell me that they are certain Ro and his lot have not crossed the border into Burundi. So, they must still be in Tanzania along with Bob Prentice and ACE.'

'I wonder how she knows that.'

'Not the slightest idea, but that's what she said.'

'If ACE is as important as everyone seems to imply, they will almost certainly have reorganised their surveillance assets to bring the main roads between here and Burundi under constant observation. When I was in the military, they had some pretty mean satellite kit. It's bound to be more sophisticated now. They probably haven't seen his convoy on the road or crossing the border, which means he's in the bush, holed up somewhere until the Tanzanian border restrictions are eased.'

'Well, that has to be good news. There's still a chance of saving Bob.'

Sam put down his knife and fork and smiled at Val who was approaching with a coffee pot. 'Please tell Mama Grace that was lovely, the best food since I don't remember when.' Val smiled an acknowledgement back.

From the kitchen came the sound of a pan banging. Mama Grace had heard the compliment. Her head appeared round the kitchen door. 'Don't you get yourself arrested again. I won't be working late a second time for nobody.' The grumpy tone in her voice was contradicted by the warm smile she was beaming towards Sam.

In the corner of her eye, Helen caught sight of Jeanie at the far end of the communal room; she had been sitting quietly on a sofa enjoying a peaceful G and T. At the sound of Mama Grace's sharp words, Jeanie shook her head, throwing her hands up in despair as the cook broke new boundaries in liberty taking. Then, with a resigned shrug, Jeanie reached forward, took a cheroot, lit it and lost herself for a few moments in a cloud of tobacco smoke.

The room settled down again; smoke dissipated, and Grace retreated back into her domain. With a smile of thanks, Sam took the coffee pot from Val and assured her they could manage themselves. She happily left them to it.

'So, if Ro has been unable to leave the country, where is he? It's a big country with lots of wild places to hide in. Did Tracy or Rupert give any hints?'

'Nothing, it's all on you I'm afraid. Though Tracy did indicate they were focusing resources.'

'Well that could mean anything. What about the British?'

'Rupert was very non-committal.'

'Huh, he seems to be able to magic fences to sit on out of nothing.'

'Don't despair, Mr Cameron, I've more to tell you.' Helen hunched forward, elbows on the table and hands stretched out to squeeze Sam's.

Sam looked at her expectantly. 'Oh?'

'While you had your little break, courtesy of the Arusha Police, I've been doing a bit of digging. I spoke with my new friend Angel. Remember when we were in Nairobi and you fell out with the British high commissioner? You said you thought it unlikely Ro would have crossed the border from Kenya into Tanzania on the main road?'

'That's right. They must have crossed the border into Tanzania through the bush. It would have been too risky on the main roads.'

'I told Angel.' She saw Sam's look of disapproval at her breach of security. 'Well, I had to speak with somebody. You'd got yourself arrested. What was I supposed to do?'

He raised his palm off the table, signalling acceptance of her reason.

'So, Angel suggested that Ro's best bet would be to get a safari guide who knows this end of the country. And he said he thought he knew where to ask around.'

'Is it safe for him to do that? Wouldn't it be better if we did it? The man has to live here after this is all over. Even if he could just point us in the right direction.'

'That's what I suggested, but he wouldn't have us do it alone. Apparently, we visitors get to see the nice cuddly side of Arusha. There's a dark underbelly too. Angel knows the place, he wouldn't tell me where to go - I think he was worried I'd go storming in single-handed and get into trouble. So, we agreed the three of us will go together.'

'That's brilliant, well done, Helen. Any more of this and I'll start to think you don't need me.'

'Oh, I need you, Mr Cameron.' She stood, leant over to kiss his forehead, and then ruffled his hair. 'Come on, we've to meet Angel at the Arusha Clock Tower in an hour. We'd better go and sit with Jeanie for a while first.'

• • •

Mauwled had turned off the clock tower roundabout into the service station forecourt, coming to a halt beyond the fuel pumps. It was quiet, only one car was filling up and two or three pedestrians wandered past. The streets around the clock tower were fairly well lit and appeared benign.

Sam opened his door and stepped out as Angel appeared. He thrust out his hand. 'Angel, good to see you again. Sorry I wasn't up to scratch this morning. But thank you, nonetheless; for getting me out of that mess and for looking out for Helen.'

'It was a pleasure to be of assistance,' said Angel as they shook hands, 'though I must confess, Helen needs little looking out for.' He laughed. 'I think if things had gone on much longer it would have been her looking out for me!'

'Well, thank you. Now, what's the plan? Where are we going, and do we need the Land Rover, or are we walking?'

'I think driving would be easiest. It's not too far, just quicker in the Land Rover.'

Mauwled had been listening through the open driver's window, and he nodded.

Sam and Angel got into the Land Rover and Helen smiled a welcome at Angel.

'Can you take us beyond the central market area?' said Angel.

Mauwled nodded and got underway.

'What's at the central market?' said Sam.

'By this time in the evening, I'm hoping not so much, it will be a bit quieter. During the day, lots of shops and stalls, but most people will have shut up shop by now. There are some places to eat, bars and nightlife too, not that I would necessarily recommend them to visitors, but I'm thinking it's where we need to be if we are to find what you want.'

'And what's that?' said Sam.

Mauwled brought the Land Rover to a halt. They were in a different Arusha now. Here the streetlights were positioned further apart. The light given by each seemed a little dimmer, leaving great pools of shadow between them.

Mauwled turned in his seat, a worried look on his face. 'This is not a place for Helen. She can stay here with me.'

'I don't think so,' said Helen. She reached across and squeezed his arm. 'Don't worry, I can look after myself.'

He did not seem convinced but gave a resigned shrug and sat back to wait. Helen noted that he kept the engine running.

Angel, Sam and Helen stood on the road and looked about. Everywhere was quiet. At some point in the past the road had been metalled but much of that had worn away. Now ruts and potholes were the prominent features. Angel led them up onto a walkway that was raised just a little above the road; it served to keep pedestrians, stallholders and their wares out of the water when the rains came. The walkway was also sheltered by the upper floor of each building, which had been built to overhang the walkway. This provided those beneath with shelter from the rains, but equally as important, it served as a sunscreen throughout the year.

They followed Angel along the walkway, passing barred doors and shuttered shop fronts. Occasional glimpses of light and muffled sounds from within made clear that the business owners and their families remained in residence. Nothing was left unattended. Here and there, rough sleepers stirred, stretching out a hand in the hope of receiving something, but Angel kept the group moving. In only a few paces they reached a lane that ran off between buildings. Stepping down into the road, they crossed the little junction then stepped back up onto the next stretch of walkway.

Angel continued in the lead. As they walked away from the junction, the streetlight behind them faded and they moved into the shadowlands. Sam switched into high alert mode, watching for danger; he unobtrusively manoeuvred so he walked on the outside and Helen had the protection of walking between him and the wall.

A moment later, he wished he had not done so. As Angel passed a doorway, shadows shifted from within the recess, emerging as Angel passed and Helen arrived. Sam immediately lunged in front of her, brushing her to the side and reaching out a restraining hand into the shadows. He grabbed one shadow and stretched out his other arm to restrain the second. There were shrieks and cries of fear as Sam momentarily felt some surprise at how little resistance the ambushers put up, but he wasn't going to take any chances.

Angel turned back and intervened before Sam could inflict any damage.

'Stop, Sam. Stop!'

Sam's fist stopped in mid-journey towards the shadow's head. He turned to look at Angel's pleading face then turned to look more closely at the shadow. Horrified, he let his hands drop.

Helen pushed past Sam to reach the girls; putting an arm around each one, she tried to reassure them they were safe.

Angel was speaking fast, none of which Helen understood but she saw the fear receding from the girls' eyes as Angel spoke.

'I'm so sorry,' said Sam. 'I thought they were attacking Helen, I didn't know they were only girls.'

'It's okay, they understand. But perhaps you should give them some money for their pains,' said Angel.

'What were they doing out here in the shadows? That was just asking for trouble,' said Helen.

'Yes, it was. But these girls must come out - they have babies to feed and are alone in the city or maybe they have husbands who send them out. They are prostitutes; this is not such a friendly place for them. They are used to being hurt, it happens a lot.'

Helen was horrified. In the half-light she couldn't gauge the girls' ages, but 'girl' was the operative word. She looked at Sam, nodding encouragement as he pulled out his wallet. She turned to Angel. 'You must do something for these girls, what can you do?'

'Not so much. There are a thousand and more scattered around, and for everyone we save, another comes along. My church aids those that come for help, but many won't come. If they are from Christian backgrounds, they are frightened of the Church's condemnation. If they have tribal religions, they are just generally suspicious and frightened.'

'Well, Angel, I want you to sort these two out, okay? And I'll see what I can do to support you in helping other girls.'

An engine purred on the street immediately behind them. Helen turned to see that Mauwled had spotted the commotion and, anticipating trouble, had quietly driven up beside them. She gave him a reassuring wave.

Angel spoke rapidly to the two girls. With Sam's money in their hands they were happy to stand and listen. They were used to beatings and worse from bad men, men who would try to steal their money too; this was proving to be a good night.

When Angel had finished speaking, the girls were smiling, real smiles. They pressed their hands together and inclined their heads towards Angel and he stretched out and touched each of their foreheads in turn. The girls then smiled to Helen and Sam before hurrying away into the night.

Angel watched them go. 'I've sent them home. With your cash they won't need to work tonight and that makes them happy. And I've told them to come to my church in the morning. I will have some work for them, so they don't have to do this again, and that made them very happy.'

'Thank you, Angel. That was awful. I'll have to speak with you about how we could do something about this. We could start a programme, maybe?'

'That would be a wonderful thing and I look forward to talking about it, but perhaps we should fix the problem we came here for first? The place we want is just ahead. You will be safe with me. My church is around the corner, and I am well known in this street. Though not in the bars,' he ended with a chuckle and led them a few steps on before pushing open a door to let light flood onto the walkway. He entered; Helen and Sam followed him in.

Several unshaded electric bulbs were strung across the ceiling, casting a harsh light that hurt as they came in from the outside. The noise that had spilled out as the door opened faded away when the bar's occupants saw the newcomers. White men were infrequent visitors, white women never called here.

As their eyes became accustomed to the light, Helen peered round. Most of the drinkers recognised Angel and clearly wondered what he wanted; those that weren't looking at him were looking at her with a very real interest. Finally, Angel spotted the man he was looking for, sat at a table with a couple of cronies. Before walking across, Angel looked over at the trestle table bar, raised four fingers towards the barman and called for four bottles of beer.

The man who Angel wanted had watched their progress towards him. When they arrived, he waved his friends away. He wiped the rough planked tabletop with his sleeve, and then swept out an expansive arm, inviting the three to join him. They sat just as the barman arrived with the beers, which he placed on the table in front of them.

Angel distributed the drinks. Helen took hers and had a sip, as did Sam, while the man they had joined looked at

Angel with steady expressionless eyes. Then he shifted his gaze to Sam and Helen, lifted his beer bottle and tilted it towards them in a salute as his face broke into a smile. Helen mirrored his actions exactly, and Sam nodded. The man reached over and touched his bottle against Angel's. 'Thanks,' he said. 'Who are your friends?'

Helen noted his well-formed English.

'This is Abe. Abe, these are my friends who need an answer to the question I asked yesterday. I got a message that you had an answer.'

Abe drank from the bottle and then looked keenly at Angel. 'I may have. It's been difficult to find what you wanted and very expensive.'

'Abe, why does everyone want money from me. Isn't it enough to be serving God's purpose?'

Abe leant back and laughed theatrically. 'Angel, you serve God's purpose for us. I have a family to keep. Now, I think what I have will help you. What will you give me?'

'Twenty dollars,' said Angel.

'I was thinking a thousand, and that would be cheap. It's good information.'

Sam leant forward a little to interrupt the discussion. 'Abe, good to meet you, I'm Sam.' He stretched across the table and shook Abe's hand. 'Angel has done well bringing us together with you. But I think you'll understand that if we are to give you even a little more than twenty dollars I need to know something about you.'

The intervention knocked Abe out of the groove he had set himself in. He looked slightly flustered.

Angel waved the barman back with more beers. 'Abe is a mechanic for one of the safari tour companies. He's based in Arusha but gets out in the bush, helping with breakdowns and such. He's the man who speaks to everyone in the business. Now, Helen said you were looking for clues about an unusual bush convoy bypassing the Kenyan border crossing.'

Abe looked at Sam. 'If you want to know who's doing what they shouldn't in the bush, I'm the man.' He leant back again, gave another excessive laugh, finished his bottle of beer and took another from the barman who had just arrived with replenishments.

Sam was not impressed with Abe, felt he was a chancer. He looked at Angel, arching a questioning eyebrow.

Angel understood and turned to speak again to Abe. 'You should be ashamed of yourself. These are my guests— you should not be trying to exploit them.' He turned to Sam and Helen. 'This man, Abe, he drinks and smokes and stays out half the night. But he is also married to a good woman, an Ethiopian woman who belongs to my church. She loves him, for all his drinking and paganism.' He threw Abe a brief scowl and Abe laughed again. 'For all that, I know he works hard, cares for his wife and feeds his family, and allows them all to attend my church. He may not look it, but he is honest. I would trust him.'

Sam looked at Abe. 'So, Angel trusts you. That says a lot for me, but how can I know what your information is worth if I don't know what you know?'

Abe had stopped laughing now. He looked very thoughtful. After a period of silence, he looked at Sam. 'My wife will not be happy if I upset her priest. But I have an answer to your question, I think it's worth a lot. A lot.'

Sam locked gaze with Abe. 'Here's my proposal. I'm going to give you fifty dollars for your information, whatever it is. If it sounds useful, I'll double it right now to a hundred. If what you tell me is right, once I've checked it out, I'll give you double that again, and I'll leave that money with Angel, so you know you'll get it. That's the best offer, the only offer, you're going to get tonight.' Sam fell silent and held Abe's gaze.

After only a short moment's hesitation, Abe laughed again. 'Sam, you are a hard man. I think you would let my children go hungry.' He shook a finger at Sam in admonishment. 'But, if Angel trusts you, then so do I.' He thrust his hand across the table. As he and Sam shook hands their grip slipped naturally to end in a thumb clasp.

'I think we should go outside to transfer the money somewhere quieter,' said Sam. He stood, and the others followed, making for the exit, Angel pausing on the way to pay the bill.

They stepped out into the shadows of the street; the warm night air was still and there was nobody in sight. Distant sounds from elsewhere in the city crossed the darkness to join with the gentle thrum of the Land Rover's engine turning over. Helen climbed into the front seat, wound the window down and followed the conversation on the walkway beside her.

Sam was counting out money. He handed Angel a hundred dollars and Abe fifty more; he kept a further fifty in his hand and them buttoned his wallet away.

'Well?' said Sam.

Abe was happy with the deal and was keen to tell all he knew. 'There's a safari driver, goes mostly to Ngorongoro and further up to the north too. Nasty piece of work. I wouldn't trust him for a minute. Last week he cancelled three days' driving, caused his company no end of headaches. Their other guides were busy, and they had to borrow a driver and vehicle guide from my boss to meet their commitments.'

'And?' said Sam.

'It was odd; the man put himself off-duty but took the vehicle. He had his company mechanic give it the full works first. Full tank, lots of extra fuel cans. If he was off sick, why did he need the vehicle? And where did he go?'

'So where did he go?'

'We don't know, but he was gone three full days and when he got back the vehicle was in a mess, all the spare fuel used. It had been worked hard.' Abe paused for a moment. 'Then when the mechanic cleared out the vehicle he found some empty lager bottles, Summit brand.' He paused and looked expectantly at Sam.

Sam waited.

'Summit is a local Kenyan lager; you don't normally get it in Tanzania. Certainly not usually out at the lodges around Ngorongoro.'

'Do you have a name for this man, where can I find him?'

For the first time Abe looked anxious. He hesitated. 'It won't come back to me will it? He's an evil man, I've heard stories ...'

'Don't worry, your part ends here,' Sam rustled the fifty-dollar note in his hand, and a moment later, Abe gave Sam the information he needed.

'He's a guide driver for African Sunrise Safaris. They have an office in Arusha, but he mostly drives the crater tours. We think he has something on the boss. Always seems to get what he wants, coming and going as he pleases. Henk. Henk Smuts.'

'South African?'

'I think so. I've never really talked much to him. He doesn't mix with the mechanics or other guide drivers.'

Sam handed over the extra fifty dollars.

Chapter 18
TUESDAY 29TH OCTOBER - AM

The orange Land Rover was making a steady speed along the highway. Jeanie had insisted that Sam and Helen take it and that Mauwled drove. They had set off at first light to be sure of getting through Arusha before the worst of the morning traffic developed. Now clear of the city and on a good road, it felt that they were making progress at last.

First, there were well-ordered farms, commercial enterprises that controlled the best land. They frequently drove past row upon row of carefully maintained coffee bushes that stretched out to dominate the environment. Further away from Arusha, family farms became more frequent with smaller fields whose shapes were formed by the natural lie of the land. With each passing mile, man's influence became less prominent as the bush imposed its might. Now the farmsteads were less frequent, mostly scattered subsistence agriculture struggling to maintain a toehold in the bush.

Everywhere was dry, with lots of browns and blacks and straw-coloured golds; those few plants that still managed to sport some green stood out as targets for browsing animals.

The bush growth had organised itself into four rough groups. There were occasional trees that had bucked the system and made it to full height. Their canopies, above browsing height, spread and flourished to create little havens of shade. Spreading out around the trees, sometimes alone, sometimes in little clusters, grew stunted trees and bushes, perhaps twice the height of a man. Between them, grew isolated thickets of shoulder-height bushes that, here and there, managed to link up and create dense patches of undergrowth. Around and between it all was open ground, carpeted with grasses; there were occasional tufts up to knee height but most had now been grazed down to the roots by passing hungry animals.

At first glance, the bush seemed to offer deceptively easy access. Regular grazers ensured clear walking paths could be found between and around most of the denser plant growth. But it was hot and dry going and visibility was significantly restricted by the plant growth ahead, to the sides and behind. In bush that could stretch a hundred miles without a break, it was easy to become lost, and just as easy to become prey for the many inhabitants who viewed humans simply as just another link in the food chain.

Mauwled explained he had once been a safari driver and guide but had got himself into some trouble. He avoided saying exactly what. Just that he'd lost his job and become a bush driver for a group that arranged to move things around the country without asking too many questions. It was clear he meant smuggling but was not going to admit it. Eventually he'd got into serious trouble and it was his Aunty, Mama Grace, who had persuaded Jeanie Albright to intervene on his behalf. She did, he was spared jail, and now worked for her.

They were making good time along the road, which seemed to stretch on endlessly. They frequently passed heavy-laden trucks and pickups whose engines struggled under the burden of hopelessly overloaded cargos. Eventually, they reached Makuyuni. Here, they branched off to the north onto a smaller though still serviceable road where the traffic noticeably reduced; anything that was heading for the western towns and Burundi, Rwanda or Uganda had stayed on the main highway that continued away to the south and west.

Where the road had been improved to enhance travel times, great gashes had been left in the landscape. The raw earth, exposed to the sun received no human landscaping. The next rains would start the process of moulding and shaping the naked earth and, with the wet, would come plant growth ensuring that it would quickly blend into the surrounding bush.

The quiet in the Land Rover was broken by the ringing of the phone. Helen pulled it from her bag and checked the caller.

'It's Elaine.' Sam watched intently as Helen's conversation progressed, seeking any sign as to progress. It sounded positive.

After a couple of minutes, Helen ended the call. 'Well, it seems your suggestion is working out. Elaine has been in touch with African Sunrise Safaris. They have you in for a tour of the Ngorongoro crater tomorrow, and they have booked you with Henk Smuts. Elaine's let them think you're a high-ranking exec who has flown in for two or three days looking for a safari tour and Smuts had been recommended by a friend as the guide to have. If anyone thinks to check, there's a nice executive aircraft sitting waiting for you back at Kilimanjaro Airport.'

'That's great. Though it would have been better to have met him this afternoon. Time's not on our side.'

'Apparently, he's away until later today.'

'I wonder where.'

'You don't need him, I can take you down into the crater, I did it years' ago.'

'Mauwled, I explained earlier, we're not here for the tour, we need to speak with this man Smuts. See if we can coax any information out of him. When we want a proper tour, I promise, you'll be the man.'

Their Land Rover was following the road that would eventually reach down onto the Serengeti plains. But first they had to drive up and over its ancient volcanic fringe. The road started to describe more turns as it followed the land's upward contours. Moving steadily upwards, greens returned to the plants, and on the areas of darker fertile soil, coffee plantations appeared more frequently, as they had done around Arusha.

Mauwled kept the Land Rover moving at a good pace, even as the gradient became steeper. The landscape ahead gave every appearance that they were driving into a mountain range. Helen glanced down to the left and caught distant glimpses of a wide flatland far below them, and still Mauwled kept moving up and on.

At last the road levelled off and it appeared to run straighter ahead. For just a moment, Helen thought the road was on a high plateau, as to her left, she gazed down onto the distant Serengeti, watching it stretch away towards the horizon like a pale biscuit-brown sea, formed by the endless dried dusty grasses.

'Wow, look at that,' said Sam, pointing to Helen's right.

She turned quickly and caught her breath. This was no plateau; they were on the broad lip of an ancient volcanic cone. The Land Rover drew to a halt at a viewing point and they all got out. The view offered a steep drop down into a crater whose flat bottom stretched for miles across. Down there, great stands of trees looked like little patches of moss while shimmering splashes of silver marked the presence of broad lakes. Her eye traced the rim of the volcano as it swept away into the distance before arcing back to complete the circle and enclose everything within.

This gave the lie to the impression they were climbing up into a mountain range; this was actually one monstrous volcano, its perfectly preserved cone rim enclosing a crater that she guessed was twenty miles across.

Helen pulled out her phone and took pictures, though she instinctively knew they would never do justice to what her eyes saw. Far below, amongst the stands of trees and the lakes were areas of dark green, that she guessed were marshlands, long ranges of yellowed grasses and dry dusty expanses. It was Eastern Africa in miniature.

'It's a great place for safari,' said Mauwled. All the animals you would want to see live in here. Look, even elephants.' He pointed towards tiny dark spots far below, no bigger than matchstick heads.

'This looks really good.' A note of concern sounded in Helen's voice. 'Are they all trapped? How did they get in there?'

Mauwled laughed. 'They got in themselves. Maybe over thousands of years, I think. There is a track down inside the crater and they can use it to get out too if they want, and even others could join them from outside.'

'Do they?' said Sam.

'Not the lions any more. On the volcano's slopes there are too many villages and farms to pass through now. But the elephants do. It's mostly bulls here. They enjoy a safe quiet life and when they want to meet ladies they go out, maybe once a year. Then they come back. The villages and farms on the outer slopes don't bother them, nobody argues with the elephants. Very dangerous.'

Helen and Sam crossed to the other side of the road and they were at last able to properly take in the sheer scale of the African savannah far below, where the lower reaches of the volcano merged into the Serengeti and then stretched off towards a far horizon. They fell silent, struck by its sheer scale.

'Brilliant,' said Sam.

'It is.' Helen did a full turn, trying to take in both the crater and the plains together. 'And Sam, isn't that odd? That 4 x 4 has stopped a little further back up the road, but there's plenty of space in the layby behind our Land Rover.'

'Yes, odd, but even more of a coincidence - it's been behind us pretty well since we left Arusha.'

'You never said.'

'No, but this is a safari destination, it may just be a coincidence.'

'I see.' Helen's voice carried no conviction.

Having absorbed the scale of their environment they returned to the Land Rover where Mauwled was waiting. Driving on, they moved away from the pinch point and the crater rim spread into a broadened and flattened expanse of land. It was permanently greened due to its high altitude microclimate. Here it really was like a high plateau and they quickly lost sight of both the crater's edges and their precipitous drops.

'The lodge accepts visitors from midday; we'll arrive about then. If you won't need me for a while, I can go and speak with some of the other drivers, see if they know anything about Smuts,' said Mauwled as they drove on towards their destination.

Chapter 19
TUESDAY 29TH OCTOBER - PM

Mauwled pulled open the back door to the Land Rover but didn't get the chance to remove Helen and Sam's bags before two smiling bellhops hurried out from the lodge reception and took them. Set in beautiful flowering gardens, the single-storey building was of new construction but used a mix of dressed dark hardwoods and white plaster to give a hint of tradition. Helen and Sam both guessed there was no wattle beneath the plaster, just modern concrete blocks. That didn't matter, this was a lovely setting, and the modern construction offered a degree of comfort that was welcome after the morning's long drive.

As they followed the bellhops into the lodge reception, their senses were refreshed by the sweet rich scents emanating from the riot of flowers and shrubs in the gardens and the climbing plants that had been trained around the entrance. Immediately they had passed through the flowering arch, they were inside reception. There they felt the welcome blast of air conditioning and were greeted by a young woman in a westernised version of Maasai dress - a white blouse with neatly tailored lightweight skirt and waistcoat in a red plaid pattern. Worn off the shoulder was a similarly patterned cloak fastened by an intricate lion's head broach.

Beyond the reception, glass doors set in an internal glass wall allowed access to the guests' area. First a broad lounge, its high white walls broken only by high set windows, small to exclude the sun's heat. The walls were decorated with clusters of artefacts - mostly spears and shields but some pots and gourds interspersed with paintings of wildlife and people in tribal dress. A bar was positioned close to the reception. At one end of the lounge was a raised performance area; at the other end was a dining room, accessed via an open archway formed into the wall. Glancing through the arch, Helen could see seating for perhaps two hundred people.

'You know, calling this place a lodge is a little misleading. It's a big hotel, but where do all the guests sleep?'

The receptionist completed their registration and with the warmest of smiles handed Helen an electronic key card. 'This is your room key. It also releases the lock on that door between reception and the lounge,' she said, waving towards the set of glass doors. The wave morphed into a clap, and from somewhere behind reception, two more smiling women appeared. Each was dressed in similar style to the receptionist but worn in place of the cloak were purple-hued tabards, added to protect their uniforms from the dust and dirt of the day.

'These maids can take you to your room now.'

'Where are the rooms?' said Sam.

'I know. Everybody asks,' said the receptionist as she released the key card into Helen's hand. 'The building is upside down. The bedrooms are all below this floor.'

'Ahh, so your building doesn't break the skyline.'

'I think so.'

'It's on the crater edge?'

'Yes, right on the edge. Your room will have a lovely view.'

'Sounds great, let's go see,' said Helen. She resisted a maid's attempt to take her little shoulder bag. 'I can manage this,' she said, then followed behind Sam, who had not been allowed to carry their bags by the women who now led them through the glass doors and beyond the bar to a discreet stairwell that Helen had not registered in her first scan of the area.

One flight down, the maids led them into a corridor and past several numbered doors. Some paces along, they stopped.

'Here we are, sir,' said the older of the two women as she used her pass card to open the door. Stepping aside, she ushered Sam forward. He thanked her then guided Helen in first.

Inside were all the standard features of an en-suite hotel room, but with plenty of space to move around. The maid took Helen's key card and slotted it into a wall-mounted holder, triggering the air-conditioning unit and making the environment altogether more welcoming. Her companion crossed the room and used a pull string to open the window blind that had been tightly shut.

The scene took Helen's breath away and instinctively she put an arm round the maid. 'This is beautiful.'

The maid nodded agreement.

The older maid told them food was available upstairs at any time through the day and the evening meal would be served from seven o'clock onwards. With more smiles the maids left, happy with the money Sam had slipped into their hands.

Sam joined Helen at the window and both stood silently for a little while. Their room was built over the crater wall with nothing to obstruct their view across and around the whole rim. And downwards, there was nothing to break a fall for a thousand feet or more. Flocks of birds circled beneath their room before spiralling out in effortless journeys over the crater, vanishing into the distance as they flew off to check out the miniature dust clouds thrown up by the tiny specks that were safari vehicles working their way across the crater floor.

• • •

Mauwled sat in the shade outside the drivers' dormitory. He had chanced upon an old acquaintance there who had been glad to see him, if only to break the frustration of a day without work. His vehicle's engine was shot, and now he could do nothing until parts arrived from Arusha.

'… and what's been going on?' said Mauwled.

'Same, same. Plenty safari customers, not enough time.' The guide paused to take a mouthful of hot tea, savoured it. Mauwled mirrored him.

'I was hearing stories back in Arusha about Smuts. He's been letting his tour company down again.'

'You know what he's like,' said the guide, glancing about him. He pulled out a packet of cigarettes and offered one to Mauwled; both men lit up and drew in deeply.

'I heard he's been taking illegal hunting trips and leaving the safari tours in the lurch. Is that right?'

The guide shrugged. 'You know nobody talks about Smuts and his business; remember how he beat that man half to death?'

Mauwled nodded. 'He's mad.'

'He's dangerous.'

The men lapsed into silence for a minute and smoked more.

• • •

Helen only half heard the jet of water kick in as Sam stepped into the shower. She watched with fascination how the scene changed outside her hotel room window as the sun dropped into the west. The crater below smoothly transitioned from bright daylight, through growing shadows, into twilight and, finally, the night. In the little time Sam spent under the water jet, the crater's beautiful daytime vista vanished into a black void; while, far into the west, way beyond the crater's rim, she could yet make out a halo from the last vestiges of sunlight that caressed the vast flat savannah of the Serengeti.

As the sound of the shower cut out in the bathroom, she gave an involuntary shiver at the depth of blackness in the crater outside. What had looked a friendly, certainly contained, environment had shifted. She felt the danger it held, the wildlife haven of the day had suddenly become a killers' trap with no exit route by night. She understood now why Mauwled had explained that safari guests were not allowed in the crater at night. The dirt track out would be too dangerous to drive after dark and to stay in that black void would be unthinkable.

Sam emerged and flicked on the main light. 'Why are you sitting in the dark?' he said, moving across the room to pick up his clean clothes.

'No reason, night just came so quickly in the crater, it took me by surprise. It was fast.'

'Yes,' said Sam, as he drew the heavy blind across the window, closing out the darkness. 'Are you set? I'm hungry.'

'Me too, let's go.'

Before they could reach the door, the phone rang. Helen checked the caller. 'It's Elaine, I wonder what's up.' She answered the phone and sat down on the edge of the bed.

Sam sat beside her, and she swung her hand round to hold the handset between them.

'Hi Elaine, it's Helen here. I've switched to speaker mode, Sam's with me.'

'Hello, to both of you. I hope you've recovered from your prison ordeal now, Sam?'

'Thanks Elaine. Yes, I'm doing fine. We're going to eat in a minute.'

'Oh good. I hope you enjoy it and I'm looking forward to seeing your pictures of Ngorongoro. Grace looked it up on the web, it seems fascinating.'

'We'll post some tomorrow. Now, what's up?' he said.

'We've had a visit. Well, actually, Scottie Brown had a visit. Then I had one a little while later. An army officer and a member of MI6 have been to see us. Scottie went back into the military sites and his digging into ACE has got some people stirred up.'

'What happened?' said Helen.

'Scottie's been told he's breached half a dozen laws and I'm taking the blame for initiating it all. They had him held in their car when they came to see me. I think they were going to take me away too. Then there was a bit of confusion when they realised our connection with you two; it became quite farcical for a little while, they were making phone calls and all the while glaring at me.

'I caught a name during one of the calls - Brigadier Starling. When he called back it was their turn to feel the heat. Then they brought Scottie in from the car, read us both the riot act and warned us not to divulge anything we knew about ACE to anyone or we'd be in big trouble. Then they were gone. Apparently, they'll be back tomorrow when I've to sign the Official Secrets Act. It seems Scottie had signed it in the past as part of his previous IT job with the police service.'

Sam leant a little closer to the phone. 'We met Brigadier Starling at a lunch meeting in the Nairobi High Commission. I think he's a big noise in the secrets department. But at least he seems to be on our side. I'm sorry you've been dragged into all this, Elaine. I'll call our contact, Rupert Peterson, later, make sure they understand you are good guys and ask him to get his people to back off.'

'Don't worry, Sam, I think the brigadier did that for you. The security men couldn't get away quick enough after he'd been on the line. They left Scottie sitting in my kitchen. Whoever this Starling is, he clearly doesn't want you upset, even from a distance.'

'Well, I'll speak to Rupert anyway.'

'I'm really sorry about all this, Elaine,' said Helen. 'How did Grace take it?'

'She's fine; she was out at college when they came. In fact, no, she's raging. Grace wishes she'd been in when the security people called. Apparently, she's just about sick of men pushing me about. She's taking the day off college tomorrow to be here when the men come back.'

'Great, but listen, tell her I don't want either her or you getting into trouble over this. Just sign the paperwork and let it be, okay?' said Helen.

'Helen, you know Grace, she gets a bit protective of her mother. But I'll tell her what you said.'

'Okay, you both take care, we'll be done here in a—'

'Hold on, don't you want to know what else Scottie found out?'

Sam instinctively leant closer to the satellite handset. 'You have more news?'

Sam switched off speaker mode. 'Hello Elaine, this is a secure handset and line, but I've taken you off speaker mode. It's hard to imagine, but if for any reason, this room is bugged, I can't let any information about ACE get out, understand?'

Helen gave Sam the slightest of scowls but was resigned to waiting for the news, whatever it was. She watched Sam's facial expressions change as he listened carefully to what Elaine said. He asked short questions that were meaningless without the context of Elaine's information and responses. Finally, he ended his conversation with a warning that Elaine really should keep it quiet. He handed the handset to Helen to say goodbye and they headed out for dinner.

'I think it would be a nice idea to go for a stroll in the

gardens in front of the lodge after we've eaten,' he said.

Chapter 20
TUESDAY 29TH OCTOBER - EVENING

Outside, the air was much cooler than when they had arrived at midday. Now, without the sun's rays, it was just pleasantly warm as altitude cooling kicked in. The gardens were discreetly floodlit, little bulbs spread apart and angled down to mark the course of the promenade through the darkened gardens. A little to their right, the course of the approach road was lit too, providing some depth to the scene and a counter to the ominous darkness of the crater that lay immediately behind the lodge.

Helen linked her arm through Sam's. 'This is nice,' she said. 'Now, come on, spill. What more did Scottie find?'

Involuntarily, Sam glanced over his shoulder and gave a little laugh at Helen's sideways glance towards him. 'Yes, I'm being paranoid, and I think probably with good reason.'

'Come on Sam, what did Elaine tell you?'

'First, I can understand why the military and security services didn't like it when they spotted Scottie's searching, and why they went to visit him and Elaine. It's very sensitive.'

'So, what's the big deal with this ACE?'

'Well, for a start it's not static and the word combat tells us something. I think it's an attack weapon.'

'What?'

'I don't know but she said they work together in packs.'

'Wolf packs?'

Sam shrugged. 'I don't know. I do know there was work being done on this years back, even before I got out. For Britain, and most of the other western countries too, the really big problem is manpower. Given so many life options today, fewer and fewer are joining the forces, and the army in particular is significantly undermanned.'

'So, it is robot soldiers then.'

'All Elaine could say was they, whatever they are, worked as part of a pack and hunted the enemy. It sounds like a form of force multiplier. For an army without enough soldiers that would be a godsend. And in the hands of some dictatorships that already have large armies, it could give them an almost incalculable advantage. In fact, there are applications at flashpoints all over. At the Line of Control between India and Pakistan, India and China, Vietnam and China, China and Russia, Russia and Iran, hell, Iran and half the world.'

'You haven't even mentioned North Korea yet!' said Helen.

'Oh, don't go there.'

'It really sounds like a game changer.'

'If it actually works, maybe. Scottie said it's a small-scale combat system, designed for tactical advantage, not strategic.'

'What does that mean?'

'Win all your tactical clashes and you eventually win the war, bit by bit. The best strategy in the world is meaningless if you can't win the individual firefights - eventually you'll lose.

'I'm thinking that since everyone is so worked up, they must have finally got a working prototype. Let's get back inside; I think we need to get some rest. Tomorrow is going to be a difficult day with our guide Smuts.'

The little pools of light marking the path ahead of them began to describe an arc as the path looped round and back towards the reception.

Chapter 21
WEDNESDAY 30TH OCTOBER - AM

It was very early when they finally encountered Henk Smuts. A tall man with a face leathered and lined through years under the African sun. Broad shouldered, his brown hair now prominently streaked with grey; his clothing was reminiscent of combat fatigues, slightly threadbare and faded through many washes. He shook Sam's hand, and then Helen's as he greeted them in a thick guttural South African accent.

Smuts was expecting his passenger to be a high-flyer wanting a whistle-stop safari. Sam met his expectations. His customer's companion, an unmarried young woman fitted too. He'd seen it plenty of times before - rich man, pretty assistant. 'A business trip'. Yes, the girl fitted Smuts' expectations too. With an only half-concealed smirk, he pointed towards his vehicle.

The safari truck was parked outside the lodge in the shade of the building. The sun was just up, and the air was still cool. Helen pulled open a rear door and held it open for Sam and he slipped in with just a nod of acknowledgement. Helen then closed the door and went around to open the door on the other side. She hoisted a rucksack in and then got in too.

They both watched the big man walk around the truck for a final inspection. He kicked a tyre, probably for effect, then got into the driver's seat and fired up the engine. A blast of cold air swept through the rear and Helen shivered, pulling her light jacket round her.

Smuts turned in his seat and smiled. His yellowed teeth, tobacco stained and in want of a thorough overhaul, showed dully beneath a thick moustache that looked sandy coloured but might equally have just been grubby.

'Well people, welcome to Ngorongoro. I'm going to leave the lid on for now,' he leant into the rear and rapped his hand on the fibreglass roofing. 'Once we are down in the crater I'll raise it up and you can have an open view of everything.'

Smuts ran through a short safety briefing and checked that they had collected water and packed lunches from the lodge. Helen patted her hand on the rucksack and turned her head to beam a devoted smile to her boss.

'Right, we should get going. I like to get ahead of the crowd, be first down. Otherwise you end up in a queue and waste half the morning.'

He put the vehicle into gear and eased away from the lodge, picking up a little speed as they went. He raised his voice so it carried into the back. 'The road's okay here, it soon turns to dirt track though. Mostly it's safe enough but if you don't have a head for heights there are a few places going down where you might want to close your eyes.' He gave a deep belly laugh as he used his mirror to eye the girl in the back seat.

Smuts reckoned she'd crack easily enough. And he knew just where to go close to the edge on the way down - that would take the smile off her face.

Smuts kept up a flow of macho safari chatter on the route down and was slightly irritated to see that Helen was not fazed by his cliff edge driving. Something caught his eye in the rear-view mirror. About a quarter of a mile behind, another safari truck was on the move.

'We've got company. Somebody else wanting to get ahead of the crowd,' he said. Then gave another confident laugh. 'Well they'd have to start pretty damned early to beat Smutsie to the bottom. I'll tell you that for nothing.'

Obligingly, Sam and Helen turned their heads to look for the following vehicle. It was familiar. Helen squeezed Sam's thigh, he patted her hand in confirmation and the two turned back to the front. It was the 4 x 4 that had travelled behind them from Arusha.

'They follow me you know. Old Smutsie is the one who delivers the goods; no customer leaves one of my safari drives unsatisfied. The other drivers try to get a tail on me, follow. That way they know they'll give their customers what they want.'

'Sounds like you're the main man around here,' said Helen.

Smuts laughed again. 'Main man? You could say that. I know this crater like the back of my hand.' He paused for a moment; let the pretty girl absorb his importance. 'Outside the crater too. I've been driving this country for twenty-five years and more. Came up after I'd finished in the South African Defence Force. Never looked back.'

'Wow,' said Helen enthusiastically.

Smuts broke off to curse a pair of young Maasai warriors who were guiding a small herd of cattle down the track. He revved his engine a little and waved a hand towards the men who sported the distinctive red plaid cloaks. They glared silent defiance back at him and then hurried to drive their cattle against the side of the crater wall. Smuts edged ahead, then when the vehicle was almost past the cattle, he gave the engine a rev, just enough to startle the beasts.

Finally, after almost a half hour of slow, sometimes bumpy descent they were safe at the crater bottom. Smuts activated the rear roof controls and the fibreglass top lifted up on struts, nearly a metre higher than its original position, now acting as a sun shield over Helen and Sam's heads. 'You can stand and get a great view, or if you prefer, the side windows will go right down so you can stay seated and just watch the world go by.'

Helen and Sam stood and watched the landscape unfold. There were no formal roads in the crater but years of safari vehicles retracing the same routes had created some well-defined tracks and Smuts steered them along his chosen route.

Not far from the foot of the track into the crater, they passed a properly constructed car park. A stopping area for lunch, according to Smuts, but he never bothered stopping there. To their right was a spread of mature acacia trees, tall with broad canopies that provided shelter from the sun for a gathering of several large male elephants. They stood in close proximity to one another, yet each in his own proud isolation was content to ignore his neighbour.

Smuts drove on, past a small lake and into extensive dried out grasslands. At this point, if it were not for the surrounding volcano walls, they might have easily imagined they were in the open space of the Serengeti.

A herd of zebra paused amidst their modest pickings to watch the vehicle pass then resumed their grazing. Beyond them, a line of wildebeest made their way steadily from one wizened patch to the next in their almost perpetual search for better growth.

A little further on, the grasslands gave out, and for a while, they travelled across what, at this time of year, was a dustbowl peppered with tufts of dry grasses.

Their safari truck came over a low rise and Helen realised they had driven round in a great arc and they were now close to a lakeside far from the exit route. Here the water was dark, almost black but shimmering in the sunlight. What she took to be a rocky outcrop suddenly moved and a great hippo reared its head, its movement was immediately mirrored by others in the group and the surface bulged and rippled under the disturbance. In just a few moments the hippos settled, the water became still and the birds that had previously perched on the hippos' backs returned to their posts to pick and scratch at their thick grey skin.

'See, over there,' said Smuts, pointing towards the lake's end. There, sitting in the open, was a big male lion. Thickset shoulders, heavy head, mane fluffed out. 'He's eaten. See all the red around his mouth and neck, that's blood, fresh blood.'

Smuts cast about, and then drove on, making for a marshy area just beyond the lake. Now he drove very slowly, watching the track ahead and to either side. 'See, to the right … in that reed bed … I'll get us a bit closer.' He gingerly nudged the vehicle further off the track and finally brought it to a halt. He turned his head to the rear and paused to admire Helen's thighs before tilting his head up to address his passengers through the skylight.

'What is it?' said Sam.

'I'm going to get us a little bit further forward - be quiet now and keep your eyes peeled. I think we should see that big boy's pride eating around here somewhere. The lionesses and, with a bit of luck, the cubs too. But don't speak now. Okay?' With a final appreciative glance at Helen's legs, he turned to face front and began to edge forward. As the vehicle flattened another round of reeds, he turned hard left and eased to a stop.

Less than five paces from the vehicle was what remained of a zebra carcass after the male lion had taken his fill. Two lionesses were methodically eating and around them were five or six cubs. The whole group was stained red, though Helen was unsure whether the cubs were actually eating or just learning a procedure. She and Sam watched in silence for a little while, fascinated by the cubs and the lionesses eating while apparently unconcerned that they had an audience.

'You're okay in the truck,' Smuts voice came to them from the cabin below, as though he knew what they were thinking. 'But believe me, if you step out you'll be on the lunch menu too.' His laugh echoed up and out. One of the lionesses turned her head for just a moment then resumed eating.

'We're going now,' said Smuts. Several more safari trucks had closed in behind him, and he wanted fresh ground to explore. 'We'll leave this lot for the amateurs.' Slowly, he pulled away, forcing the truck through the reed bed and leaving the other safari trucks to manoeuvre for spots around the pride and its kill.

As they pulled away, Sam watched the vehicles behind him; he had to admit to Helen that Smuts was right. He did seem to have a knack, and the other drivers were certainly following him around.

Helen nudged Sam's side, and he looked to see what was interesting her. She nodded towards a vehicle that was cutting out from the following pack, seemingly intent on keeping pace with them. Once again, it was the 4 x 4 that had been dogging their tracks over the past day or so. He raised his binoculars to his eyes and casually did a slow sweep of the landscape. As the following vehicle came into view, he paused his scan and tried to see who was on board. He felt a tightening in his stomach.

He could see the driver and front passenger clearly, couldn't make out who was in the rear but guessed they too would be Asian. Somewhere along the line, their Nairobi tail had switched the inconspicuous city car for a big 4 x 4. He kept the sham of his wildlife scan up, and after a few moments of peering absently into the bush, he lowered the glasses and turned to Helen. 'Korean,' he said. 'It's them.'

'How did they find us?'

'I don't know. I guess the other question has to be why did they find us? I don't think we've done anything to attract attention.'

'No, but they're here.'

Smuts' voice came up to them from the driver's seat. 'I think I'll find an open spot to stop for lunch. What do you say, hungry yet?'

They both agreed, and Smuts drove towards his planned location. While maintaining a discreet distance behind, the other vehicle followed on.

'Ha! I see we've still got one follower. Not much I can do about it now, but I'll shake them off after lunch.'

Chapter 22
WEDNESDAY 30TH OCTOBER - PM

The spot Smuts chose for lunch had a stark beauty; a long flat stretch of dusty yellowed earth that lay between a shrunken lake and a stand of trees. Once the rains came it would become lakebed again, today it was bone-dry hard pack. They could make out more elephants standing in the shade of the trees, their heads weighed down with long tusks that rocked gently from side to side as they stared out quietly towards the waters of the lake.

A little more disconcerting was the family of hyenas that had emerged from the woods and spread out to walk slowly and silently towards the water.

'Oh, oh, look at this. These beauties have spotted something,' said Smuts pointing towards the hyenas. He scanned the lakefront ahead of them as Helen and Sam followed his direction.

'There. See? At the water's edge. That wildebeest, it shouldn't be at the water on its own. It's a herd animal. Something's wrong for sure.'

Some instinct made the wildebeest look up, and it registered the danger. The hyenas realised they had been spotted and suddenly began to move much quicker. As they sped up, their bouncing, almost comic, gait became more pronounced. The wildebeest started to move away but slowly, too slowly.

'He's lame, the old boy's lame. He doesn't stand a chance,' said Smuts. Helen could hear the excitement growing in his voice as death approached.

'These hyenas are brutal, once they've got you in their sights, you may as well give up. A hyena clan can see off a lion if push comes to shove. Look at those shoulders, heavyset to carry that big head. And the jaws, strong, crack right through a bone in a single bite.' Smuts' South African accent became more pronounced as he became engrossed in the hunt.

'Go on, run old man. Run!' He kept his eyes on the wildebeest as it started in one direction then changed its mind and turned to run through the shallows in the opposite direction then stopped, that escape route closed by a great beast of an animal. The wildebeest backed a little into the water, half turned one way then the other. Knew it was dead.

'Look! See the wildebeest's back end? It's all raked and red. It must have dodged a lion attack last night. It'll wish the lion had got it now. That would have been a cleaner kill.'

The wildebeest chose its direction of flight far too late, and then stopped; its head lowered, its horns waving in a last desperate defence. As the hyenas milled about, their yip, yip, yipping cries worked towards a crescendo and the wildebeest, losing its nerve, decided to run.

Helen averted her gaze in revulsion as Smuts cheered on the attackers. The sound of splashing, excited cries of the hyenas and frightened screams from the doomed wildebeest rushed up from the water's edge.

'Go on, have him. Have him down. Ha! They've got him. See how they do it? That's one wildebeest that'll sire no more calves.' He laughed out loud.

When the wildebeest had made its final ill-fated break, its damaged quarter had faltered, making the animal stumble. Immediately, one huge hyena had thrust her head between his rear legs and bitten deep into the wildebeest's groin. Jaws clamped tight on her favoured point of first contact, the wildebeest's own motion provided the energy to simultaneously emasculate it and rip open its rear end. As the wildebeest struggled forward in its agonising death throes, an umbilical of intestine unravelled to maintain a deadly tether with its attacker. The hyena chewed and bit on its mouthful of flesh as the others closed in, darting forward and back stressing and tiring the crippled wildebeest.

Now unable to move its rear at all, the wounded animal could no longer face off the hyenas. It couldn't kick out, couldn't turn its head to face an attacker without becoming unstable and falling. Life struggles to the very end, but the end was here.

'Go on, have him down. Have him down!' Smuts was lost in the moment, bloodlust blocking out every civilising thought.

The wildebeest's cries turned to squeals of fear and agony as one hyena took its damaged rear leg between its jaws, the sound of crunch and crack racing across the beach while the attacker ripped the leg away and loped off to enjoy its prize. The wildebeest was finally down on its back, three remaining legs kicked spasmodically in the air; two legs were seized by juvenile hyenas who did not yet have the jaw strength to sever the limbs cleanly, so they engaged in a tug of war, chewing through flesh and bone, still yipping through their clamped jaws.

Having swallowed her first mouthful, the big female returned and sniffed at the supine animal's belly, which jerked from side to side under the leg pulling of the juveniles. Nosing about, she paused for a moment to select the perfect spot and then sank her teeth in. Jerking back, she tore open the belly, and then she thrust her muzzle deep into the wound, bit hard and pulled, drawing out what remained of the wildebeest's intestines. The little ones crowded round for a taste of the kill as the wildebeest's eyes rolled. All hope gone, its one free leg kicked out vainly. Then it was still, and the hyenas piled in to dismember the carcass.

Smuts reached over the back of his seat and gripped Sam's arm. 'There man! Africa in the raw. Beautiful animals, they know how to kill for sure. You wouldn't have got that with any of those follow-on drivers. You come to me, you get the best.' He laughed out loud, then releasing Sam's arm, he waved a dismissive hand towards Helen. 'Your assistant doesn't look so good. Come on girly, you've got a nice trip to Africa with your boss, time to realise what the bush means.' Smuts turned back to look at the scene by the lakeside.

'Tell me, man, why did you really insist to my tour company that I was the only driver you'd accept? Not many people do that.'

Sam had spent much of the morning wondering when he should broach the subject. Smuts had done it for him, and he was ready.

'I was told you were the man I wanted.'

'Told by who?'

'Friends, well no, business connections in Europe, and out in the East too. I'm not giving you their names. I'm sure you know some people like to avoid being named. People who name them might as well go and play with those hyenas.'

Smuts continued looking at the beach. One or two hopeful vultures had landed. He could see other black specs circling above, coming lower, but there would be little left once the hyenas had finished.

'I know more than one European that could describe.' Smuts looked over his shoulder towards Sam. 'Anything in particular you're interested in?'

'Well, my friends tell me you're the man for most tricky things. I heard, if a man wanted to shoot with something heavier than a camera, you had a handle on that.'

Smuts said nothing, but Sam saw his slight nod.

'My friends say you can do more than that.'

Smuts turned back to Sam. 'Look, let's not dance about. You've heard I can fix things out here in the bush, maybe that's true and maybe it's not. I've done a bit of checking too. I know you're rich, a private jet sitting on the runway over at Kilimanjaro.' He turned and looked at Helen who was struggling to conceal her distaste for the man. 'You're doing alright for yourself, girly. A boss with a private-'

'Let's stay focused on the business in hand, shall we? And you've been checking on me too, interesting,' said Sam. He felt a tingle in his spine. It had been a gamble to allude to unnamed acquaintances, but Smuts was greedy, and he moved in a dirty world. He wasn't going to play down his links and status if there was a chance of money to be made.

'I knew there was something more about you,' said Smuts. 'Ordinary folk don't request specific guides. Hey, ordinary folk don't have private planes. And I know you're not police or wildlife protection investigators. If you were undercover, you might have been able to front up this trip, but the private jet? That's out of their league. So, what are you wanting? And remember, I live in a cash world. That's cash dollars, American. Tell me again, who are your friends?'

Sam leant forward. 'Friends like mine don't have names, but they know you and you know them. I'm interested in hunting for real, off-piste you might say. But the main reason I'm down here is I need to set up a transport route. One that doesn't attract too much attention.'

'Transport what to where? Internal or crossing borders?' Smuts' business mind was suddenly in top gear. He gave Helen a cautious look.

'Don't worry about the girl,' said Sam. He placed his hand on Helen's shorts, slid it on to the bare flesh of her thigh. 'She does as she's told.'

Smuts' eyes traced the hand's progress and he gave a deep throaty laugh as Sam squeezed the bare flesh hard.

'That's how it should be, hey, yes? Make sure the little woman knows her place. Good man. Now what are we talking?'

'I want some private shooting; I'll pay big for the right beasts. I'm thinking the man that can set that up in this wilderness is the man who can sort my little transport problem too. Think of one as the test for the other. Show me you're the man to deliver.' Sam released Helen's thigh and snapped his fingers in front of Helen's face. 'Cash, girl. Quickly.'

'Yes, sir.' Helen kept her face down and bit her lip as she raised her top a little and pulled at the money belt Sam had made her wear. She was furious, could feel Smuts' eyes on her midriff as she pulled the belt up and out a little. Unzipping it, she withdrew a wad of US dollars; she handed them to Sam and, with some relief, tucked her top back into her waistband again.

'Good girl,' said Sam, flicking through the cash wad then looking up to catch Smuts' eye. 'One thing you should know, money's no problem. Here, take this, treat it as a goodwill gesture.' He thrust the money forward.

Smuts took it eagerly. 'You can rely on me. Smutsie always delivers, I'm your man.'

'Another thing. Be aware my business contacts don't like to be messed with, I think you know what I mean.' Sam pointed down to the shore where the wildebeest's carcass was now just scraps of bone and hide that the disappointed vultures squabbled over. 'There are no prisoners and no second chances in my line of business.'

'Don't worry about me. As long as you can deliver the cash, I can deliver the services. So, tell me more of what you want.'

'If somebody needed to move things across the borders around these parts and wanted to avoid the roads and border checks how would you recommend they go about it?'

'Which border and how big is your package?'

'I'd need some flexibility on destinations and big, think truckloads big.'

'Hmm, that's not easy. I'm sure there are bush drivers who could get packages across for you no problem, but a truck-sized delivery. That's a challenge, man. A big challenge. Plenty of the smaller bush tracks won't support a truck. No, you've got yourself a problem there.'

'That's what I thought.'

'Why can't you just go to one of the smaller crossings and bribe the border guards? That's what some folk would do in this country.'

'So I've heard, but I need a belt and braces approach. I can't risk chancing upon an honest border guard or running into a spot check, you understand?'

'I sure do, man. Matter of fact, there's been a similar problem for somebody else recently.'

'I see, and how did that get fixed?'

Smuts looked back out of the window towards the beach. The carcass had been cleared now and the vultures who had missed out on scraps were taking off one by one with empty bellies and angry squawks.

'That sort of problem gets fixed with lots of money, and plenty of skills and knowhow. Those sorts of skills are valuable out here.'

'I'll bet,' said Sam.

'You've got to know the bush, man. Know how the land lies, know who to trust, who to pay, who to hide from.' He paused and looked at Sam with a pointed stare. 'Not that Smutsie hides from many.'

'So, what's the solution?'

'You'd need to keep way off the beaten track. If it's as big as you say, and maybe attracts attention, then there's no point in even trying to get it over a border crossing. You're going to need to go off-road.'

'You said bush tracks wouldn't support a big truck.'

'I did, and I didn't say I'd go by bush tracks either.'

'Well?' said Sam, he was becoming sick of the charade and wanted out of the situation as soon as possible. He could sense Helen's anger as she sat beside him playing the compliant personal assistant. She needed out too.

'Think man, no road, no bush track, what's left?'

'Look, I'm not the bush expert, I'm asking you. Now is there a way or have I wasted that goodwill payment I've just given you?'

'Alright man, alright. It's simple, you fly it out.'

Sam looked at him askance. 'Fly? It's not a bundle of newspapers I want to shift. A plane big enough to take my load will need a proper runway. Not some bush landing strip. Any airport is going to have security, customs, and the works.'

The tainted moustache parted to show yellow teeth again. 'You're spot on, man; except not for Henk Smuts. I've got a runway, tucked away in the middle of nowhere. Some mining company had great plans, thought it was on the Tanzanite mother lode. They built the infrastructure, a runway to fly in their kit and months later - Pop'—Smuts clapped his hands—'the surveyors had screwed up big time. Deposit was a dud, finished before they'd really got started. Place just abandoned.'

'I see,' said Sam. 'And it's yours to use?'

'Well, the locals have reclaimed the whole area. It's just bush, miles and miles and miles of it. Pastoralists, they won't let their land go a second time. And sure as hell, the Tanzanian Government doesn't want to be reminded of the flop.'

'I'm interested Mr Smuts, you might be able to help me. Where exactly is your runway?'

Smuts faced forward and fired up the engine. 'Now, man, it's been nice talking with you. I'm thinking we might work together, but first, I'll need to do a little more checking, a runway's a valuable commodity.'

Sam stayed calm. 'As you wish. But be under no illusions, you're not my only iron in the fire.'

'No problem, we all have to be careful. But I tell you, I've got a thing going with the local headman - big game, big guns, no questions. For you, it would be sweet, man. Come right down on to my runway in that beautiful little exec plane you've got sitting at Arusha. I'll sort your hunting - lion, buffalo, elephant, whatever you want. Then fly right back out again, man, perfect, we'll make a real team.'

'It all sounds good. But look, my assistant's looking off colour; I'd like to head back to the lodge now please. We can talk as we go.'

Helen nodded an acknowledgement.

Smuts pushed the accelerator and selected a course that offered the shortest route back to the only way in and out of the crater. 'No problem, man. We're on our way. You got to keep the little lady sweet, hey?'

'You're right, Mr Smuts, I have.' Sam leant forward again. 'But, for the avoidance of doubt, Mr Smuts, I don't play team games. If we go ahead, you will work for me, not with me, and so kindly drop the *man*. It's sir to my staff, understand?'

Smuts shrugged, flashed his yellows at Sam in the rear-view mirror and feigned calm acceptance, but he couldn't hide how his eyes burned with anger. 'No problem, sir it is.'

Helen turned to look out of the side window, smiled to herself, just a tiny bit of the anger she felt dissipating when she heard Smuts being pulled into line.

'Ha! That safari truck's still following us. Well, they got a real treat with the hyena kill at lunch, but they're wasting their time now, we're heading straight out. Some of these drivers aren't worth their lunch, much less their fee.'

• • •

Sam held the hotel room door open for Helen and followed her in; taking care to make sure the door was securely locked behind them. He walked past Helen and dropped their shoulder bag on the floor beside the occasional table. 'Well, that was interesting …'

Helen pushed him in the back, and as he turned to face her, she punched his arm, hard. 'Don't *interesting* me, Sam Cameron.' She punched his arm again. 'And don't ever do that to me again, right?'

'Whoa, hold on, we were just setting the scene, luring him in. He's that sort of man.'

'Set any scene you like, but see these?' Helen stretched her hands down below her shorts and gripped her thighs. 'These are not lures to get some sleazebag on board, right?' She punched Sam's arm again. 'Never. Now, fix me a drink please. I'm going to shower.' She disappeared into the bathroom. As the sound of water spraying emerged into the bedroom, Sam gave a resigned shrug and headed for the fridge to pour Helen's drink.

Chapter 23
WEDNESDAY 30TH OCTOBER - EVENING

Mauwled sat on the low wall that ran beside the driveway. Half in shadow, he waved his beer bottle in salute as Helen and Sam approached.

'Mauwled, good to see you,' said Helen, as she sat on the wall beside him. 'Why won't you come into the lodge for a drink?'

Sam handed him a fresh bottle of beer. Mauwled quickly finished off his original bottle and placed it at his feet. He clinked the replacement against Sam's bottle and Sam sat on the wall too.

'Thank you. The lodge doesn't like the drivers to come into the guest areas, so it's easier out here. Did you have a nice safari with Smuts?' Mauwled sounded sceptical.

'It was very useful,' said Sam.

'But we had to cut it short. You were right; he's not a nice man. There's stuff we need to ask you, Mauwled.'

'Sure, how can I help you?'

Helen fixed Mauwled's gaze. 'It's about your past, when you were off the rails. Sam's keen to understand what you used to do, it's important.'

'See, Mauwled, I'm trying to track down something that can't be driven across the border. Well, not officially.'

Mauwled's eyes widened and he half laughed in disbelief. 'Are you trying to smuggle, Sam?'

Sam gave a little grin. 'No, that's not my bag. Somebody's trying to smuggle something out of the country and I want to stop them.'

'I can't break any laws, Sam, if I do, I'll go straight to prison.'

Helen rested her hand on Mauwled's forearm for a moment. 'We know that Mauwled, don't worry. The thing is, one of Sam's friends has been snatched ...'

'By Smuts?'

'Well, we think by friends of his.'

'Smuts doesn't have friends. Only money and enemies.'

'I can understand that,' said Sam, 'but he told me he had a private runway, to fly things in or out without any questions. A proper runway, not a landing strip.'

'No there are no runways here. Not private anyway. There's the tourist strip for light planes to land.'

'No, that won't be it. The place I'm looking for has to be remote, abandoned, and built for big aircraft. Linked to a disused mine.'

Mauwled shook his head. 'Nothing like that here.'

Sam sat quiet for a minute, thinking carefully as they drank their beers.

'There's the illegal hunting, Sam,' said Helen.

'That's right, Mauwled, apparently he could arrange private hunting in the district around the runway.'

Mauwled shook his head again. 'No, Sam. Here at Ngorongoro, it's too protected for illegal hunting, same for the Serengeti and Tarangirie too. You need bush away from the national parks.'

'Is there much of that?'

Mauwled nodded and stretched his hands out. 'Plenty, but not here.'

'Hell, where can it be? You can't just hide a runway.'

'There's a lot of empty land, Sam,' said Mauwled with another quite solemn nod.

'What was that stuff he said they were trying to mine, could that be a clue?' said Helen.

'Tanzanite. It's a gemstone mineral that is found only in Tanzania,' said Sam. Even in the shadows, she could see the expression on his face lifting. 'It's found in very limited areas. I know Smuts said the mine struck out, but surely, it would have to be in one of the recognised prospecting areas. The company that built it would never have been able to raise its initial funding otherwise. Helen, I think you might just have cracked it. Mauwled, do you know about Tanzanite?'

'Yes, but it's not found around here.'

'Where is it found, is it far?'

'I know of some areas. Way over, south of Arusha. Deep in the bush, very lonely places.'

'Right, do you know the areas well?'

Reluctantly, Mauwled nodded. It was a time and place in his life he didn't want to revisit. 'There are some mines over there, but you can travel for days and not see one. I don't know them, but there is illegal hunting there for sure.' He looked down at the ground. 'I know that.'

'Okay, good. Now, Mauwled, think, did you ever see a runway for airplanes when you were there?'

After a long moment, Mauwled nodded, cautiously. 'Maybe. I didn't see it, but I remember some talk of it when I was there once. A rich man was coming in and my friend was to collect him and drive for him. I had thought he was making it up, to make me jealous - for the tips. I didn't get to do the fancy jobs. I did the long-distance ferrying. But I remember where, I think.'

'Brilliant, where exactly was all this happening?'

'Simanjiro District. It's wild land. I think it was near a place called Moypo.'

'What's there? Can we go there?'

'It's a long drive. I think more than a day, maybe.'

Sam stood, took a couple of steps from the little wall and turned to face Helen and Mauwled. 'I've got some phone calls to make. Mauwled, would you plan a route? We're in a hurry, but I don't want to risk a night drive; actually getting there is the most important thing. So, we'll need to break our journey overnight.'

'We could go through Tarangire, stop there in a lodge or campsite; you'd need to book though. Then travel on next morning. I think we could be in Simanjiro by the middle of the next day.'

'Okay, let's do it. Mauwled, can you recommend a lodge in Tarangire to Helen? Helen, would you contact Elaine? Have her book an overnight stop with the lodge; at least we will be maintaining our innocent tourist façade.

'Mauwled, we will want to get away before dawn. Can you get the Land Rover ready and pick us up from reception without causing a disruption?' Sam waited for Mauwled's response. He was mindful of the vehicle that had been following them. This seemed like a good moment to shake off their tail.

Chapter 24
THURSDAY 31ST OCTOBER - AM

The sun was just coming over the horizon when a silhouetted man ran across the drivers' compound beside the Ngorongoro lodge. He pushed open a dormitory door and shouted. It took the other three occupants only moments to jump up and hurry to the door.

All four men stepped out into the car park and looked around anxiously. Then their leader barked orders. One man sprinted for the lodge reception, another hurried to the crater's rim to peer down and check for any traffic descending into the crater. The third man opened up his vehicle and started doing the essential pre-drive checks that ensured vehicles didn't become stranded in the bush. Park Jae-In, the leader, went back into the cabin to prepare himself for what he felt was going to be a very big day.

News came quickly. First, the man who went to check the crater edge reported back. He could see a vehicle heading down towards the crater floor. It was Smuts'. There were no other vehicles on the way down.

A couple of minutes later, the other runner returned; Cameron and the woman had already checked out, they had left well before sunrise in their orange Land Rover, not with Smuts.

It was a big country; there would be time to catch up with Cameron. First though, Smuts was close, and Park knew it was important to find out what the two men had talked about the previous day.

• • •

Park Jae-In sat in the front passenger seat and berated his driver. From time to time, his angry shouts would spill over into violence and he would strike the driver on the side of the head or lean round and use the strap of a binocular case to slap the legs of the men standing behind him, their heads and shoulders protruding through the skylight.

To Park, it seemed that his boss Ro Soo-Ann had been right not to place too much trust in the South African. The previous evening, there had been no opportunity to get Smuts alone in the dormitories, and now he had slipped off ahead of them.

All morning, frustration had been building. His team had driven quickly down into the crater to question Smuts, but he had vanished. Now the sun was almost at its height, the heat was intolerable, and still, Smuts was missing. The crater was so large, it was almost impossible to find an individual vehicle.

Park's mind flicked back to the previous day. He thought of Smuts taking Cameron on that long drive around the crater floor. Why stop for lunch in that isolated spot? What had they talked about? Had Smuts betrayed them? What did he say? Had he told Cameron about Ro? Was it a double-cross? Park shouted out in fury and slapped his driver's head. 'Find him! Find Smuts now!'

This morning Cameron was gone. Given a head start, he could be anywhere by now. So, he had to focus on Smuts; his location was known. There were enough questions to put to him, and not least would be - where had Cameron gone? Park's problem now was Smuts had vanished too.

He shouted at his lookouts, whipped their legs again, then turned to bang his fist on the dashboard.

'Hell,' he shouted, 'where is he?'

The driver braced himself for another blow but just as they came over a little ridge in the rolling grasslands that covered this part of the crater, he shouted out in glee. Park looked in the direction his driver was pointing and saw Smuts' vehicle drawn into the shade of a solitary tree. Here, in the remotest, most isolated part of the crater floor, they had found him. They had their man.

A watercourse trailed down from the crater wall. Fed by the high-altitude microclimate at the top of the cone it kept a trickle of water flowing even in the driest of times. The stream passed behind Smuts' 4 x 4, rounded the solitary tree and spilled into the adjacent reed bed, which it sustained throughout the year. The dark green of the reed bed providing a cool sanctuary for its residents.

Park could see Smuts regaling his customers with some story or other. An older woman and, what was probably, her adult daughter, the two women were about to eat lunch while politely listening to their guide.

Park pointed at Smuts' vehicle and shouted an order. His driver executed the instruction to perfection, bringing his vehicle alongside Smuts' and turning his front end in before he stopped so the bonnets almost touched, forming a V-shaped space between the two vehicles.

Smuts looked across in surprise and was about to shout an insult at the careless driver when he noticed they were Korean. 'Hey, what's up? What brings you out here?'

Park did not answer, just maintained a blank stare as he made a hand signal to his guards to get out. They jumped down into the V-shaped space between the vehicles and pulled open the driver's door on Smuts' vehicle. Smuts began to shout an objection, then he reached down beside his seat for the rifle he kept there. His action was too late; he was already half out of the seat and falling towards the ground.

Smuts grunted as he hit the earth. 'What the hell are you doing, man?' he said. Then his voice changed into a furious snarl as a man's boot pressed down hard on the side of his face. He felt the boot turn and tilt as the heel was worked under his chin and pressed in against his windpipe. He fell silent.

In the rear of Smuts' vehicle, the two passengers were crying, holding onto each other in fear. They gasped as the door was pulled open then shrank back in fear.

Park appeared at the open door. 'Silence!' He thrust his pistol towards the women. 'Silence now or you die.' Silence fell immediately. He smiled. 'Good. Now listen carefully, women. You are nothing to me. Live or die, it doesn't matter. Understand?'

Two very frightened ladies nodded back at him.

'Women, give me your phones now. Give me your water bottles.' He thrust his hand out and the women scrabbled to comply.

Park put the phones in his pocket and emptied the water bottles over the parched earth. Then he stepped over the prostrate Smuts to climb into the driver's seat. There he took the ignition keys then rummaged around, found Smuts' phone and pocketed it. He bent down to gather up the rifle, looking at it approvingly. Pulling open the bolt, he saw the magazine was full. Finally, he got out and, standing by the open driver's door, raised the rifle and fired a single shot. The women screamed again; he turned cold eyes on them and they fell silent. The radio fitted to Smuts' dashboard seemed wrecked. To be sure, he grabbed the microphone tethered on its coiled lead and ripped it out.

Park gave an order and watched as his men hoisted Smuts to his feet and pushed him into the back of their 4 x 4 where he was held at gunpoint.

Pushing the doors to Smuts' vehicle shut again, Park raised the rifle. The women ducked down in terror as he shot out the side windows, shattering them. He put shots through the front and rear screens too then stepped back as his second man hurried to smash the screens in, clearing all the frames.

Park leant in through the open window frame. 'Women, be quiet.' The frightened crying subsided, and the women watched in silent and growing terror as Park got into his 4 x 4 and it drove off, leaving them alone in the bush.

Chapter 25
THURSDAY 31ST OCTOBER - PM

As they bounced along the dirt track, Smuts remained firmly held between the two guards on the rear passenger seat. He had undergone a thorough interrogation. His face was bloodied but his confidence had not wavered.

'I'm telling you, man, he was just a safari customer, some high roller from the UK. Nothing more. Now come on, I'm on your side, for God's sake.'

Park wiped blood from his skinned knuckles, examined the damaged skin carefully, annoyed to see little beads of his own blood seeping out. He should have worn gloves.

'So you keep saying, but Mr Ro will be concerned. I was watching you, why did I see Cameron give you this money? It's a lot. You must have given him something in return.' Park allowed Smuts' wad of cash to flick through his fingers.

'No, I'm telling you, it was a deposit for some big game hunting I'm going to arrange for him. That's all.'

'We are very anxious that you have not betrayed our situation.'

'Why would I do that? Ro's paying me a stack of money to get you guys out of Tanzania. I wouldn't risk that, would I?'

'Mr Ro doesn't know what you'd risk for money. He will want to know exactly what you told Cameron.'

'I've told you what was agreed. Now let's call it quits, hey? I've still got those tourists to take out of the crater.'

The vehicle came to a halt and Smuts looked out of the window. Puzzled.

'Ah, good, we've arrived,' said Park. He barked an order to the driver who reached under his seat and produced a machete.

Smuts flinched; very quickly, concern was turning to fear.

'What's this man? Steady on now ...' his words trailed off into relieved silence when the driver hurried away. Smuts looked again at the location. They were on the lakeside beach where he had stopped with Cameron the day before. It was quiet here, it always was. 'Why are we here?'

'Because I don't think you've told me everything, and I want you to do it now. In fact, I'm going to make you. You had your chance.' The sound of chopping coming from a thicket of young trees distracted Smuts; he craned his neck to see what the driver was doing.

'Look, get Ro on the phone. You've gone right overboard, let him decide.'

'You know I can't do that. We are observing broadcast and telephone silence. No broadcast messages. You have never been able to call Ro Su-Ann; have always spoken face-to-face. The British spies will be listening for us from their GCHQ. No, never. They must not locate us! No phones!' Park's voice rose to a shout of indignant fury then lapsed into silence. His hand reached back to slap across Smuts' face.

Smuts knew this was as bad as it gets. He glanced around, eyed the nearest thicket of undergrowth. If he could fight his way out of the vehicle, shake them off and make it there, he'd be able to use his bushcraft skills. That would give him an edge, weapons or not. The idea withered as the driver emerged from the thicket, cutting off his escape route. He wondered what the driver was carrying. As the man got nearer, Smuts saw he carried the trunks of half a dozen young saplings that had taken advantage of the thicket's protection to gain a little height on the wildlife whose steady grazing constrained the growth of most trees and bushes.

'Ah, good, he's back. Now, Smuts, I think it's time you shared with me properly.'

'What's going on? What are those poles for?'

Park did not bother answering; he smiled a cold little smile and watched through the window as his driver set to work. Smuts watched too.

The driver selected three of the poles, tested and flexed them. Content, he crossed to the vehicle and got a ball of strong twine from the survival box. Using a length of the twine, he bound the three pole ends together, forming a tripod that might have served as a rudimentary tent frame. Spreading the free ends apart, he pressed them into the ground, and then applied his weight to each in turn, ensuring they were secure.

'There's no need for all this, man. I can keep you in the loop, tell you everything.' There was clear pleading in Smuts' voice. He didn't know what was planned but knew it involved him, and it didn't look good. Park ignored him, concentrating only on his driver's construction activity.

The driver took the three remaining poles and, one by one, tied them as supporting cross struts, from one leg to the next, locking the tripod frame. The man stood back and admired his work. The apex of the frame met at around twelve feet off the ground. The legs buried into the earth were equidistant apart. It was a solid construction. He turned and, with a smile, bowed his head very slightly to Park.

A barked order from Park had Smuts hustled out onto the ground.

'What the hell?' Smuts, now very frightened, protested and struggled as his wrists were tied together in front of him.

The tone in his voice rose higher when the two guards produced knives and swiftly cut away his clothes. 'No, no, please stop.'

From a few paces' distance, Park watched impassively. For a moment, the struggle became fiercer as they pulled Smuts to his feet. When he realised he could not escape, Smuts stilled. The driver stepped forward with thicker rope he had taken from the vehicle.

'What are you going to do, Park? Hang me?' Knowing it was over for him gave Smuts a little confidence, things couldn't get any worse.

'In a manner of speaking, yes,' said Park.

His driver stepped up and secured one end of the rope around Smuts' wrists. He yanked the other and the guards manhandled Smuts beneath the tripod frame. The driver threw the rope's free end up and over the frame's apex; he caught the falling end and began to pull. Smuts resisted but was distracted by a heavy blow in the midriff. As he gasped, the driver jerked the rope and Smuts' bound hands shot up. Quickly, the two guards lifted Smuts up off the ground and the driver pulled again, taking in the slack. Then he tied off the rope on one of the supporting cross struts, leaving Smuts dangling naked, his feet no more than a foot off the ground.

One of the guards took hold of Smuts' right leg, dragged it out to one of the tripod uprights where the driver bound the leg tight to the pole. The four men gathered in front of Smuts. His fear was visible, and they laughed while the driver accepted congratulatory claps on the back from the two guards.

'Please, I beg you, stop this. Anything you want, I promise …'

'We already have what we want.' Park took a step towards Smuts. 'You gave us our exit route, and we appreciate that. Mr Ro is very pleased with the runway. You should know a cargo plane has been organised, it will reach

Burundi on Friday evening and fly into Simanjiro the next morning to collect Mr Ro and our cargo. You delivered, Mr Smuts. You have our thanks.'

'So why this? What's this all for?' Smuts twisted his head up, looking at his hands bound tight above his head. 'You have what you wanted, let me go.'

'Unfortunately, you broke the rules. You spoke with Cameron and we're still not sure what you said. That's dangerous for us.'

'I've told you, I've told you. He's a big-shot businessman who wanted some hunting arrangements. I didn't know his name was Cameron, or anything else. All I agreed was that I'd arrange it for him. There's nothing for Ro to worry about.'

'Mr Ro to you - show respect to your betters. And Cameron is not a businessman. He's British; he's come across the border from Kenya. He's here, and he's looking for our cargo. Mr Ro is concerned about Cameron.'

Smuts dropped his head. 'Oh hell.'

'Yes, oh hell! I need to know exactly what you told Cameron.' Taking another pace forward, Park let his hand gently caress one of the tripod poles. 'You are going to die today Smuts. The only question is how. You can choose, easy or hard.' Park smiled, he could see tears of fear running down Smuts' face, hear a little moan of fear. He stood quietly for a minute listening.

'This framework is my driver's speciality. Let me tell you. Normally he would light a little fire beneath your free leg. The foot would get hot and you'd struggle to keep it from the flame. The stronger you are the longer you can keep it away. Keeping your free foot away from the flames, lets the heat rise up and reach your manhood. Very painful.' He stepped within the frame and cupped Smuts' genitals in his hand, squeezed and jerked, watching Smuts convulse in pain, bringing a murmured ripple of approval from his men.

Park stepped back and allowed Smuts a moment to compose himself. 'I tell you, in the end you would choose to let your foot burn. But it's only a little fire. It won't be quick. Once the flames kill the nerves in your foot, you won't feel anything there, but you will smell your own flesh as it roasts off the bone. Then you'll feel the heat move up your leg and the pains grow again and will slowly keep spreading up and up. And then, no matter what you do, your manhood burns. You will scream and cry and beg, and still it will burn.

'For a strong man like you, I've seen my driver make that process last an hour, more. Once it reaches your belly you'll die, but by then that is what you will want more than anything before in your life.'

Smuts lost control of his bladder and the driver spotted it. Pointing and shouting, the guards joined him in applauding Smuts' fear.

'God, just shoot me, man. Have a heart.'

'But I haven't finished. I could shoot you, if I was certain you'd told me everything, but I'm not. So today my driver has a different plan for you. Something new.'

Smuts raised his head eagerly. 'Yes, what? I'll do anything, just say the word.'

Park smiled and pointed up. Smuts looked into the sky and baulked, turning away quickly. High in the sky were several black dots, describing a slow circle around the beach. Vultures: they had spotted the commotion. In the bush, commotion means death, and they were circling, waiting for their share of any leftovers.

'Please don't do this. I'm yours, forever, anything you want, any damned thing.'

'I can make it quick,' Park waved his pistol. 'Or you can take the slow route. I just need to know what you told Cameron.'

'I've told you, told you everything.' Smuts was shaking his head, crying and forcing his words out between sobs. 'Please, just end it. I … I—'

'Yes, you what? Last chance, Smuts.'

Smuts jerked his head up. 'I did tell him something else …' Smuts let his head drop again. 'I told him there was a runway, one he could fly into, when he came for a private hunting party.'

'Where? Where did you say it was?'

'I didn't. I promise, I didn't need to. Why would I? He didn't need to know the details. Now you know everything. Please, just shoot me. Please!'

Park nodded. He accepted Smuts had nothing left to tell. Glancing along the beach behind Smuts, he saw the clan of hyenas had come from a thicket where they had been sheltering from the sun. The sounds of distress interested them, they hovered perhaps a hundred paces away, weighing up the situation.

Park pointed to the clan and his men greeted its appearance with excited murmurs of anticipation.

'What is it? What's there?' Smuts' voice took on a whole new level of fear. 'Tell me, what is it?' He tried to turn but couldn't. He looked at the guards and fear coursed through him as they began to yip, yip. He knew exactly what was there.

Park and his team retreated to the vehicle, followed all the way by Smuts' cries, begging them to end it. Park blanked him. Once safely on board, the driver manoeuvred them closer to Smuts and came to a halt. The occupants opened their windows for a better look, and the driver cut the engine. They were close now, within spitting distance, as proven by one of the guards. Park leant out of the window with his pistol and pointed it at Smuts.

'Oh, thank you. Thank you. Do it now. God bless you,' Smuts was almost euphoric at the sight of the pistol.

Park took careful aim and fired. The report startled the hyenas who had been edging closer. They darted away along the beach; their alarmed yipping still filled the air after the sound of gunfire had subsided.

'Damn you! Damn you to hell, Park ...' Smuts' words faded into a groan as he struggled to come to terms with his fate. His tied leg was now dripping blood from a calf wound.

One of the guards opened a cool box and passed out bottles of cold beer, and the men sat back to watch the show. Thick cigarette smoke billowed through the windows as they lit up their smokes.

Smuts glared at Park, and then his focus shifted to his immediate environment. In the still air of the afternoon, he could hear something behind him. He tried to turn, to see but could not turn far enough. Then the pain that was coursing up his leg from the calf wound suddenly diminished, his mind distracted by a peculiar bristling sensation he felt sweep over the back of his bound ankle.

He felt warm breath stroke his calf and something rough and wet ran across his skin, removing the blood that had already started to congeal on his leg. Absolute fear had him attempting to turn again, and this time, he twisted just far enough to see a big hyena jump back, startled at his movement. A few paces off, it stopped and gave its yipping laugh as it reappraised the situation. His heart sank when human bio-mechanics compelled his head to return to its starting position, and he lost sight of the beast.

Inside Park's vehicle, the driver and guards were excitedly exchanging bets. What part of the body would be bitten first? Would Smuts put up a fight? How long would it last? Enthralled, the men watched carefully as another round of beers was distributed.

Smuts lifted his head and looked towards Park in a final desperate appeal then he let his eyes drop again. It was clear

Park would not relent; he was filming the event on his phone - fulsome evidence for Ro of Smuts' punishment.

Smuts wondered where the hyena had got to, knew he didn't have long. Then a shadow crossed his head and a rustle sounded above him. He looked up to see the first vulture had landed and decided to get a head start on the hyenas by hopping up onto the tripod. It was now perched on the apex, its long neck arched out and down projecting its bald head and cruel beak to assess the food. A second vulture fluttered up on to one of the tripod's cross-supports, close to Smuts' tied ankle. For some moments, the air was filled with the deep throaty hiss and cackle of the vultures as they appraised each other. The noise ended in a sudden flurry of retreating feathers when the hyenas returned.

The big female worked her way round the tripod and was followed by two youngsters. The rest of the family completed the encirclement from the other direction. Some emitted their laughing yips. The big female stayed silent until finally baying out her identity call as she came to a halt, square in front of Smuts.

He felt a tugging on his hanging leg and looked down to see one of the youngsters was nuzzling his foot. Instinctively he kicked out and the youngster gave a cry and scurried away behind its mother. She paced forward and Smuts knew what was coming. Throat or groin? It couldn't reach his throat. He looked once more towards the vehicle, a final plea for some release. The occupants had fallen silent, fascinated; along with the rest of the hyena pack they watched, waited.

The big female gave her call again and closed in. Smuts felt her breath hard in his groin. Felt her enormous head twist for position, sensed the mouth open and then the firm contact as she took full advantage of her trapped prey to position her teeth for maximum affect. Smuts cringed up and back. The female moved a little forward, repositioning her open mouth. Then gravity took effect and returned Smuts' body to its starting point, so pressing his groin more firmly into the grateful beast's gaping mouth. For just a moment, all along the beach, only Smuts' frightened wail of anticipation could be heard.

Then she bit. Accompanied by a throaty growl her jaws enclosed Smuts' groin. The lower jaw teeth reached far between his legs to sink into a buttock, the upper jaw teeth cutting into his lower belly. The bite clamped hard and her shoulders started to shake as she backed away ripping at Smuts' groin. Smuts let out a fearful cry as the hyena reversed, tearing the flesh from his body, her little ones pressing and nuzzling at her mouth hoping to share in the feast. The pack closed in, and bit and snapped at Smuts' legs and belly.

Park's vehicle echoed with cheers and cries of excitement as bets were won and lost, and he finally switched off the camera phone. He turned with a big grin towards his team. They were grinning back when suddenly one of the guards pointed him back to the tripod.

The boldest of the vultures had realised Smuts' head was beyond the hyenas' reach and hopped back to the tripod apex from where its long neck carried the unforgiving butcher's beak down and into line with Smuts' face. The hyena bites below were tearing the life from his body; he had no capacity to resist the vulture. He just closed his eyes and waited for the inevitable strike. It came, accompanied by renewed cheering from the men in the vehicle.

Park's men finished their beers then he gave a brief order. Break-time over, the men returned to a more balanced demeanour, bets were settled, and the driver got the vehicle going. He retraced their route, heading back to Smuts' vehicle and the women.

• • •

An hour had passed since Mauwled had steered the orange Land Rover off the main road and onto a dusty track. Since then, it had been heavy going along the deeply rutted route. Now, he was guiding it carefully up a gentle slope between thorn trees and a scattering of bushes. The land seemed empty of animals. All that could, were lying low, sheltering from the unforgiving mid-afternoon heat. Helen took a mouthful of water from her bottle and returned her gaze to the passing countryside. The land had levelled out into a little ridge that ran at right angles to the track. About thirty paces ahead the track ended, and the land fell away in a steep escarpment, dropping almost sheer to a small river that was not much more than a trickle while the land waited for the rains.

'We're here,' said Mauwled, pointing along the ridge to their left. A little way along was a welcome site and Helen let out a cheer, Sam picked it up and Mauwled joined in. Ridge Top Lodge was exactly what they needed - a safe place to stay the night ready for an early start next morning in their push towards Simanjiro District.

• • •

Park stared straight ahead while nodding an acknowledgement to the guard who had leant forward between the driver and front passenger seats. The man's finger pointed to Smuts' abandoned vehicle. They were back where it had all started; Park wondered what they would find.

As they approached, he looked for the two women. They were still sat in the back seat where he had left them. He witnessed their initial joy at the approach of a vehicle, saw it turn to despair when they recognised it was his.

Park's driver gave a long blast on the horn. It shocked in the vicinity but was quickly lost in the vastness of the crater.

'Goodbye, women. Night is coming!' Park laughed. He knew that, at this time in the afternoon, there was no prospect of rescue. The few, if any, safari trucks that ventured to this remote corner, so favoured by Smuts, would be long gone. By lunchtime, they would have begun working their way steadily towards the crater's distant exit track. He shouted an order and the 4 x 4 started to pull away to a series of horn blasts and the taunting cheers of his men.

The noise had disturbed the nearby reed bed residents. Now, sandy gold coloured fur worked itself imperceptibly to the edge of the green. Yellow eyes watched Park's vehicle retire up the slope. In the ensuing quiet, attentive ears focused on the renewed distress and crying from across the clearing. Sensitive noses twitched in response to the scent of fear drifting on the air.

Chapter 26
THURSDAY 31ˢᵗ OCTOBER - EVENING

Helen and Sam sat in easy chairs, carefully positioned on their private veranda to provide the best of views. As the sun dropped low in the sky, they had a perfect sightline over the ridge and down the steeply sloping flank, across the shrunken little river and out over the level stretch of plain beyond. The plain was dotted with scrubby bushes, stands of broad-topped acacia trees, and the occasional baobab - dark, solid and heavyset, their leafless boughs stretching up into the sky like overstated caricatures of ghoulish Halloween witches' trees.

Enthralled, they watched as the whole landscape appeared to shift. Two or three elephant herds were moving in close proximity, all eager to get to what little water still trickled along the riverbed. Sixty or more animals moved in unison through the landscape - great matriarchs, heavily pregnant females, teenagers and youngsters. Unconcerned babies would appear from behind bushes, darting here and there, only to vanish from sight behind the next, their location always signposted by the looming presence of protective mothers and aunts.

Helen leant forward, tilted her sunhat back and pulled off her sunglasses.

'What's next, Sam?' she said.

'We move out first thing in the morning. I'd much rather have pushed on through the night, but the bush roads are just too dangerous after dark. Easy to get lost, easy target for robbers - and we might just run into some of them.' He pointed towards the elephants.

'Hmm, that would be more than scary.'

'I've checked my map, there's no sign of a runway in the area that Mauwled's highlighted. It's just bush, endless bush.'

'Why isn't it on the map?'

'Mauwled's not sure. But he is sure there's a runway and he believes a support building, a warehouse or some such. Some of this bush activity is just so haphazard; it might just be the mining company didn't bother telling the cartographers about the development.'

'Or it's not there.'

'That's an eventuality I'd rather not think about just now.'

'Have you tried Google Earth?'

'I tried with the lodge's computer last night, after you'd gone to bed. No joy, I'm afraid. There is simply too much empty land to check - a million hectares, more, and the image scale available lacks the magnification on offer in Europe and the States.'

'So, we're counting on Mauwled.'

'Oh, I've set a plan B in motion, but I'm not sure how we can implement it in the time available. If Mauwled's got the wrong spot we could still be a day or two's travel away from Bob, wherever he is. I called Rupert last night and got him to start looking for the runway too.'

'Can't they get a satellite to look and just tell you where it is?'

'Well, I hope so that's my plan B, but it seems there's a bit of a resource conflict blown up. Rupert seems to think

Tracy is having some problems calling in the additional resources she needs, and there's no way he'll have any resources to speak of available to him - anything he wants will have to go through a committee.

'I'm guessing, once the first flush of reaction to the theft of ACE passed, there will have been a political argument over who pays the eventual bill for this mess. The British politicians are hopeless at stepping up quickly. This is a British problem, but if the politicians can shift any part of the recovery bill by stalling or passing costs elsewhere, they'll try. Never mind the consequences of delay in the meantime for people on the ground.'

'That's an awful attitude to have.'

'That's a nice way of describing it. Rupert expects it will all be sorted quickly. But budget holders only want to spend according to guidelines and this is a case sure to be beyond any guidelines.'

'What'll happen?'

'They'll play poker eyes for a while, the Americans will sit tight on their satellite archive until the British fold and agree to pay their fair share - then both countries will pile in and do their bit to resolve the problem. I'm just hoping it won't be too late. We've lost people in the past because of penny-pinching.'

'How is that a way to protect a country?'

'Hmm. Anyway, that's out of our hands. I'm backing Mauwled right now. He's what we've got here and now. If Smuts' runway exists, there will be satellite photos of it somewhere. In the meantime, let's hope Mauwled's right - that's our best, fastest option.'

Helen waved beyond Sam and called out to Mauwled who had just emerged from his lodge tent. 'Mauwled, we're over here. Come and join us for a drink. Grab a chair and bring it over.'

Mauwled waved an acknowledgement.

'I'll go and get you a beer,' said Helen, standing. 'Do you want another, Sam?'

'I'm fine, thanks.'

Before Helen could move, there was the sound of an elephant trumpeting, just once, then silence. She glanced across the flat plain, which was suddenly still. The elephants had stopped. Another trumpet sounded, longer this time, more strident. She couldn't quite work out where the sound had come from.

'Someone's not happy,' said Mauwled, pointing towards the big adult female nearest the river. She was standing square to something that none of them could make out from up on the ridge. Ears out wide, trunk up and a further trumpet blast rang out; then the female began to retrace her steps, backing away from the water. Other leading females watching her took up the sound; shrieked alarm calls began to sound throughout the herds. Then the bush burst into life as the elephants turned and ran away from the water as one. Dust clouds kicked up across the plain and the sound of scores of pounding feet reached across the river and up the rise to meet them.

'What caused that?' said Helen staring intently, hands on hips. 'Wow!'

The elephant herds continued their retreat as Sam and Mauwled stood beside her to watch.

'Maybe lions at the water. Maybe nothing. Who knows? Elephants do as they choose,' said Mauwled. He shrugged and smiled at the same time.

Helen laughed. 'I wouldn't try to stop them for sure. Now, a beer for you.'

Chapter 27
FRIDAY 1ST NOVEMBER - AM

They had risen early, eaten breakfast and were driving away from Ridge Top Lodge just as the sun was coming up.

After an hour's driving, they moved out of the reserve and joined with a transit road that Sam was reluctant to credit with the name 'highway'. Mauwled headed in a south-easterly direction, and as the road deteriorated into a rutted track, the landscape quickly adopted a familiar pattern. From time to time, the vast expanse of bush would suddenly be broken by a fencing line that separated the wild rangelands from great cultivated fields; today just tracts of barren earth, cleared of bush by fire and bulldozer then ploughed and, Sam assumed, seeded. Now, as with everything else, just waiting for the rains. No sooner did the fields come into view then they were left behind, nature and the bush closing all around them again.

'Why are some of the field fences broken? Is it elephants?' said Helen.

'Well, I suppose it might be. But I think some of the people here feel cheated. This is the land they need for their cattle, and little by little, it's being fenced in,' said Sam.

'That's not fair.'

'No, it's not.'

Mauwled explained that much of the bushland here was home to the Maasai pastoralists - people who lived semi-nomadic existences, moving their cattle through the bush in a traditional seasonal pattern as they followed the available pasture and water. Their home was the bushland that their families had used and protected for generations. Now, sometimes, as the seasons changed, and they returned to their bomas they might find some of their family's ancestral land had been taken for farming.

Occasionally, the travelling trio would get a fleeting glance of a boma set back from the track - the traditional homesteads comprising of a mixed cluster of rectangular and round huts, their thick wicker walls coated with dung. Each roof was formed using a framework of branches over which were fixed thick bundles of dried grasses, tightly packed to exclude rainwater. Frequently, the huts were contained between two concentric circles of thorn tree bushes, reinforced with more cut boughs, woven into high impenetrable fences to keep out predators. The inner circles were empty by day but, at night, served as a corral in which to pen the livestock safely.

Sam leant forward between the driver and passenger seats. He thrust out his arm and waved a map of Tanzania in Mauwled's direction.

'I've given up looking for the runway, Mauwled. I'm going to have to rely on your local knowledge; there is just no sign of anything like it in the Simanjiro District.'

'Probably, once the mine company went bust, there was nobody to report the runway was ever built.'

'Well, wherever it is, it's well hidden.'

The morning continued in a never-ending round of rocking and bumping as the Land Rover slowly worked its way along the dirt road, jockeying from one side to the other in a bid to pick out the least rutted route. Eventually, the land started to rise in a gentle incline that continued unbroken to the horizon. The sun had climbed high in the sky and it beat down incessantly; in spite of the air conditioning, it was hot, sticky and dusty inside the Land Rover. It was exhausting enough as a passenger, and Sam recognised the effort Mauwled was making as the driver.

Just before midday, they reached the top of the escarpment and Mauwled pulled in to the side. 'Here's a good view for you,' he said, opening his door and climbing out. He stretched and groaned even as he beckoned them out.

Helen and Sam joined him. Nothing moved in the simmering midday heat.

Helen looked forward, towards their destination, and caught her breath. Immediately ahead, the road dropped away and started a precarious zigzag, working its way down the face of the escarpment. She couldn't gauge how far it dropped - hundreds of feet, maybe much more - the heat-driven rippling in the air made focusing difficult.

Beyond, the bushlands stretched out into the distance. Perhaps five miles off, she could see a break in the bush where a vast flat pan imposed itself, a clearing devoid of any plant growth; it appeared a little over a mile wide and she couldn't guess how long - more than five, perhaps nearer ten miles in length. The far side of the pan was tightly fringed with taller trees and bush, and even from here, she could see they were greener than the surrounds - a riverbank.

Beyond the line of green trees, the colour faded back to browns as the dry bush reasserted itself, running away unchanging into the far distance until it merged into the smudge of a black line of hills that defined what she took to be the other side of the valley.

'Beautiful,' said Helen. 'Beautiful and very lonely.' From their vantage point she could see nothing was moving, anywhere.

Sam put an arm round her shoulder; she leant into him a little. 'It's hard to imagine such empty places still exist in the world,' he said.

Mauwled stuck out his arm, pointing to beyond the furthest end of the flat pan. 'Moypo is over there,' he said. 'We should go.'

Sam switched on the satellite phone. There was a message from Rupert - confirmation that Mauwled's information about a runway was right. They were heading in the right direction. And news of an abandoned flatbed like the one locals had seen near Nanyuki on the day of the abduction. Sam punched the air in delight.

'So we're on the right track then?' said Helen.

'I'm sure of it.'

'What's so special about the flatbed truck?'

'Apparently the ACE vehicle has a very distinctive shape. A flatbed would be great for moving the ACE quickly and discreetly. Cover it with a tarpaulin and nobody would ever guess what's under - untraceable.'

'But why abandon it?'

'ACE is a modified Land Rover, excellent for rough terrain. The flatbed probably dropped it off before the Kenyan border post, let it run through the bush with some other 4 x 4s and planned to collect it again further south in Tanzania before making a dash for Burundi. Once the Tanzanian authorities closed their borders Ro had to change his plan - stay out of sight in the bush. From that moment on the flatbed was useless to him.'

'We're really going to catch them?'

'Maybe, whether we get there in time will depend what flight arrangements Ro has made so we need to keep going while we can.'

Chapter 28
FRIDAY 1ST NOVEMBER - PM

The drive down the side of the escarpment had taken well over an hour as the Land Rover wove back and forth following the line of the track. Mauwled didn't speak. This was a drive that demanded complete concentration. Finally, they reached the bottom, he visibly relaxed as the ground levelled out and he pushed on, slow and steady, the only way to be sure of not breaking the suspension or an axle on the rough bush track.

The winding track they followed through the bush was sunk half a man's height below ground level, having been hollowed out by countless journeys to and fro across the soft-packed sandy earth that dominated here. It gave a sense of the bush closing in on them, limiting their horizons to just a strip of vivid blue sky.

Suddenly, the bush cleared and the heavily rutted track they were following split into various separate routes, dispersing in a dozen different directions across the flat pan that Helen had admired from the top of the escarpment. One by one, the individual tracks faded to nothing, each disappearing into the emptiness of the pan. Mauwled drove a short way out onto the pan and stopped.

Now they were on the pan, Helen could see it was not pure white. An underlying light sandy colour was coated in a greyish surface layer of what she thought might be salts. Where the powdery surface had been broken by previous tyre tracks, the disruption was superficial. Beneath was a hard-packed layer that gave nothing to passing vehicles. Looking across the pan, she could now clearly see to the far side where the river's course was marked with a line of verdant trees and bush.

Mauwled pointed along the length of the pan. 'We're going that way.'

Viewed from ground level the far end vanished into a flat sameness. It seemed the pan had no end. 'How long is it?'

'More than ten miles. You want to drive a bit?' he looked at her with a grin. 'It's fun.'

Helen let her eyes scan the pan. It really was flat, empty, a surface unbroken other than by an occasional stunted tuft of some tough grass. In the distance a dust devil spiralled up from nothing. It filled and moved across the pan, leaving a trail of dust behind it. Then, just as suddenly as it appeared, it faded down and out.

'What formed all this?' she said.

'It's the flood plain. The river bursts its banks upstream over there and washes out. Normally twice every year, so it's kept clear and flat and baked dry by the sun. Leaving a crust of silt and salts - nothing gets a chance to grow. Drive. It's safe; go as fast as you want.'

'Okay, I will,' said Helen. The chance to drive like a madwoman, ignoring every rule in the book, no roads, no restrictions, and knowing nobody would get hurt, was just too tempting.

Helen started off slowly, making sure she had full control then she opened up, pushing the Land Rover faster and faster across the smooth and unbroken surface of the pan. She gave a whoop of pleasure and gunned it still harder.

'You're throwing up a real dust storm behind us,' said Sam as he peered out of the back window.

'I can't see it.'

'Look in your mirror.'

Helen looked in the rear-view mirror and could see nothing but grey. Glancing to either side, the pan was flat and clear and topped by the bright blue sky right across to its distant edges. 'I can't see a thing behind.'

'Do a loop,' said Mauwled, laughing. 'A big loop, and maybe a little slower?'

Helen looked at him and smiled enthusiastically. She glanced over her shoulder towards Sam, 'Hold on to your hat. Here we go!' She turned the wheel just a little and the Land Rover veered slightly off to the right, describing an enormous circle. As the turn progressed, Helen continued to glance through her side window. At first there was nothing to see but as the turn continued she spotted the dust cloud, rising and billowing to hang in the still air, hovering above the track of their journey and stretching back into the distance, marking the exact course they had followed.

Helen whooped again and laughed out loud. Sam and Mauwled joined in. As the turn continued, Helen realised they would cut across their own track and run through the dust cloud. She glanced at Mauwled, raised a questioning eyebrow.

He nodded, smiled again, and with a shrug pointed towards the looming dust cloud. 'Go for it. But make sure your window is shut tight.'

She kept the slight turn on the wheel and moments later they plunged into the wall of dust and visibility vanished. No phased loss, no gradation, just plunged into greyness. Mauwled had leaned over and switched off the ventilation just before they reached the dust cloud, which helped to keep out most, but not all, of the dust.

For a moment, Helen's foot waivered on the accelerator - it was disconcerting to have no visual cues.

'Keep going,' said Sam, from the rear seat. 'You're doing great.'

She restored pressure on the pedal, and suddenly, they burst out of the dust cloud and into bright sunshine. Helen kept the turn on the wheel a little longer, bringing them back onto their original track. 'Now that was fun,' she said. 'Again?'

'I think we'd better keep going now, we are running against the clock,' said Sam. He cracked open a small bottle of water and passed it forward over Helen's shoulder. 'Here, take a drink.'

She took the bottle and settled into the first period of smooth driving they had experienced in quite a while.

• • •

Park stood beside his vehicle, binoculars in hand. He looked down the escarpment into the valley. He cursed to himself; in the distance, out on the flat pan, he could see a dust cloud. It stretched far off. Like the vapour trail of a jet plane, it reached out from a moving needle point source, expanding to mark its route.

He brought his binoculars up and focused on the distant vehicle. It was too far away to make out details. But one thing he could be sure of, it was orange in colour.

Another movement caught his eye as he lowered his binoculars and he quickly brought them back up to check it out. Far below, another vehicle had just emerged from the bush track onto the pan. He watched its progress for a few moments before turning towards his vehicle and ordering the long drive down to begin.

• • •

As they approached the far end of the pan, Mauwled had got behind the wheel again and manoeuvred the Land Rover towards an almost imperceptible track that fed from the pan back into the bush line. While driving the length of the pan, they had also traversed it from side to side. They were much nearer the river now.

'How much longer now, Mauwled?' said Sam, when they were once again driving through the bush. At this end of the pan, the track was rutted though much less sunken than the track they had followed leading in. This was a yet quieter place with very little traffic.

'Not far … five, ten minutes maybe.'

'How would you approach this?' said Sam, keen to push on but mindful that breaching any local protocols would not be helpful. In his experience, pretty well throughout Africa no matter what you were proposing, it always paid to have the local chief or headman on board. Without their blessing, no locals were going to raise a hand to help.

'We should go straight to the village to meet the local chief. We won't ever make it to the runway without his say so.'

'Right, and what's this man like?'

'I haven't seen him for a couple of years, more. Not since I stopped driving for the smuggling gangs. But we got on fine then.'

'Is he involved in the smuggling?' said Helen.

'No, no. But nothing can happen in his area without his blessing. He's okay, don't worry.'

Moments later Sam gave a sudden cry of surprise. 'What's that Mauwled? Over on the left.'

Mauwled swung off the track, worked his way between some clumps of bush before coming to a halt. They were in a manmade clearing and the bush was obviously kept at bay by regular cutting. In the middle of the clearing was what had caught Sam's attention. A building. A single-storey modern building with concrete foundations, whitewashed breeze-block walls, and a tiled roof that hung out over the front by eight or nine feet to provide the cover for a concrete-based veranda.

'What is this?' said Sam, opening the Land Rover door to go get a better look.

Mauwled beckoned him back. 'Let's visit the chief first, Sam.'

Sam hesitated for a moment then nodded, getting back into the vehicle. 'I thought there was nothing here.'

'It's an old health clinic for the peoples of the area. It was closed. It's always been closed as long as I've known it.' Mauwled made a chopping sign with his hand. 'Government cuts, everything was closed. Now it's a community centre and used for visitors to stay.'

'What visitors?'

'NGO workers mostly, but not very often. The local people sometimes use it when they need to gather.' He got the Land Rover moving again, edged back onto the track and continued along the way.

The bush began to thin perceptibly. Then, after a hundred yards or so, it gave way completely to a clearing of dry and dusty earth that was held in place only by grasses, mostly grazed down to a rough stubble. The track continued in an arc as it crossed the clearing, skirting round a big boma in the centre before continuing on and disappearing back into the bush on the far side.

Twenty paces from the boma, Mauwled stopped the Land Rover. They all looked ahead. They were being watched by a group of people standing at an opening in the outer ring of thorn-bush fencing.

It was the biggest boma they had passed on their journey. The high thorn-bush fence described a great circle, within which was a circle of twenty or more huts, identical in construction to others they had passed. Some were rectangular shapes, others round, some constructed in close proximity to one another, edges touching, to convert their shape from circular to figure-of-eight - twin-roomed huts.

Within the circle of huts was another ring of thorn bush that was formed to enclose the livestock. It seemed that on the wide flat valley floor this enclosure was the only significant raised ground they had passed. Helen commented on it and Sam agreed it was an odd feature in the landscape.

'I will go and speak with them,' said Mauwled. 'You should stay here. Don't get out of the Land Rover without me.' And he was gone before there was any opportunity for debate.

Sam leaned his head forward into the gap between the front seat headrests, so he could get a better view of proceedings. Mauwled approached the gap in the outer thorn bush where the stooped figure of an old man had appeared. He was flanked by a tall young man who leant on a long thin staff. Helen realised it was a spear, and not for show.

Hands were shaken, words spoken. Mauwled pointed back at the Land Rover, the old man nodded then pointed away in the other direction. At some point, the little children of the boma became emboldened and started to appear. A mixture of toddlers and little ones, some naked, some in tee shirts, some in shorts. The children demurely took up places behind the old man and the warrior.

After a little while, some youngsters moved forward and happily wove themselves around Mauwled's legs. As the adults' conversation wore on, a few of the bolder ones edged beyond Mauwled to get a closer look at the orange Land Rover and its occupants. A sharp word from the old man had them scurrying back into line.

Eventually, Mauwled reached out his hand, shook the older man's hand, then the warrior's. Helen noted how, on each occasion, the palm shake morphed into a thumb grip and then Mauwled turned and headed back for the Land Rover.

Mauwled got in and turned to face Sam. 'We can't do anything for now. That was one of the elders; it's his son who has assumed leadership now, we need to speak with him. He won't be back until much later. We are to come back in the morning.'

'Hell, are you sure? Is there nothing we can do?'

'We must wait. If you try to push ahead without his son's authority, it is bad. In fact, it's all bad. The old man thinks we will not get permission to travel to the runway. They have already made an arrangement with somebody else.'

'It has to be Ro, he's bought them off,' said Sam.

'So, what now?' said Helen.

'The elder's son is the leader now. He will decide when he returns. We can stay in the old health centre tonight, but I think he's just being kind because there's no time for us to reach anywhere else before dark falls. He will send word when we should call in the morning.'

· · ·

The old clinic had four rooms leading off the veranda. A quick inspection had identified that two rooms were bedrooms, each filled with four sets of bunk beds, the third a store-cum-washroom and the largest - which must once have been the clinic's treatment area - was now cleared except for a few tables and chairs stacked at one side.

Helen had picked a bedroom, and she and Sam had given it a once over for unwanted snakes and insect visitors. Then they went out to see what Mauwled was doing. He had opted not to use the other bedroom; instead, he had taken a little tent from the back of the Land Rover and had pulled it up on to the vehicle's roof. They watched as he popped it up and secured it.

'What are you doing Mauwled?' said Helen.

'I like to stay with the Land Rover, security.' Then he gave a little laugh. 'And it's safer up here.'

'Safer from what?'

He spread his hands wide and looked about. 'Snakes, lions, people. I don't like to sleep on the ground in the bush, if I can avoid it.'

'You know best, I guess,' said Helen, 'but given a choice, I'll settle for indoors.'

'We're going down to the river, want to come?' said Sam.

'Sure, I'll come. But you must be careful at the river, never go close to the edge. You must watch for crocodiles.'

The walk through the bush here was easy. Livestock from the boma made their way out every day and kept the bushes and the undergrowth well down. It took only a few minutes' walking before the bush began to turn greener where the roots were able to tap down to the river's underground water table. When they reached the riverbank, it was immediately clear just how low the water level had dropped.

Much of the riverbed that would normally have been under three or four feet of water was now dry pebble beach. What remained of the shrunken flow moved slow and muddy brown through only the deepest part of the bed. On its surface, fallen leaves and clumps of water plants, dislodged upstream by drinking animals, floated slowly past. Sam guessed that right now, even at its deepest, the river would be only four or five feet deep.

They settled down on some big rocks under the shade of the green-leaved trees to enjoy the calm and relative cool, listening to what remained of the river as it flowed by.

A little while later, the tranquillity was broken by the arrival of a herd of animals. There were a number of goats and about forty young cattle, all immature, little more than calves. Some of the livestock were fitted with roughly fashioned bells round their necks that gave a gentle clunking sound as they walked.

Herding the livestock were half a dozen boys. Helen guessed their ages at around ten or eleven, certainly none more than twelve. All carried thin wooden-shafted spears, pointed with sharp metal tips; these were rested over the shoulders of some, while others had them reversed, using the shafts to guide wandering animals back into the herd. The boys called to one another and whistled to the livestock, comfortably at ease with the environment as they guided their wards down to the water for a last drink before returning to the boma at the end of the day.

'They're very young,' said Helen.

'Yes, by our standards, but I've seen exactly the same in Kenya. The children and the animals grow up together. The little ones we saw earlier, soon they'll be responsible for the goat kids and youngest calves, which are kept in and around the boma, where there's always an adult around if a predator turns up. Then, about nine or ten, they'll move up to caring for the older calves and goats; they'll move a bit further from the boma.'

'That progression kind of makes sense, I guess. I saw something similar in West Africa, but they still seem so young,' said Helen.

'It's what they're brought up to expect. Once they graduate from this lot, it's rituals and initiations and before you know it they're propelled headlong into adulthood. Then they'll join the young men to take the main cattle herds away for part of the year to their seasonal pastures. And the senior warriors remain here with the breeding herds.'

Once down the side of the riverbank, the goats and calves hurried across the dry riverbed bleating their joy at the smell of water. They quickly lined up along the river's edge, their mouths all down to the water, taking a long drink. The sun cut through the tree canopy above them to dapple the water and animals with sparkling light. The young boys wandered up and down the line, still calling out to one another, pausing to check a calf's hindquarters here, making sure a weaker animal fitted into the drinking line there.

As Sam tried to plan a route through their problems, Helen took in the bucolic scene. She opened her water bottle and took a drink, absorbing the atmosphere and relaxing, letting the ordered harmony of nature wash over her.

Suddenly, the calm of the riverbank was shattered in a rush of water as a shape exploded out of the river and grabbed one of the drinking calves by the throat. The calf tried to retreat with the rest of the herd but was held tight in the crocodile's jaws.

The two-metre crocodile immediately began its inexorable reverse back into the water; the screaming calf fighting for its life. The calf's resistance could only slow the monster's retreat into the water; it was no match for the reptile's strength and there was only one possible outcome.

The nearest boy hurried to the calf, jabbed his spear at the crocodile then abandoned his weapon to grab the calf and throw his weight into the struggle.

The other boys all arrived in a hurry, each one jumped into the shallows beside the crocodile's head, there they mounted a constant jabbing, jabbing, jabbing with their spears. All the time aiming for its eyes or trying to force their spears into the beast's mouth.

Helen, Sam and Mauwled were on their feet, running for the riverbank.

A spear penetrated the crocodile's eye socket. It jerked its head but kept hold of the calf, which was now dragged knee deep into the bloodied river.

Finally, one of the boys managed to thrust his spear into the crocodile's mouth. Shouting in triumph he leant his weight against the shaft, driving it in. A second boy got his spear in too and pressed it home into the croc's soft inner flesh. The boys were making a terrific noise. The distracted beast, facing an unexpected attack, opened its mouth in defiance and the calf was immediately dragged back on to dry land by the first boy, who had steadfastly clung on to it throughout.

The crocodile was maddened by the unexpected assault. As it retired to midstream, it swung its tail, smashing into the head of one boy who had knelt to retrieve a dropped spear. He fell like a stone into the water and immediately disappeared beneath the surface. For the first time, the other boys looked stunned; this was beyond their expectations.

Sam shouted over his shoulder to Helen, telling her to stay away from the water as he rushed to where the boy had disappeared. The water only came to his waist. He plunged under, reaching for the bottom, feeling around until his hands made contact with the boy. Surfacing with a desperate gasp for air, Sam pulled the youngster back to the surface.

He turned to make for the bank, only to find Helen in the water beside him. She grabbed the boy too and together they dragged him to safety. Around them was an escort of excited jabbering boys, stabbing their spears into the water to deter any further attack and retreating in pace with Helen and Sam.

On the bank, Helen took charge and called on her earlier years of nursing experience to check the boy. She rolled him over and applied compression to his back, squeezing water out of his lungs and onto the dry riverbank. She squeezed again, getting more out, and was about to roll the boy over and start CPR when he coughed, wheezed and cried out in distress. Helen looked up and grinned at Sam; the boy would live.

One boy tended to the injured calf, while one remained with their fallen friend. The others were busy gathering their herd together again, but always keeping a watchful eye on Helen's actions. They all heard their watching friend's shout as he saw Helen's grin and read the signal. Cheers and shouts rang out amongst the boys, and once they had the herd back together, they clamoured round Helen and Sam shouting their thanks.

After a little while, the injured boy stood. Helen protested that he should not be walking anywhere but Mauwled explained he needed to. His pride and honour demanded he go home on his own feet.

Helen, Sam and Mauwled walked up the riverbank with the boys and their herd. There they paused to watch as the boys drove their livestock in a slow procession through the bush back to the boma. The injured young boy, still a little unsteady on his feet, brought up the rear. He paused just before disappearing into the scrub with his herd, turned to look back at the three adults and raised his arm and spear in salute. Then he turned again and vanished from sight.

They made their way back to the clinic in silence. The lazy pleasure of a still, dry, African afternoon was gone. Here they were at the sharp end of nature.

Entering the clearing beside the clinic, Helen eyed Mauwled's tent pitched on the Land Rover's roof. 'You know, I think you're right Mauwled. This is not a place to take even half a chance.'

'I'll get a fire started so you two can get dried out. And I'll see what rations there are for a meal. At least you won't be in the dark here, there's a solar lighting cell. It worked when I was here last. Enough to see by but not enough light to read.'

Helen smiled a thank you and sat down on the edge of the concrete veranda's patio where it still caught the late afternoon sun's rays. Its warmth was welcome as she suddenly found herself shivering.

Sam sat beside her and put his arm round her. 'Come on, we'd better get dried off. I think we're going to stink a bit after that dip.'

Helen nodded but didn't move. 'What I don't understand is why those boys didn't just let the calf go. It wasn't worth risking their lives for, it was madness.'

'It's their life and honour. The Maasai live for their cattle. The boys couldn't have gone home had they not at least tried to save the calf. It's just that simple. For the Maasai, cattle are everything - part of the family group. No halfway house.'

Chapter 29
FRIDAY 1ST NOVEMBER - EVENING

Mauwled was busy trying to get a fire alight in the open-air firepit set to the side of the clinic. In spite of his repeated efforts, the flames were reluctant to do more than flicker and glint before fading away. As darkness pushed out the twilight, the solar lighting came up on the veranda, casting just enough light for Helen and Sam to see one another - they were still sitting cold and wet, quietly coming to terms with nature's brutality and the boys' bravery, their attempt to catch warmth from the setting sun having failed.

'Come on, let's make a move,' said Sam, standing. As he did, he tensed; there was a sound of movement beyond the clearing. Looking round, he saw Mauwled was on the alert too.

'What's up?' said Helen, rising to join Sam while giving an involuntary shiver. The boy's close escape had brought bush life into sharp focus. She glanced towards Mauwled, wishing he could get the fire blazing. She saw he was looking off into the darkness; saw Sam was looking in the same direction. 'Is there something there?'

'Yes, I heard something. I have no idea what. Listen ...'

They stood in silence, straining their ears. And the sound came again. Movement - it was coming closer.

Mauwled joined them, taking up a position beside Helen. She noticed that he had a machete in his hand and wondered where it had come from. He reached across her and handed Sam a heavy stick. Sam took it and hefted it in his hand, finding the balance point and shifting his grip.

'What have you got for me?' she asked.

'You just keep back,' said Sam.

'I don't think so, Cameron,' she said, jumping down from the veranda. In the half-light of the veranda's solar lights she cast about, selected a large stone and then stepped back onto the veranda, standing between the two men. They all stared towards the approaching sounds.

A shape separated from the dark of the bush. Then another and another. Men coming closer, closing on the clinic. The leading man paused, waved his hand and called out. Helen couldn't understand and Sam, for all his language skills, grasped none of it. But Mauwled understood. It was Maa, the Maasai language. By the time the speaking man had finished his second sentence, Mauwled had stepped down from the veranda, thrust his machete into his belt and reached out a welcoming hand.

The shadow man advanced and Helen saw it was the elder from the boma gate. He shook hands with Mauwled as others followed him into the dim solar-powered light. A second old man appeared, and then four tall men, morani, each carrying a spear and a rungu, the Maasai throwing club, so lethal in the hands of an experienced moran. She knew that the cloaks they wore were bright red patterned though there was no hint of colour in the closing darkness. Then came two women, leading donkeys burdened down with large water drums and supplies strapped to their backs. Last came two more morani.

Mauwled shook the second elder's hand. Once again, Helen noted how the conventional handshake morphed seamlessly into a thumb clench. She and Sam looked expectantly as Mauwled and the two older men came up onto the veranda; the morani followed them up and gathered behind their elders. Meanwhile, the two women led the donkeys off towards Mauwled's failed fire.

'They have come to greet you, to thank you,' said Mauwled. 'The boys have told how you both went into the water to save their friend's life. That was brave, that is what the morani would have done.'

'Morani?' said Helen.

'The morani are the Maasai warriors. They will always stand to protect their people and their animals.'

The older men stepped forward and reached out their hands; in turn, they shook Sam's, him making the morph to thumb grip with ease, having mastered it years before. They reached out to Helen, each shook her hand. She muffed the thumb grip, but they showed no sign other than warmth.

One of the elders plucked at Helen's still damp top, spoke to his companion then shouted off into the shadows. A female voice answered. Helen turned to see the two women had been busy. A fire was now flickering in the firepit, flames rising as it grew in strength, and a huge pot was suspended above the flames, a second smaller one beside it.

Mauwled and the elders talked a little, pausing now and then to keep Sam and Helen informed.

'The boy you saved was one of the elder's grandsons. A son of the chief and from his senior wife. They owe you a great debt and wish to honour you. There will be a welcoming ceremony for you in the morning.'

Sam and Helen both smiled towards the elders.

'Please tell them it will be an honour to meet the chief. We did only what any good person would do to help a child in need, and we are pleased the boy is well,' said Sam.

After Mauwled passed on the message, the elders shook their heads at Sam and laughed before replying.

'They say what you did needed the courage of a lion. You cannot deny it. They honour you.'

The elders spoke again, and Mauwled listened carefully before translating.

'It seems you are now their guests. The elders are going back to the boma now. The morani will stay to ensure your safety through the night and will bring you to the boma in the morning.'

'Wow, that's great,' said Helen.

The elders smiled and nodded to her. One reached out again to her damp top and tweaked at it once more, showing it to the other. Then he turned and shouted at the women.

A woman's voice came back again. Helen looked towards the firepit. The women were standing beside it. One was pouring the smaller pan of boiling water into an enormous teapot, which she placed on the table beside the fire; in the flickering light, Helen could see a row of mugs arranged beside it. The other was calling instructions to two of the morani as they shuffled from the shadows behind the clinic, dragging an old galvanised bathtub towards the flames.

'There is tea for you to drink,' said Mauwled. 'The elders are returning to the boma now and will see you in the morning.'

Goodbye salutes were exchanged, and the two elders disappeared into the darkness as Mauwled led Sam and Helen across to the fire.

Tea was served, and Helen was happy to sip the hot, sweet brew while standing by the fire to catch a little heat.

Mauwled chatted to the morani who had all happily taken tea from the two women. Then he turned to Helen and Sam. 'Helen, you are to bathe now, then Sam.'

'What?' said Helen.

'The women have heated water for you.'

Two of the morani had taken leather patches in their hands and carried the giant pan of boiling water to the bath, where they poured it in. The women hoisted another pan of water over the fire.

Helen looked round at the ring of watching morani. 'I'm not stripping off for a crowd. Forget it. I'd rather be dirty and cold.'

The women had been watching her and understood exactly what the problem was. They laughed and shouted at the morani, pointing towards the clinic's veranda. The men looked at one another and laughed too but didn't move. One of the women moved towards them, scolding, and the men retired to the veranda. A woman picked up the giant teapot and handed it to Mauwled, then pointed him and Sam towards the retreating morani.

Helen stood alone by the fire, wondering what would happen next. She threw frequent glances back at the veranda where she could see the shadows of the men moving about. Then the two women swung into action.

From the back of one donkey, they lifted a roll of stitched cowhides, it unfurled into a long strip with four wooden stakes attached. They banged the stakes into the earth, creating a three-sided vanity screen. It enclosed the bathtub and was positioned to block out the line of sight to the clinic while the open side faced close to the roaring fire.

The women took Helen by the hands and led her behind the screen where they began gently pulling at her clothes. Suddenly, Helen felt tired, weak and dirty. She didn't resist as her clothes were peeled off and she was hustled into the hot bath. She lay back and closed her eyes, letting the heat warm her body. At the sound of giggles, she opened her eyes. The women were standing over her; one held a bar of soap the other a smaller pan of hot water.

Helen sat up as the hot water was added, topping up her bath. Then the senior woman leaned behind Helen and vigorously scrubbed at her dirty back. Back clean, she straightened up and handed Helen the soap. More hot water was added, and the two women allowed Helen to complete her bath while they inspected her dirty clothes.

Bath over, Helen decided it was time for bed and happily retired to her chosen room while the morani organised a bath for Sam. The women left with all the river-dirtied clothes, their donkeys and an escort of two morani.

Eventually, Sam made it to bed too. Mauwled climbed up to his tent on the Land Rover roof, and the two morani left behind to guard the guests squatted down on the clinic's veranda; the muttered noise of their low voices the only sound in the quiet of the night.

Chapter 30
SATURDAY 2ND NOVEMBER - AM

It was dark and still outside. Through the dormitory's mesh-covered window frame, from which the glass had vanished long ago, Sam could hear the first stirrings of nature preparing for the dawn. He sat up, lifted the side of his mosquito net and flipped it over his head, letting it fall back onto the bed behind him. Slipping a hand back under the net, he pulled out the clean set of clothes he had placed under it the previous evening, and he dressed. Then, flicking on his torch he looked down at his boots, lifted them up and shook them one at a time. Nothing nasty came out, and he pulled the boots on. Having spent some hours beside the fire the previous evening, they were almost dry.

The coming of the dawn had been one of his favourite times of day when he'd served in Kenya. Now he wanted a little quiet time to revisit the experience while thinking through the impending meeting. He opened the door and stepped out onto the veranda. Closing the door quietly, he passed a moran who was sitting on a tiny three-legged stool.

Sam wandered across the clearing, coming to a halt beside the remains of the fire. He sat quietly at the table and let the emerging sounds of dawn envelop him. At first, it was quiet, almost silent. With each passing minute, the noise rose as more and more birds and insects roused and started their rituals to welcome the new day. Bit by bit, the soundscape developed as different creatures chipped in. He lay flat on the bench. In the east, the skyline was lightening. Sam knew it was going to get much louder as morning broke.

The moran on the veranda stood, glanced over in Sam's direction then walked to the far end. He looked out across the clearing, beyond Mauwled's Land Rover to where he knew his friend was standing in the shadows, watching. He saw the shape of his friend and silently returned to his little stool and sat, waiting. In a little while, their long watch would be over.

The sound of approaching footsteps seemed too heavy to him, he knew it was not his friend. It must be Sam, returning, having walked right round the clinic. The moran looked up to greet Sam but could do nothing as a knife flew across the veranda and sunk into his chest. He stood, cried out, staggered forward and then fell with a thump, groaning. A dark stain spread out from his body across the pale concrete surface.

One of Park's guards hurried across the veranda. Stopping at the groaning moran, his hands reached down. One clamped over the dying man's mouth, the other trailed across his chest, seeking the dagger handle. Found, it was wrenched out and the moran shuddered in pain. Then the suffering ended as the blade was drawn across his throat.

Night watch over, the second moran, returned to the clinic in response to his brother warrior's stirrings. He turned the corner in time to see the killing cut and shouted out in anger.

The crouching guard turned in surprise; he had seen only one warrior. In a single motion, he stood and drew back his knife hand. He had to pause for a moment to adjust his grip on the bloodied weapon. And it dropped from his fingers. He took an involuntary half step backwards, looked down at his chest and cried out in shock and pain. That lost moment had cost him his life. The head of the moran's spear was embedded in his chest, seven feet of shaft sticking out in front of him. He gripped the shaft and collapsed to his knees, he screamed only once.

At the first sound of trouble, Sam's moment of indulgence was dismissed, and he ran for the clinic. He reached the end of the veranda in time to see two men running towards him from the bush line. They had passed the Land Rover and were crossing the clearing in front of the clinic: each held a pistol and was firing as they ran. Sam grabbed the moran and pulled him down and off the end of the veranda as several rounds bit into the clinic wall punching little holes in the plaster.

The moran was furious at Sam's intervention and struggled free. Sam signed him to keep down and then crawled to the corner. He peered round to assess the situation and found himself looking at a man's legs. He turned his head to look up and was confronted by a Korean man pointing a pistol directly into his face. It was Park's driver. The driver spoke into a communication headset, Sam recognised the language, Korean. It was a language he didn't speak but he didn't need to understand the words. From his captor's elated tone, it was clear he was reporting a success.

The remaining Korean guard was peering over the edge of the veranda, looking for the surviving moran, but he had vanished.

'Are you Cameron?' said the driver. His pistol pointed unwaveringly at Sam.

Sam remained silent.

'Are you Cameron? Boss is coming now, don't move.'

Sam stayed still, weighed up his options; they were limited. He wondered who the boss was. Ro Soo-Ann? Here? Or was it Park?

The Korean guard was checking his fallen colleague for signs of life while still glancing about for the missing moran. He pronounced his colleague dead and stood up as another Korean appeared. Park walked quickly towards the clinic from the bush beyond the Land Rover.

As Park strode past the vehicle, there was a flurry of motion and Mauwled leapt out of his tent and down from the roof on to the passing Korean. The confusion was racked up as the tent came down to earth too, deflecting Mauwled's machete carrying hand. Nonetheless, he still drew a deep wound across Park's arm. Standing over Park, Mauwled lifted his blade and made to chop at Park's prostrate body.

The Korean guard shouted in anger and aimed at Mauwled. The first shot hit Mauwled's shoulder, the second grazed his head. Mauled dropped like a stone landing on Park's legs and pinning them to the ground.

The driver had made the mistake of looking away for a moment in an effort to assess what was happening and Sam struck. From the ground, he couldn't overpower the guard, but he could reach up just high enough to grab the pistol barrel tight. He did, twisting its aim away from his head. The weapon fired twice, the rounds punched harmlessly into the dry earth.

Then, as Sam clung on to the weapon and tried to get to his feet the driver kicked him hard in the chest. Kicked again. Sam had control of the weapon's direction but was unable to get up. Each kick weakened him further.

From his vantage point on the veranda, the guard glanced at the driver and reckoned he had it under control. He knew Park needed assistance and took a step forward. While he had been looking away from the building towards where Park lay, Helen had opened the bedroom door, her only available weapon was the moran's abandoned little stool. She stooped, picked it up and with a shriek of effort swung it hard at the back of the guard's head.

It proved only a glancing blow, but it was enough to propel the guard off the veranda. As he stepped clear of the building, he was dropped on by the surviving moran who had scaled the veranda roof. The guard fell to the ground, rolled over but never got up as the moran's rungu crushed his skull, twice.

A blood lust showed in the warrior's eyes as he turned his attention towards the driver, who having seen the ferocity of the moran's attack, stopped kicking Sam and panicked. He released his grip on the pistol and turned to flee. He had only gone three paces when the rungu struck him in the middle of his back, knocking him forward and down.

As he struggled to his feet, the moran caught him, forcing him to the ground. Pulling a knife from under his red cloak, he let the blade slice across the back of the driver's hamstring. The driver screamed in pain and fear and rolled onto his back, reaching up in an effort to defend himself. The moran decided he would not take a chance on the driver having a hidden weapon. In a single motion, he kicked the Korean's outstretched arms away and stooped to plunge his knife into the man's chest. Instantly blood coughed and spluttered from the man's mouth and then he went limp, dead.

Helen helped Sam up. He took the driver's abandoned pistol and together they hurried across the clearing towards Mauwled. Park was gone, a trail of blood leading away into the bush. Helen knelt down to assess Mauwled while Sam got the first aid kit from the Land Rover and then stood guard in case Park resurfaced.

• • •

Less than five minutes after the Korean guard's gunshots had filled the dawn air, a flurry of movement occurred on the path leading towards the boma as, signed by an array of red cloaks and glinting spearheads, a troop of morani trotted into the clearing. They fanned out, some working round the edges of the clearing, weaving in and out of the bush border, searching for threats. Others moved directly to the clinic. At their head was a tall slender man, his cloak bright red in the now risen sun.

The surviving moran of the guard detail bowed his head slightly towards the tall man and pointed at the dead moran on the veranda. Watching from where she was tending Mauwled's wounds, Helen could see the anguished response of the chief as he knelt beside the dead moran and paid his respects.

Accompanied by several morani, the chief crossed the clearing to Helen and Sam. He stopped, looked down at Mauwled, assessing the condition of his wounds. Satisfied that Mauwled would live, the chief looked at Sam.

'You may call me Charles, Charles Shanlan. I am the chief here.' He spoke slowly, gently. A man who had to measure his words, but his English was perfect. 'I am sorry for what has happened to your friend,' he waved his club towards Mauwled. 'You are all welcome here. These people have shamed me; my father had made you our guests, under our protection. This will be avenged.'

Registering the anglicised name, Sam reached out his hand and the two men shook solemnly. As he let go, Sam pointed to the blood trail leading away into the bush. 'One got away,' he said.

The chief knelt down and inspected the trail. Followed the track for half a dozen paces then stopped. He beckoned over a senior moran and, pointing to the trail, spoke briefly. The senior moran looked at the blood splatter and turned back to the morani that had followed Charles across the clearing. He said just a few words then turned and headed into the bush, followed by a group of the morani.

Charles turned his attention back to the visitors. 'You must come back to the boma. We can talk there. Will you need help with your friend?'

Sam glanced at Helen, then down to Mauwled. 'No, thanks. I think we'll manage in the Land Rover.'

Charles nodded and spoke in Maa to his men. Two stepped forward and gently lifted Mauwled, sliding him onto the rear passenger seat of the Land Rover. Sam thanked them, then stretched into the rear and patted Mauwled's pockets, searching for the ignition keys - finding them.

Straightening up, Sam closed the rear door and turned back to Charles. 'We'll see you over there then,' he said.

Charles waved them on. A moran leapt onto the rear of the vehicle as it moved off. He gripped hold of the roof rack with one hand, held his spear in the other and worked one leg over the rear door's mounted spare wheel. He hung on as the vehicle left the clearing and made its slow bumpy progress along the rutted dirt track through the bush towards the boma.

'Do you think they'll catch the guy who ran off?' said Helen.

'I would think so. These morani will know the lie of the land like you know your home town.'

'What will happen to him?' said Helen.

'I don't know. I've a feeling we probably don't want to.'

Helen remembering some of the awful things she had seen during her time working as a nurse in West Africa, before she joined the Church. 'Should we do something?'

'Helen, I don't want to do anything that will obstruct my finding the runway and rescuing Bob Prentice. Mauwled's out of the picture now so I need these people; it's certain they know exactly where it is.'

'Okay, but it's not nice to think what will happen to that man, even if he's a killer.' Deep down, Helen knew there was nothing they could do. Justice in the bush was a blunt instrument. It had to be, the nearest law officers might be a hundred miles and more away. It was simple, people defended themselves and theirs in every way they could.

As they drove across the open space in front of the boma, they could see a herd of livestock just disappearing into the bush - their escorts needing to do nothing to encourage them onwards as the animals hurried towards the riverbank and their first drink of the day.

The Land Rover veered off the track and came to a halt to one side of the boma's entrance. They got out and pulled open the rear passenger doors. Mauwled was conscious though decidedly groggy. As they prepared to lift him out, Helen and Sam were pulled away by the moran who had journeyed back with them. He pointed towards the boma from where several women were emerging.

The women lifted Mauwled out and carried him off. Helen insisted on following, and she took the first aid kit, leaving Sam to deal with the moran.

Glancing about as she walked through the boma's gateway opening, she saw that there was a stack of cut thorn bush to one side, guessed it was a gate they would close at night. Directly ahead of her was another stack of cut thorn bush that presumably represented the gate to the inner ring of thorn bush where the cattle stayed. She could see through the opening that the corral was almost empty. Two or three cows stood on the top of the strangely domed hillock that was the livestock pen. Close up, the space was much bigger. She thought that it would easily hold three hundred cattle, perhaps more.

The women carrying Mauwled had turned off to the left, walking past a line of huts that arced round, following the curved space between the two thorn tree fences. Helen moved quickly to catch up. Passing successive huts, she became more aware of the children, lots of children. Toddlers hurried, and frequently fell over, in their rush to join the bigger children; the fours and fives and sixes who were running, determined to be close to Helen. As they hurried, they made little lion roars and raised their hands, clenching and opening their fingers like lion claws.

She came to a halt outside a hut through whose arched entranceway the women had just ducked. Taking a little breath, she stooped to enter. Pushing aside the heavy leather flap, she stepped into the gloomy interior and paused to allow her eyes to adjust.

Mauwled had been placed on a raised sleeping frame where the women were making him comfortable. Amongst the women, she recognised the two she had met the previous evening. They smiled and beckoned her across the floor of the hut.

Then the flap behind her was pushed to the side and little faces appeared, anxious not to be left out. The bravest of the little boys slipped into the hut and stood beside Helen. He made a roaring sound and continued to clench and flex his fingers. Helen mimicked him, and the children crowded at the entrance squealed in delighted mock fear. One of the older women rattled off a blast of Maa that immediately had the children fall quiet.

The women all laughed, and the little boy's mother crossed the hut and cuddled him. Then she looked at Helen, made the same roar her little boy had done, reached out her hand, took a strand of Helen's hair in her hand, and made a roaring sound again. Her son mimicked her and all the children in the doorway laughed and joined in, and they found the courage to edge into the hut too.

The young woman stroked Helen's hair again. Finally, Helen realised what was happening; the children saw her red hair as lion hair. They were completely fascinated by it. The young woman smiled at Helen, and her little boy tentatively reached out his hand and gave her hair the briefest of touches. He quickly pulled his hand back even as all the other children gasped at his courage. When they saw that Helen had permitted the contact they all excitedly crowded round to take their chance to touch, twirl, and stroke her auburn hair.

After a minute, the older woman, who clearly had a position of authority, spoke sharply to the children, and reluctantly, with final touches of Helen's mane, they left the hut.

As the entrance flap fell shut, excluding the children and the sunlight, the old woman put her hand on Helen's shoulder, drawing her across the hut to be welcomed into the group. Pulling a torch from the first aid kit, Helen started to take a closer look at Mauwled's condition.

• • •

Sam was sat on a solid old dining-room chair. Helen sat next to him. He had no idea where the chair came from, but he could see three or four more dotted amongst the range of other seating including benches, logs and several sturdy, if roughhewn, handmade seats. They were all arranged in an approximate square. Each seat was occupied by a serious-faced man. The elders and the morani. Beyond the square was a table on which women had placed rows of big mugs. Enormous teapots appeared, and the women began pouring hot thick tea, which was passed round.

Helen and Sam got their drinks at the same time as the chief, who was sat directly opposite. They thanked the woman who handed them their mugs. Then Sam took a double take, they were old British Army issue pint tea mugs. The steaming liquid soon heated the enamel-coated tin to blister point and he was pleased to put his on the ground beside Helen's. How the mugs had ended up in a Maasai boma was a mystery.

Helen spoke quietly to Sam. 'We need to get Mauwled proper medical attention. The bullet went right through his shoulder. All the bleeding's stopped and I've stitched up his head too. But it's a certainty his wounds are going to become infected. Can we get him to a doctor or hospital?'

Sam did not get a chance to answer her as Charles' father stood to speak and everyone fell silent. He spoke in Maa for a couple of minutes. Whatever he said elicited a murmured round of approval, and the men drank a mouthful of tea. Sam and Helen joined them in drinking, then smiled and nodded their approval of the brew. The elder smiled back and was supported by a further round of murmurs. In faltering English, he welcomed Sam and Helen before reaching out a hand to where Charles, his son, was seated. Then the elder sat down.

Charles stood and looked around the gathering, then focused on Helen and Sam.

'I want to apologise again for what happened at the clinic. My nephew is dead, and our peace has been broken. Those were bad men and not of us. They will all pay a heavy price. What they have done is not the Maasai way, but we will settle it our way.' He paused and spoke to the audience in Maa, repeating his message. The men cheered approval and clapped their hands.

Charles turned his attention back to Sam and Helen. 'First, although this is a bad day, I must thank you both for my son's life. I am in your debt. You were brave as the morani would be. Anything we can do to help you, please just ask.

'My father has told me that you want permission to visit the runway, though Mauwled did not tell him why. He and the other elders indicated yesterday that they thought I would not allow such a thing, and they were right.' He paused for a moment as he saw Sam shift in his seat. 'They were right because I had agreed to allow another man the sole use of the runway. It would have been wrong to dishonour my word.' Charles stopped talking and thought deeply for a moment.

Then he resumed. 'Those men who attacked this morning, they are from the runway. When they attacked, they breached our trust. When they killed my nephew, they became my enemy, became all my people's enemy.' He stopped, looked round the assembly and repeated what he had said in Maa. Again, the men clapped and stamped their feet in agreement.

Returning to English, Charles reached out both his hands towards Sam and Helen. 'You are both brave, brave like the morani. You risked your lives to save one of our children, my child. This morning, you both fought with the morani against an enemy. Yesterday, you stood for us, and today, you stood with us. I promise, we are one. You are morani; you, Sam, and you, the Lion Lady.'

The assembled men read the spirit of Charles' words, clear in any language, and they stood as one to cheer when Charles crossed the space between them to shake Sam and Helen's hands and welcome them into his family. First Sam's hand, then Helen's. She was delighted at the outcome; at last, they were making progress towards recovering Sam's friend. Secretly delighted, too, at having finally got the handshake right but delighted most of all by her Maasai name, Lion Lady.

As the meeting broke up, Sam got the satellite phone out. They needed to organise medical treatment for Mauwled, and it was time to report to the authorities. Just as he flicked the phone on, a cry went up from the children hovering around the entrance to the boma. Others picked up the shout and morani began to rush for the gate, clutching a variety of spears and clubs.

Sam looked at Helen and flicked the phone off again. 'Come on; let's see what's going on here.' They both hurried to the entranceway, arriving at the same time as Charles and the elders. Everyone stared out across the clearing. Three of the morani who had set off earlier in the morning on the blood trail were returning and they had two prisoners. As they approached, it was clear that both men were very frightened and had experienced some rough treatment at the hands of their captors. It was also clear these men were not Koreans but Africans.

The morani threw their prisoners to the ground at the boma entrance; the senior moran stood square to Charles and addressed him in Maa. He waved his finger in front of him, pointed his spear behind him, towards the direction they had just come from, described an arc across the bush with his spear and returned it to the front, to point it at the two men lying before him. When he finished speaking, he raised his spear, the morani beside him raised theirs and the crowd cheered.

One of the prisoners raised his head and called to the chief, his voice quickly drowned out by a round of heckling from the crowd. Helen felt a twinge of recognition, she knew that voice. She pushed herself forward through the crowd to get a better look. One of the prisoners had raised his head and was trying to address the chief, with little success.

'Angel? Angel, what are you doing here?' said Helen. She stepped forward and then knelt beside the priest. 'Sam! I need you here.'

Sam had followed her through the crowd and now joined her. The senior moran was looking concerned over their intervention. He glanced at the chief, and Charles stepped forward.

'Who is this man? Is he a friend?' said Charles.

Helen looked up to Charles. 'Yes, he's an Ethiopian Orthodox Tewahedo Church priest. He's a friend of ours.'

'Hold on,' said Sam. 'We think he's our friend, but what's he doing out here? Perhaps we'd better hear his story before vouching for him. Don't you think?'

Helen had pulled Angel up to his knees and pressed her water bottle into his hand. 'Well, okay, but remember what he's done for us. I'm giving him the benefit of the doubt for now.'

Charles spoke a line of Maa to the senior moran while raising his open palmed hand in an *up* gesture. The warrior and his team responded at once, pulling the prisoners up to their feet.

'You can join us,' said Charles to Sam and Helen as he turned to make his way through the crowd. The morani followed with their prisoners, though now their control was less domineering. Sam and Helen came next then the crowd rolled in behind - in only a couple of minutes they were seated back in their places at the square. Now though, the clear space in the middle was occupied by the two prisoners and the morani who had caught them stood to one side, spears to hand should anything threaten to get out of hand.

At a respectful distance, behind the seated morani and elders, were gathered most of the women of the boma. The children milled about excitedly, finding vantage points where they could. One little boy sidled up behind Helen and was pressing against her. His hand reached forward to be held in hers, his head peeping round her shoulder. His other hand, free behind her back, crept up to her hair and once again wrapped little fingers into the lion's mane. There was a ripple of giggles from his friends. It was silenced by an older woman's voice that demanded order.

Helen felt the little boy go in an instant as his mother hurried forward and snatched him up and away. The senior moran, whose men guarded the captives, had been speaking quietly and hurriedly into Charles' ear. He finished, straightened up and joined the rest of his team. Then silence fell when the chief rose from his seat. He addressed the gathering in Maa, speaking for several minutes, then he looked at Helen and Sam.

'I understand this man might be your friend, but one of my warriors was killed this morning. I, my people, need to understand what these men were doing here and why. Were they involved?'

Sam stood. 'Charles, let me thank you for taking the time to investigate this. It is a wise thing to do. I hope we can help.' He waved his hand towards the prisoners. 'We do not know that man, but we know this one, his name is Angel. He has been good to us and helped us before. He is a priest of our God, not a man of war. We don't know why he is here. That we will have to establish - we must question Angel. But first, how did your warriors find him?'

Charles looked at Angel, then over to Sam. He gave a dry little laugh. 'I think Angel is a good name for a man of your God, yes?'

'Yes, a good name,' said Sam.

Charles looked around the assembly and translated what Sam had said. The words were met with murmuring and nods of acknowledgement. Then Charles turned his attention back to Sam and Helen.

'The morani followed the blood trail as I ordered. It led to a big off-road vehicle, 4 x 4. We know the man who ran got there. He left lots of blood on the driver's seat but didn't drive away. He set off into the bush again. This time there was no blood trail, he must have bandaged his wound. So, following him was not so easy, but our morani can do this. I don't understand why he didn't drive away.'

The morning's action triggered a thought in Sam's mind and he raised a hand. Charles stopped talking and gestured for Sam to speak.

'He may not have been the driver. The driver would have had the keys in his pocket, so this other man could never have driven the vehicle away. Remember Mauwled, our driver, had his vehicle keys in his pocket.'

Charles nodded and then translated for the gathering. They looked from one to another and nodded agreement.

'The morani continued the hunt. Eventually, they found him. He was with these two, in a little bush clearing, getting ready to drive away in another vehicle. When my warriors challenged them, the wounded man tried to fight. He pointed his weapon at my senior moran, but never got the chance to shoot as he was speared by the others. These ones surrendered. Unlike their friend, they did not try to fight back so the morani did not kill them at once. They thought I might want to speak to them first.'

Helen stood, while giving an involuntary shiver; the morning's death toll continued to rise. And the chief's, *at once*, implied it hadn't finished yet. She looked at Angel, could not work out why he would have sided with Ro and the Koreans. He knew how important this all was to Sam and her. 'Charles, thank you. Your warriors have shown great skill and courage, and please tell them how I admire them. But I am sure there is more to learn. Can Angel speak?'

Again, Charles translated for his people, and then looked back to Helen.

'Of course, since our Lion Lady wishes it.'

'I do. Thank you, Charles.' Helen looked down to Angel, read his worried face. 'Now, Angel, you've got some explaining to do. Please tell us how you are mixed up in all this and, please, why are you even here?'

Angel made to stand and was halted when one of his captors reversed his spear and pressed the shaft down on to Angel's shoulder. He remained kneeling. He glanced from the chief and back to Helen.

'This is all a misunderstanding. I had nothing to do with the man the warriors speared. I had never met him before. Not in all God's creation did I know he existed until this morning. I swear it on all the saints. Please, Helen, tell them I am your friend, I beg you.'

'Angel, stop jabbering. Three questions. Who is that man kneeling next to you? Why were you with the Korean when the morani caught up with you? And why were you out in the bush, as far from your Arusha church as you like?'

Angel hesitated for a moment. Helen had already bought him a breather; if he answered wrong, she wouldn't be able to do so again. He knew of the Maasai's fearsome reputation.

'This man is a member of my church; he is my driver, nothing more. Whatever else happens he does not deserve to be involved.'

'Okay, I could buy that one,' said Helen, casting a glance across the floor towards Charles.

'We were not with that man. I had never seen him before he came running out of the bush towards us. He made my driver get into our vehicle; he wanted to be taken somewhere. I don't know where. When the warriors arrived, he was about to get on board. I think he was about to shoot me. The warriors thought we were together, but we were his prisoners.'

'Alright, so misunderstandings can happen, sometimes. But Angel, if you didn't know the man, why were you parked up in an area close to his vehicle? Are you trying to tell me it was a coincidence?'

'Yes, a coincidence, that's it. A coincidence. I've never seen him before. My driver and I were just having our breakfast when we heard shouts and screams and gunfire. Then everything went quiet, so we were just about to drive closer to the building when the Asian man burst into the clearing. He pointed a gun at us, like I said. He made the driver get in, then the warriors arrived. That's it, I promise.'

'Drive closer to the clinic, why? Why were you in the bush there anyway?'

'I was instructed to watch you. I've been on your trail since you left Arusha.'

'Why, what's going on? I thought we were friends.'

'We are, that's why I've been following you. Bishop Ignatius—'

'The bishop! Ignatius put you up to this?'

Angel nodded. 'Yes, he said I was to watch over you. Make sure no harm came to you.'

'Who is the bishop?' said Charles.

'Bishop Ignatius. He has a history of sending people to protect me.'

'And his choice of guardians tends to leave something wanting,' said Sam. 'You know, Charles, I can believe his story. The bishop has form in this department.'

'But why would the bishop want to protect you, Sam?' said Charles.

'It's not him. Helen is the bishop's concern,' said Angel. 'I was told to watch out for her, to intervene if necessary.' He gave a shrug. 'I can cope with drunks in Arusha or road crashes, but I don't know what he expects me to do against gunmen or … or them,' he nodded towards his captors. 'It's not exactly covered in our training.'

'But why you?'

'Because I'm the only one in Arusha he could organise and trust at short notice. His own assistants had already been exposed and found wanting.'

Helen stood up. 'You know what, Charles? I believe him. It sounds lame, but his bishop has already had people follow me, to *protect me*. I just wish he wouldn't.'

Angel looked at her. 'I am just a priest running a church. I am not in the bishop's confidence so much. All he would tell me is our Church had once made a promise, and it falls to us to honour that undertaking.'

Sam tugged gently on Helen's wrist; she looked at him, then sat. Sam stood. 'Charles, I believe this man. What he says is full of coincidence, but I know him. He helped Helen and me in Arusha with no thought for gain. Helen and I trust him, and Charles, look at him. He wouldn't know which end of a spear to hold, much less what to do with it. He is a good man of peace and of God. I will be happy to stand for him.'

Chapter 31
SATURDAY 2ND NOVEMBER - PM

Helen straightened up. Mauwled seemed to be doing okay. The young woman who was maintaining a watch on his progress had reported, through some confused signing, that he had been awake for a little while, or at least Helen thought that was what was meant. She noticed the woman was heating something in a little pot, perhaps getting something ready for when Mauwled awoke next. That was unremarkable, what surprised her was that the young woman was using a gas burner. Its little blue flame burned away beneath the pot. How did they get gas out here?

Helen pointed at the burner and shrugged her shoulders, then waved her hands about as though searching for something. The young woman realised what Helen was asking and proudly pointed her towards the back of the hut. Helen went to have a look and flicked on her torch. Here was something she had missed in the gloom, a second entrance. She lifted the leather flap, looked in and struggled to believe what she saw. There was a second hut attached to the first - semi-detached. The hut she was looking into was filled with a huge balloon, a gas balloon whose pipe was feeding fuel direct to the burner. She let the flap fall - that was a room she didn't particularly want to go in. Helen hurried out into the daylight.

Behind the hut, she found where a plastic hose fed into the hut and continued to trace it back towards its source. The hose ran beneath the inner circle of thorn bush, which at this point branched out to form a smaller partitioned section within the corral. Peering through the hedge, she saw what looked like a long, narrow cement channel covered with plastic sheeting. Puzzled, she set off to find Sam, following the course of the inner circle of thorn bush as it wound round the enclosed central hillock.

She spotted him on the far side of the hillock, standing alone, halfway up. He was using the phone. Helen passed through the open thorn bush entranceway and walked up the slope towards him. She caught the end of his conversation.

'… okay, sir, I'll do what I can. It won't be easy, but I'm on it. I'll hear back from you later. Shall we say this evening, seven o'clock - nineteen hundred hours? We have to keep the phone off whenever possible in case of charging problems. Thank you, sir, we'll speak again then. Goodbye.' He hung up and powered down the phone.

'Who was that?' said Helen.

'Brigadier Starling. Everything's brewing up. Seems GCHQ Cheltenham have intercepted various messages. Ro has got his flight sorted out; it's coming in tomorrow morning.'

'Where does that leave Bob Prentice?'

'In a mess. They are still working on getting a special ops unit into the country, but it's not certain they will make it in time. It seems the brigadier is expecting me to impede Ro somehow.'

'Can we?'

'We can try. I need to think a little about how we might do something. Charles has told me the runway is only about three miles away; it's on the other side of the river. So, there's plenty of time to get there, we just need a plan.

'Oh, by the way, some good news. The High Commission in Nairobi has been able to persuade the Kenyan authorities that the killing at the university was nothing to do with me, that it's down to Ro's boys. They unearthed some evidence at the university. Professor Ngure has given a statement that confirmed he'd had a telephone conversation with Susan Curtis after I had left her that evening.'

'That's great, but make sure they've got it in writing. Getting you out of African prisons is an expensive process.' She reached out her hand for the phone. 'I'll call Elaine, she'll be worried. I'd better call Tracy too, I'm meant to be keeping her posted on what you're up to.'

'So, I've definitely got a spy in the camp now.'

'That's right, you'd better behave yourself. Oh, talking of spying, I've discovered the hut next to where Mauwled is being kept has a gas balloon in it. Do you think it's safe? And where does the gas come from?'

'Yes, Charles told me about it a little while ago - he's quite proud of it. Seems an NGO built a concrete slurry tray that some of the cattle droppings are directed into. The slurry gives off gas, methane I guess, which is trapped beneath the plastic and piped into their gasbag, where it's stored for cooking.'

'Wow, that's neat. But is it safe?'

'As safe as anything else is out here. Plus, it saves having to cut down the bush for firewood. Oh, and see this?' Sam pointed to the ground beneath their feet.

'Uhuh,' said Helen.

'This isn't a hill at all. Underneath this, the land's just as flat as the surroundings. It's just cattle droppings that have been added to every night and baked dry in the daytime sun, building up over decades, perhaps centuries, into this hill.'

Helen gazed around. 'Wow, that is one heap of whatever you want to call it. One big heap.'

'Look, why don't you make your calls now? I'm going to think through Brigadier Starling's instructions. Charles has said he will support us any way he can. Turns out Smuts had visited him with Ro a few days ago and agreed that Ro could use the runway at a generous price. That's why we weren't welcome. He'd made an exclusive deal with Ro, and the elders knew he wouldn't break it.'

'Not until Ro's men killed one of the morani.'

'That certainly sealed it for us.'

He paused for a moment, looked up at the sky. For the first time during their journey, the sun was shielded by a cloud - a big, plump cloud.

Helen looked up too. 'Is that what everyone's been waiting for?'

'It's a start, but they'll need a lot more than that to break the drought.' As if on cue, the solitary cloud moved on and the sun burned down again.

Chapter 32
SATURDAY 2ND NOVEMBER - EVENING

The orange Land Rover set off after dark with Sam at the wheel. By his side were Helen and Charles; in the rear seats and cargo store were five morani. Following behind was Angel's vehicle. His driver had been escorted back to collect it from the bush during the afternoon. This vehicle carried six more morani.

The patchy cloud of the day had been gathering through the evening. Now the sky was overcast, blocking out the stars and moon that Helen had become so familiar with in recent days. There was just a blanket of black beyond the vehicle's lights as Sam carefully followed what little of the bush track was lit by their headlights.

Suddenly, Charles ordered Sam to stop. There was nothing in front of them. The track had vanished, and the headlights seemed to be pointing into a void, like searchlights staring out in the hope of picking out some aerial attackers. Instead, just highlighting moths and other flying insects of the night that were drawn to the beams.

Charles jumped out, moved a step away from the Land Rover, and from nowhere, a moran appeared. There were lowered voices and the warrior jabbed his spear into the black ahead. Charles nodded an acknowledgement, the warrior bowed his head very slightly and turned away, vanishing as if by magic as Charles returned to the vehicle.

'The bush beyond the river is clear now. There was a patrol from the runway, but it passed before sunset. Some of my people followed it, but now is a good time to cross the river; it's all clear.'

'You've sent people ahead?' said Helen.

'Yes, all the morani want revenge for their dead brother. There are some here watching the ford, others have crossed ahead to ensure we are not surprised. Now, we should go.'

Sam edged forward, trusting Charles' knowledge but unsure of what lay in the void ahead. With a jerk, the front of the Land Rover lurched over the crest of the riverbank and headed down. As it progressed, the lights picked out the dried bed and beyond that the shrunken river itself. This location was four or five hundred paces upstream from where they had encountered the young crocodile; here the watercourse was broader and shallower - a fording place. Immediately upstream from the ford, on the boma side of the river, the river course bulged out to form a broad side pool that, though much shrunken through the dry times, still held water.

The headlights shimmered on the water and, across the river, picked out another moran, standing motionless facing them. He raised an arm in salute, then beckoned them on.

'Drive at the moran,' said Charles. 'He is marking the course of the ford. Drive straight at him and you will be fine. He will step aside in good time, only stop once you are beyond him.'

Sam complied. The Land Rover bumped and splashed through the darkness, aiming always for the solitary man who continued to wave them across. With a growl, the vehicle pulled out of the river and rolled to a halt beyond their guide who was ignoring them, now concentrating on guiding the second vehicle across.

Charles got out and spoke words into the darkness.

Helen heard a voice respond in hushed Maa. A few moments later, morani appeared; they slapped mud across the front and rear lights, then vanished into the black.

She could just make out a shape standing directly in front of the Land Rover. It stooped and wiped a narrow stroke of mud from the lowest point on the driver's side headlight, letting the slightest of beams shine onto the ground ahead. The shape straightened up again and walked round to the passenger door. It was Charles.

He leaned close to the open window. 'We can follow the track for now. The last part, we will need to walk. Sam, slowly follow the moran who will step in front of the little beam. His body will block the light as long as you stay close.'

'Wouldn't we be quicker walking?' said Sam.

'Yes, but the bush at night has its own dangers, and later you might need the vehicles to get away fast.'

Moving through the blackness, Sam's only steer was a little patch of illuminated red cloak leading them through the night.

• • •

Nearly an hour had passed as they edged forward at less than regular walking pace. Finally, the moran guide stopped, and with relief, Sam stopped at once; his legs had been working the pedals without a break. He reached down and rubbed his calf muscles. Then they reversed both the vehicles a little off the track and into the bush, ready for a quick getaway.

Switching off the engine, Sam left the keys in the ignition and, as he got out, lifted the machine pistol they had liberated from Park's truck. He hung it over his shoulder and felt for the pistol he had picked up at the clinic.

Helen grabbed the first aid kit; she hitched it onto her shoulder and stood beside Sam. Angel appeared at her side. Helen was aware of others standing close by in the dark; the morani from the vehicles, and others, she couldn't be sure how many. She could only hear the breathing and sense the humanity close packed around her.

They all listened carefully as Charles gave instructions to his men. The Maa he spoke meant nothing to her, other than now familiar sound sequences, but others understood. Helen's sense of bodies gathered around her started to diminish, the morani silently dispersing in response to Charles' words.

'Keep close now, we will move up to the runway perimeter. We are only four hundred paces from there, so be very quiet,' said Charles, his whispered English a welcome sound in the dark bush night.

It took quite a while to weave through the bush to the runway. Some thickets were impenetrable and required detours, in other places there were wide spaces between the bushes and stunted trees where grazers had kept the growth in check. The moran leading the column knew exactly where he was going; Helen might as well have been blindfolded for all she could see. Each step was a step into black, and the walk seemed to take forever. Eventually, they came to a halt.

Charles invited them all to kneel then they crawled forward, edging round the shape of yet another bulging mound of bush. Beyond it, after carefully parting a final stand of the ubiquitous grasses, Helen saw this was different; here the environment changed.

She became aware of the steady grumbling tut, tut, tut of a distant generator. There was a clearing between her and some electric lights that shone from a building on the other side. As her eyes started to pick out detail, she could tell the clearing was the runway. The electric lights were shining from two adjacent locations, the first a two-storey office unit, the second an open-sided warehouse shelter for cargo. The only things inside it were a little wire-fenced lockup and vehicles, neatly parked in a row.

Charles shuffled across and settled between Sam and Helen. He pointed to the wire lockup. Helen focused on it and realised there were two men seated close beside it - guards.

'That's where they used to keep a supply of fuel,' said Charles.

'Right, and I'm thinking there's really no need to mount a guard on a bunch of oil drums out here.'

'You are correct, no need,' said Charles.

'So, they are guarding something special. I'll guess that lockup would be the perfect little jail to keep Bob Prentice hemmed in.'

'Correct.'

'What's the plan?' said Helen.

Charles carefully pointed to the end of the runway at what looked like a mound of earth. Slowly, she became aware of little movements, two heads showing above a defensive earthwork, probably talking to each other, certainly vigilant.

Then Charles swung his hand in an arc towards the opposite end of the runway, pointing out two small figures patrolling along its length. 'We have counted eight guards rotating their duties every half hour.'

'Smart, every guard has to stay alert. No one gets the chance to be lulled into any false sense of familiarity. Whoever set this up was on the ball. Look, Charles, I need to get a closer look at the lockup, make sure our man is inside. Can we work our way round to the other side?'

'Of course, it will take a little while and we will need to be very quiet. Perhaps, just you and I should go?'

'Let's do it,' said Sam.

Helen felt Sam's hand squeeze her shoulder and then, before she could object to being left behind, he was up and gone into the black.

Chapter 33
SUNDAY 3RD NOVEMBER - AM

Helen had counted off the sequences of guard changes in Sam's absence. While he had been away, Angel had crept forward into Sam's space. She had welcomed his whispered chat as a distraction from worry over where Sam had got to, and what was going to happen next. To her other side a moran lay silent, intently staring across the runway.

'Angel, I still don't really understand why you're here.'

'Truth is I don't understand either. Bishop Ignatius said I was to come, and I was to ensure you were safe.'

'Yeah? And what does your bishop think you could do against this lot,' she said while gazing across the runway towards the guards.

The silence that followed made it clear Angel had no idea.

'Angel, you're a decent guy, you helped us out in Arusha, I'm thankful for that. We would never have got Sam out of jail in time without you. And we sure wouldn't have found a lead to Smuts and Ngorongoro either. So, you've done a lot to help us, but out here, it's a different ballgame. The bishop asked you to help us in Arusha, you helped us, and I appreciate that. Really, I do. But why would he send you into such danger? That, I don't understand.'

She felt Angel's shoulder rise against hers as he shrugged. 'All I can say is the bishop insists you are precious to him and to the Church. He told me if anything happened to you … Well nothing must happen to you.'

'So here we are.'

'Yes, here we are …' Angel fell silent.

• • •

A gentle rustling sound behind them did not cause any concern to the moran who lay motionless in the grass beside Helen. Moments later, Sam and Charles appeared, moving shadow shapes in the dark. They crouched down beside Helen and Angel. Charles' senior moran moved closer. It would be dawn in a couple of hours. Now was the time to learn of plans.

Together, they all pulled back from the edge of the bush and into deeper cover. There they sat in a circle as Sam detailed his plan.

'There are four pairs of guards, regularly rotating through the tasks. When one group goes inside for their break, the next comes out. That pair goes directly to the hangar to take over responsibility for guarding the ACE and Bob in the lockup. The guards they relieve then patrol up the far side of the runway to the defensive position at the end, and they take over that position. Finally, the two guards relieved at the defensive position patrol the full length of the runway's edge on our side, passing just in front of us, before crossing over and heading back up the runway to the office for their break, and then the sequence repeats.'

'Are you sure Bob is in the lockup?' said Helen.

'Yes, the lockup's really just a giant wire cage, he's there alright. We saw him.'

'Is he hurt?'

'Can't say for sure, looks as though they have him tied to the fencing.'

'I thought he was probably asleep,' said Charles.

'Now here's my plan. I and four of Charles' morani will work back around to a spot behind the warehouse and wait.

'Charles, your senior moran,' Sam rested a hand on the shoulder of the warrior crouched next to him, 'should take four men to the end of the runway and get in a position to attack the dugout. Their job is to take out the defenders there to prevent them firing down the runway at us when we cross back here with Bob. Now this is very important - you'll remember as we went round together, I pointed out the shoulder-launched rockets, the tubes they have placed beside their dugout. I need them brought back to this point as quickly as possible.'

Sam paused to allow Charles a chance to translate for the warriors.

'Charles, I would like you to get to the other end of the runway, to the very end. You'll have cover there where the bush has regrown right back to the edge. When the two guards patrolling the runway's edge reach the corner, you and your men take them out. Your only targets are the two patrolling guards. Then, as soon as you strike - but not before, I want the senior moran to go into action at the dugout end. Then we'll move on the guards at the warehouse. Finally, once we've grabbed Bob we will come directly back across the runway to here.

'I don't know how long we'll have before the guards on their break kick back into action or how many more men Ro has in the office building. We will be lucky to have two minutes before reinforcements start to turn out. So, let's make every second count.'

'What's the rocket for?' said Helen.

'My goal is to rescue Bob. The military want ACE rescued. Right now, we don't have the tools to get it away from Ro, so the next best thing will be to destroy it - at least that will keep it out of other people's hands. There won't be time to rescue Bob and destroy it while I'm over there. Once back here, I'll use a rocket to blow the damned thing up. That should satisfy everyone - except Ro.'

'What about Ro and the rest of his men?' said Helen.

'As soon as we've snatched Bob, we'll fall back to this location, and then carry on to the vehicles. I'll follow as soon as I've blown up ACE. Then it's hell for leather to the river and across at the ford. We should be able to hold them off from the other side for a while. I'm guessing once Ro sees the ACE is destroyed, a desire for revenge will be trumped by the need to get out of here ahead of any authorities that he must know will be closing in on him.'

Again, Charles provided a translation for the morani. It was clear they were delighted, welcoming the opportunity to dole out punishment for the death of their brother warrior.

'So, timing is going to be critical. All three attacks must be launched in strict order or we lose the element of surprise. If we get the timing right, they won't have time to put up any resistance. Those of us attacking the warehouse and the defensive position will get into our positions, wait, and watch. We will strike only after the patrolling guards reach the corner and turn at the far end of the runway, where you will be waiting, Charles. Exactly as they turn, you attack. Everyone happy with the plan?'

The shadows dispersed into the night leaving Helen with Angel and two morani, who were to act as a rear guard. The minutes slipped by, and while maintaining the strict silence that Sam had ordered, Helen, Angel and the rear guard crawled the short distance back to the edge of the bush. The runway was close enough to touch. Then the silence was broken by a whispered voice.

'What if it goes wrong?' said Angel.

'It won't,' said Helen.

'But it's all such a patchwork, so many variables.'

'It'll work, stop worrying. Sam understands these things.'

There was an anxious hiss from the shadows as one of the morani expressed displeasure at their talking. Angel fell quiet, and Helen settled down to wait and watch.

• • •

Sam was tucked in to the immediate rear of the open-sided warehousing. From his vantage point, he could see the lockup with Bob lying inside, and the row of vehicles. One long wheelbase Land Rover was in British Army camouflage colours, and its peculiarly shaped fibreglass superstructure marked it out. The others were a selection of civilian 4 x 4s. Two men sat beside the lockup, their seating positions ensuring they could see along the line of vehicles. Away to his right, at the end of the runway, Sam could just make out the little raised mound of earth that marked the defensive position. The intermittent glow of a cigarette indicated that the guards there were relaxed.

To Sam's left and immediately beyond the warehousing was the office building. It was quiet now, but he knew there were two guards taking a break inside. Sam was unsure how many other men were inside, and he recognised that not knowing was a danger. He had to live with that as best he could.

Low and intermittent, the sound of the dawn was just starting to splutter into life as the first light crept into the eastern sky. He knew, in only a few minutes, the bush world would be filled with singing and rustling in the growing light. He let his eyes cast across the runway, knew Helen and the others would be watching from directly opposite his position. Then he turned his head to check on the mobile patrol's progress. Approaching the farthest end of the runway, now too far away for detail to be discernible, only their torches played clearly against the bush line, where the once cleared land had regenerated growth back to the runway's edge. They would be turning at any moment now. He glanced to the morani ranged to either side of him. Using hand gestures and facial expressions he had signed their tasks as best he could. They had nodded understanding; he had to trust they had picked up what he needed.

• • •

Charles squatted in the bush, two morani to either side of him. The lightening sky had done nothing yet to illuminate them in the still darkened shadows of the bush. They remained invisible to the two guards whose torches had steadily worked their way along the edge of the runway; now the guards were close, very close, just three or four paces from the corner. They would turn at any moment.

Twisting the shaft of his spear slightly, Charles allowed the long-bladed head to rest against the upper thigh of the young moran who knelt to his left. He gently pressed the flat of his blade against the moran's flesh until he felt a slight resistance. With his other hand he brought the balled end of his rungu to rest on the thigh of the moran to his right. He could sense the anticipation in the air as his young morani tensed, ready for the off. He maintained a steady pressure.

A torch beam flicked past them, failed to pick them out; but had it done so, Charles could tell it would not have mattered. The guards were not even looking now - their senses were relaxing with the approaching daylight and the reassuring calls of the dawn chorus. They just wanted their break. The torch beams swung away, forming an arc as the guards started to change direction.

At the same instant, Charles lifted his spearhead and rungu from the flesh of his men, releasing them. Like greyhounds loosed from the trap, both men leapt up and, in silence, stepped clear of the bush, launching their spears towards the unguarded backs of the two guards.

A lifetime of practice ensured the spear hands that needed to be steady in the face of a charging lion launched their missiles true. Simultaneously, the long-bladed spearheads reached their targets' backs. One died instantly, dropping to the ground without a sound, the spear point having plunged through the back of his ribcage and straight through his heart.

The second guard dropped forward to his hands and knees, the shaft sticking up from his back, straight to the sky, its blade embedded in his left lung. The man had no breath to cry out and just moaned as the young moran closed on him. Pulling the rungu from his waistband the moran raised it high and brought it down on the guard's head. He died instantly, his skull collapsing under the blow.

Charles signalled the second pair of morani forward. They moved out from cover to help the first two warriors carry the guards away into the bush. Charles retrieved the abandoned torches and switched them off before he too stepped back into the anonymous bush where his young warriors were busy extracting their spears from the dead men's bodies.

• • •

The senior moran was kneeling on the ground. Head up, he had been staring intently down the length of the runway, maintaining an unwavering watch on the slow bobbing beams of the guards' torches, toy-like in the distance as they worked round the runway perimeter. He was also aware of the cigarette smoke and sounds of quiet chatter emanating from the dugout that was just a few paces in front of him.

He saw the beams of the distant torches swing round as the patrol reached the far end of the runway and began its turn. A moment later the distant beams tilted, shuddered and rolled as though they had been dropped to the ground. The beams caught a moment of movement and then went out. It had begun.

Bringing his focus closer to home, he began to crawl forward. The morani who were spread out to either side did the same and the warrior line rapidly advanced on the defensive position. Reaching the edge of the little trench, the senior moran stood and leapt over the earthwork, dropping down into the trench.

He landed between the two guards who had been sitting peacefully on upturned wooden boxes, their weapons resting against the side of the trench. Both men cried out in shock and one leapt up, reaching for his weapon. The other couldn't move. The senior moran had angled his spear down towards the man's belly as he dropped. The spearhead sliced through flesh and vitals. Driven by the senior moran's bodyweight the long broad blade kept moving down, finally emerging from deep between the guard's legs to embed itself in the wooden box on which the guard sat.

The guard did not understand what had happened, with one hand he gripped the spear shaft, with the other he reached between his legs. Instantly, both hands were bloodied and foul, he tried to stand but couldn't. The pain signals at last reached his brain and he screamed loud. A young moran standing above the trench swung his rungu and shattered the man's jaw to stop the noise. He swung again and broke the guard's skull, killing him.

The senior moran grappled with the surviving guard, preventing him from picking up his firearm. Two more morani dropped into the trench and the guard realised it was all up for him. His shouted alarm call died on his lips when one of the newly arrived morani thrust a sharp knife into his throat.

Blood pumped out of the opened throat and sprayed across the morani who revelled in this further revenge for yesterday's death of their brother moran. As the blood flow ended and the guard's body went limp, the senior moran let it fall to the bottom of the trench. He pointed to the tubes sticking up at either end of the trench and ordered his men to remove them. The men grabbed a tube each and clambered out of the trench.

Time was tight with the daylight growing minute by minute but the senior moran took a moment to look across at the open-sided warehouse, trying to gauge Sam's progress before he led his band in a run directly down the runway, to carry the shoulder-launched rockets to their rendezvous point.

• • •

Sam had watched the silhouette of a moran appear behind the defensive trench then drop out of sight, he guessed into the trench. No gunfire followed. Then more morani appeared and they too dropped into the trench. He thought he heard a cry, knew he had, but was thankful that the dawn chorus was now cranking itself up; to the unaware, the distant cries had merged into the steadily building wall of noise from a myriad of different birds and animals and insects. Today it sounded different, louder than he had heard before, as though an unconscious sense of anticipation permeated the bush.

The coming of daylight revealed another change. The long days of blue skies and burning sun were gone. Yesterday's patchy clouds had been harbingers of change. This morning's sky was a mass of grey and black cloud, piling up high, bulging fit to burst, heavy with rain and just waiting for nature's cue to release its load.

While he'd watched the distant morani move into action there had been a tightness in his stomach, something he always felt just before action. Now, as he raised a hand to trigger his attack, the tightness subsided, as it always did. He looked to left and right, saw the morani were ready, waiting for the signal. His hand dropped, and they swung into action.

Sam and the four morani stood as one; while two morani paused to launch their spears at the guards, Sam and the other two closed in at the run. The morani were to deal with the guards while Sam needed to find the key to the lockup cage.

The sitting men were caught completely off guard. All they could do was turn their heads in response to the movement at the rear of the warehousing and note the blurs that were the spears hurtling across the open space towards them.

One spearhead punched through its target's breastbone, slicing through the lung behind and emerging through the ribcage at the rear to embed itself in the chair back. The man groaned and dropped his cigarette. He coughed and, volcano-like, a puff of smoke emerged from his mouth, followed by a flow of frothy red. Vainly, he clawed at the spear shaft where it had entered his chest. He looked at it, then up at the moran rushing across the concrete floor towards him.

There was no time for his consciousness to register the pain he felt in his chest before the heavy end of the moran's swinging rungu met the side of his head, shattering his skull. The second blow was unnecessary but was delivered regardless, coming down from above and splitting the skull in two to leave the brain exposed to nature and the first of the morning flies that were quick to settle on the exposed jelly.

The second spearhead met more resistance in the stock of the guard's machine pistol; it was deflected to one side while knocking the guard off his chair and onto the ground. His weapon still secure on its strap, the guard looked up at the moran closing on him, raised the barrel of his weapon and pulled the trigger. The burst of fire put three rounds into the moran: leg, groin, belly, the wounded warrior dropped to the ground. And then snarling, he raised himself on to his forearms and tried to continue his attack, dragging himself towards the grounded guard.

In complete fear, the guard fired again, determined to kill his attacker, and without thinking, he allowed his high-speed machine pistol to empty its magazine, in the process, the grounded moran's head simply disintegrated. Then the guard wished he had exercised more control with his trigger finger. He saw his friend, still seated, skewered with a spear and being beaten with a club. In desperation, he tried to get up, but slipped in the splattered remains of the dead warrior's head. He screamed and shouted for help while scrabbling across the concrete floor.

Sam's plan A, the stealthy opening of the cargo cage and rapid dash away to safety, had vanished with the firing of the guard's weapon and his desperate shouts for help. There was no advantage now in pausing to search the guards for the access key. Leaving the morani to deal with the still breathing guard, Sam changed direction and headed for the cargo cage.

As he approached, Sam could see his friend Bob, lying on the ground, hands secured and tied to the inside of the fence. He aimed his pistol at the padlock that held the gate shut.

'Turn your eyes away,' he shouted.

He saw Bob avert his gaze and immediately brought the muzzle close to the lock and fired. He fired again, and the broken lock dropped to the ground.

As Sam swung the gate open there was a scream behind him, it rose and fell in intensity several times. While crossing the cage, he chanced a glance in the direction of the scream. The second guard would never get the chance to shoot another Maasai. One moran was stood over the guard, repeatedly plunging his long-bladed spear into the guard's back. Simple justice - the guard had killed his brother, now he killed the guard.

Turning his attention back to the cage, he belted the pistol, produced his pocketknife and knelt beside Bob Prentice. 'Hold still, sir,' said Sam, while cutting at the rope around Bob's wrists.

'Cameron? Sam Cameron, is that you?' Bob was sitting up, twisting his wrists to offer the best cutting profile.

'It's me. Don't ask why, long story. We're on a tight line here.'

'Right, right, I'm with you. But Sam, you know who's behind this? It's Ro.'

The rope fell away. Then Sam cut the ties from Bob's ankles and pulled Bob to his feet. He realised Bob could hardly walk. Pushing an arm beneath his old commanding officer's shoulder, he began to lead him from the cage. The morani saw the problem and hurried to help as Bob collapsed to the ground.

One moran stood between Bob's legs, bent and took a leg in each hand. The other two morani each took an arm. They lifted Bob off the ground and set off at a run across the runway towards the rendezvous point. Sam swung the machine pistol off his shoulder and followed the morani out onto the runway. A few paces behind the group, he provided cover, running backwards, keeping his weapon trained on the office doorway.

He had not retreated twenty paces before the tea-break guards got their act together. The office door burst open and the two men ran out. They did not get the chance to fire as Sam put them down with a crisp burst of fire.

Still retreating, he spotted movement at an upper floor window and fired; saw through the remnants of shattered glass that he'd made contact. Then a weapon fired from a window further along. Sam heard a cry from one of the group behind him and immediately sprayed the offending window, hoping he'd got his man but couldn't be sure - certainly made them keep their heads down for a moment. He fired again, emptying the magazine.

Turning his back on the office, he threw down the empty weapon and ran to catch up with the retreating morani. One was wounded and hobbled along while the other two rushed ahead with Bob; they were almost at the bush line. As Sam caught up with the wounded moran, he forced his arm round and under the man's shoulder, supporting and pulling him ahead. 'Come on, man, we'll make it,' he said.

The moran grunted a response and both men focused on reaching the bush.

From the corner of his eye, Sam caught a glimpse of the senior moran leading his attack team at the run back from the end of the runway. They each had a bulky tube slung over their shoulder. Sam's heart sank - that team should already have been safe at the rendezvous point and under cover of the bush. They were taking too long to get back. There was nothing he could do.

Just as Sam and his team reached the bush, gunfire resumed behind them. Dust kicked up around their feet, leaves twitched and flicked, and Sam felt his shirt tugged as a round whizzed past, too close to think about. Then they were in cover and out of sight. The gunfire stopped for a moment, its sound replaced by the shouts of the senior moran urging his men on.

Sam handed the wounded moran on to his colleagues. A little ahead, he could see Helen leaving Bob and moving towards the wounded man, first aid kit in her hand. He turned back towards the runway and, dropping to his hands and knees, quickly crawled back to the bush line. Charles was already there; they nodded at one another just as the patta patta sound of automatic fire resumed.

Sam and Charles watched in horror as, one by one, the senior moran and his team dropped on to the runway. In only seconds, they were all down. Sam gritted his teeth and reached out to restrain Charles from running out into the open as the guns worked up and down the line of wounded men three times. By the third pass, it was clear there would be nobody left to save. All the morani were dead. Sam could feel the rage pulsing through Charles.

'They must all die,' said Charles. 'All of them.' The restrained balance that normally played through all his spoken English was missing now. This was a chief needing to avenge his fallen warriors. 'That was murder, no need to shoot them three times.'

Sam understood Charles' pain and was furious at the loss of such good proud men. But his concern was different. He needed the shoulder missile launchers that were now lying abandoned amongst the dead. Without them, he could not destroy ACE. Now Koreans were darting from the office door and heading for the warehouse. Sam couldn't make out exactly what they were doing.

There was a rustling behind Sam then Bob Prentice, his untethered legs slowly regaining mobility, was lying between him and Charles.

Bob saw the bodies lying on the runway. 'Damn, Ro. That's always the way with him, he's a butcher.'

'He will pay,' said Charles. He turned his head to look at Bob. 'I hope you were worth it.'

Bob didn't reply, just rested his hand on the chief's shoulder.

Sam rolled onto his side and stuck out his hand. Bob took it and they shook warmly. 'Charles, this is Colonel Bob Prentice, my good friend and one-time commanding officer.'

Charles and Bob shook hands.

'So, Sam, we can catch up later, I'll look forward to learning why it's you leading a rescue mission after your years away. Right now, though, where are the troops? We need to deal with Ro at once.'

'No troops, just me, Charles and his warriors - the morani.'

'Hell, no backup at all?'

'Sorry, it's down to us.'

'Look at those,' said Charles. 'What are they?' He pointed across to the warehouse where the backdoor to the oddly shaped British military Land Rover had opened. A little ramp had slid out and, one after the other, four what looked like big shoeboxes on wheels were rolling down. They assembled in an orderly line beside their control vehicle.

'They're Rollers and that's their control vehicle. We need to move now,' said Bob. 'We need to be away before they get started.'

'What are they?' said Sam.

'Come on, I'll tell you as we go. We must fall back now.'

'What's the panic Bob?'

'It's ACE. Ro's going to …' His voice trailed off as a percussive whooshing sound came from the Land Rover, which had been manoeuvred out from beneath the warehouse roof to launch a series of smoke bombs into the sky. More whooshing sounds followed as more smoke bombs flew high overhead.

Helen joined them. 'What is it Sam? What's going on?' She pointed up into the sky where a pattern of smoke bombs hung in the air, each suspended on a miniature parachute, and they all dispersed billowing clouds of light brown smoke. 'Look at them all.'

The billowing smoke was spreading as the bombs dropped slowly down. Sam reckoned they were dispersing along the whole length of the runway and he couldn't work out how far back, perhaps all the way back to the vehicles.

'How far to your vehicles?' said Bob.

'Three, maybe four hundred yards.'

'We won't make it in time,' said Bob.

'What are we running from? Is it a gas attack? Is that what your ACE is, a chemical weapon?'

'No, not chemicals.'

Bob reached round and pulled Sam's pistol from his waistband. Sam looked startled, then puzzled.

'What's going on Bob?'

Bob thrust the weapon into Sam's hand. 'Shoot me, kill me now. It's your only chance to get away. Shoot me now before ACE becomes fully active.'

Charles stretched across with his spear and pressed it lightly down on to Sam's forearm. 'Many morani just died to keep him alive. Nobody is going to kill him now, he must live.'

'Don't worry, Charles; I have no intention of shooting him.'

Bob's face contorted with anxiety, he glanced out across the runway to where the four little vehicles remained motionless on the ground. 'Look, kill me or you're all done for. It's that simple. ACE stands for Autonomous Combat Entity. Those little monsters over there will take you all.' He waved his hand up into the sky. That's not a smoke bomb cloud, it's a mote cloud.'

'Mote cloud?' said Helen.

'Yes. A multitude of tiny manufactured motes. Think of the house dust motes you see drifting down through a shaft of sunlight, only here each one is a tiny sensor that can pick up movements and share the knowledge with the surrounding motes. They only communicate a couple of paces but that's all that's needed. By the time that lot settle, they will have blanketed this area, a half mile in every direction. We'll never make it to the vehicles.'

'Bob, slow down, you're not making sense,' said Sam.

'Look it's simple. The motes form a detector grid. They're far too small for you to see them but very numerous; they all just sit there and register every footstep, every rolling wheel that passes by. They tell their neighbours who tell theirs and so on. That control vehicle unleashes the four Rollers into the mote grid and they just work their way through it, communicating with and through the motes. Hunting any walking man or moving vehicle, always calculating the most efficient intercept routes. Working independently, in pairs, all together, they decide what'll work best. Believe me, you can't hide. They'll know where you are, where you're going and when you're changing direction. The motes are already settling now, the network will be forming as we speak. There's no time. Just shoot me while you can.'

Charles threw Bob a look of disdain. 'We came to help you. If it's so bad, stay and help us, why take the coward's way out?'

Bob sighed in exasperation, put his head in his hands and shook it. 'No, no, no. Listen, right now everyone in the mote grid, except me, is on borrowed time. I think it's already too late. Any moment now the motes will complete their network, tell the control vehicle and then it's a turkey shoot and you are the turkeys. No escape, period.'

'Not you?' said Helen.

'No, I'm a living key, what the monster feeds off. Listen, ACE is so lethal it's fitted with the latest bio-security measures. An ACE unit is programmed to its controller. The mote network is constantly scanning for the controller's biorhythms. The system only works if the motes are aware of the controller's presence, that's why Ro has needed me. Fire it up without my presence, and it will auto-fry everything. The kit is useless without the controller. It will simply self-destruct. It's a failsafe to ensure the system can't be used against us by an enemy.'

'Bob Prentice, what the hell have you been doing since I left you?'

'You don't want to know, believe me. But believe me, too, your only hope now is to shoot me. Once I'm dead, there are no biorhythms for the motes to detect and the weapon will start a phase down, within two minutes the message will have filtered through the whole mote grid, the control vehicle and the Rollers and then it will simply self-destruct completely, burn itself out. And that will leave Ro with nothing.'

'We haven't come this far to lose you now. There must be something we can do,' said Sam.

'But if you're the controller, how is it working now without your instructions?' said Helen.

'Anyone with the operator's handbook can activate the system from the control vehicle; the system just needs to be aware of my living presence in the theatre. Oh, and of course, the Rollers know not to shoot their controller.'

'Look, your little Rollers are moving. They're fast,' she said.

'Yes, electric, and they have solar power capacity, like the motes, so once deployed they look after themselves.' Bob shouted into the surrounding bush areas. 'Everyone listen - nobody move, do not walk under any circumstances, and just stay still.'

Charles realised his morani would not understand and translated the message, shouting it into the bush. He couldn't be sure his message was heard by his warriors who he had already directed back to the vehicles with their wounded comrade.

Helen, Sam, Charles and Bob stood in motionless silence for a few moments. Angel hovered immediately behind Helen. From their position, just inside the bush line, they were concealed but still had a clear view out across the runway; a direct line of sight over the bodies of the dead morani to the office block on the far side. More bodies lay there, dead, Ro's men. The rear door to the oddly shaped Land Rover was still open; a man appeared at the doorway, a bullhorn in his hand.

'Ro,' said Bob.

'Hmm, he hasn't changed,' said Sam. 'I wonder if he knows it's me here to rescue you.'

Bob looked at him. 'If he does, then guaranteed he will have something nasty lined up for you. Last time we crossed paths you messed up his little scheme in Brunei, remember?

And I don't have Ro marked down as the forgiving type. Oh, and how exactly is this a rescue?' He gave a dry laugh, Sam joined in.

'Come on guys,' said Helen. 'This is not the time for laughing. And Sam, this *is* the time for you to come up with some great plan to get us off the hook. Let's focus guys.' Helen put her arm round a very nervous looking Angel. 'Don't worry, Sam will come up with something, he always does.'

Angel gave her a smile that lacked conviction.

Sam was eyeing up the shoulder-launched rocket tubes lying scattered amongst the dead morani. 'If I could get one of those and take out the control vehicle, that might do the trick.'

The Rollers were buzzing to and fro across the runway, weaving crazy patterns, sometimes independently, and sometimes in concert.

'No, once the system is activated and up and running, the Rollers have all the computing power necessary to interact independently with the mote network. If you take out the control vehicle, all you do is destroy the off switch not switch it off. It's only a few moments before they are ready, that little dance they're doing is a calibration procedure.'

'I could try to take the Rollers out.'

'Yes, you might get one, two if you are very lucky before they get you.'

'Well if that's all we've got, let's hope I'm lucky,' said Sam, preparing to make a dash for the rocket launch tubes.

The bullhorn cracked and whistled as Ro raised it to his mouth. 'Colonel Prentice. I know you can hear me. I can see where you are on the control vehicle's display panel. There is no hiding place. I want you to step out into the open now. If you do, I will spare your friends. On that you have my word.'

Just as Ro stopped speaking, the four Rollers stopped their dance, coming again to a halt in a neat line in front of their control vehicle.

Four heavily armed men, each dressed in camouflage fatigues, had emerged from the office building and lined up beside the Rollers. Ro shouted an order at them and pointed to the 4 x 4 parked beside his control vehicle. Two men got into the vehicle; the other two stepped out onto the runway, beside the Rollers.

'Why aren't they worried about being shot by the Rollers?' said Sam.

'They'll have ID recognition tabs on. That's how the Rollers can distinguish between friend and foe while moving through the grid.'

One of the Koreans stooped to place something on a Roller. Ro raised the bullhorn again. 'Colonel Prentice I'm sending you a package.'

Suddenly, the Roller started to move. It pulled away from the pack, moved directly out to the middle of the runway and then paused momentarily before running twenty yards up the centreline, turning and retracing its route.

'What's it doing?' said Sam.

'Deciding where it wants to go. It must have a mission.'

'I thought they were autonomous.'

'Yes, but they can be instructed from the control vehicle too. Look it's on the move.'

The Roller suddenly darted forward, faster than a man could run. It moved silently over the runway and disappeared into the bush around thirty paces to Sam and Helen's left.

'I get that the motes form a detector matrix on the ground, so the Rollers know where people are relative to their own positions, but how are they able to manoeuvre round things? How do they know where rocks or trees and bushes are?' said Sam.

'That sounds hard, but it was actually one of the easier design issues to resolve. In fact, it fixed itself. As the dust motes settle, they land on everything, not just the ground. Rocks bushes, old tree stumps. If it's out there, it will get covered. The motes are constantly fixing their positions relative to the grid. Not just left and right, behind and ahead, it's up and down too. So, it's forming a three-dimensional map. It doesn't know if the bump ahead is a rock or a tree stump; just knows it's an obstacle and drives round ...' Bob stopped talking. The colour had drained from his face and he directed a meaningful stare beyond Sam.

Cautiously, Sam turned - his heart sank. The Roller, that only moments before had entered into the bush further along the runway, had plotted a course through the wild undergrowth, around rocks, trees and bushes and was now moving directly towards them. In size, the squat little construct was similar in proportions to a big shoebox fitted with four disproportionately large wheels that kept the box well clear of the ground. On the top was mounted a little device that looked for all the world as though it had been modelled on a frigate's automatic gun turret.

'Nobody move,' said Bob.

The Roller stopped directly in front of Bob. The walkie-talkie resting behind the gun turret squawked and then Ro's voice came through. 'Colonel Prentice. Pick up the radio.'

'Hello, Ro. Prentice here.'

'Good, Colonel Prentice. Now let's not waste any time, I've got a tight schedule to keep. I want you to walk out of the bush and onto the runway right now.'

'And I'll do that because?'

'Because if you don't, I will shoot all the pathetic little rescue party around you, and then my men will still be able to bring you in. Now, please, come out onto the runway.'

'What's the big hurry, Ro? We're all out here in the middle of nowhere, isn't there some other way to handle this?'

'No.'

The Roller suddenly kicked into action; executing a smart turn, it rolled silently off, deeper into the bush, and vanished from sight.

'Colonel Prentice, can Captain Cameron hear me?'

'He can hear you.'

'Good. It's been a long time Captain Cameron. I've often thought how nice it would be for our paths to cross again.'

'It's just Cameron now, Ro. I'm a civilian.'

'And yet, here you are. Once again, intruding into my world. It has to stop, and I think today is the day for stopping.'

'Get on with it Ro. I won't give you any ground.'

Helen was listening intently. She knew that Sam's time in the military had involved some tricky moments, but he had never talked too much about it. Being in the Intelligence Corps covered a lot of ground. Anything from interpreting aerial photographs and deciphering codes all the way up the scale to, well, clearly to this.

'No, I know you won't give ground. But my spotters in Nairobi picked up that you don't travel alone any more. It seems you have come on an accompanied posting to a combat zone. I think that was a mistake. Out here, you're in my domain, I will call the shots, quite literally, Mr Cameron. And she's very pretty, if you like redheads. Which I do.'

'Leave her out of this, Ro. She's nothing to do with you and me.'

'Oh, but she is. Any special friend of yours merits special treatment from me. And she will have it.'

Charles let out a shout. Pointing onto the runway. 'I think one of the morani is still alive, I saw a movement.' He didn't hesitate and sprinted out from the bush onto the runway where he hurried to his surviving warrior.

'No! Stay still!' said Bob,' but Charles was already gone. Ignoring Bob's instruction, Helen immediately followed with the first aid kit. Angel was torn between the illusory comfort afforded by the bush and his bishop's instruction to find and protect Helen. He hesitated, but after a moment the bishop won, and he too hurried into the open to join Helen. She was kneeling beside the surviving moran, already assessing his wounds and applying dressings. Charles knelt by the man's head, cradling it.

'He stroked the young man's face. His hands were gentle, but when Helen glanced up to his eyes, they were full of anger.

Sam turned his attention away from the runway and back to the walkie-talkie as it squelched and crackled. 'Well this is a turn up. I hadn't thought you would give up the girl so easily,' said Ro.

'Butt out, Ro. Don't even think of harming her or believe me there are no rules of engagement anywhere that will protect you, ever.'

'A raw nerve, I see. Well, before you make any threats, you'd better understand just what power I wield now I have ACE active. I'm watching the scanners, it won't be long now.'

Sam glanced at Bob, 'What does he mean?'

'There are scanners in the control vehicle that display the Rollers' progress around the grid. The Rollers can be left to clear and defend the grid independently. They can also be directed to complete specific tasks; once given a task the Rollers will work independently to achieve it. He must have instructed the Roller that just left us to do something ...'

The reports of controlled gunfire from deeper in the bush suddenly dominated the environment. The firing stopped as abruptly as it had started and was replaced by the cries of wounded men. It was immediately clear that the group of morani who had set off with their wounded comrade for the vehicles had not made it.

Sam and Bob turned and gazed in the direction of the noise.

'Hell, it's caught up with the morani.'

'What are their chances? Will any survive?'

'Oh, they'll still be alive - listen to the cries. The Rollers are programmed to put two rounds into their target's lower leg. Bang, bang; rapid fire and certain hits. Sure as hell, puts the target down. Immobilises them. If they manage to get up and walk, they'll get another two rounds.'

'Why the lower leg?'

'Practicality and efficiency. The Roller is working on information from the mote network; at any given moment, it knows exactly where a biped's feet are and hence its lower leg. So, it targets what it knows. No point in going for body shots or headshots unless it knows how high above the ground the man is and that's entirely unpredictable from the information available to them. Plus, heads and bodies are invariably well armoured these days. Might even miss, depending on the way a man is leaning or facing. Go for the lower legs, a certain hit every time. Then your victim's out of the battle and perfect ambush bait to draw in rescue parties - more targets.'

'This is one sick weapons system, Bob. How the hell did you get involved in it?'

On the runway, Charles could hear Sam and Bob's voices, but he ignored them as he stood and gazed back over the bush line towards the more distant cries of his morani. He knew exactly what it meant. Angel stood in silence beside him. Helen remained on her knees and continued to patch up her patient.

The radio squelched. 'Colonel Prentice. You know what just happened. Eight men down, and by the way, one made the mistake of getting up - now he's got four bullet holes in his legs. Now, can I expect your co-operation, or do I need to issue more instructions?'

Just as Bob raised the walkie-talkie to reply there came the sound of gunfire close by on the runway, it was followed by suddenly familiar cries of pain. A more distant sound reached them as a 4 x 4 engine revved and tyres screeched. Sam and Bob hurried to where the bush gave way to the runway's edge.

Charles and Angel were both down with bullet wounds to their lower legs.

A 4 x 4 raced across the runway, halting beside the downed morani. Two Koreans leapt out and snatched Helen. She was struggling, fighting to get back to the wounded moran who was once more motionless on the ground.

Bob caught Sam's arm and forcefully checked him, preventing him from leaving the bush line.

'Let me go, damn it,' said Sam.

Bob kept tight hold and threw his gaze out across the runway. 'Don't go out or you'll be downed, look.'

While still struggling, Sam followed the direction Bob had indicated. No more than ten paces ahead was a Roller - motionless, its gun barrel facing towards them.

'It must have come across the runway while the first one was shooting up Charles' morani back there. They can move very fast on a flat surface.'

In frustration, Sam looked beyond the Roller to where the guards were manhandling Helen. Each man had taken a grip of one of her arms and they were propelling her towards the open door of their 4 x 4.

'Let me go,' said Helen. 'That man will die without attention.' The Koreans ignored her. She continued to struggle, wedging a foot against the doorframe in an attempt to avoid being forced into the rear seats. Her head banged against the opened door slicing a wound above her temple and blood started to trickle down the side of her face. She still pushed back with her foot, refusing to enter. 'No! No, I'm not going in there.'

She leaned forward and bit one guard's hand, hard, kept biting harder to force him to release her. The man cried out as her teeth drew blood; she gagged slightly but bit on, even as the taste of iron in the man's blood registered on her taste buds. Then she felt a blow to the back of her head and everything went black.

Sam shouted in anger and, once again, struggled against Bob's restraining arms while an unconscious Helen was bundled into the 4 x 4 and driven away across the runway.

Sam and Bob stood at the bush line alone. Out on the runway, the Roller was motionless as Angel and Charles lay on the ground bleeding. It was clear that Angel had no intention of moving, lying curled up so he could hold his now blood-red shirt pressed against his leg wounds. He was losing a lot of blood.

Charles rose to his knees; the anger on his face had not been diminished by the pain he felt.

'Don't stand up!' Sam's warning cut over Angel's gentle moaning. 'Charles, do not stand up. The Roller shoots at legs. Don't give it a target.'

'What the hell are we going to do, Bob? This is your monster.'

'There's nothing we can do; the little blighters are pretty well invincible when …' Bob fell silent as Sam shook his arm.

Out on the runway, Charles, still kneeling, had drawn his rungu from his waistband and lifted it above his head.

'He'll never hit that little thing from there,' said Sam.

They both watched spellbound as the chief took careful aim. He drew his arm back then flashed it forward to let the rungu fly. It hissed through the air and caught the Roller squarely on its side. The little machine rocked and then toppled over.

'Yes,' said Sam, starting forward to help Charles and Angel.

'Wait.' Bob gripped Sam's arm for a second time, holding him back. Then he stepped close beside him before shouting across to Charles who was struggling to his feet. 'Stay down, it's not safe.'

Sam could just see what was causing Bob concern. From the sides of the Roller, little rods had started to extend out - like telescopic aerials. In seconds, its side lying on the ground was tilted, angling off the surface, until finally enabling the wheels to fall back onto the ground. The rods protruding on the other side prevented any continuance of the roll and the Roller was upright again. The rods withdrew back inside the Roller, then the machine executed a neat little circle, reorienting itself before halting exactly where it had started.

'Self-righting, really? Didn't you think to build in a failsafe?'

'I've already told you what it is,' said Bob as the walkie-talkie squelched again.

'I'm afraid the time for games is over. I've got a flight to catch. So, here's the deal. I have the girl here. If you want her to survive, I need Colonel Prentice to walk over here now. Otherwise there's going to be a bloodbath ...'

Ro's voice from the walkie-talkie was lost to the roar of a big cargo plane's engines as it flew low overhead, attempting to reconnoitre the runway that now lay beneath the heavy black blanket of cloud that had continued to build and lower. As the plane passed by, the bush rippled, and Sam felt the air thrust back towards him, having to brace himself to keep his footing, seeing the red cloaks of the dead morani fluttering on the runway.

The aircraft banked and came round, lining up to land. They watched it touch down, thunder along the runway, smoke trailing behind from tyre burns, and slowly, the monster came to a halt.

'Bob, go with me on this one.' Sam pulled the pistol from his pocket and pressed it against Bob's temple and the two men moved clear of the bush at the runway's edge.

One hand holding the pistol, the other holding the walkie-talkie, Sam called Ro.

The reply was instant. 'I hear you, Mr Cameron. I see you have my prize under guard. Please, do not harm my goods.'

'I want a trade, Prentice for Helen. No clauses, a straight trade.'

Sam heard a laugh come over the walkie-talkie. 'You are in no position to negotiate. If you kill Colonel Prentice, there is a two-minute close-down sequence before the grid and equipment self-destructs. Plenty of time for the Roller to shoot you and those remaining morani guarding the vehicles, oh yes, I've seen them on the grid. And I'll still be taking this female with me. Believe me, Cameron; she will live long enough to pay for the harm you have done me a thousand times over. Every time I punish her, she will wish for death, but I will never grant it. She will linger and suffer and be cursing your name to hell before I let her die. Now give me the colonel.'

The plane had taxied to a halt beside the warehouse. Its great tail door lowered to form a rear access ramp. Sam saw the control vehicle manoeuvre to the rear of the aircraft, line up on the ramp and stop. He saw the little ramp on the rear of the control vehicle lower again, watched as the two Rollers that had remained near the warehouse whizzed across and up the little ramp to their housing inside the control vehicle.

'He's right; you are going to have to let me go over there. The Rollers won't shoot you right now because they can't differentiate between your legs and mine. Remember, they are programmed not to shoot me. But we can't run forward or back, if we do we will separate and your legs will immediately become target practice. Believe me, you cannot outrun the

Rollers. They'll put you down in moments. And for me on the grid, there's no hiding place, Ro's men can take me easily.'

The undergrowth rustled close by and the first Roller that had shot down the retreating morani appeared; it took up station a few paces from the second Roller.

'It's Hobson's choice, I'm afraid. I'll just have to go over there,' said Bob. 'Fact is, even now he could just send his men over here. I'm betting he's got one or two left who are good shots. They could pick you off even while you're holding that pistol to my head. I'm guessing the only reason he hasn't sent them over is he wants to get on that plane now. Air traffic control up at Arusha will certainly have been watching the flight. I'm sure it will be an unauthorised entry from Burundi. Now it's just dropped off the radar, they will be sending out an investigation flight for sure. Ro won't want to be caught on the ground.'

Sam lowered the pistol. Immediately, the walkie-talkie started up.

'Well done, Mr Cameron. I can deal with you another day. In fact, take that as a promise, I'll look forward to it. Now send Colonel Prentice across at once. And don't try anything silly. I'm going to leave one of the Rollers on the ground. I've programmed it to shoot anyone who steps onto the runway. All I'm prepared to promise in return is that the woman won't be killed. Now hurry along please, we have a plane to catch and I don't want to waste any more time.'

'He's not kidding, Sam. Remember, once activated the Roller doesn't need the control vehicle. It will function autonomously on the grid.' Bob shook Sam's hand. 'I'm sorry it's come to this. If I get the chance, believe me, I'll make sure Helen can get away.' Bob stepped out on to the runway as drops of rain started to fall.

Sam watched Bob walk away. One of the Rollers broke off and matched Bob's pace for a few moments, providing an otherworldly escort. Then it rushed ahead and disappeared up the control vehicle's rear ramp where it self-stowed beside the other Rollers. The remaining Roller seemed to bristle slightly, its little gun turning to scan along the bush line; it came to rest, pointing at Sam. He took a pace back from the runway.

The raindrops began to fall more frequently. The first shower of the year's Little Rains. He knew from past experience that the word little was relative. Relative to the Big Rains, which should normally come in the springtime. After a few preliminary showers, the clouds would burst, and everything would be soaked. He thought about their vehicles, parked up on this side of the river. If they weren't moved back across the river this afternoon, it would flood, and they would be stuck for the duration. He put the thought to one side. There were other more pressing things to deal with.

Across the runway, the control vehicle was driven up the airplane's rear ramp into the cargo bay and then Helen was hustled onto the ramp by two of Ro's men; though still groggy, she had resumed her resistance. He watched Ro step down the ramp to where his men struggled with her.

Ro raised his walkie-talkie and beat Helen on the back of the head, she was stunned for a moment and Ro pushed her hat off. Reaching his free hand behind her head, he gripped her ponytail and jerked it. Sam could see Ro shouting at her, could not hear the words. Ro let go of her hair, and as she was hustled onto the plane, Ro continued down the ramp to join his remaining men who were waiting for Bob to reach them.

Sam turned his attention back to Bob, who for some reason had turned round and was walking backwards towards Ro and his men. With every step now, he was hit by another huge individual raindrop, the wetness darkening the silver of his hair to black. The first proper shower wasn't far away now. Then Sam saw why Bob was walking backwards - he was discreetly signalling. Pointing towards the sky, then waving wiggly fingers towards the ground, he pointed at the stationary Roller and gave Sam a thumbs up.

Bob pointed skyward again, and Sam traced the direction. Nothing, just black clouds and raindrops. He knew the sun would be high now, but the cloud was too thick for even an equatorial sun to burn through. He had no idea what Bob was signing.

He watched Bob being seized, his hands bound and then pushed towards the ramp. One of his guards kicked him to encourage speed as Ro hurried ahead up the ramp. Halfway up the ramp, Bob resisted, stopped and turned again to Sam pointing his bound hands into the air then giving a thumbs up. The signal was brought to an abrupt end as the guards forced him onto the plane. Immediately, the ramp began to close and the aircraft started to taxi for take-off even while the ramp was closing. The signal meant nothing to Sam.

By the time the aircraft had reached the far end of the runway the first shower had commenced. In moments, Sam was soaked. He looked despairingly at the aircraft as it prepared for take-off. There was nothing he could do.

Out on the runway, Charles and Angel lay unable to move to shelter as the deluge developed. First wounded, now soaking. Around them, the heavy raindrops were splashing back up off the surface. The two wounded men raised their heads to catch some of the falling drops of rain in their mouths.

A little beyond lay the shot morani. Sam didn't know if the moran Helen had patched up had survived, but the others were dead for sure. The rainwater was beginning to flow in little rivulets across the surface, pausing at the fallen bodies, then building and flowing round them.

He glanced down at the malevolent Roller that had sat motionless waiting to intercept any intrusion. He thought it moved, just a little jerk backwards, a hand's width, no more. Sam looked again, saw it move forward. Then back. Suddenly the Roller was trundling backwards and forwards in larger and faster sweeps. He watched it for a few moments more then, as the sound of the airplane's engines began to grow to a roar at the far end of the runway it came to him. He knew exactly what Bob's signals had meant.

Sam took a breath then sprinted out onto the runway. At once, the Roller's gun barrel turned to align with his legs, only to jerk backwards again, the gun barrel rotated wildly before nuzzling down into a neutral position while the Roller moved off to describe an ever-widening spiral.

As Sam ran past Charles and Angel, he shouted at them. 'It's safe to stand. The rain's washing the motes off the runway, the network's breaking up. The Roller doesn't know where it is any more.' He saw Charles struggling up and heading towards Helen's first aid kit.

The airplane was starting to roll down the runway as Sam reached the warehouse. Without hesitation, he jumped into the abandoned 4 x 4. Thankfully, the keys were still in the ignition. Starting up, he gunned the engine and tyres screeched as he forced the vehicle into a hard U-turn inside the warehouse, emerging at full throttle as the aircraft continued its take-off run.

Sam flicked on the windscreen wipers while he drove the 4 x 4 out into the centre of the runway and turned to face the oncoming aircraft. Gripping the wheel tight, he prepared to charge, to play dare with the pilot. He could see the plane racing down the runway. It was now or never; he had to make the pilot abort the take-off.

Pressing the accelerator to the floor, he felt the 4 x 4 jump ahead with the engine's full power being released. The sense of exhilaration it generated was lost at once as, up ahead of him, the plane began to rise, struggling into the sky, its engines obliterating every other sound as they roared an agonised protest at the early lift off. Crawling higher into the air, the plane seemed to hang for a moment and then it pulled up and away, almost immediately disappearing into the black cloud that lowered across the runway.

Sam lifted his foot from the accelerator allowing the 4 x 4 to glide to a halt. He banged his fist on to the steering wheel, three, four times. Then let his forehead rest on the wheel, where he remained still for a long moment.

Sam gave himself a shake. He couldn't help Helen now, but there were men down here he could help. Then he would track the plane down, and whatever it took, he swore to himself, he'd find Ro and Helen, and Bob. Once she was safe, he'd make sure Ro could never hurt anyone else again.

Pushing the 4 x 4 into gear, Sam drove across the runway to where Charles was ignoring his own wound while trying to patch up Angel.

Chapter 34
SUNDAY 3RD NOVEMBER - PM

The aircraft's fuselage was partitioned internally by a transverse bulkhead that was fitted with a single door designed to allow flight crew access from the flight deck and crew cabin at the front end of the plane into the much larger cargo bay at the rear.

A single row of six seats was fixed at the front of the cargo bay, three set to either side of the crew's access door. Facing forward, they offered only the uninspiring view of the solid dividing bulkhead, just an outstretched arm's length in front. A single porthole was positioned in the plane's side at either end of the row - offering a glimpse of the world outside and a little natural light for passengers. The rest of the cargo bay depended for light on two rows of electric lights, spaced evenly along the full length of the bay - they had not been switched on.

At the rear of the otherwise empty cargo bay, amidst the shadows and the half-light afforded by the two distant passenger portholes, the control vehicle was secured.

Helen sat at one end of the row of seats, staring out through the porthole, her face pressed up against the window glass, trying forlornly to make space between herself and Ro who had taken the seat next to her. Ro had freed her ponytail and fanned her hair out, allowing his fingers to trawl repeatedly through the auburn tresses. Each time she raised her bound hands to push his away, he slapped her face and forced her hands back down into her lap.

Sat on Ro's other side was one of his team; the other surviving members sat in the three seats on the other side. She could see Bob Prentice's shoeless feet sticking out into the aisle marking where, in the absence of a seventh passenger seat, he had been forced onto the deck in the space between the bulkhead and seats. The Korean guards rested their boots on his body. His frequent groans signalled each occasion the guards chose to kick or stamp on him.

She braced herself against another lurch and gravity pulled at her stomach as the plane continued its struggle up through the rainclouds. As the bumping and rocking continued, Helen bit her lip, she had known smoother take-offs. She braced her feet against the bulkhead in front of her against a particularly violent bump. After what seemed like an age, they pulled clear of the clouds and brilliant sunlight flooded through the pair of little portholes. She blinked for a moment at the sudden brightness.

Focus returned in a hurry when she felt a hand fumbling in her lap.

'What do you think you're doing?' she said, pressing her hands down to resist Ro's.

In silence, he reached his other hand round, took a grip on her wrist binding and jerked her hands up leaving her lap exposed. With his other hand, he completed the release of her seatbelt. He stood, dragged her up and, having ordered the seated guard next to him out of the way, pulled Helen out of her seat before propelling her deeper into the cargo bay.

He half pushed, half dragged her onwards. She tried to stop herself by gripping the driver's side door of the control vehicle. Ro just banged down on her fingers and continued to move her deeper into the bay. Reaching the darkest shadows at the rear of the control vehicle, he pressed her back against it and gripped her by the throat. 'You were Cameron's special lady. Now you are my little redhead bitch. I'm going to teach you how a woman should behave.' He brought his free hand round and slapped Helen's face hard. 'Never speak back to me again, slut, or I'll beat you until you cry tears of blood.' He slapped her face again.

She couldn't help the tears, they were involuntary, but she bit her lip, no way was she going to cry out.

Ro released Helen's throat and reached for the control vehicle's rear door handle. 'Today is a great day. I intend to celebrate, starting with you. Get in there. Now,' he said, pulling open the rear door. Helen turned on him, kicking hard between his legs, but Ro had a full array of martial arts moves, defensive as well as offensive. He parried her kick, caught her heel in his hand, lifting it high. With bound hands, she was unable to break her fall and fell with a violent jolt onto her back.

Lying in pain, she felt Ro grab her bound wrists and drag her up. He shoved her towards the vehicle's rear access door.

Then he paused and looked back along the cargo bay towards a member of the flight crew who had just appeared at the access doorway set in the bulkhead.

'Ah, beer, I'll take one of those.' He pushed Helen hard, sending her sprawling onto the floor of the control vehicle. Then he hurried forward to get his drink.

Taking the bottle from the flight attendant, he took a mouthful and waved it towards the control vehicle. 'Bring me more over there, and plenty of it.' The attendant gave a smile of acknowledgement and disappeared back through the access door to get more beer.

Ro looked down at his men, each holding a beer; they raised their bottles to salute him for a successful mission. Stooping slightly, he reached along the row and clinked his bottle against each of theirs in turn. 'Now we party,' he said leering in the direction of the control vehicle. His men gave a raucous cheer as he headed back to the rear of the cargo bay and the control vehicle.

Inside the vehicle, Helen was searching frantically, scanning the worktops fitted down each side of the vehicle's interior for anything that might cut her bonds or serve as a weapon. There was nothing. She glared defiantly at Ro as he entered through the rear door. She knew exactly what Ro intended and had no intention of making it easy for him.

Two steps inside, Ro paused and looked at her thoughtfully, then he laughed before taking a long drink from the beer bottle and let out a contented sigh. He stood in front of her. 'Now you will obey me,' he said. Reaching out a hand, he stroked her cheek. Helen jerked her head away. Ro returned his hand to her face. Now the gentleness was gone. He gripped her face hard, using all his strength to force it round so he could see her eyes. His thumb and index finger sought out the soft flesh of her cheeks, pressed in hard between her upper and lower jaw, driving her lower jaw down and fixing her mouth open. He laughed again.

Turning his own face slightly, he raised his bottle up and took a mouthful of beer, then turned back to stare into Helen's eyes. He swilled the beer in his mouth and finally swallowed. Leaning in close to Helen's face, he let out a long theatrical gasp of pleasure that released a blast of warm moist beer fumes into Helen's open mouth. She forced back the overwhelming urge to vomit and knew now was the moment she had to act.

Helen clenched her fists and brought her bound hands up sharply, catching Ro hard under the chin. His lower jaw jerked up, catching his tongue between upper and lower teeth, an unintentional bite that drew blood. Ro cried out in pain and instinctively released his grip on Helen's face to tend his wound.

Before Ro's hand could reach his bleeding face, Helen banged her fists up a second time. Tooth bit on tooth and a splinter of tobacco-yellowed incisor fell unseen onto the floor. Suddenly the plane banked sharply as though executing an unexpected manoeuvre. Helen and Ro were both thrown to the side. Still facing one another, less than a breath apart, she jutted out her elbow to steady herself against the worktop.

Searching for stability, Ro leant his bottle holding hand on to the same worktop while clutching at his damaged face with his other hand. Helen could see blood trailing from his mouth; knew she had prodded the dragon and had to follow through before Ro's shock at her actions turned to rage. Still bracing on the worktop against the plane's sharpening turn; she shifted her bodyweight onto one leg and brought her knee up hard into Ro's groin. Spluttering blood, he gasped in pain at this new assault, he dropped to his knees. His hands abandoned their other duties and grasped at his privates in a vain attempt to diminish the agony.

Glimpsing the beer bottle now rolling away towards the rear door, Helen lunged across the worktop to grab it. She looked at it, reversed her grip so the neck was in her hand and raised it high before bringing it down hard on Ro's head. There was a hollow thudding sound as the bottle made contact and bounced back from his head. Ro roared and began to force his body up.

Helen brought the bottle down again, putting every ounce of her strength into the strike. The shock of impact ran up to her elbow, hurting. She knew it was hurting much worse for Ro. This time, the sound was of breaking glass, the bottle breaking across his head. Ro collapsed back down to his hands and knees, his initial moan transposing into a rising growl.

She raised the bottle again and looked at the wicked edge on the broken bottle's neck - all she had left as a weapon.

Helen tried to work out how she could hold the glass at an angle that would allow her to cut her wrist bonds. She needed to get free quickly. Having spotted the pistol in Ro's waistband, she wanted it, knew it was her only hope against the rest of his men.

A hand gripped the waistband of her bush shorts and applied drag. Ro began to pull himself up. She looked down and saw his angry eyes staring back at her as he rose from the deck. Another hand reached up and took a tight fistful of her top, pulling it down while he began to lever himself up.

'You're dead, bitch. You're going to die; die a hundred deaths, starting right now.'

Helen looked down in horror at the face rising towards her, she felt the hand levering up from her waistband, saw his bulging fist dragging on her top. There was no escape, only one option. She swung her hand down, driving the sharp edge of the bottleneck into the back of Ro's hand. For just a moment, he didn't feel any pain. Helen's top turned red with his blood. She twisted her wrist, and as glass scraped bone, he screamed. His hand immediately released her top and dropped away, his other hand released her waistband and clutched at its sliced-up twin. Ro's head was beside her feet; she stamped, and he writhed away.

Reaching her still bound wrists down, she brought the bottleneck against Ro's belly and twisted so her empty hand could snatch his pistol. Gripping it, she straightened up. She had to get out of the vehicle. All she had was surprise and a pistol to overcome Ro's guards and free Bob Prentice, so he could untie her. And it had to be now, before they realised something was amiss.

Still steadying herself against the destabilising motion of the banking plane Helen edged to the rear and took a breath, readying herself to go on the offensive.

Leading with the pistol, she reached the vehicle's rear door and came to an abrupt halt. Her pistol was pointing at the midriff of the flight attendant who was just about to enter the vehicle's rear. She could see three bottles of beer in the attendant's left hand, just as Ro had ordered; they shielded the pistol held in the attendant's right.

'You!' said Helen. 'What are you doing here?' She thrust her pistol forward into the attendant's face. 'Move and you're dead.'

The attendant froze, then gradually allowed her left hand holding the beer bottles to drop down by her side. Helen could see the attendant's pistol was pointing directly at her chest.

'It's not how it looks. Let's stay calm here, Helen, and everything will work out just fine,' said the flight attendant.

'I don't think it will; you've lied to me. Have you been in with Ro all along?'

'You've got it wrong, honey. Come on out, and I'll show you.' Tracy backed off a pace; the bottles dangling between the fingers of her lowered left hand clinked as she moved. The pistol in her right hand still pointed in Helen's direction.

Helen glanced down towards Tracy's pistol then back to fix eye contact. She saw Tracy suck her lip in slightly as she weighed the situation, then with a disarming smile the CIA agent lowered her weapon.

Helen's confusion deepened when a familiar voice reached her from outside the vehicle.

'Ro, give it up, man. Your boys are taken, there's no way out for you.'

'Rupert? Rupert is that you?' Helen kept her pistol pointed at Tracy as she glanced sideways, striving without success to confirm the identity of the voice.

'Helen?'

This time she recognised his voice and, confused, brought her eye contact back to Tracy. 'What is this?'

'It's okay, Rupert,' Tracy called over her shoulder, 'crisis averted. She's already put Ro down.'

'What? How in heaven's name did she manage that?' Rupert's smiling face appeared round the doorframe. He grimaced slightly as Helen's pistol turned on him. Then, reading Helen's confusion, he smiled again and waved Helen's gun aside. 'Come on now, Helen, we're all on the same side.' He looked down at Ro and gave an approving nod. 'Good work there, but I think we need to get him tied up now, don't you?' Rupert glanced over his shoulder towards Tracy. 'That's a very impressive piece of handiwork down there. Are you sure she's not one of your assets?'

'Nope. She's a civilian. American civilian.'

Rupert repeated his languid smile to Helen then turned his head round towards Tracy. 'Natural talent then; a bit like another American lady I know. I assume you'll be making her your protégé?'

'What is happening?' said Helen. She sensed that neither Rupert nor Tracy presented a threat to her, they seemed as friendly as in her past contacts with them and unfazed by her pointing pistol, but she still maintained her guard.

'Well, it's really quite simple,' said Rupert, slowly reaching out a hand to guide Helen's pistol muzzle away and down. 'Once we knew Ro had no choice other than to use a plane to get ACE out of Tanzania, we had to set up an intercept plan.' He climbed through the rear doorway of the control vehicle and pointed towards Ro. 'Would you mind, please? I'd very much like to get him secured.'

Helen turned sideways and allowed Rupert space to pass.

'Thank you, and now, perhaps you'll allow me?' He paused while squeezing past Helen, quickly loosening her wrist ties. 'I can reuse these ties now.' Then he stooped over Ro.

'Well, old man, looks like we've finally got you where we want you. It's taken a long time; I think you bit off more than you could chew this time, don't you?'

Ro mumbled an incoherent response through his broken teeth, and Rupert gripped his arms, tying them tightly together with Helen's ties. He glanced up at her and smiled while tugging on the bindings to make sure they were secure. 'A pleasant irony here, don't you think?'

'You've taken over the plane? How did you manage that? I never heard a thing.'

Standing up, Rupert shooed her out of the vehicle. 'We didn't do anything of the sort; we can't go leaving things to chance like that. Come on, let's get a seat and we'll tell all.'

Tracy reached out a guiding hand to help Helen down and they all headed back to the row of seats. The sense of immediate relief grew when Helen saw Ro's men trussed up and secured against a bulkhead - they were going nowhere. Two armed men in civilian clothes stood at the seats that were all empty save one, which was occupied by Bob Prentice.

'What about Sam?' said Helen. 'Ro left him on the runway.'

Tracy and Rupert exchanged glances. 'We're going back right now,' she said.

Helen was suddenly aware of the plane's descent and felt the bumping and turbulence start to build.

'Come on, let's get seated,' said Rupert, waving them towards the seating. He rested a hand on Bob's shoulder.

Bob raised his beer bottle in acknowledgement.

Helen sat between Rupert and Tracy. This time she was in charge of her own seatbelt. 'So, if you didn't take over the plane, you'd better explain what's happened.'

Rupert leant forward, looked round her towards Tracy. 'It can't do any harm now,' he said.

Tracy gave a little nod of agreement and Rupert switched his attention back to Helen.

'Once Ro needed to charter a cargo plane, we knew he was limited for choice. There are air charter companies with planes of the right capacity and loading facilities spread all around the world. But only a very few of them that would be prepared to take on a dodgy black flight contract like his. Fewer still who actually had planes in the right place; in fact, there were only two possible planes available. Thankfully, once our governments' little spat over ultimate financial responsibility was resolved, our people have deep enough pockets to move pretty quickly when it comes to covering up embarrassing problems. We used anonymous front companies to charter the two available planes and got them flying off to wherever—'

'Leaving a CIA front company plane as the only one Ro could charter at short notice,' said Tracy with some satisfaction. She leant across Helen and bumped beer bottles with Rupert.

They smiled at one another. 'Perfect international teamwork,' said Rupert, and they both drank. Helen was silent for a long moment while her neighbours exchanged further self-congratulatory accolades.

'Do you mean you had Sam and I go through all that for no reason? Seriously? People have been killed, wounded, and we don't know for sure how Sam is right now. There's a bunch of wounded Maasai down there, desperate for medical help, all unnecessary casualties. You were always going to intercept Ro; that was your plan from the outset.'

The pair fell silent for a moment. Then Rupert tried to calm her. 'No, no, you misunderstood. Not from the beginning. At first, we did need Sam to trace Ro through Kenya. Local politics meant we really couldn't put anyone in to do that. Then it was pure serendipity that the terrorist attack snarled up the Tanzanian border, trapping Ro inside the country. It gave us more time to find him and implement a recovery plan. Once you and Sam had rumbled his plan to fly out and you delivered the runway tip-off we were able to get our charter plane to the front of the queue and Ro jumped at it because you were closing in on him.

'You and Sam found the runway. And it was Sam's presence in theatre that propelled Ro to take the first available charter plane rather than wait for one he knew and trusted.' Rupert looked to Tracy for backup.

'Yeah, Ro had to assume Sam would catch up with him, and then Sam's masters would know exactly where he was. You and Sam broke his cover and created the urgency that moved Ro along. Then we just made sure his first best exit flight option was us.' Tracy leant back in her seat, satisfied.

'Sam's masters? You don't own him. He only helped in the first place to save his old friend.' She leant forward and called across the aisle to Bob. 'Did you know about all this?'

'I've been held prisoner for days, trussed up like a turkey.'

'Well, Sam is not going to like this one bit, believe me.'

The aircraft's continued bumpy descent suddenly dropped it below cloud level and the pilot immediately began some final manoeuvring to achieve the best approach on the fast closing runway. Instinctively, Helen broke off from the conversation as all the passengers craned to see what was outside.

• • •

Sam was driving Ro's 4 x 4 back towards the runway; he had casualties on board. Wounded morani were packed into the rear cargo space, the back seats and up front beside Angel's driver who had made the mistake of wandering away from his vehicle into the grid and been shot for his error. Each had bullet wounds to the lower leg, none of them would be walking anywhere for the next week or two. One had a shattered tibia bone, which needed sorting quickly or the man might end up crippled. Sam had applied some emergency first aid, but they all needed proper treatment.

Ahead, as the first solid bout of rain eased away to only sporadic flurries, he could see Angel resting under the warehouse cover, just where Sam had left him. He glanced about wondering where Charles was. Then he saw him, standing motionless near the office doorway, looking across the runway towards the shapes scattered here and there on the far side. His fallen clansmen. Nephews, cousins, friends. He was leaning part of his weight on his club as though it were a walking stick, and from somewhere the chief had retrieved a spear which he clutched in his other hand for further support.

The two bullet holes in his leg should have kept him down. But Charles had work to do and little time to do it in. Sam shook his head; Charles should not be standing. He tooted the 4 x 4's horn as he approached, and the chief turned towards him. As Sam neared, he saw Charles' face lighten at the sight of his morani in the vehicle.

Pulling to a halt, Sam leant out. 'Found them, they'll live. And I've been back to our own vehicles, the four morani you left on guard there were unhurt. Angel's driver was hit because he thought it was okay to go walkabout! Your boys are coming through the bush now, should be here in a few minutes.'

'Let's get you and Angel inside now. I'll drive across the runway and, when your men get here, we'll load your dead on the roof. Sorry, it's not very respectful, the alternative is we leave them here, otherwise we'll all be trapped on this side of the river pretty soon.'

Charles was not looking at him. Sam thought, he's not even listening. The chief raised his spear and pointed it along the runway. Sam turned to see what had captured the chief's attention. Perhaps two miles off and closing fast, was the cargo plane.

'Holy Christ,' said Sam. He jumped back into the driver's seat and hurried the 4 x 4 off the runway and beneath the warehouse roof; he paused beside Angel, jumped out, lifted the groaning priest and, without ceremony, shoved him inside. Then Sam drove the 4 x 4 out of the far side of the warehouse and slewed to a halt behind the first growth of bush beyond. He hoped it would go unnoticed in the poor weather.

Getting out, he hurried back through the warehouse, pausing to pick up a pistol that its dead owner would not need again and hurried back to join Charles. 'Come on, man. We need to get to cover.' Charles would not budge.

Suddenly, the roar of the landing aircraft deafened them as it bounced, skidded, and settled into its route along the runway amidst a trail of splash and spray. It hurtled past them, engines screaming, while the pilot fought to slow his charge before he ran out of runway. Eventually, the expertise of a seasoned pilot began to have an effect, and just as Sam thought there was no chance left, it began to slow, stopping a few paces short of the end. Sam gave a sigh, he didn't care about Ro and his men, but Helen was on board.

Sam pulled at Charles' arm. 'Come on, let's get to some cover, in the office building, we can assess things from there.' He felt the man resist his pull for a moment, then Charles acceded and followed Sam inside, just as the plane completed its turn and began to taxi back.

It was a struggle for Charles to get up the flight of steps to the upper-level office and Sam helped as best he could. Once there, they saw dead men lying on the floor beneath the windows. Sam didn't take pleasure in shooting people, never had, but, in this moment, was pleased they were dead. Wounded men would have presented a dilemma: should he administer first aid just when Ro was returning or focus on the coming conflict?

He looked at Charles, saw the hatred in his eyes and realised it wouldn't have been an issue. In rural Africa, justice was rough and ready, if the men had still been alive, Charles may well have administered summary justice. As it was, Sam could tell it was all Charles could do now to stop himself from stabbing the dead bodies with his spear.

He guided Charles past the bodies to one of the windows. 'You watch from here, I'm going to the next window along. Keep your head down.' Stooping to pick up a dropped machine pistol, Sam grabbed a spare magazine from its dead owner and reloaded the weapon. By the time he was in position, the plane had come to a halt directly outside the office building.

The rear cargo bay door lowered, and Sam brought his weapon to bear on the widening opening. A movement within drew his attention, and he readied himself as people began to appear on the ramp. He aimed, then hesitated.

He watched Helen run down the ramp. She glanced about then called out his name, shouting and looking around her anxiously. She was joined by Bob Prentice who called his name too. Sam was puzzled. Where was Ro? Was it a trap? Then Rupert strolled down the ramp. Sam did a double take, what was he doing here? Never mind weapons, the man was still carrying his umbrella, in a combat zone.

'Sam, where are you? We've got Ro, it's all okay.'

Sam rose and cautiously leant around the window frame. 'Helen! Up here. What's going on?'

Sam could see she was genuinely at ease. This was not a set-up. He leant out of the window. 'We'll be down in a moment.' Ducking back inside he helped Charles up and made for the stairs.

'That lady of yours has something about her. The children in the boma were right you know; a real lioness.'

'Hmmm,' said Sam. 'Don't let her hear you say she's mine. Or we'll both be facing a lioness.'

Charles laughed. 'Your ways are so different. She is a strong lioness, yes, but in our world, the lioness must always belong to the lion. A strong lion.'

'Well, trust me - that one belongs to no one. Come on, let's get down and find out what's happened.'

• • •

Helen met Sam at the office entrance, and they hugged. She took a moment to ask Charles how he was, then quickly explained what had happened. Sam showed no emotion as she explained how they had been used by MI6 and the CIA.

'You're alive, Helen, that's the most important thing to me right now. Come on, let's see what Rupert and your CIA friend have in mind.' Charles waved them on. In public, he would not accept help, so he shuffled along behind them.

Approaching the ramp, Sam called out, 'Rupert, you've cut this all a bit fine. And I'm thinking you could have handled it a bit differently; it all got a little hairy for a while.'

'A little hairy?' hissed Helen. 'They hung us out to dry. Charles lost men.'

Sam shushed her gently, then as they reached the ramp, he looked at Rupert expectantly. 'Well? What's the story?'

'Yes, it wasn't the easiest of rides, I'll grant you. I'm afraid enlisting your assistance was the only way we could see of manoeuvring Ro, so we could tidy things up.'

Helen pointed across the runway. 'Look! There are dead men over there. Good men who died because you took the easy option. That's not tidy. That's heartless and low, low. Dirty low!'

She saw Rupert's pained look. 'No, no, Helen. Never the easy option. We took the urrg ... the safest option, yes that's it, the safest option.'

'And you know, Helen, it was the only way we could be absolutely sure of stopping Ro from getting ACE out to some pretty nasty regimes,' said Tracy, walking down the ramp to join them.

Helen glared at her, then looked away in exasperation. On the far side of the runway, she saw Bob Prentice hurrying back towards the aircraft followed closely by their two civilian-dressed rescuers who struggled to keep up while carrying his now dormant Roller between them.

Sam rested a hand on Helen's shoulder then moved slightly in front of her. 'In any event, Rupert, let's worry about recriminations later. You're here, we at least are safe, you have ACE back, and you've got Ro, which has to be a bonus in anyone's book. Now, I've got a bunch of wounded men who need medical treatment and once that rain resumes I'm betting your pilot will refuse to take off again. So, let's all get on board and get the hell out of here.'

Tracy stepped up beside Rupert. 'I'm sorry, that's not how we're planning to play it,' she said.

'What?'

'Listen, Sam, we're sorry but we have to follow security protocols.'

'No! We all need to get out of this environment quickly.'

'Oh, you will, Sam. Just not on our plane,' she said.

'I'm an American citizen, you can't just leave me, leave all of us out here. You know that,' said Helen, pushing past Sam. 'You know, I think you've only landed again just to dump me off. Now you let us all on that plane and fly us up to Arusha, then you can go wherever you choose.'

'Sorry, can't do it,' Tracy looked at her expressionlessly.

'You can, you just won't.'

'No. This plane has an unlogged flight plan. It's been bobbing up and down like a yoyo,' said Rupert. 'Wherever we land in East Africa, the authorities are going to take a very keen interest. And I'm afraid we can't let that happen, otherwise it will put ACE out into the public domain, which is what we've been struggling to avoid.'

Sam had gently eased Helen back. 'Okay, I understand your security position, I really do. But you have to land somewhere, where? And what do you mean; we will get out, how?' he said.

Rupert cleared his throat a little. 'You will recall our phone conversation of yesterday? You asked for medical help for your wounded driver. Well, we currently have an airborne British Army medical team doing joint training with the Tanzanian military. I took the liberty of speaking with their commanding officer last night, and I anticipate an Army Air Corps helicopter and medical team should be reaching the boma quite soon. They will treat your boys and then fly you back to Arusha, discreetly.'

A few big drops of rain fell. Sam put his hand out and one splashed into his palm. He looked up at the clouded sky, gently squeezed Helen's shoulder. 'When it rains next, the plane won't be able to take off and pretty soon the ford is going to be unpassable too.'

'So, all the more reason to get moving,' said Rupert.

'You didn't say where you were going,' said Helen.

'Where we originally came from,' said Tracy. 'Diego Garcia.'

Helen looked at Sam. 'Where's that?'

'Indian Ocean island base. A British sovereign territory. It's leased to the States as a secure naval base. They don't like visitors there.'

'You got that right, now we need to go,' said Tracy as Bob hurried past them up the ramp. He threw Sam a warm wave in greeting then disappeared into the cargo bay, eager to ensure his helpers stowed the Roller securely in its space in the control vehicle.

'What about Ro and his men?' said Charles.

Rupert looked at him a little disdainfully. 'You can let us worry about that.'

'No. He has committed murder in my lands. He must face justice here.'

'Not going to happen, friend. Ro's coming with us,' said Tracy, a note of impatience creeping into her voice. 'We've got a long flight over the Indian Ocean and I'm thinking Ro and his friends will want to try some open water swimming, no witnesses, no bodies, no questions. That's how it has to be. Now we've got to take off and you've got a river to cross. Let's go, huh?'

Charles spoke a few quiet words in Maa. Then, resting his whole bodyweight on his uninjured leg and spear shaft, he raised his rungu and pointed it at Tracy and Rupert.

Tracy laughed. 'I don't know whether that's a blessing or a curse, but we're going now, anyway.'

Helen tried hard to keep the elation from showing in her face as Tracy and Rupert turned to walk up the ramp only to stop short with long glinting spear points pressed close into their bellies. She had watched the four morani emerge from the bush on the far side of the runway and cross silently to arrive just in time to respond to Charles' quietly spoken command.

'Whether it is a blessing or a curse for you will depend on what you do next, I think,' said Charles. 'Now, I want Ro. He must face the justice of my people; it is the way. Bring him out. The rest you can have.'

'You'd better do as he says,' said Sam.

The group at the foot of the ramp remained a frozen tableau while Tracy shouted instructions up into the cargo bay, to the men helping Bob restore some order inside his control vehicle. They had trouble obeying her instructions, as they emerged from the control vehicle to be greeted by very sharp spear points. It took less than a minute for Ro to be dragged down the ramp and deposited on the runway. His mouth was a mess of blood and broken teeth, his hand still bleeding, but he had regained his air of arrogant contempt.

Tracy looked angrily at Sam. 'Get this, Cameron; Ro has been a thorn in our side for years. He must not get out of the bush; do you understand me? He ends here, and I'm holding you responsible.'

'Whoa there, I'm just a civilian, remember? The civilian you left on a runway to die. Remember that too? I'm not on your payroll and not about to take any orders from you. I'm just a guest here; I don't have any influence on what happens.'

'Don't smart mouth me, Cameron.'

'You need not worry yourself about this man. Justice will be done, and the bush will swallow everything,' said Charles.

'It sure as hell better or—'

'Or our masters will be rather disappointed,' said Rupert, unfurling his umbrella and flipping it up as the rain began to fall. 'Perhaps the answer to all our problems is for Charles and his people to have their justice, and for Sam to see that justice is done. I'm sure that would meet all our needs, don't you think?' He looked towards Tracy.

She still looked defiant. The raindrops were falling steadily now.

'For God's sake, Tracy, if we don't take off now we'll all be trapped here for days. By which time the authorities will be looking for the plane that dropped off their radar and it's guaranteed they'll take a great interest in our cargo. Let's take the deal and go!' They all waited for Tracy's decision while the drumbeat of falling raindrops landing on Rupert's umbrella grew louder.

'Okay, let's go,' she said.

Charles issued an order. His men allowed their spears to drop away from Tracy and Rupert and all stepped back from the ramp. Grabbing their captive, they manhandled him off the runway. Tracy and Rupert boarded, and the plane immediately began to taxi away as the cargo bay ramp started to close.

• • •

Just before the crest of the riverbank, Sam stopped the 4 x 4 and pulled on the handbrake. He left Charles in the front passenger seat and got out. Standing still in the rain, which now fell at a steady pace, he looked about. From his vantage point at the top of the bank, he could see down towards the river and, immediately below him, could see a moran standing at the foot of the bank. Across the river was another - they were marking the river crossing's entrance and exit points. Necessary even in daylight now, as the appearance of the banks was changing with the rising river level. The men gave him a wave of greeting and beckoned him on.

Sam acknowledged them then turned away. He walked to the rear of the vehicle, passing the watching morani who filled the 4 x 4's back seats. Squeezed amongst them was Ro, looking very uncomfortable.

Ro saw Sam looking in through the side window at him and, in a fit of defiance, spat. It splatted on the glass between them, and Sam turned away without responding while the morani to either side of Ro indignantly punched him.

Sam surveyed the bodies of Ro's dead men; the morani had dragged them from where they fell and bundled them up onto the 4 x 4's roof rack where they had been lashed down tight. Rivulets of red trickled down the sides of the vehicle, evidence of where the rain was steadily rinsing through wounds and stained clothes. A lot of bodies. He looked back at the rising river and worried that his vehicle might prove too top heavy for the crossing. He glanced again at Ro; Sam didn't like it but knew there was a price to be paid. He knew that Ro knew it too. Sam hurried on.

Parked behind his 4 x 4 was the orange Land Rover. At the wheel was Helen. She poked her head out of the window as he approached.

'How's it looking?'

'Water's up quite a bit already. How are you all doing?'

'We're fine ... well, we will be once we're across.'

Sam glanced into the interior. Beside Helen was Angel, next to him was his driver looking sorry for himself and occasionally emitting a little groan. In the rear were the wounded morani; all transferred from the 4 x 4 to the Land Rover, which offered a little more space for the journey. He smiled encouragement at them. They grinned back, stoically. A lifetime of training demanded they show no weakness or pain. If Sam had not known all of the men had bullet wounds, he would not have been able to tell from their demeanour.

'I think we've made it in time. You pull ahead of me. Go straight down the slope, slowly. There are men marking the entrance and exit to the crossing, just steer a straight line between the two. Once you're in the water, don't stop for anything.'

'Sam, I spent years in West Africa, I've driven Land Rovers through more river crossings than I can remember. I'll be fine.'

'Okay, I know, but this water is rising, and it looks to be picking up speed. And don't forget, you've got extra weight up top.'

He broke off to check the ties that secured the dead morani to her roof rack. The bodies were covered, protected from the rain by Mauwled's little tent that the warriors had found scrunched up in the rear of the Land Rover.

'Drive past me then pause at the bank. I'm going to hook the steel cable from the 4 x 4's front winch to the back of the Land Rover, if the river does take you we might be able to stop you being carried away completely. When you are on the other side, go right up the bank to solid ground and then we'll use the cable as an anchor point for me - if necessary you can drive ahead to pull the 4 x 4 out if I get stuck.'

'Great, see you on the other side.'

Sam slid his hand through the driver's side window and squeezed Helen's shoulder lightly. 'Helen, take care.'

'I'll be fine, stop worrying. Now go and get me hooked up.' She revved the Land Rover's engine and edged ahead of the 4 x 4.

Once Sam had the cable hooked on to the back of the Land Rover he banged on its side and waved it on. Helen's drove forward, allowing the vehicle to edge down the bank, pausing for just a moment at the foot. Then, as the moran on the bank beckoned her on, Helen drove out into the water. She didn't stop, executing a textbook crossing. The vehicle struggled for only a moment as it started to pull up the bank on the far side.

Sam let out a little sigh of relief as the orange Land Rover crested the far bank and stopped on the level. Helen got out for a moment, gave him a wave and then jumped back in the driver's seat, ready to edge ahead and take any slack out of the steel cable that linked the two vehicles as Sam crossed towards her.

The 4 x 4 was not as sturdy as the Land Rover but its raised snorkel exhaust and well-built water seal doors kept the rising waters out and Sam made it across too. At the top of the bank, he stopped and got out. He was immediately joined by the moran who had been marking the far bank and had clung on to the back of Sam's 4 x 4 when it had entered the water. Everyone was over.

Some yards ahead, he saw Helen unhooking the tow cable and he wound it back in on the winch. She followed the hook back along the track, and as it clunked to a stop against the winch bar, she arrived next to him.

Sam grinned at her. 'Piece of cake.'

'Told you not to worry.' She gave him a hug, he hugged her back. They touched lips in a brief kiss then separated when Charles hobbled from the passenger door to join them.

'What now?' said Helen.

Sam pointed off along the track. A group of elders and the small number of Charles' morani who had remained behind at the boma when their expedition had set off were now emerging through the blur of the rain.

'I think you should get back to the boma with the wounded now. The sooner they get treatment the better. And there are families who will want their dead.'

Helen hesitated for just a moment. She sensed there was business afoot at the riverbank.

'Really, you should go now,' said Sam, reaching out a hand and resting it on her forearm, he squeezed. 'Please.'

Helen realised that Sam was not really asking; there was an urgency in his voice that she rarely heard.

'Okay,' she said. With a rueful glance around, she turned and walked back to the Land Rover. A moment later, Sam heard the engine kick into life and it rolled away, quickly disappearing into the rain gloomed bush.

• • •

In the clearing outside the boma, Helen drove the Land Rover past a large helicopter. It had red, white and blue roundels together with little Union Jacks painted on the nose, and on the fuselage were large red crosses set against white circles. The flight crew was sat inside the aircraft, watching her pass. If nothing else, it confirmed that Rupert had told the truth about the medical team.

She pulled to a halt just outside the boma gates. A rainproof shelter had been rigged by the medical team - an open-sided tent, a sheet of canvas for a floor and a trestle table set up in the middle. She was quite impressed that they had such a portable shelter kit with them. As Helen got out of the Land Rover, she was met by the medics.

'I've got wounded. All gun shots.'

'Great, thanks. We'll take it from here. Have you been in a war zone or something?' The military medics kicked into action, using the Land Rover as a holding area where they did a quick triage assessment of the injuries and began taking the wounded one at a time for treatment.

Standing off to one side of the treatment area but still under the canvas, Helen listened as the steady drum of rain on the canvas above her head provided a back score to the wailing and crying of the women of the boma as they carefully lowered the dead morani down and carried their bodies away. When the last of the bodies had disappeared inside the boma, she turned her attention back to watch the team efficiently treat one wound after another. The moran with a shattered leg was carried off to the helicopter - he needed more complex treatment that was beyond their field service resources.

'I guess we're your ride,' came a voice from behind her.

Helen turned to see the pilot. 'I sure hope so, otherwise we're in trouble.'

'Looks to me like you've already been in a bit of trouble.'

'Ha, something and nothing,' said Helen lightly.

'More something than nothing, I'm thinking. Don't worry, I've been told not to ask questions.'

Helen gave him a grateful smile. She was suddenly feeling very drained. Right now, she didn't need questions.

'Come and wait in the aircraft, it's not luxury but better than this. And I've got coffee.'

'Oh, coffee, I'll go for that,' said Helen. 'I don't suppose you've anything a bit stronger by any chance? I could manage a glass for sure.'

The pilot laughed. 'Sorry, no alcohol. I might have some chocolate though. If you friend hasn't eaten it all.'

'My friend?'

'Yes, African guy, shot in the shoulder and has a little head scratch, seems to like chocolate.'

'Mauwled! They've fixed him up already? Great, let's go see.'

• • •

The morani were ranged along the bank - just upstream from the fording point, beside the natural pool Sam had spotted the previous evening. It was so valued because it stayed wet even during the driest times of the year. It was also here that the biggest of the crocodiles necessarily gathered through the dry months. With the steady dropping of the water levels, their opportunities for ambush had diminished. Some had not eaten for months; they were hungry and now, with the coming of the rains, they would quickly spread out to their favoured spots, upstream and down. But first, an unexpected feast.

It was raining, first water and then men. One after another, bodies had dropped into the pool. The first splash had alerted them, then the taste of man had spread through the water like a sounding dinner gong, and from all across the pool, they came. Closing in on the Korean cadavers, jaws snapping, tails swiping, hissing, all vying for a good grip; then the spinning and rolling, the ripping of flesh as, one by one, the Koreans' bodies were torn apart.

It had not taken long for the larger crocodiles in the pool to take their share. Then the meat was gone, and the waters fell still. The only visible movements remaining were from the smaller crocodiles who were just too far down the pecking order to have eaten. They hovered, still hoping that the man-rain might resume.

Sam had stood two or three paces back from the morani while the scene unfolded. Solutions to problems in the bush were uncompromising and swift. It was not nice, nature at its most brutal; but he had to admit to himself, Charles had been as good as his word to Rupert. The bush had taken the Koreans; there would never be any evidence of their presence here.

He wondered what fate Charles had in store for Ro and turned to look back towards the vehicle where Ro had been left. He was standing outside it, exactly where his morani guards had left him while they helped carry the bodies to the bank. His hands remained tied, and before leaving him, they had tied his feet too. The defiance of before was gone now; Ro, too, had watched the show.

Charles stood in the middle of the row of men who were gathered along the bank, he leant heavily on his spear shaft, his face expressionless.

Sam stepped across to join him. 'What about Ro? You can't do that to him too, he's alive.'

'No, there must be a meeting of the elders to decide. I do not know what will happen. When a Maasai kills, there is a bill to pay: many cattle and goats and the families must agree. But this is different, he is an outsider - we will have to see.'

As they turned and started towards the vehicles, Sam shouted an alert. Ro had clearly decided he was not waiting for the Maasai to reach a decision on his fate. He'd stooped, managed to untie his feet and was running off along the bankside. The morani took up Sam's cry and set off in pursuit.

With tied hands, Ro was at a disadvantage as he hurried along the bank above the pool, heading for the fording place beyond. After only a few paces, his plan collapsed. The leading moran had paused for just a moment to raise his rungu and, with the precision that came from years of practice, hurled it at Ro. It caught him square in the back and sent him tumbling forward.

Gasping for breath, Ro raised his head and saw the next moran about to seize him. He rolled to one side and Sam caught the look of surprise on Ro's face when he dropped away from the closing moran. Sam saw the surprise turn to fear as Ro comprehended what was happening. Having rolled over the lip of the bank, he was sliding down towards the pool. The wet earth now offered no resistance, and even as his hands scrabbled at the muddy bank, he began to gather speed on the slide down.

Ro hit the surface with a splash. What had been dried earth just four hours before was now under a foot of water. He struggled to his hands and knees, getting his head and back clear of the surface. Then quickly rose to his feet and glanced about. Other than the falling rain's pattern on the surface, here the water around him seemed still. Immediate anxiety easing, he turned to face the bank then looked up to see the gathered morani and Sam looking down at him.

Ro directed a slightly manic laugh towards his audience and then started to hurry round the edge of the ever-deepening pool. The water reached to just below the knee and it seemed Ro fancied his chances of making the fording point beyond the pool before it became completely unusable.

Sam had learnt long ago that still waters were no sign of safety. Just as he was about to call a warning, Ro realised that too. From the shallows directly in front of him, a young six-foot crocodile leapt and snapped. Ro was moving towards his attacker and could not evade it. His motion carried him directly towards the opening jaws. In despair, he cried out and raised his bound hands in futile defence. The crocodile closed its jaws on his hands, tight.

Sam saw the ugly predator, saw an empty eye socket; he knew exactly how that had been lost.

Ro was still on his feet though bent at the waist, the crocodile holding his bound hands and forearms tight, trying to drag him into deeper water while Ro desperately strained to work his legs back to the pool's edge and out onto the bank.

He was caught in a deadly tug of war with the crocodile and his arms were the rope. He screamed for help and glanced back up the bank, cried again for assistance.

The morani stood impassively watching the struggle
unfold. Sam could not. With a curse under his breath, he
started for the lip of the bank. Bad as Ro was, nobody
deserved to die like that.

Charles shouted and two morani grabbed Sam just as he
went over the lip. Holding tight, they pulled him back to his
feet at the top. Pinned between the two warriors, Sam looked
angrily at Charles and was about to unleash a tirade in his
direction when he suddenly became aware that Ro was silent.
Charles pointed his club down towards the pool, and Sam
traced the direction of his point. He shivered.

Ro was standing upright now. He hadn't won the tug of
war; the small crocodile had thought better and released him
before slipping backwards quietly beneath the water, all the
while its good eye glaring angrily at the one that got away.

Sam and the morani were all silent, looking down into the
pool. Any sense of justice and anger that even the toughest of
the warriors felt was replaced by a morbid horror as their
darkest nightmares played before them.

The indignation Sam felt at Charles having stopped him
vanished when he recognised his life had just been saved.
Sam realised he was holding his breath and forced air into his
lungs as, below them in the water, nature played out its
eternal cycle. Ro's entry splash and the commotion of the
struggle with the smaller crocodile had alerted the big boys,
and they were back for more.

Ro had given up shouting for help that couldn't come.
He was standing facing the pool's edge, which he knew he
could never reach. A huge crocodile had slid between him
and the bank, cutting off his retreat. The monster was so big
that, here in the shallows, even when pressed to the bottom
its bulk was above the surface. It watched Ro and gave a hiss
that carried up the bank to the audience.

Ro slowly turned his head, looked back out towards the
deep, could see two other big boys had closed on him and

were holding off for a moment, assessing his potential as a meal. He turned quickly back to look at the bankside crocodile. Sam realised Ro was not silent, he was whimpering to himself.

One of the crocs behind him flicked its tail and glided silently in. It turned its head slightly and nuzzled the back of Ro's leg, letting its front teeth brush against trouser. Ro felt the touch and jerked his leg away. The crocodile instantly responded by snapping hard on the leg above the knee and dragging him back. Now Ro let out an uncontrollable scream of fear and pain, falling forward towards the water, instinctively reaching his bound hands out to break his fall.

Up on the bank Sam shrugged off the hands of the restraining morani. This was not something he wanted to be part of. They let him go just as the pool-edge monster decided Ro was his meal, and leapt forward, mouth open wide to catch the falling prey. Ro's scream of terror stopped abruptly as his head and shoulders were engulfed, disappearing into the crocodile's maw. Ro's free leg continued to kick out in an uncontrollable though futile response as the two crocodiles vied for supremacy and hurriedly moved into deeper water.

Sam had already turned away when the crocodiles sank beneath the surface. In the deep, Ro's free leg kicked just once more as the two giants began to spin, their death rolls ripping his still living body in two. The sound of churning water reached Sam, he knew what it meant. Didn't need to look back to know the water would be frothing white and red. He hurried to his vehicle.

Pulling open the driver's door, he looked back. 'Come on, Charles. There's a doctor waiting to treat you and I really need to go.'

Chapter 35
MONDAY 4TH NOVEMBER - PM

Helen put down her cutlery, lifted her glass and drained its last drops of rosé wine. As soon as she put the glass down, John Guthrie hurried to fill it.

'I'm sure Sam won't be long now,' he said.

'Well, I hope that a courtesy visit was the right thing to do. I've had my fill of bailing him out of African police stations.'

'Oh, absolutely, the very best course of action. In fact, the authorities here are actually decent enough really, you know. It's the local politics that are just a bit sticky at present. It'll come good soon enough. In the meantime, Sam visiting police headquarters to apologise for his abrupt departure will help us in the, urrgh, the normalisation process.'

'If you say so. But remember, John, if the Nairobi police lock him up, I'm holding you responsible.'

'Don't worry; he'll be along in no time. His contrite apology will boost the local police chief's self-esteem no end. And of course, it's the High Commission that's facilitated it, so we'll benefit as the restorer of harmony. Do remember, Sam's only transgression was to leave the country faster than the people chasing him. He hadn't actually committed a crime in the first place. It's all just about showing up, allowing local authorities to save face, and building bridges. We really are so very grateful you stopped off.'

'Okay, I'm trusting you.' She glanced around the Thorn Tree Café. The atmosphere was exactly as it had been when she and Sam had visited for afternoon tea just a few days before. It was the perfect picture of stability in a changing world; yet so much had happened in those past few days, she gave a little shiver. Then laughed to herself; Sam had promised she would come here to eat. He could never have guessed it would be with John.

John suddenly tensed, and Helen looked up to see a group of men approaching. It was Bishop Ignatius with his assistant and an escort. This time, not junior priests; now the bishop was followed by three of the burliest guards she had seen. John stood and moved to create a barrier between Helen and the newcomers. 'Can I help you?' he said.

Though outnumbered and outsized, Helen could tell that John would stand his ground. She reached out a hand and rested it on his forearm. 'It's okay, John. These are friends of mine.'

John looked doubtful. 'Really?' He looked at the guards. 'Friends?'

'Yes, really,' said Helen, though she had still not really reconciled her relationship with the bishop.

'Helen, we meet again, what fortune,' said Bishop Ignatius.

'Well, knowing you, your Grace, I'm not sure luck will have been a factor. But please join me.' She waved a hand towards one of the seats, and with a chuckle, the bishop sat.

'Thank you, Helen. And I must confess, you're right - no fortune. As soon as I learnt you were travelling to Nairobi, we came to meet with you.' He waved away a waiter who had hurried across to serve. 'Now I need a quiet word with you. A private word. Perhaps your friend could excuse us for a few minutes?'

Helen thought carefully for a moment. 'Okay, I think we both deserve a few words after everything that's happened. Please, John, would you mind taking another table for a little while?'

John started to object.

'It'll be fine John. Church business.'

Overruled and not entirely convinced, John retired to a nearby table from where he monitored the bishop and his entourage. He watched the bishop's assistant sit too. One guard stood his ground immediately behind the assistant while the other two were waved away to sit in chairs at another nearby empty table.

'So, your Grace, I haven't forgotten you had us followed. How's the poor man's foot now? I hope he's recovering.'

'Oh yes, he's fine.'

'And Angel?'

'Yes, another unfortunate casualty. He will be fine too. I must say, those news reports from Europe that I followed clearly were not exaggerated. It seems you really do lead quite the dangerous existence. You almost appear to attract trouble. And perhaps that is fitting with your history.' Ignatius gave a theatrical laugh and briefly rested his hand on his assistant's shoulder, shaking it. Dutifully, the assistant joined in.

'Well, please pass my best wishes on to them, and I hope they recover quickly. Now, your Grace, I really want to be getting home. What can I do for you?'

'The picture of the box I showed you in Arusha. How do you feel about it?'

'Interested,' said Helen. 'I've got one quite similar.'

Bishop Ignatius smiled broadly. 'As I expected.'

'You did?'

'Of course. It was as we expected.'

'Hold on there. As you expected?' said Helen. 'You'd better rewind a bit, I think we're missing something.'

'Rewind?'

'Tell me what you expected.'

'There are two boxes - individually just pretty trinkets, worth very little. Together, priceless. One is the key and one is the lock.'

Bishop Ignatius reached a hand across the table and rested it on Helen's for a moment, squeezed it and smiled at her. Then leant back again. 'I am happy you are who we want. The instruction speaks only of the ring; you have the ring. Your story also bears out the news reports; it could not be fabricated. You are whom we have waited for. Though I must say, we had always thought to look for a man.'

'Times change,' said Helen.

'They do,' said Bishop Ignatius, 'and times roll on too. It has been a long wait, and now it falls to me to honour the covenant made so long ago.'

'A covenant?'

'I told you in Arusha how your Templar helped the Copts, and in return, we kept his box safe until his return. The ring bearer was to collect the box. You are the ring bearer, you are the collector. Now it falls to me to close that bargain, to redeem our debt. The box is yours.'

'Thank you, Ignatius, but please explain a bit more,' said Helen.

'Now you and I meet just as our predecessors did.'

'And what of this box or package that my predecessor needed to keep away from Rome?'

Ignatius beckoned towards his assistant. The man immediately rummaged within his robes, and his hand emerged holding the slim wooden case that Helen had seen in Arusha. She knew it contained an engraved gold plaque. He then produced a second larger box, and after a moment's hesitation, he laid it on the table beside the first. The woods were identical, and shiny and smooth through repeated polishing.

She lifted the second wooden box and turned it in her hand, pulled off the lid and looked inside. Then she tipped the box to allow its contents to slide gently out onto her hand.

'This is really beautiful,' she said, admiring the beautifully ornate box that slipped out.

She took it in her hands and turned it, looking carefully at the patterning. So similar to her own box, they must be a pair. 'I wonder what is so important about this that it had to leave Europe,' she said, tracing the now familiar Moorish pattern inlaid into the surface. 'Do you know how to open it?'

Ignatius shook his head. 'No, the priest that brought it from Edinburgh did not show how. He made our Pope and his bishop each swear an oath never to attempt to open it.'

'What do you think, your Grace?' she said.

The bishop gave his trademark laugh while raising his hands and shaking his head. 'I think nothing. We made a promise and have kept it. Just as your predecessor made a promise and kept it when it would have been easier to sail away and never return. He averted a tragedy for our people and provided the resources that enabled them to continue through some very dark days. It is my honour to see the bargain completed, we have honoured our pledge.'

'But what is it for?'

'All I can say are the words of our oath that each bishop in turn has sworn: *To keep the key that turns the lock that turns the key to show the way.* I have often thought about what it means, have never reached any conclusion. The words mean we take care of the key, but how is a box a key? How does a box turn a lock? I don't know. That is for you to resolve.'

'What now?' said Helen.

'Now we will leave you to continue your journey. You have our eternal thanks for your predecessor's kindness; if you have just an ounce of his quality, I know you will be a fine person. I see you are.'

'And the boxes?'

'They are yours,' said Bishop Ignatius. 'You must take them to complete the covenant.'

Ignatius and his assistant stood. Helen joined them. 'Ignatius, I still don't know what this is for, but thank you. I think it would have been far less trouble for you to have let us pass by without saying a thing.'

'Doing the right thing is often the hardest thing. But it is right to do.'

Helen lifted the slim wooden box and its plaque of gold so carefully engraved with the image of her ring. 'Well Ignatius, thank you again, and please keep this to mark that you and your Church have honoured our covenant.'

Ignatius bowed his head very slightly and took the box, passing it to his assistant. Then he took a step towards Helen as she moved towards him. They embraced. With a kiss to the bishop's cheek, she pulled back.

'We will meet again and under less stressed circumstances, I'm sure. And I hope then you will share with me the secret of my key, your box, once you solve it,' he said.

'You can count on that. In fact, when Sam and I finally have a chance to relax and solve the riddle of your box I'll definitely visit and tell you everything. That's a promise.'

'And I will look forward to it. You will always be welcome.' Ignatius waved his hand to gather his entourage together and then they were gone.

John returned to her table and sat in the seat Bishop Ignatius had just vacated. 'That all looked a little intense. Is everything alright?'

'Oh, believe me, John. In my life, intense is normal. There's always one more thing. But yes, everything is just fine, really. And thank you for standing up for me; I appreciated that and your concern too. Look, I think I'll just go through to reception for a quick look. I saw some hotel souvenirs and I'd quite like to get something.'

'By all means,' said John, standing. 'Please, feel free. Though, if you don't mind, I'll stay here at the table. I've seen enough souvenirs to last me a lifetime.'

Helen stood too. 'Sure, you stay put, I won't be long. Truth to tell, I'm keen to get away now. Once Sam gets here, we're going across to the gold stores in Kimathi Lane to buy presents for a couple of special friends back home and then it's straight out to the airport.'

John smiled, inclined his head very slightly and pushed a guiding arm out towards the reception. 'And you have a private plane waiting at the airport - very impressive, I must say.'

'Oh, it's only borrowed.'

'Yet, still impressive. Now, please do go, I'll await your return.'

'Great, I won't be long.'

With Ignatius' box secure in her shoulder bag, Helen walked briskly out into the reception and spent five minutes browsing the display, only to conclude that none of the expensive trinkets on offer could do justice to their experience.

A little wistfully, she turned and headed back to join John at the table. As she passed the Thorn Tree message board, an impulse stopped her - she wanted to check her message for Sam was still there. She couldn't see it. Scanning the board again in case it had been moved, she still couldn't see it. With a growing sense of disappointment, her search finished back where she had started, the message had definitely gone. Then she stopped, almost gasped in surprise. Just beside where she had left her message for Sam was another neatly folded paper note, with her name on it.

In disbelief, she stretched out her hand and let a finger trace across the handwriting, it was Sam's. When did he put this up? Was it him who had taken her message? It must have been. She quickly unpinned the note and read the message. Helen smiled to herself, thoughtfully, then tapped the note against the board before tucking it into her trouser pocket. She smiled again and turned at the sound of Sam's voice calling to her from the hotel reception.

Author's note.

Thank you for reading The Temple Covenant. I do hope you enjoyed the story. If so, I would be most grateful if you would take a moment to give The Temple Covenant a rating and a sentence or two of review. Reader ratings are so important in supporting and enabling authors in today's reading world.

Thank you. D.C.

D.C. MACEY

D. C. Macey is an author and lecturer based in the United Kingdom.

A first career in the Merchant Navy saw Macey's early working life devoted to travelling the globe. In the process, it gave an introduction to the mad mix of beauty, kindness, cruelty and inequality that is the human experience everywhere. Between every frantic costal encounter was a trip across the ocean, which brought the contrast of tranquil moments and offered time for reading, writing and reflection. Those roving days came to a close, however, with Macey serving as a ship's officer in the North Sea oil industry.

Several years working in business made it apparent that Macey's greatest commercial skill was the ability to convert tenners into fivers, effortlessly and unerringly - a skill that ensured Macey had the unwelcome experience of encountering those darker aspects of life that lie beneath the veneer of our developed world and brought fleeting glimpses into the shadows where bad things lurk.

Eventually, life's turbulence, domestic tragedy and impending poverty demanded a change of course. As a result, the past decade and more has been spent in lecturing and producing predominantly corporate media resources, so allowing Macey the opportunity to return to the written word.

Throughout it all Macey is certain that a happy home and laughter have proven time and again to be the best protection against life's trials.

BOOKS IN THE TEMPLE SERIES

The Temple Legacy (The Temple - Book 1) Published August 2015

The Temple Scroll (The Temple - Book 2) Published August 2016

The Temple Covenant (The Temple - Book 3) Published April 2018

The Temple Deliverance (The Temple - Book 4) Publication late 2018

For more information:

www.dcmacey.com

or

contact@dcmacey.com

Temple Legacy

(The Temple - Book 1)

Seven hundred years ago, in a time of war and betrayal, Europe's greatest treasure disappeared amidst a frenzied and brutal grab for power. The men who guarded it vanished into history.

In Edinburgh today, former élite British Military Intelligence officer Sam Cameron has turned to the quieter world of archaeology. Together with young church minister Helen Johnson, he leads his students on a field trip. What they unearth raises exciting questions. What are the mystery objects? What is their connection to the Knights Templar?

But others are asking the same questions and the thrill of discovery is quickly clouded by the brutal killing of a retired church minister and a spreading rage of violence and death.

Now Helen and Sam must race to unravel an ancient mystery, find how it links to the murdered minister, and fend off a very modern threat. Failure will cost their lives and the lives of many more. Success will answer the greatest unresolved mystery of the medieval world.

The Temple Scroll

(The Temple - Book 2)

A lost treasure, an impenetrable puzzle and a psychopathic killer: a deadly combination.

The Temple Scroll is a rollercoaster ride of danger, mystery and murder. From New England to the islands of the Mediterranean, it follows the deadly hunt for the Templars' lost treasure.

Archaeology lecturer Sam Cameron and church minister Helen Johnson thought their old problems were done. They were wrong. Killers are set on finding the Templars' treasure and they believe Sam and Helen hold the key.

As the psychopathic Cassiter directs his team of killers towards their goal, the calm of summer vanishes in an explosive bout of blood and suffering.

Under pressure from every side, Sam and Helen must draw on all their instincts and professional skills to stay alive as they attempt to crack the puzzle that protects the Templars' treasure.

As the search for the Templar hoard moves inexorably to a conclusion, Sam and Helen must risk all in a frantic bid to save their friends, the treasure, and the priceless holy relics of the early Church. Now there is no mercy and no escape - there is only win or die.

The Temple Covenant

(The Temple - Book 3)

A quiet sabbatical spent visiting archaeological sites in the Great Rift Valley offers Helen Johnson and Sam Cameron the perfect opportunity to unwind and put the violent climax to their recent adventures behind them. But where they go trouble isn't far away. Alarm bells ring when Helen attracts the attentions of the mysterious Bishop Ignatius of the Ethiopian Orthodox Tewahedo Church. He is desperate to meet with her and will not take no for an answer.

Elsewhere, news breaks that senior British Intelligence Corps Colonel Bob Prentice is missing in Nairobi and security chiefs have cause for concern. Concern turns to panic when it's realised an operational prototype of the British Army's latest super-weapon has vanished too.

In a last gasp attempt to retrieve the situation the British Government turns to former Intelligence Corps officer Sam, hoping that his civilian status can keep him under the radar and his old skills might just turn the problem round.

Meanwhile, Helen is co-opted into a role that goes against her every belief – a role that her patriotism demands she fulfil even as she struggles to evade the determined attentions of Bishop Ignatius and his men.

Far from the cloudy skies of Edinburgh, a frightening and bloody hunt plays out beneath the burning sun of the East African bush. Racing against the clock, and with scant support, Sam and Helen must risk everything to resolve the challenge of the enigmatic Bishop Ignatius while fighting to preserve the West's place in a dangerous world.

The Temple Deliverance

(The Temple - Book 4)

Jolted out of their holiday season calm, Helen Johnson and Sam Cameron find they must play one last hand in a deadly game.

The final hunt is on to unpick an ancient code that hides the incredible nature of the Templars' greatest secret. From the depths of northern winter to the sun-kissed beaches of North Africa, Helen and Sam must hurry to piece together the final clues in a race against time to save themselves, their loyal friends and Christianity's greatest heritage.

Beset by new enemies, they must also contend with the return of old foes who are hell bent on vengeance and determined to snatch the ultimate prize they have coveted for so long. As violence and death sweep across the continents, innocence is no protection; knowledge and grit are the only currencies of survival. Calling on trusted allies, Helen and Sam struggle against the odds, knowing that this time only one side can walk away.

Printed in Poland
by Amazon Fulfillment
Poland Sp. z o.o., Wrocław